"Every so often, a work of popular fiction vaults over its humble origins as entertainment, grasps the American imagination and stirs up the volcanic subtexts of our daily life. *Uncle Tom's Cabin* was that kind of book; so was Laura Z. Hobson's *Gentleman's Agreement*. Michael Crichton's eighth novel, RISING SUN, a thriller set against the background of current American-Japanese tensions, is likely to be another.... A shocking and ominous polemic, RISING SUN is at heart a rallying cry.... That Mr. Crichton effortlessly weaves a mesmerizing mystery comes as no surprise. Witty and erudite, he can already lay claim to one of America's heavyweight titles: Most Serious Suspense Novelist. That he should now write so passionately and engagingly on matters of Japanese culture and the survival of a free and productive America—that is the surprise of RISING SUN. . . . RISING SUN exposes the raw nerves of a country in profound economic distress, of a people with declining faith in themselves, their leaders and their past, a people very uneasy about their future. Despite the book's provocative tone, Mr. Crichton is no xenophobe, no fool, no ranting bigot. The questions he poses are of great consequence in the debate about America's condition at the end of the American century. What more could one ask of popular fiction?"

The New York Times Book Review
(Front page review)

**Please turn the page
for more reviews. . . .**

"EXTRAORDINARY . . .

Where Crichton really excels [is] the detailing of the many ways in which Japan has penetrated America, and the very real dangers this poses. The Japanese make no bones that to them business is war, and that a part of the war is conducted by neutralizing public opinion."

Chicago Sun-Times

"Remarkably timely . . . The plot of RISING SUN thicken[s] at a satisfying pace. . . . Let us hope that Mr. Crichton's assiduously researched fantasy does not turn out to be too extremely timely."

The New York Times

"[A] tense, fast-paced murder mystery."

Playboy

"FASCINATING . . .

Suspenseful . . . Technologically riveting . . . Bound to attract controversy and a huge readership."

The Kirkus Reviews (starred review)

"Enough mystery and suspense to keep the reader hooked . . . [The] glimpses into the deep-rooted otherness of Japanese mores are fascinating. So is the book's science, as one might expect from an author with an M.D. degree and a long line of bestsellers with high-tech plots."

USA Today

"[This] entertaining, well-researched thriller cannot be easily dismissed as Japan-bashing because it raises important questions about that country's adversarial trade strategy and our inadequate response to it."

Publishers Weekly (starred review)

RISING SUN

Michael Crichton

BALLANTINE BOOKS • NEW YORK

All rights reserved under International and Pan-American Copyright Conventions. Published in the United States by Ballantine Books, a division of Random House, Inc., New York, and simultaneously in Canada by Random House of Canada Limited, Toronto.

Grateful acknowledgment is made to Warner/Chappell Music, Inc. for permission to reprint excerpts from "Great Balls of Fire" by Otis Blackwell and Jack Hammer. Copyright © 1957 by Unichappell Music, Inc. & Chappell & Co. All rights reserved. Used by permission.

This is a work of fiction. Characters, corporations, institutions, and organizations in this novel are either the product of the author's imagination or, if real, used fictitiously without any intent to describe their actual conduct, except as noted below.

References in this novel to events and activities concerning certain Japanese corporations (Matsushita, Minolta, Mitsubishi, Nintendo, Panasonic, Sumitomo Corp., and Toshiba), to former Japanese prime ministers (Takeshita and Tanaka), and to certain American corporations (Cray Research, Emerson, Fairchild, General Electric, Houdaille, RCA, and Sears) are true.

Library of Congress Catalog Card Number: 91-53173

ISBN 0-345-38037-1

The edition published by arrangement with Alfred A. Knopf, Inc.

Manufactured in the United States of America

First Ballantine Books Edition: January 1993
Twenty-first Printing: June 1993

To my mother,
Zula Miller Crichton

We are entering a world where the old rules no longer apply.
—Phillip Sanders

Business is war.

—Japanese motto

LOS ANGELES POLICE DEPARTMENT
CONFIDENTIAL TRANSCRIPT
OF INTERNAL RECORDS

Contents: Transcript of Video Interrogation
Detective Peter J. Smith
March 13–15

re: "Nakamoto Murder" (A8895-404)

This transcript is the property of the
Los Angeles Police Department and is
for internal use only. Permission to copy,
quote from, or otherwise reproduce or
reveal the contents of this document is
limited by law. Unauthorized use carries
severe penalties.

Direct all inquiries to:

Commanding Officer
Internal Affairs Division
Los Angeles Police Department
PO Box 2029
Los Angeles, CA 92038-2029
Telephone: (213) 555-7600
Telefax: (213) 555-7812

Video Interrogation: Det. P.J. Smith   3/13–3/15

Case: "Nakamoto Murder"

Description of interrogation: Subject (Lt. Smith) was interrogated for 22 hours over 3 days from Monday, March 13 to Wednesday, March 15. Interview was recorded on S-VHS/SD videotape.

Description of image: Subject (Smith) seated at desk in Video Room #4, LAPD HQ. Clock visible on the wall behind subject. Image includes surface of desk, coffee cup, and Subject from the waist up. Subject wears coat and tie (day 1); shirt and tie (day 2); and shirtsleeves only (day 3). Video timecode in lower right corner.

Purpose of interrogation: Clarification of Subject role in "Nakamoto Murder." (A8895-404) Officers in charge of the interrogation were Det. T. Conway and Det. P. Hammond. Subject waived his right to an attorney.

Disposition of case: Filed as "case unsolved."

INT: Okay. The tape is running. State your name for the record, please.

SUBJ: Peter James Smith.

INT: State your age and rank.

SUBJ: I'm thirty-four years old. Lieutenant, Special Services Division. Los Angeles Police Department.

INT: Lieutenant Smith, as you know, you are not being charged with a crime at this time.

SUBJ: I know.

INT: Nevertheless you have a right to be represented here by an attorney.

SUBJ: I waive that right.

INT: Okay. And have you been coerced to come here in any way?

SUBJ: (long pause) No. I have not been coerced in any way.

INT: Okay. Now we want to talk to you about the Nakamoto Murder. When did you first become involved in that case?

SUBJ: On Thursday night, February 9, about nine o'clock.

INT: What happened at that time?

SUBJ: I was at home. I got a phone call.

INT: And what were you doing at the time you got the call?

FIRST NIGHT

FIRST NIGHT

◆ Actually, I was sitting on my bed in my apartment in Culver City, watching the Lakers game with the sound turned off, while I tried to study vocabulary for my introductory Japanese class.

It was a quiet evening; I had gotten my daughter to sleep about eight. Now I had the cassette player on the bed, and the cheerful woman's voice was saying things like, "Hello, I am a police officer. Can I be of assistance?" and "Please show me the menu." After each sentence, she paused for me to repeat it back, in Japanese. I stumbled along as best I could. Then she would say, "The vegetable store is closed. Where is the post office?" Things like that. Sometimes it was hard to concentrate, but I was trying. "Mr. Hayashi has two children."

I tried to answer. "*Hayashi-san wa kodomo ga fur . . . futur . . .*" I swore. But by then the woman was talking again.

"This drink is not very good at all."

I had my textbook open on the bed, alongside a Mr. Potato Head I'd put back together for my daughter. Next to that, a photo album, and the pictures from her second birthday party. It was four months after Michelle's party, but I still hadn't put the pictures in the album. You have to try and keep up with that stuff.

"There will be a meeting at two o'clock."

The pictures on my bed didn't reflect reality any more. Four months later, Michelle looked completely different. She was taller; she'd outgrown the expensive party dress my

7

ex-wife had bought for her: black velvet with a white lace collar.

In the photos, my ex-wife plays a prominent role—holding the cake as Michelle blows out the candles, helping her unwrap the presents. She looks like a dedicated mom. Actually, my daughter lives with me, and my ex-wife doesn't see much of her. She doesn't show up for weekend visitation half the time, and she misses child-support payments.

But you'd never know from the birthday photos.

"Where is the toilet?"

"I have a car. We can go together."

I continued studying. Of course, officially I was on duty that night: I was the Special Services officer on call for division headquarters downtown. But February ninth was a quiet Thursday, and I didn't expect much action. Until nine o'clock, I only had three calls.

Special Services includes the diplomatic section of the police department; we handle problems with diplomats and celebrities, and provide translators and liaison for foreign nationals who come into contact with the police for one reason or another. It's varied work, but not stressful: when I'm on call I can expect a half-dozen requests for help, none of them emergencies. I hardly ever have to roll out. It's much less demanding than being a police press liaison, which is what I did before Special Services.

Anyway, on the night of February ninth, the first call I got concerned Fernando Conseca, the Chilean vice-consul. A patrol car had pulled him over; Ferny was too drunk to drive, but he was claiming diplomatic immunity. I told the patrolmen to drive him home, and I made a note to complain to the consulate again in the morning.

Then an hour later, I got a call from detectives in Gardena. They'd arrested a suspect in a restaurant shooting who spoke only Samoan, and they wanted a translator. I said I could get one, but that Samoans invariably spoke English; the country had been an American trust territory for years. The detectives said they'd handle it. Then I got a call that mobile television vans were blocking fire lanes at the Aerosmith concert; I told the officers to give it to the fire department. And it was quiet for the next hour. I went back to my textbook and my sing-song woman saying things like, "Yesterday's weather was rainy."

Then Tom Graham called.

"It's the fucking Japs," Graham said. "I can't believe they're pulling this shit. Better get over here, Petey-san. Eleven hundred Figueroa, corner of Seventh. It's the new Nakamoto building."

"What is the problem?" I had to ask. Graham is a good detective but he has a bad temper, and he tends to blow things out of proportion.

"The problem," Graham said, "is that the fucking Japs are demanding to see the fucking Special Services liaison. Which is you, buddy. They're saying the police can't proceed until the liaison gets here."

"Can't proceed? Why? What have you got?"

"Homicide," Graham said. "Caucasian female approximately twenty-five years old, apparent six-oh-one. Lying flat on her back, right in their damn boardroom. Quite a sight. You better get down here as soon as you can."

I said, "Is that music in the background?"

"Hell, yes," Graham said. "There's a big party going on. Tonight is the grand opening of the Nakamoto Tower, and they're having a reception. Just get down here, will you?"

I said I would. I called Mrs. Ascenio next door, and asked her if she would watch the baby while I was gone; she always needed extra money. While I waited for her to arrive I changed my shirt and put on my good suit. Then Fred Hoffmann called. He was watch commander at DHD downtown; a short, tough guy with gray hair. "Listen, Pete. I think you might want help on this one."

I said, "Why is that?"

"Sounds like we got a homicide involving Japanese nationals. It may be sticky. How long have you been a liaison?"

"About six months," I said.

"If I was you, I'd get some experienced help. Pick up Connor and take him downtown with you."

"Who?"

"John Connor. Ever heard of him?"

"Sure," I said. Everyone in the division had heard of Connor. He was a legend, the most knowledgeable of the Special Services officers. "But isn't he retired?"

"He's on indefinite leave, but he still works cases involving the Japanese. I think he could be helpful to you. Tell you what. I'll call him for you. You just go down and pick him up." Hoffmann gave me his address.

"Okay, fine. Thanks."

"And one other thing. Land lines on this one, okay, Pete?"

"Okay," I said. "Who requested that?"

"It's just better."

"Whatever you say, Fred."

Land lines meant to stay off the radios, so our transmissions wouldn't be picked up by the media monitoring police frequencies. It was standard procedure in certain situations. Whenever Elizabeth Taylor went to the hospital, we went to land lines. Or if the teenage son of somebody famous died in a car crash, we'd go to land lines to make sure the parents got the news before the TV crews started banging on their door. We used land lines for that kind of thing. I'd never heard it invoked in a homicide before.

But driving downtown, I stayed off the car phone, and listened to the radio. There was a report of a shooting of a three-year-old boy who was now paralyzed from the waist down. The child was a bystander during a 7-Eleven robbery. A stray bullet hit him in the spine and he was—

I switched to another station, got a talk show. Ahead, I could see the lights of the downtown skyscrapers, rising into mist. I got off the freeway at San Pedro, Connor's exit.

What I knew about John Connor was that he had lived for a time in Japan, where he acquired his knowledge of Japanese language and culture. At one point, back in the 1960s, he was the only officer who spoke fluent Japanese, even though Los Angeles then had the largest Japanese population outside the home islands.

Now, of course, the department has more than eighty officers who speak Japanese—and more, like me, who are trying to learn. Connor had retired several years before. But the liaison officers who worked with him agreed he was the best. He was said to work very fast, often solving cases in a few hours. He had a reputation as a skilled detective and an extraordinary interviewer, able to get information from witnesses like nobody else. But most of all, the other liaisons praised his even-handed approach. One said to me, "Working with the Japanese is like balancing on a tightrope. Sooner or later, everybody falls off on one side or the other. Some people decide the Japanese are fabulous and can do no wrong. Some people decide they're vicious pricks. But Connor always keeps his balance. He stays in the middle. He always knows exactly what he is doing."

John Connor lived in the industrial area off Seventh Street, in a large brick warehouse alongside a diesel truck depot. The freight elevator in the building was broken. I walked upstairs to the third floor and knocked on his door.

"It's open," a voice said.

I entered a small apartment. The living room was empty, and furnished in the Japanese style: tatami mats, shoji screens, and wood-paneled walls. A calligraphy scroll, a black lacquer table, a vase with a single splash of white orchid.

I saw two pairs of shoes set out beside the door. One was a man's brogues. The other was a pair of women's high heels.

I said, "Captain Connor?"

"Just a minute."

A shoji screen slid back and Connor appeared. He was surprisingly tall, maybe a hundred and ninety centimeters, well over six feet. He wore a *yukata,* a light Japanese robe of blue cotton. I estimated he was fifty-five years old. Broad-shouldered, balding, with a trim mustache, sharp features, piercing eyes. Deep voice. Calm.

"Good evening, Lieutenant."

We shook hands. Connor looked me up and down, and nodded approvingly. "Good. Very presentable."

I said, "I used to work press. You never knew when you might have to appear in front of cameras."

He nodded. "And now you're the SSO on call?"

"That's right."

"How long have you been a liaison?"

"Six months."

"You speak Japanese?"

"A little. I'm taking lessons."

"Give me a few minutes to change." He turned and disappeared behind the shoji screen. "This is a homicide?"

"Yes."

"Who notified you?"

"Tom Graham. He's the OIC at the crime scene. He said the Japanese were insisting on a liaison officer being present."

"I see." There was a pause. I heard running water. "Is that a common request?"

"No. In fact, I've never heard of it happening. Usually, officers call for a liaison because they have a language problem. I've never heard of the Japanese asking for a liaison."

"Neither have I," Connor said. "Did Graham ask you to bring me? Because Tom Graham and I don't always admire each other."

"No," I said. "Fred Hoffmann suggested I bring you in. He felt I didn't have enough experience. He said he was going to call you for me."

"Then you were called at home twice?" Connor said.

"Yes."

"I see." He reappeared, wearing a dark blue suit, knotting his tie. "It seems that time is critical." He glanced at his watch. "When did Graham call you?"

"About nine."

"Then forty minutes have already passed. Let's go, Lieutenant. Where's your car?"

We hurried downstairs.

* * *

I drove up San Pedro and turned left onto Second, heading toward the Nakamoto building. There was a light mist at street level. Connor stared out the window. He said, "How good is your memory?"

"Pretty good, I guess."

"I wonder if you could repeat for me the telephone conversations you had tonight," he said. "Give them to me in as much detail as possible. Word for word, if you can."

"I'll try."

I recounted my phone calls. Connor listened without interruption or comment. I didn't know why he was so interested, and he didn't tell me. When I finished, he said, "Hoffmann didn't tell you who called for land lines?"

"No."

"Well, it's a good idea in any case. I never use a car phone if I can help it. These days, too many people listen in."

I turned onto Figueroa. Up ahead I saw searchlights shining in front of the new Nakamoto Tower. The building itself was gray granite, rising up into the night. I got into the right lane and flipped open the glove box to grab a handful of business cards.

The cards said Detective Lieutenant Peter J. Smith, Special Services Liaison Officer, Los Angeles Police Department. Printed in English on one side, in Japanese on the back.

Connor looked at the cards. "How do you want to handle this situation, Lieutenant? Have you negotiated with the Japanese before?"

I said, "Not really, no. Couple of drunk driving arrests."

Connor said politely, "Then perhaps I can suggest a strategy for us to follow."

"That's fine with me," I said. "I'd be grateful for your help."

"All right. Since you're the liaison, it's probably best if you take charge of the scene when we arrive."

"Okay."

"Don't bother to introduce me, or refer to me in any way. Don't even look in my direction."

"Okay."

"I am a nonentity. You alone are in charge."

"Okay, fine."

"It'll help to be formal. Stand straight, and keep your suit jacket buttoned at all times. If they bow to you, don't bow back—just give a little head nod. A foreigner will never master the etiquette of bowing. Don't even try."

"Okay," I said.

"When you start to deal with the Japanese, remember that they don't like to negotiate. They find it too confrontational. In their own society they avoid it whenever possible."

"Okay."

"Control your gestures. Keep your hands at your sides. The Japanese find big arm movements threatening. Speak slowly. Keep your voice calm and even."

"Okay."

"If you can."

"Okay."

"It may be difficult to do. The Japanese can be irritating. You'll probably find them irritating tonight. Handle it as best you can. But whatever happens, don't lose your temper."

"All right."

"That's extremely bad form."

"All right," I said.

Connor smiled. "I'm sure you'll do well," he said. "You probably won't need my help at all. But if you get stuck, you'll hear me say 'Perhaps I can be of assistance.' That will be the signal that I'm taking over. From that point on, let me do the talking. I'd prefer you not speak again, even if you are spoken to directly by them. Okay?"

"Okay."

"You may want to speak, but don't be drawn out."

"I understand."

"Furthermore, whatever I do, show no surprise. *Whatever* I do."

"Okay."

"Once I take over, move so that you're standing slightly behind me and to my right. Never sit. Never look around.

Never appear distracted. Remember that although you come from an MTV video culture, they do not. They are Japanese. Everything you do will have meaning to them. Every aspect of your appearance and behavior will reflect on you, on the police department, and on me as your superior and *sempai*."

"Okay, Captain."

"Any questions?"

"What's a *sempai*?"

Connor smiled.

We drove past the searchlights, down the ramp into the underground garage.

"In Japan," he said, "a *sempai* is a senior man who guides a junior man, known as a *kōhai*. The *sempai-kōhai* relationship is quite common. It's often assumed to exist whenever a younger man and an older man are working together. They will probably assume it of us."

I said, "Sort of a mentor and apprentice?"

"Not exactly," Connor said. "In Japan, *sempai-kōhai* has a different quality. More like a fond parent: the *sempai* is expected to indulge his *kōhai*, and put up with all sorts of youthful excesses and errors from the junior man." He smiled. "But I'm sure you won't do that to me."

We came to the bottom of the ramp, and saw the flat expanse of the parking garage ahead of us. Connor stared out the window and frowned. "Where is everybody?"

The garage of the Nakamoto Tower was full of limousines, the drivers leaning against their cars, talking and smoking. But I saw no police cars. Ordinarily, when there's a homicide, the place is lit up like Christmas, with lights flashing from a half-dozen black and whites, the medical examiner, paramedics, and all the rest.

But there was nothing tonight. It just looked like a garage where somebody was having a party: elegant people standing in clusters, waiting for their cars.

"Interesting," I said.

We came to a stop. The parking attendants opened the doors, and I stepped out onto plush carpet, and heard soft music. I walked with Connor toward the elevator. Well-dressed people were coming the other way: men in tuxedos, women in expensive gowns. And standing by the elevator, wearing a stained corduroy sport coat and furiously smoking a cigarette, was Tom Graham.

When Graham played halfback at U.S.C. he never made first string. That bit of history stuck like a character trait: all his life he seemed to miss the crucial promotion, the next step up a detective's career. He had transferred from one division to another, never finding a precinct that suited him, or a partner that worked well with him. Always too outspoken, Graham had made enemies in the chief's office, and at thirty-nine, further advancement was unlikely. Now he was bitter, gruff, and putting on weight—a big man who had become ponderous, and a pain in the ass: he just rubbed people the wrong way. His idea of personal integrity was to be a failure, and he was sarcastic about anybody who didn't share his views.

"Nice suit," he said to me, as I walked up. "You look fucking beautiful, Peter." He flicked imaginary dust off my lapel.

I ignored it. "How's it going, Tom?"

"You guys should be attending this party, not working it." He turned to Connor and shook his hand. "Hello, John. Whose idea was it to get you out of bed?"

"I'm just observing," Connor said mildly.

I said, "Fred Hoffmann asked me to bring him down."

"Hell," Graham said. "It's okay with me that you're here. I can use some help. It's pretty tense up there."

We followed him toward the elevator. I still saw no other police officers. I said, "Where is everybody?"

"Good question," Graham said. "They've managed to keep all of our people around back at the freight entrance. They claim the service elevator gives fastest access. And they

17

keep talking about the importance of their grand opening, and how nothing must disrupt it."

By the elevators, a uniformed Japanese private security guard looked us over carefully. "These two are with me," Graham said. The security man nodded, but squinted at us suspiciously.

We got on the elevator.

"Fucking Japanese," Graham said, as the doors closed. "This is still our country. We're still the fucking police in our own country."

The elevator was glass walled and we looked out on downtown Los Angeles as it went up into the light mist. Directly across was the Arco building. All lit up at night.

"You know these elevators are illegal," Graham said. "According to code, no glass elevators past ninety floors, and this building is ninety-seven floors, the highest building in L.A. But then this whole building is one big special case. And they got it up in six months. You know how? They brought in prefab units from Nagasaki, and slapped them together here. Didn't use American construction workers. Got a special permit to bypass our unions because of a so-called technical problem that only Japanese workers could handle. You believe that shit?"

I shrugged. "They got it past the American unions."

"Hell, they got it past the *city council*," Graham said. "But of course that's just money. And if there's one thing we know, the Japanese have money. So they got variances on the zoning restrictions, the earthquake ordinances. They got everything they wanted."

I shrugged. "Politics."

"My ass. You know they don't even pay tax? That's right: they got an eight-year break on property taxes from the city. Shit: we're *giving* this country away."

We rode for a moment in silence. Graham stared out the windows. The elevators were high-speed Hitachis, using the latest technology. The fastest and smoothest elevators in the world. We moved higher into the mist.

I said to Graham, "You want to tell us about this homicide, or do you want it to be a surprise?"

"Fuck," Graham said. He flipped open his notebook. "Here you go. The original call was at eight thirty-two. Somebody saying there is a 'problem of disposition of a body.' Male with a thick Asian accent, doesn't speak good English. The operator couldn't get much out of him, except an address. The Nakamoto Tower. Black and white goes over, arrives at eight thirty-nine p.m., finds it's a homicide. Forty-sixth floor, which is an office floor in this building. Victim is Caucasian female, approximately twenty-five years old. Hell of a good-looking girl. You'll see.

"The blue suits stretch the tape and call the division. I go over with Merino, arriving at eight fifty-three. Crime scene IU and SID show up about the same time for PE, prints, and pics. Okay so far?"

"Yes," Connor said, nodding.

Graham said, "We're just getting started when some Jap from the Nakamoto Corporation comes up in a thousand-dollar blue suit and announces that he is entitled to a fucking conversation with the L.A.P.D. liaison officer before anything is done in their fucking building. And he's saying things like we got no probable cause.

"I go, what the fuck is this. We got an obvious homicide here. I think this guy should get back. But this Jap speaks excellent fucking English and he seems to know a lot of law. And everybody at the scene becomes, you know, concerned. I mean, there's no point in pushing to start an investigation if it's going to invalidate due process, right? And this Jap fucker is insisting the liaison must be present before we do anything. Since he speaks such fucking good English I don't know what the problem is. I thought the whole idea of a liaison was for people who don't speak the language and this fucking guy has Stanford law school written all over him. But anyway." He sighed.

"You called me," I said.

"Yeah."

I said, "Who is the man from Nakamoto?"

"Shit." Graham scowled at his notes. "Ishihara. Ishiguri. Something like that."

"You have his card? He must have given you his card."

"Yeah, he did. I gave it to Merino."

I said, "Any other Japanese there?"

"What are you, kidding?" Graham laughed. "The place is swarming with them. Fucking Disneyland up there."

"I mean the crime scene."

"So do I," Graham said. "We can't keep 'em out. They say it's their building, they have a right to be there. Tonight is the grand opening of the Nakamoto Tower. They have a right to be there. On and on."

I said, "Where is the opening taking place?"

"One floor below the murder, on the forty-fifth floor. They're having one hell of a bash. Must be eight hundred people there. Movie stars, senators, congressmen, you name it. I hear Madonna is there, and Tom Cruise. Senator Hammond. Senator Kennedy. Elton John. Senator Morton. Mayor Thomas's there. District Attorney Wyland's there. Hey, maybe your ex-wife is there, too, Pete. She still works for Wyland, doesn't she?"

"Last I heard."

Graham sighed. "Must be great to fuck a lawyer, instead of getting fucked by them. Must make for a nice change."

I didn't want to talk about my ex-wife. "We don't have a lot of contact any more," I said.

A little bell rang, then the elevator said, "*Yonjūsan kai.*"

Graham glanced at the glowing numbers above the door. "Can you believe that shit?"

"*Yonjūyon kai,*" the elevator said. "*Mōsugu de go-zaimasu.*"

"What'd it say?"

" 'We're almost at the floor.' "

"Fuck," Graham said. "If an elevator's going to talk, it should be English. This is still America."

"Just barely," Connor said, staring out at the view.

"*Youjūgo kai,*" the elevator said.

The door opened.

Graham was right: it was a hell of a party. The whole floor had been made into a replica forties ballroom. Men in suits. Women in cocktail dresses. The band playing Glenn

Miller swing music. Standing near the elevator door was a gray-haired, suntanned man who looked vaguely familiar. He had the broad shoulders of an athlete. He stepped onto the elevator and turned to me. "Ground floor, please." I smelled whiskey.

A second, younger man in a suit instantly appeared by his side. "This elevator is going up, Senator."

"What's that?" the gray-haired man said, turning to his aide.

"This elevator's going up, sir."

"Well. I *want* to go *down*." He was speaking with the careful, over-articulated speech of the drunk.

"Yes, sir. I know that, sir," the aide replied cheerfully. "Let's take the next elevator, Senator." He gripped the gray-haired man firmly by the elbow and led him off the elevator.

The doors closed. The elevator continued up.

"Your tax dollars at work," Graham said. "Recognize him? Senator Stephen Rowe. Nice to find him partying here, considering he's on the Senate Finance Committee, which sets all Japanese import regulations. But like his pal Senator Kennedy, Rowe is one of the great pussy patrollers."

"Oh, yeah?"

"They say he can drink pretty good, too."

"I noticed that."

"That's why he's got that kid with him. To keep him out of trouble."

The elevator stopped at the forty-sixth floor. There was a soft electronic ping. "*Yonjūroku kai. Goriyō arigatō gozaimashita.*"

"Finally," Graham said. "Now maybe we can get to work."

The doors opened. We faced a solid wall of blue business suits, backs turned to us. There must have been twenty men jammed in the area just beyond the elevator. The air was thick with cigarette smoke.

"Coming through, coming through," Graham said, pushing his way roughly past the men. I followed, Connor behind me, silent and inconspicuous.

The forty-sixth floor had been designed to house the chief executive offices of Nakamoto Industries, and it was impressive. Standing in the carpeted reception area just beyond the elevators, I could see the entire floor—it was a gigantic open space. It was about sixty by forty meters, half the size of a football field. Everything added to the sense of spaciousness and elegance. The ceilings were high, paneled in wood. The furnishings were all wood and fabric, black and gray, and the carpet was thick. Sound was muted and lights were low, adding to the soft, rich quality. It looked more like a bank than a business office.

The richest bank you ever saw.

And it made you stop and look. I stood by the yellow crime-scene tape, which blocked access to the floor itself, and got my bearings. Directly ahead was the large atrium, a kind of open bullpen for secretaries and lower-level people. There were desks in clusters, and trees to break up the space. In the center of the atrium stood a large model of the Nakamoto Tower, and the complex of surrounding buildings still under construction. A spotlight shone on the model, but the rest of the atrium was relatively dark, with night lights.

Private offices for the executives were arranged around
the perimeter of the atrium. The offices had glass walls
facing the atrium, and glass walls on the outside walls as
well, so that from where I was standing you could look
straight out to the surrounding skyscrapers of Los Angeles.
It made you think the floor was floating in midair.

There were two glass-walled conference rooms, on the left
and right. The room on the right was smaller, and there I
saw the body of the girl, lying on a long black table. She was
wearing a black dress. One leg dangled down toward the
floor. I didn't see any blood. But I was pretty far away from
her, maybe sixty meters. It was hard to see much detail.

I heard the crackle of police radios, and I heard Graham
saying, "Here's your liaison, gentlemen. Now maybe we can
get started on our investigation. Peter?"

I turned to the Japanese men by the elevator. I didn't
know which I should talk to; there was an awkward moment
until one of them stepped forward. He was about thirty-five
and wore an expensive suit. The man gave a very slight bow,
from the neck, just a hint. I bowed back. Then he spoke.

"*Konbanwa. Hajimemashite, Sumisu-san. Ishiguro desu.
Dōzo yoroshiku.*" A formal greeting, although perfunctory.
No wasted time. His name was Ishiguro. He already knew
my name.

I said, "*Hajimemashite. Watashi wa Sumisu desu. Dōzo
yoroshiku.*" How do you do. Glad to meet you. The usual.

"*Watashi no meishi desu. Dōzo.*" He gave me his business
card. He was quick in his movements, brusque.

"*Dōmo arigatō gozaimasu.*" I accepted his card with both
hands, which wasn't really necessary, but taking Connor's
advice, I wanted to do the most formal thing. Next I gave
him my card. The ritual required us both to look at each
other's cards, and to make some minor comment, or to ask
a question like "Is this your office telephone number?"

Ishiguro took my card with one hand and said, "Is this
your home phone, Detective?" I was surprised. He spoke the
kind of unaccented English you can only learn by living here
for a long time, starting when you're young. He must have
gone to school here. One of the thousands of Japanese who

studied in America in the seventies. When they were sending 150,000 students a year to America, to learn about our country. And we were sending 200 American students a year to Japan.

"That's my number at the bottom, yes," I said.

Ishiguro slipped my card into his shirt pocket. I started to make a polite comment about his card, but he interrupted me. "Look, Detective. I think we can dispense with the formalities. The only reason there's a problem here tonight is that your colleague is unreasonable."

"My colleague?"

Ishiguro gave a head jerk. "The fat one there. Graham. His demands are unreasonable, and we strongly object to his intention to carry out an investigation tonight."

I said, "Why is that, Mr. Ishiguro?"

"You have no probable cause to conduct one."

"Why do you say that?"

Ishiguro snorted. "I would think it's obvious, even to you."

I stayed cool. Five years as a detective, and then a year in the press section had taught me to stay cool.

I said, "No, sir, I'm afraid it's not obvious."

He looked at me disdainfully. "The fact is, Lieutenant, you have no reason to connect this girl's death to the party we're holding downstairs."

"It looks like she's wearing a party dress—"

He interrupted me rudely. "My guess is you'll probably discover that she has died of an accidental drug overdose. And therefore her death has nothing to do with our party. Wouldn't you agree?"

I took a deep breath. "No, sir, I wouldn't agree. Not without an investigation." I took another breath. "Mr. Ishiguro, I appreciate your concerns, but—"

"I wonder if you do," Ishiguro said, interrupting me again. "I insist that you appreciate the position of the Nakamoto company tonight. This is a very significant evening for us, a very *public* evening. We are naturally distressed by the prospect that our function might be marred by unfounded allegations of a woman's death, especially this, a woman of no importance . . ."

"A woman of no importance?"

Ishiguro made a dismissing wave. He seemed to be tired of talking to me. "It's obvious, just look at her. She's no better than a common prostitute. I can't imagine how she came to be in this building at all. And for this reason, I strongly protest the intention of Detective Graham to interrogate the guests at the reception downstairs. That's entirely unreasonable. We have many senators, congressmen, and officials of Los Angeles among our guests. Surely you agree that such prominent people will find it awkward—"

I said, "Just a minute. Detective Graham told you he was going to interrogate everybody at the reception?"

"That is what he said to me. Yes."

Now, at last, I began to understand why I'd been called. Graham didn't like the Japanese and he had threatened to spoil their evening. Of course it was never going to happen. There was no way Graham was going to interrogate United States senators, let alone the district attorney or the mayor. Not if he expected to come to work tomorrow. But the Japanese annoyed him, and Graham had decided to annoy them back.

I said to Ishiguro, "We can set up a registration desk downstairs, and your guests can sign out as they leave."

"I am afraid that will be difficult," Ishiguro began, "because surely you will admit—"

"Mr. Ishiguro, that's what we're going to do."

"But what you ask is extremely difficult—"

"Mr. Ishiguro."

"You see, for us this is going to cause—"

"Mr. Ishiguro, I'm sorry. I've just told you what police procedure is going to be."

He stiffened. There was a pause. He wiped some sweat from his upper lip and said, "I am disappointed, Lieutenant, not to have greater cooperation from you."

"Cooperation?" That was when I started to get pissed off. "Mr. Ishiguro, you've got a dead woman in there, and it is our job to investigate what happened to—"

"But you must acknowledge our special circumstances—"

Then I heard Graham say, "Aw, Christ, *what is this*?"

Looking over my shoulder, I saw a short, bookish Japanese man twenty meters beyond the yellow tape. He was taking pictures of the crime scene. The camera he held was so small it was nearly concealed in the palm of his hand. But he wasn't concealing the fact that he had crossed the tape barrier to take his pictures. As I watched, he moved slowly back toward us, raising his hands for a moment to snap a picture, then blinking behind his wire-frame spectacles as he selected his next shot. He was deliberate in his movements.

Graham went up to the tape and said, "For Christ's sake, get out of there. This is a crime scene. You can't take pictures in there." The man didn't respond. He kept moving backward. Graham turned away. "Who is this guy?"

Ishiguro said, "This is our employee, Mr. Tanaka. He works for Nakamoto Security."

I couldn't believe what I was seeing. The Japanese had their own employee wandering around inside the yellow tapes, contaminating the crime scene. It was outrageous. "Get him out of there," I said.

"He is taking pictures."

"He can't do that."

Ishiguro said, "But this is for our corporate use."

I said, "I don't care, Mr. Ishiguro. He can't be inside the yellow tape, and he can't take pictures. Get him out of there. And I want his film, please."

"Very well." Ishiguro said something quickly in Japanese. I turned, just in time to see Tanaka slip under the yellow tape, and disappear among the blue-suited men clustered by the elevator. Behind their heads, I saw the elevator doors open and close.

Son of a bitch. I was getting angry. "Mr. Ishiguro, you are now obstructing an official police investigation."

Ishiguro said calmly, "You must try to understand our position, Detective Smith. Of course we have complete confidence in the Los Angeles Police Department, but we must be able to undertake our own private inquiry, and for that we must have—"

Their own private inquiry? The *son of a bitch.* I suddenly couldn't speak. I clenched my teeth, seeing red. I was furious. I wanted to arrest Ishiguro. I wanted to spin him around, shove him up against the wall, and snap the cuffs around his fucking wrists and—

"Perhaps I can be of assistance, Lieutenant," a voice behind me said.

I turned. It was John Connor, smiling cheerfully.

I stepped aside.

Connor faced Ishiguro, bowed slightly, and presented his card. He spoke rapidly. "*Totsuzen shitsurei desuga, jiko-shōkai wo shitemo yoroshii desuka. Watashi wa John Connor to mōshimasu. Meishi o dōzo. Dōzo yoroshiku.*"

"John Connor?" Ishiguro said. "*The* John Connor? *Omeni kakarete kōei desu. Watashi wa Ishiguro desu. Dōzo yoroshiku.*" He was saying he was honored to meet him.

"*Watashi no meishi desu. Dōzo.*" A graceful thank you.

But once the formalities were completed, the conversation went so quickly I caught only an occasional word. I was obliged to appear interested, watching and nodding, when in fact I had no idea what they were talking about. Once I heard Connor refer to me as *wakaimono*, which I knew meant his protégé or apprentice. Several times, he looked at me severely, and shook his head like a regretful father. It seemed he was apologizing for me. I also heard him refer to Graham as *bushitsuke*, a disagreeable man.

But these apologies had their effect. Ishiguro calmed down, dropping his shoulders. He began to relax. He even smiled. Finally he said, "Then you will not check identification of our guests?"

"Absolutely not," Connor said. "Your honored guests are free to come and go as they wish."

I started to protest. Connor shot me a look.

"Identification is unnecessary," Connor continued, speaking formally, "because I am sure that no guest of the

Nakamoto Corporation could ever be involved in such an unfortunate incident."

"Fucking A," Graham said, under his breath.

Ishiguro was beaming. But I was furious. Connor had contradicted me. He had made me look like a fool. And on top of that, he wasn't following police procedure—we could all be in trouble for that later on. Angrily, I shoved my hands in my pockets and looked away.

"I am grateful for your delicate handling of this situation, Captain Connor," Ishiguro said.

"I have done nothing at all," Connor replied, making another formal bow. "But I hope you will now agree it is appropriate to clear the floor, so the police may begin their investigation."

Ishiguro blinked. "Clear the floor?"

"Yes," Connor said, taking out a notebook. "And please assist me to know the names of the gentlemen standing behind you, as you ask them to leave."

"I am sorry?"

"The names of the gentlemen behind you, please."

"May I ask why?"

Connor's face darkened, and he barked a short phrase in Japanese. I didn't catch the words, but Ishiguro turned bright red.

"Excuse me, Captain, but I see no reason for you to speak in this—"

And then, Connor lost his temper. Spectacularly and explosively. He moved close to Ishiguro, making sharp stabbing motions with his finger while he shouted: "*Iikagen ni shiro! Soko o doke! Kiiterunoka!*"

Ishiguro ducked and turned away, stunned by this verbal assault.

Connor leaned over him, his voice hard and sarcastic: "*Doke! Doke! Wakaranainoka?*" He turned, and pointed furiously toward the Japanese men by the elevator. Confronted with Connor's naked anger, the Japanese looked away, and puffed anxiously on their cigarettes. But they did not leave.

"Hey, Richie," Connor said, calling to the crime unit

photographer Richie Walters. "Get me some IDs of these guys, will you?"

"Sure, Captain," Richie said. He raised his camera and began moving down the line of men, firing his strobe in quick succession.

Ishiguro suddenly got excited, stepping in front of the camera, holding up his hands. "Wait a minute, wait a minute, what is this?"

But the Japanese men were already leaving, wheeling away like a school of fish from the strobe flash. In a few seconds they were gone. We had the floor to ourselves. Alone, Ishiguro looked uncomfortable.

He said something in Japanese. Apparently it was the wrong thing.

"Oh?" Connor said. "*You* are to blame here," he said to Ishiguro. "*You* are the cause of all these troubles. And *you* will see that my detectives get any assistance they need. I want to speak to the person who discovered the body, and the person who called in the original report. I want the name of every person who has been on this floor since the body was discovered. And I want the film from Tanaka's camera. *Ore wa honkida.* I will arrest you if you obstruct this investigation further."

"But I must consult my superiors—"

"*Namerunayo.*" Connor leaned close. "Don't fuck with me, Ishiguro-san. Now leave, and let us work."

"Of course, Captain," he said. With a tight, brief bow he left, his face pinched and unhappy.

Graham chuckled. "You told him off pretty good."

Connor spun. "What were you doing, telling him you were going to interrogate everybody at the party?"

"Aw, shit, I was just winding him up," Graham said. "There's no way I'm going to interrogate the mayor. Can I help it if these assholes have no sense of humor?"

"They have a sense of humor," Connor said. "And the joke is on you. Because Ishiguro had a problem, and he solved it with your help."

"*My* help?" Graham was frowning. "What're you talking about?"

"It's clear the Japanese wanted to delay the investigation," Connor said. "Your aggressive tactics gave them the perfect excuse—to call for the Special Services liaison."

"Oh, come on," Graham said. "For all they know, the liaison could have been here in five minutes."

Connor shook his head. "Don't kid yourself: they knew exactly who was on call tonight. They knew exactly how far away Smith would be, and exactly how long it would take him to get here. And they managed to delay the investigation an hour and a half. Nice work, detective."

Graham stared at Connor for a long moment. Then he turned away. "Fuck," he said. "That's a load of bullshit, and you know it. Fellas, I'm going to work. Richie? Mount up. You got thirty seconds to document before my guys come in and step on your tail. Let's go, everybody. I want to get finished before she starts to smell too bad."

And he lumbered off toward the crime scene.

With their suitcases and evidence carts, the SID team trailed after Graham. Richie Walters led the way, shooting left and right as he worked his way forward into the atrium, then going through the door into the conference room. The walls of the conference room were smoked glass, which dimmed his flash. But I could see him inside, circling the body. He was shooting a lot: he knew this was a big case.

I stayed behind with Connor. I said, "I thought you told me it was bad form to lose your temper with the Japanese."

"It is," Connor said.

"Then why did you lose yours?"

"Unfortunately," he said, "it was the only way to assist Ishiguro."

"To *assist* Ishiguro?"

"Yes. I did all that for Ishiguro—because he had to save face in front of his boss. Ishiguro wasn't the most important man in the room. One of the Japanese standing by the elevator was the *jūyaku*, the real boss."

"I didn't notice," I said.

"It's common practice to put a lesser man in front, while

the boss stays in the background, where he is free to observe progress. Just as I did with you, *kōhai*."

"Ishiguro's boss was watching all the time?"

"Yes. And Ishiguro clearly had orders not to allow the investigation to begin. I needed to start the investigation. But I had to do it in such a way that he would not look incompetent. So I played the out-of-control *gaijin*. Now he owes me a favor. Which is good, because I may need his help later on."

"He owes you a favor?" I said, having trouble with this idea. Connor had just screamed at Ishiguro—thoroughly humiliating him, as far as I was concerned.

Connor sighed. "Even if you don't understand what happened, believe me: Ishiguro understands very well. He had a problem, and I helped him."

I still didn't really understand, and I started to say more, but Connor held up his hand. "I think we better take a look at the scene, before Graham and his men screw things up any more than they already have."

It'd been almost two years since I worked the detective division, and it felt good to be around a homicide again. It brought back memories: the nighttime tension, the adrenaline rush of bad coffee in paper cups, and all the teams working around you—it's a kind of crazy energy, circling the center where somebody is lying, dead. Every homicide crime scene has that same energy, and that finality at the center. When you look at the dead person, there is a kind of obviousness, and at the same time there is an impossible mystery. Even in the simplest domestic brawl, where the woman finally decided to shoot the guy, you'd look at her, all covered in scars and cigarette burns, and you had to ask, why tonight? What was it about tonight? It's always clear what you are seeing, and there's always something that doesn't add up. Both things at once.

And at a homicide you have the sense of being right down to the basic truths of existence, the smells and the defecation and the bloating. Usually somebody's crying, so you're listening to that. And the usual bullshit stops; somebody died, and it's an unavoidable fact, like a rock in the road that makes all the traffic go around it. And in that grim and real setting, this camaraderie springs up, because you're working late with people you know, and actually know very well because you see them all the time. L.A. has four homicides a day; there's another one every six hours. And every detective at the crime scene already has ten homicides dragging on his backlog, which makes this new one an intolerable burden, so he and everybody else is hoping to solve it on the spot, to get it out of the way. There is that kind of finality and tension and energy all mixed together.

And after you do it for a few years, you get so you like it. And to my surprise, as I entered the conference room, I realized that I missed it.

The conference room was elegant: black table, black high-backed leather chairs, the lights of the nighttime skyscrapers beyond the glass walls. Inside the room, the technicians talked quietly, as they moved around the body of the dead girl.

She had blond hair cut short. Blue eyes, full mouth. She looked about twenty-five. Tall, with a long-limbed, athletic look. Her dress was black and sheer.

Graham was well into his examination; he was down at the end of the table, squinting at the girl's black patent high heels, a penlight in one hand, his notebook in another.

Kelly, the coroner's assistant, was taping the girl's hands in paper bags to protect them. Connor stopped him. "Just a minute." Connor looked at one hand, inspecting the wrist, peering closely under the fingernails. He sniffed under one nail. Then he flicked the fingers rapidly, one after another.

"Don't bother," Graham said laconically. "There's no rigor mortis yet, and no detritus under the nails, no skin or cloth fibers. In fact, I'd say there aren't many signs of a struggle at all."

Kelly slipped the bag over the hand. Connor said to him, "You have a time of death?"

"I'm working on it." Kelly lifted the girl's buttocks to place the rectal probe. "The axillary thermocouples are already in place. We'll know in a minute."

Connor touched the fabric of the black dress, checked the label. Helen, part of the SID team, said, "It's a Yamamoto."

"I see that," Connor said.

"What's a Yamamoto?" I said.

Helen said, "Very expensive Japanese designer. This little black nothing is at least five thousand dollars. That's assuming she bought it used. New, it's maybe fifteen thousand."

"Is it traceable?" Connor asked her.

"Maybe. Depends on whether she bought it here, or in Europe, or Tokyo. It'll take a couple of days to check."

Connor immediately lost interest. "Never mind. That'll be too late."

He produced a small, fiber-optic penlight, which he used to inspect the girl's scalp and hair. Then he looked quickly at each ear, giving a little murmur of surprise at the right ear. I peered over his shoulder, and saw a drop of dried blood at the pierced hole for her earring. I must have been crowding Connor, because he glanced up at me. "Excuse me, *kōhai*."

I stepped back. "Sorry."

Next, Connor sniffed the girl's lips, opened and closed her jaw rapidly, and poked around inside her mouth, using his penlight as a probe. Then he turned her head from side to side on the table, making her look left and right. He spent some time feeling gently along her neck, almost caressing it with his fingers.

And then, quite abruptly, he stepped away from the body and said, "All right, I'm finished."

And he walked out of the boardroom.

Graham looked up. "He never was worth a damn at a crime scene."

I said, "Why do you say that? I hear he's a great detective."

"Oh, hell," Graham said. "You can see for yourself. He doesn't even know what to do. Doesn't know procedure. Connor's no detective. Connor has *connections.* That's how he solved all those cases he's so famous for. You remember the Arakawa honeymoon shootings? No? I guess it was before your time, Petey-san. When was that Arakawa case, Kelly?"

"Seventy-six," Kelly said.

"Right, seventy-six. Big fucking case that year. Mr. and Mrs. Arakawa, a young couple visiting Los Angeles on their honeymoon, are standing on the curb in East L.A. when they get gunned down from a passing car. Drive-by gang-style shooting. Worse, at autopsy it turns out Mrs. Arakawa was pregnant. The press has a field day: L.A.P.D. can't handle gang violence, is the way the story goes. Letters and money come from all over the city. Everyone is upset about what happened to this fresh young couple. And of course the detectives assigned to the case don't discover shit. I mean, a case involving murdered Japanese nationals: they're getting *nowhere*.

"So, after a week, Connor is called in. And he solves it in one day. A fucking miracle of detection. I mean, it's a *week later*. The physical evidence is long gone, the bodies of the honeymooners are back in Osaka, the street corner where it happened is piled high in wilted flowers. But Connor is able to show that the youthful Mr. Arakawa is actually quite a bad boy in Osaka. He shows that the street-corner gangland shooting is actually a *yakuza* killing contracted in Japan to take place in America. And he shows that the nasty husband is the innocent bystander: they were really gunning for the wife, knowing she was pregnant, because it's *her* father they wanted to teach a lesson. So. Connor turns it all around. Pretty fucking amazing, huh?"

"And you think he did it all with his Japanese connections?"

"You tell me," Graham said. "All I know is, pretty soon after that, he goes to Japan for a year."

"Doing what?"

"I heard he worked as a security guy for a grateful Japanese company. They took care of him, is what it amounted to. He did a job for them, and they paid off. Anyway, that's the way I figure it. Nobody really knows. But the man is not a detective. Christ: just look at him now."

Out in the atrium, Connor was staring up at the high ceiling in a dreamy, reflective way. He looked first in one direction, and then another. He seemed to be trying to make up his mind. Suddenly, he walked briskly toward the elevators, as if he were leaving. Then without warning, he turned on his heel, and walked back to the center of the room, and stopped. Next, he began to inspect the leaves on the potted palm trees scattered around the room.

Graham shook his head. "What is this, gardening? I'm telling you, he's a strange guy. You know he's gone to Japan more than once. He always comes back. It never works out for him. Japan is like a woman that he can't live with, and can't live without, you know? Myself, I don't fucking get it. I like America. At least, what's left of it."

He turned to the SID team, which was moving outward from the body. "You guys find those panties for me yet?"

"Not yet, Tom."

"We're looking, Tom."

I said, "What panties?"

Graham lifted the girl's skirt. "Your friend John couldn't be bothered to finish his examination, but I'd say there's something significant here. I'd say that's seminal fluid oozing out of the vagina, she's not wearing panties, and there's a red line at the groin where they were ripped off. External genitals are red and raw. It's pretty clear she had forcible intercourse before she was killed. So I'm asking the boys to find the panties."

One of the SID team said, "Maybe she wasn't wearing any."

Graham said, "She was wearing them, all right."

I turned back to Kelly. "What about drugs?"

He shrugged. "We'll get lab values on all fluids. But to the eye, she looks clean. Very clean." I noticed that Kelly was distinctly uneasy, now.

Graham saw it, too. "For Christ's sake, what are you hangdog about, Kelly? We keeping you from a late-night date, or what?"

"No," Kelly said, "but to tell you the truth, not only is there no evidence of a struggle, or of drugs—I don't see any evidence that she was murdered at all."

Graham said, "No evidence she was murdered? Are you kidding?"

Kelly said, "The girl has throat injuries that suggest she may have been into one of the sexual bondage syndromes. She has signs beneath the makeup that she's been tied up before, repeatedly."

"So?"

"So, technically speaking, maybe she wasn't murdered. Maybe she experienced sudden death from natural causes."

"Aw, Christ. Come on."

"It's quite possible this is a case of what we call death from inhibition. Instantaneous physiological death."

"Meaning what?"

He shrugged. "The person just dies."

"For no reason at all?"

"Well, not exactly. There's usually minor trauma involving the heart or nerves. But the trauma isn't sufficient to cause death. I had one case where a ten-year-old kid got hit in the chest with a baseball—not very hard—and fell down dead in the school yard. Nobody within twenty meters of him. Another case, a woman had a minor car accident, banged into the steering wheel with her chest, not very hard, and while she was opening the car door to get out, she dropped dead. It seems to happen where there is neck or chest injury, which may irritate the nerves running to the heart. So, yeah, Tom. Technically, sudden death is a distinct possibility. And since having sex is not a felony, it wouldn't be murder."

Graham squinted. "So you're saying maybe *nobody* killed her?"

Kelly shrugged. He picked up his clipboard. "I'm not putting any of this down. I'm listing the cause of death as asphyxiation secondary to manual strangulation. Because the odds are, she was strangled. But you should file it away in the back of your mind that maybe she wasn't. Maybe she just popped off."

"Fine," Graham said. "We'll file it. Under medical examiner's fantasies. Meanwhile, any of you guys got an ID on her?"

The SID team, still searching the room, murmured no.

Kelly said, "I think I got a time of death." He checked his temperature probes and read off a chart. "I register a core of ninety-six point nine. In this ambient room temperature, that's consistent with up to three hours postmortem."

"Up to three hours? That's great. Listen Kelly, we already knew she died *sometime* tonight."

"It's the best I can do." Kelly shook his head. "Unfortunately, the cooling curves don't discriminate well for under three hours. All I can say is death occurred sometime within three hours. But my impression is that this girl has been dead a while. Frankly, I would say it's close to three hours."

Graham turned to the SID team. "Anybody find the panties yet?"

"Not so far, Lieutenant."

Graham looked around the room and said, "No purse, no panties."

I said, "You think somebody cleaned up here?"

"I don't know," he said. "But doesn't a girl who's coming to a party in a thirty-thousand-dollar dress usually carry a purse?" Then Graham looked past my shoulder and smiled: "Well, what do you know, Petey-san? One of your admirers to see you."

Striding toward me was Ellen Farley, the mayor's press secretary. Farley was thirty-five, dark blond hair cropped close to her head, perfectly groomed as always. She had been a newscaster when she was younger, but had worked for the mayor's office for many years. Ellen Farley was smart, fast on her feet, and she had one of the great bodies, which as far as anyone knew she retained for her own exclusive use.

I liked her enough to have done a couple of favors for her when I was in the L.A.P.D. press office. Since the mayor and the chief of police hated each other, requests from the mayor's office sometimes passed from Ellen to me, and I handled them. Mostly small things: delaying the release of a report until the weekend, so it'd run on Saturday. Or announcing that charges in a case hadn't been brought yet, even though they had. I did it because Farley was a straight shooter, who always spoke her mind. And it looked like she was going to speak her mind now.

"Listen, Pete," she said. "I don't know what's going on here, but the mayor's been hearing some pretty strong complaints from a Mr. Ishiguro—"

"I can imagine—"

"And the mayor asked me to remind you that there is no

excuse for officials of this city to be rude to foreign nationals."

Graham said loudly, "Especially when they make such large campaign contributions."

"Foreign nationals can't contribute to American political campaigns," Farley said. "You know that." She lowered her voice. "This is a sensitive case, Pete. I want you to be careful. You know the Japanese have a special concern about how they are treated in America."

"Okay, fine."

She looked through the glass walls of the conference room, toward the atrium. "Is that John Connor?"

"Yes."

"I thought he was retired. What's he doing here?"

"Helping me on the case."

Farley frowned. "You know the Japanese have mixed feelings about him. They have a term for it. For somebody who is a Japan lover and goes to the other extreme, and turns into a basher."

"Connor isn't a basher."

"Ishiguro felt roughly treated."

"Ishiguro was telling us what to do," I said. "And we have a murdered girl here, which everybody seems to be forgetting—"

"Come on, Pete," she said, "nobody's trying to tell you how to do your job. All I'm saying is you have to take into account the special—"

She stopped.

She was looking at the body.

"Ellen?" I said. "Do you know her?"

"No." She turned away.

"You sure?"

I could see she was rattled.

Graham said, "You saw her downstairs earlier?"

"I don't—maybe. I think so. Listen, fellas, I've got to get back."

"Ellen. Come on."

"I don't know who she is, Pete. You know I'd tell you if

I did. Just keep it cordial with the Japanese. That's all the mayor wanted me to say. I've got to go now."

She hurried back toward the elevators. I watched her leave, feeling uneasy.

Graham came over and stood beside me. "She's got a great ass," he said. "But she ain't leveling, buddy, even with you."

I said, "What do you mean, even with me?"

"Everybody knows you and Farley were an item."

"What are you talking about?"

Graham punched me on the shoulder. "Come on. You're divorced now. Nobody gives a shit."

I said, "It's not true, Tom."

"You can do what you want. Handsome guy like you."

"I'm telling you, it's not true."

"Okay, fine." He held up his hands. "My mistake."

I watched Farley at the other end of the atrium, ducking under the tape. She pressed the elevator button, and waited for it to come, tapping her foot impatiently.

I said, "You really think she knows who the girl is?"

"Damn right she does," Graham said. "You know why the mayor likes her. She stands by his side and whispers everybody's name to him. People she hasn't seen for years. Husbands, wives, children, everyone. Farley knows who this girl is."

"Then why didn't she tell us?"

"Fuck," Graham said. "Must be important to somebody. She took off like a shot, didn't she? I tell you, we better figure out who this dead girl is. Because I fucking hate being the last one in town to know."

Connor was across the room, waving to us.

"What does he want now?" Graham said. "Waving like that. What's he got in his hand?"

"Looks like a purse," I said.

"Cheryl Lynn Austin," Connor said, reading. "Born Midland, Texas, graduate of Texas State. Twenty-three years old. Got an apartment in Westwood, but hasn't been here long enough to change her Texas driver's license."

The contents of the purse were spread out on a desk. We pushed them around with pencils.

"Where'd you find this purse?" I asked. It was a small, dark, beaded clutch with a pearl clasp. A vintage forties purse. Expensive.

"It was in the potted palm near the conference room." Connor unzipped a tiny compartment. A tight roll of crisp hundred-dollar bills tumbled onto the table. "Very nice. Miss Austin is well taken care of."

I said, "No car keys?"

"No."

"So she came with somebody."

"And evidently intended to leave with somebody, too. Taxis can't break a hundred-dollar bill."

There was also a gold American Express Card. Lipstick and a compact. A pack of Mild Seven Menthol cigarettes, a Japanese brand. A card for the Daimatsu Night Club in Tokyo. Four small blue pills. That was about it.

Using his pencil, Connor upended the beaded purse. Small green flecks spilled out onto the table. "Know what that is?"

"No," I said. Graham looked at it with a magnifying glass.

Connor said, "It's *wasabi*-covered peanuts."

Wasabi is green horseradish served in Japanese restaurants. I had never heard of *wasabi*-covered peanuts.

"I don't know if they're sold outside Japan."

Graham grunted. "I've seen enough. So what do you think now, John? Is Ishiguro going to get those witnesses you asked for?"

"I wouldn't expect them soon," Connor said.

"Fucking right," Graham said. "We won't see those witnesses until day after tomorrow, after their lawyers have briefed them on exactly what to say." He stepped away from the table. "You realize why they're delaying us. A Japanese killed this girl. That's what we're dealing with."

"It's possible," Connor said.

"Hey, buddy. More than possible. We're *here*. This is their building. And that girl is just the type they go for. The

American beauty long-stemmed rose. You know all those little guys want to fuck a volleyball player."

Connor shrugged. "Possibly."

"Come on," Graham said. "You know those guys eat shit all day long at home. Crammed into subways, working in big companies. Can't say what they think. Then they come over here, away from the constraints of home, and suddenly they're rich and free. They can do whatever they want. And sometimes one of them goes a little crazy. Tell me I'm wrong."

Connor looked at Graham for a long time. Finally he said, "So as you see it, Tom, a Japanese killer decided to dispatch this girl on the Nakamoto boardroom conference table?"

"Right."

"As a symbolic act?"

Graham shrugged. "Christ, who knows? We're not talking normality here. But I'll tell you one thing. I'm going to get the fucker who did this, if it's the last goddamned thing I do."

The elevator descended rapidly. Connor leaned against the glass. "There are many reasons to dislike the Japanese," he said, "but Graham knows none of them." He sighed. "You know what they say about us?"

"What?"

"They say Americans are too eager to make theories. They say we don't spend enough time observing the world, and so we don't know how things actually *are*."

"Is that a Zen idea?"

"No," he laughed. "Just an observation. Ask a computer salesman what he thinks of his American counterparts, and he'll tell you that. Everyone in Japan who deals with Americans thinks it. And when you look at Graham, you realize they're right. Graham has no real knowledge, no first-hand experience. He just has a collection of prejudices and media fantasies. He doesn't know anything about the Japanese—and it never occurs to him to find out."

I said, "Then you think he's wrong? The girl wasn't killed by a Japanese?"

"I didn't say that, *kōhai*," Connor replied. "It's very possible Graham is right. But at the moment—"

The doors opened and we saw the party, heard the band playing "Moonlight Serenade." Two party-going couples stepped into the elevator. They looked like real estate people: the men silver-haired and distinguished looking, the women pretty and slightly tacky. One woman said, "She's smaller than I thought."

"Yes, tiny. And that . . . was that her boyfriend?"

"I guess. Wasn't he the one in the video with her?"

"I think that was him."

One of the men said, "You think she had her boobs done?"

"Hasn't everybody?"

The other woman giggled. "Except me, of course."

"Right, Christine."

"But I'm thinking about it. Did you see Emily?"

"Oh, she did hers so *big*."

"Well, Jane started it, blame her. Now everyone wants them big."

The men turned and looked out the window. "Hell of a building," one said. "Detailing is fantastic. Must have cost a fortune. You doing much with the Japanese now, Ron?"

"About twenty percent," the other man said. "That's way down from last year. It's made me work on my golf game, because they always want to play golf."

"Twenty percent of your business?"

"Yeah. They're buying up Orange County now."

"Of course. They already own Los Angeles," one of the women said, laughing.

"Well, just about. They have the Arco building over there," the man said, pointing out the window. "I guess by now they have seventy, seventy-five percent of downtown Los Angeles."

"And more in Hawaii."

"Hell, they *own* Hawaii—ninety percent of Honolulu, a hundred percent of the Kona coast. Putting up golf courses like mad."

One woman said, "Will this party be on *ET* tomorrow? They had enough cameras here."

"Let's remember to watch."

The elevator said, "*Mōsugu de gozaimasu.*"

We came to the garage floor, and the people got off. Connor watched them go, and shook his head. "In no other country in the world," he said, "would you hear people calmly discussing the fact that their cities and states were sold to foreigners."

"Discussing?" I said. "They're the ones doing the selling."

"Yes. Americans are eager to sell. It amazes the Japanese. They think we're committing economic suicide. And of course they're right." As he spoke, Connor pressed a button on the elevator panel marked EMERGENCY ONLY.

A soft pinging alarm sounded.

"What'd you do that for?"

Connor looked at a video camera mounted in the corner of the ceiling and waved cheerfully. A voice on the intercom said, "Good evening, officers. Can I help you?"

"Yes," Connor said. "Am I speaking to building security?"

"That's right, sir. Is something wrong with your elevator?"

"Where are you located?"

"We're on the lobby level, southeast corner, behind the elevators."

"Thank you very much," Connor said. He pushed the button for the lobby.

☀ The security office of the Nakamoto Tower was a small room, perhaps five meters by seven. It was dominated by three large, flat video panels, each divided into a dozen smaller monitor views. At the moment, most of these were black rectangles. But one row showed images from the lobby and the garage; another row showed the party in progress. And a third row showed the police teams up on the forty-sixth floor.

Jerome Phillips was the guard on duty. He was a black man in his midforties. His gray Nakamoto Security uniform was soaked around the collar, and dark under the armpits. He asked us to leave the door open as we entered. He appeared noticeably uneasy to have us there. I sensed he was hiding something, but Connor approached him in a friendly way. We showed our badges and shook hands. Connor managed to convey the idea that we were all security professionals, having a little chat together. "Must be a busy night for you, Mr. Phillips."

"Yeah, sure. The party and everything."

"And crowded, in this little room."

He wiped sweat from his forehead. "Boy, you got that right. All of them packed in here. Jesus."

I said, "All of who?"

Connor looked at me and said, "After the Japanese left the forty-sixth floor, they came down here and watched us on the monitors. Isn't that right, Mr. Phillips?"

Phillips nodded. "Not all of 'em, but quite a few. Down here, smoking their damn cigarettes, staring and puffing and passing around faxes."

"Faxes?"

"Oh, yeah, every few minutes, somebody'd bring in another fax. You know, in Japanese writing. They'd all pass it around, make comments. Then one of 'em would leave to send a fax back. And the rest would stay to watch you guys up on the floor."

Connor said, "And listen, too?"

Phillips shook his head. "No. We don't have audio feeds."

"I'm surprised," Connor said. "This equipment seems so up-to-date."

"Up-to-date? Hell, it's the most advanced in the world. These people, I tell you one thing. These people do it right. They have the best fire alarm and fire prevention system. The best earthquake system. And of course the best electronic security system: best cameras, detectors, everything."

"I can see that," Connor said. "That's why I was surprised they don't have audio."

"No. No audio. They do high-resolution video only. Don't ask me why. Something to do with the cameras and how they're hooked up, is all I know."

On the flat panels I saw five different views of the forty-sixth floor, as seen from different cameras. Apparently the Japanese had installed cameras all over the floor. I remembered how Connor had walked around the atrium, staring up at the ceiling. He must have spotted the cameras then.

Now I watched Graham in the conference room, directing the teams. He was smoking a cigarette, which was completely against regulations at a crime scene. I saw Helen stretch and yawn. Meanwhile, Kelly was getting ready to move the girl's body off the table onto a gurney, before zipping it into the bag, and he was—

Then it hit me.

They had cameras up there.

Five different cameras.

Covering every part of the floor.

I said, "Oh my God" and I spun around, very excited. I was about to say something when Connor smiled at me in an easy way, and placed his hand on my shoulder. He squeezed my shoulder—hard.

"Lieutenant," he said.

The pain was incredible. I tried not to wince. "Yes, Captain?"

"I wonder if you'd mind if I asked Mr. Phillips one or two questions."

"No, Captain. Go right ahead."

"Perhaps you'd take notes."

"Good idea, Captain."

He released my shoulder. I got out my notepad.

Connor sat on the edge of the table and said, "Have you been with Nakamoto Security long, Mr. Phillips?"

"Yes, sir. About six years now. I started over in their La Habra plant, and when I hurt my leg—in a car accident— and couldn't walk so good, they moved me to security. In the plant. Because I wouldn't have to walk around, you see. Then when they opened the Torrance plant, they moved me over there. My wife got a job in the Torrance plant, too. They do Toyota subassemblies. Then, when this building opened, they brought me here, to work nights."

"I see. Six years altogether."

"Yes, sir."

"You must like it."

"Well, I tell you, it's a secure job. That's something in America. I know they don't think much of black folks, but they always treated me okay. And hell, before this I worked for GM in Van Nuys, and that's . . . you know, that's *gone*."

"Yes," Connor said sympathetically.

"That place," Phillips said, shaking his head at the memory. "Christ. The management assholes they used to send down to the floor. You couldn't believe it. M.B. fucking A., out of Detroit, little weenies didn't know *shit*. They didn't know how the line worked. They didn't know a tool from a die. But they'd still order the foremen around. They're all pulling in two hundred fucking thousand a year and they didn't know shit. And nothing ever worked right. The cars were all a piece of shit. But here," he said, tapping the counter. "Here, I got a problem, or something doesn't work,

I tell somebody. And they come right down, and they know the system—how it works—and we go over the problem together, and it gets *fixed.* Right away. Problems get fixed here. That's the difference. I tell you: these people *pay attention.*"

"So you like it here."

"They always treated me okay," Phillips said, nodding.

That didn't exactly strike me as a glowing endorsement. I had the feeling this guy wasn't committed to his employers and a few questions could drive the wedge. All we had to do was encourage the break.

"Loyalty is important," Connor said, nodding sympathetically.

"It is to them," he said. "They expect you to show all this enthusiasm for the company. So you know, I always come in fifteen or twenty minutes early, and stay fifteen or twenty minutes after the shift is over. They like you to put in the extra time. I did the same at Van Nuys, but nobody ever noticed."

"And when is your shift?"

"I work nine to seven."

"And tonight? What time did you come on duty?"

"Quarter to nine. Like I said, I come in fifteen minutes early."

The original call had been recorded about eight-thirty. So if this man came at a quarter to nine, he would have arrived almost fifteen minutes too late to see the murder. "Who was on duty before you?"

"Well, usually it's Ted Cole. But I don't know if he worked tonight."

"Why is that?"

The guard wiped his forehead with his sleeve, and looked away.

"Why is that, Mr. Phillips?" I said, with a little more force.

The guard blinked and frowned, saying nothing.

Connor said quietly, "Because Ted Cole wasn't here when Mr. Phillips arrived tonight, was he, Mr. Phillips?"

The guard shook his head. "No, he wasn't."

I started to ask another question, but Connor raised his hand. "I imagine, Mr. Phillips, you must have been pretty surprised when you came in this room, at a quarter to nine."

"You damn right I was," Phillips said.

"What did you do when you saw the situation?"

"Well. Right away, I said to the guy, 'Can I help you?' Very polite but still firm. I mean, this *is* the security room. And I don't know who this guy is, I've never seen him before. And the guy is tense. *Very* tense. He says to me, 'Get out of my way.' Real pushy, like he owns the world. And he shoves past me, taking his briefcase with him.

"I say, 'Excuse me, sir, I'll have to see some identification.' He don't answer me, he just keeps going. Out the lobby and down the stairs."

"You didn't try and stop him?"

"No, sir. I didn't."

"Because he was Japanese?"

"You got that right. But I called up to central security— it's up on the ninth floor—to say I found a man in the room. And they say, 'Don't worry, everything is fine.' But I can hear they're tense, too. Everybody is tense. And then I see on the monitor . . . the dead girl. So that's the first I knew what it was about."

Connor said, "The man you saw. Can you describe him?"

The guard shrugged. "Thirty, thirty-five. Medium height. Dark blue suit like they all wear. Actually he was more hip than most of them. He had this tie with triangles on it. Oh—and a scar on his hand, like a burn or something."

"Which hand?"

"The left hand. I noticed it when he was closing the briefcase."

"Could you see inside the briefcase?"

"No."

"But he was closing it when you came in the room?"

"Yes."

"Was it your impression he took something from this room?"

"I really couldn't say, sir."

Phillips's evasiveness began to annoy me. I said, "What do you think he took?"

Connor shot me a look.

The guard went bland: "I really don't know, sir."

Connor said, "Of course you don't. There's no way you could know what was in somebody else's briefcase. By the way, do you make recordings from the security cameras here?"

"Yes, we do."

"Could you show me how you do that?"

"Sure thing." The guard got up from the desk and opened a door at the far end of the room. We followed him into a second small room, almost a closet, stacked floor to ceiling with small metal boxes, each with stenciled notations in Japanese *kanji* script, and numbers in English. Each with a glowing red light, and an LED counter, with numbers running forward.

Phillips said, "These are our recorders. They lay down signals from all the cameras in the building. They're eight-millimeter, high-definition video." He held up a small cassette, like an audio cassette. "Each one of these records eight hours. We change over at nine p.m., so that's the first thing I do when I come on duty. I pop out the old ones, and switch over to the fresh ones."

"And did you change cassettes tonight, at nine o'clock?"

"Yes, sir. Just like always."

"And what do you do with the tapes you remove?"

"Keep 'em in the trays down here," he said, bending to show us several long, thin drawers. "We keep everything off the cameras for seventy-two hours. That's three days. So we keep nine sets of tapes all together. And we just rotate each set through, once every three days. Get me?"

Connor hesitated. "Perhaps I'd better write this down." He produced a small pad and a pen. "Now, each tape lasts eight hours, so you have nine different sets . . . ."

"Right, right."

Connor wrote for a moment, then shook his pen irritably. "This damn pen. It's out of ink. You have a wastebasket?"

Phillips pointed to the corner. "Over there."

"Thank you."

Connor threw the pen away. I gave him mine. He resumed his notes. "You were saying, Mr. Phillips, that you have nine sets . . ."

"Right. Each set is numbered with letters, from A to I. Now when I come in at nine, I eject the tapes and see whatever letter is already in there, and put in the next one. Like tonight, I took out set C, so I put in set D, which is what's recording now."

"I see," Connor said. "And then you put tape set C in one of the drawers here?"

"Right." He pulled open a drawer. "This one here."

Connor said. "May I?" He glanced at the neatly labeled row of tapes. Then he quickly opened the other drawers, and looked at the other stacks of tapes. Except for the different letters, all the drawers looked identical.

"I think I understand now," Connor said. "What you actually do is use nine sets in rotation."

"Exactly."

"So each set gets used once every three days."

"Right."

"And how long has the security office been using this system?"

"The building's new, but we've been going, oh, maybe two months now."

"I must say it's a very well-organized system," Connor said appreciatively. "Thank you for explaining it to us. I have only a couple of other questions."

"Sure."

"First of all, these counters here—" Connor said, pointing to the LED counters on the video recorders. "They seem to show the elapsed times since the tapes began recording. Is that right? Because it's now almost eleven o'clock, and you put in the tapes at nine, and the top recorder says 1:55:30 and the next recorder says 1:55:10, and so on."

"Yes, that's right. I put the tapes in one right after another. It takes a few seconds between tapes."

"I see. These all show almost two hours. But I notice that

one recorder down here shows an elapsed time of only thirty minutes. Does that mean it's broken?"

"Huh," Phillips said, frowning. "I guess maybe it is. 'Cause I changed the tapes all one after another, like I said. But these recorders are the latest technology. Sometimes there are glitches. Or we had some power problems. Could be that."

"Yes. Quite possibly," Connor said. "Can you tell me which camera is hooked to this recorder?"

"Yes, of course." Phillips read the number off the recorder, and went out to the main room with the monitor screens. "It's camera four-six slash six," he said. "This view here." He tapped the screen.

It was an atrium camera, and it showed an overall view of the forty-sixth floor.

"But you see," Phillips said, "the beauty of the system is, even if one recorder screws up, there are still other cameras on that floor, and the video recorders on the others seem to be working okay."

"Yes, they do," Connor said. "By the way, can you tell me why there are so many cameras on the forty-sixth floor?"

"You didn't hear it from me," Phillips said. "But you know how they like efficiency. The word is, they are going to *kaizen* the office workers."

"So basically these cameras have been installed to observe workers during the day, and help them improve their efficiency?"

"That's what I heard."

"Well, I think that's it," Connor said. "Oh, one more question. Do you have an address for Ted Cole?"

Phillips shook his head. "No, I don't."

"Have you ever been out with him, socialized with him?"

"I have, but not much. He's an odd guy."

"Ever been to his apartment?"

"No. He's kind of secretive. I think he lives with his mother or something. We usually go to this bar, the Palomino, over by the airport. He likes it there."

Connor nodded. "And one last question: where is the nearest pay phone?"

"Out in the lobby, and around to your right, by the restrooms. But you're welcome to use the phone here."

Connor shook the guard's hand warmly. "Mr. Phillips, I appreciate your taking the time to talk to us."

"No problem."

I gave the guard my card. "If you think of anything later that could help us, Mr. Phillips, don't hesitate to call me." And I left.

Connor stood at the pay phone in the lobby. It was one of those new standing booths that has two receivers, one on either side, allowing two people to talk on the same line at once. These booths had been installed in Tokyo years ago, and now were starting to show up all over Los Angeles. Of course, Pacific Bell no longer was the principal provider of American public pay phones. Japanese manufacturers had penetrated that market, too. I watched Connor write down the phone number in his notebook.

"What are you doing?"

"We have two separate questions to answer tonight. One is how the girl came to be killed on an office floor. But we also need to find out who placed the original call, notifying us of the murder."

"And you think the call might have been placed from this phone?"

"Possibly."

He closed his notebook, and glanced at his watch. "It's late. We better get going."

"I think we're making a big mistake here."

"Why is that?" Connor asked.

"I don't know if we should leave the tapes in that security room. What if somebody switches them while we're gone?"

"They've already been switched," Connor said.

"How do you know?"

"I gave up a perfectly good pen to find out," he said. "Now come on." He started walking toward the stairs leading down to the garage. I followed him.

"You see," Connor said, "when Phillips first explained

55

that simple system of rotation, it was immediately clear to me that there might have been a switch. The question was how to prove it."

His voice echoed in the concrete stairwell. Connor continued down, taking the steps two at a time. I hurried to keep up.

Connor said, "If somebody switched the tapes, how would they go about it? They would be working hastily, under pressure. They'd be terrified of making a mistake. They certainly wouldn't want to leave any incriminating tapes behind. So probably they'd switch an entire set, and replace it. But replace it with what? They can't just put in the next set. Since there are only nine sets of tapes all together, it would be too easy for someone to notice that one set was missing, and the total was now eight. There would be an obvious empty drawer. No, they would have to replace the set they were taking away with an entirely new set. Twenty brand-new tapes. And that meant I ought to check the trash."

"That's why you threw your pen away?"

"Yes. I didn't want Phillips to know what I was doing."

"And?"

"The trash was full of crumpled plastic wrappers. The kind that new videotapes come wrapped in."

"I see."

"Once I knew the tapes had been replaced, the only remaining question was, which set? So I played dumb, and looked in all the drawers. You probably noticed that set C, the set Phillips removed when he came on duty, had slightly whiter labels than the other sets. It was subtle, because the office has only been active two months, but you could tell."

"I see." Somebody had come into the security room, taken out twenty fresh tapes, unwrapped them, written new labels, and popped them into the video machines, replacing the original tapes that had recorded the murder.

I said, "If you ask me, Phillips knows more about this than he was telling us."

"Maybe," Connor said, "but we have more important things to do. Anyway, there's a limit to what he knows. The murder was phoned in about eight-thirty. Phillips arrived at quarter to nine. So he never saw the murder. We can assume the previous guard, Cole, did. But by a quarter of nine, Cole was gone, and an unknown Japanese man was in the security room, closing up a briefcase."

"You think he's the one who switched the tapes?"

Connor nodded. "Very possibly. In fact, I wouldn't be surprised if this man was the killer himself. I hope to find that out at Miss Austin's apartment." He threw open the door, and we went into the garage.

A line of party guests waited for valets to bring their cars. I saw Ishiguro chatting up Mayor Thomas and his wife. Connor steered me toward them. Standing alongside the mayor, Ishiguro was so cordial he was almost obsequious. He gave us a big smile. "Ah, gentlemen. Is your investigation proceeding satisfactorily? Is there anything more I can do to help?"

I didn't get really angry until that moment: until I saw the way he toadied up in front of the mayor. It made me so mad I began to turn red. But Connor took it in stride.

"Thank you, Ishiguro-san," he said, with a slight bow. "The investigation is going well."

"You're receiving all the help you requested?" Ishiguro said.

"Oh, yes," Connor said. "Everyone has been very cooperative."

"Good, good. I'm glad." Ishiguro glanced at the mayor, and smiled at him, too. He was all smiles, it seemed.

"But," Connor said, "there is just one thing."

"Just name it. If there is anything we can do . . ."

"The security tapes seem to have been removed."

"Security tapes?" Ishiguro frowned, clearly caught off guard.

"Yes," Connor said. "Recordings from the security cameras."

"I don't know anything about that," Ishiguro said. "But let me assure you, if any tapes exist, they are yours to examine."

"Thank you," Connor said. "Unfortunately, it seems the

crucial tapes have been removed from the Nakamoto security office."

"Removed? Gentlemen, I believe there must be some mistake."

The mayor was watching this exchange closely.

Connor said, "Perhaps, but I don't think so. It would be reassuring, Mr. Ishiguro, if you were to look into this matter yourself."

"I certainly will," Ishiguro said. "But I must say again. I can't imagine, Captain Connor, that any tapes are missing."

"Thank you for checking, Mr. Ishiguro," Connor said.

"Not at all, Captain," he said, still smiling. "It is my pleasure to assist you in whatever way I can."

"The son of a bitch," I said. We were driving west on the Santa Monica freeway. "The little prick looked us right in the eye and *lied*."

"It's annoying," Connor said. "But you see, Ishiguro takes a different view. Now that he is beside the mayor, he sees himself in another context, with another set of obligations and requirements for his behavior. Since he is sensitive to context, he's able to act differently, with no reference to his earlier behavior. To us, he seems like a different person. But Ishiguro feels he's just being appropriate."

"What burns me is he acted so confident."

"Of course he did," Connor said. "And he would be quite surprised to learn that you're angry with him. You consider him immoral. He considers you naive. Because for a Japanese, consistent behavior is not possible. A Japanese becomes a different person around people of different rank. He becomes a different person when he moves through different rooms of his own house."

"Yeah," I said. "That's fine, but the fact is he's a lying son of a bitch."

Connor looked at me. "Would you talk that way to your mother?"

"Of course not."

"So you change according to context, too," Connor said. "The fact is we all do. It's just that Americans believe there is some core of individuality that doesn't change from one moment to the next. And the Japanese believe context rules everything."

"It sounds to me," I said, "like an excuse for lying."

"He doesn't see it as lying."

"But that's what it *is*."

Connor shrugged. "Only from your point of view, *kōhai*. Not from his."

"The hell."

"Look, it's your choice. You can understand the Japanese and deal with them as they are, or you can get pissed off. But our problem in this country is that we don't deal with the Japanese the way they really are." The car hit a deep pothole, bouncing so hard that the car phone fell off the receiver. Connor picked it up off the floor, and put it back on the hook.

Up ahead, I saw the exit for Bundy. I moved into the right lane. "One thing I'm not clear about," I said. "Why do you think the man with the briefcase in the security room might be the killer?"

"It's because of the time sequence. You see, the murder was reported at eight thirty-two. Less than fifteen minutes later, at eight forty-five, a Japanese man was down there switching the tapes, arranging a cover-up. That's a very fast response. Much too fast for a Japanese company."

"Why is that?"

"Japanese organizations are actually very slow to respond in a crisis. Their decision-making relies on precedents, and when a situation is unprecedented, people are uncertain how to behave. You remember the faxes? I am sure faxes have been flying back and forth to Nakamoto's Tokyo headquarters all night. Undoubtedly the company is still trying to decide what to do. A Japanese organization simply cannot move fast in a new situation."

"But an individual acting alone can?"

"Yes. Exactly."

I said, "And that's why you think the man with the briefcase may be the killer."

Connor nodded. "Yes. Either the killer, or someone closely connected with the killer. But we should learn more at Miss Austin's apartment. I believe I see it up ahead, on the right."

The Imperial Arms was an apartment building on a tree-lined street a kilometer from Westwood Village. Its fake Tudor beams needed a paint job, and the whole building had a run-down appearance. But that was not unusual in this middle-class section of apartments inhabited by graduate students and young families. In fact, the chief characteristic of the Imperial Arms seemed to be its anonymity: you could drive by the building every day and never notice it.

"Perfect," Connor said, as we walked up the steps to the entrance. "It's just what they like."

"What who likes?"

We came into the lobby, which had been renovated in the most bland California style: pastel wallpaper with a flower print, overstuffed couches, cheap ceramic lamps, and a chrome coffee table. The only thing to distinguish it from a hundred other apartment lobbies was the security desk in the corner, where a heavyset Japanese doorman looked up from his comic book with a distinctly unfriendly manner. "Help you?"

Connor showed his badge. He asked where Cheryl Austin's apartment was.

"I announce you," the doorman said, reaching for the phone.

"Don't bother."

"No. I announce. Maybe she have company now."

"I'm sure she doesn't," Connor said. "*Kore wa keisatsu no shigoto da.*" He was saying we were on official police business.

The doorman gave a tense bow. "*Kyugo shitu.*" He handed Connor a key.

We went through a second glass door, and down a carpeted corridor. There were small lacquer tables at each end of the corridor, and in its simplicity, the interior was surprisingly elegant.

"Typically Japanese," Connor said, with a smile.

I thought: a run-down, fake Tudor apartment building in Westwood? Typically Japanese? From a room to the left, I heard faint rap music: the latest Hammer hit.

"It's because the outside gives no clue to the inside," Connor explained. "That's a fundamental principle of Japanese thinking. The public facade is unrevealing—in architecture, the human face, everything. It's always been that way. You look at old samurai houses in Takayama or Kyoto. You can't tell anything from the outside."

"This is a Japanese building?"

"Of course. Why else would a Japanese national who hardly speaks English be the doorman? And he is a *yakuza*. You probably noticed the tattoo."

I hadn't. The *yakuza* were Japanese gangsters. I didn't know there were *yakuza* here in America, and said so.

"You must understand," Connor said, "there is a shadow world—here in Los Angeles, in Honolulu, in New York. Most of the time you're never aware of it. We live in our regular American world, walking on our American streets, and we never notice that right alongside our world is a second world. Very discreet, very private. Perhaps in New York you will see Japanese businessmen walking through an unmarked door, and catch a glimpse of a club behind. Perhaps you will hear of a small sushi bar in Los Angeles that charges twelve hundred dollars a person, Tokyo prices. But they are not listed in the guidebooks. They are not a part of our American world. They are part of the shadow world, available only to the Japanese."

"And this place?"

"This is a *bettaku*. A love residence where mistresses are kept. And here is Miss Austin's apartment."

Connor unlocked the door with the key the doorman had given him. We went inside.

It was a two-bedroom unit, furnished with expensive oversized rental pieces in pastel pink and green. The oil paintings on the walls had been rented, too; a label on the side of one frame said Breuner's Rents. The kitchen counter was bare, except for a bowl of fruit. The refrigerator contained only yogurt and cans of Diet Coke. The couches in the living room didn't look as if anybody had ever sat on them. On the coffee table was a picture book of Hollywood star portraits and a vase of dried flowers. Empty ashtrays scattered around.

One of the bedrooms had been converted to a den, with a couch and a television, and an exercise bike in the corner. Everything was brand-new. The television still had a sticker that said DIGITAL TUNING FEATURE diagonally across one corner. The handlebars of the exercise bike were covered in plastic wrap.

In the master bedroom, I finally found some human clutter. One mirrored closet door stood open, and three expensive party dresses were thrown across the bed. Evidently she had been trying to decide what to wear. On the dresser top were bottles of perfume, a diamond necklace, a gold Rolex, framed photographs, and an ashtray with stubbed-out Mild Seven Menthol cigarettes. The top dresser drawer, containing panties and undergarments, was partially open. I saw her passport stuck in the corner, and thumbed through it. There was one visa for Saudi Arabia, one for Indonesia, and three entry stamps for Japan.

The stereo in the corner was still turned on, an ejected tape in the player. I pushed it in and Jerry Lee Lewis sang, "You shake my nerves and you rattle my brain, too much love drives a man insane. . . ." Texas music, too old for a young girl like this. But maybe she liked golden oldies.

I turned back to the dresser. Several framed color enlargements showed Cheryl Austin smiling in front of Asian backgrounds—the red gates of a shrine, a formal garden, a street with gray skyscrapers, a train station. The pictures seemed to be taken in Japan. In most of the pictures Cheryl was alone, but in a few she was accompanied by an older Japanese man with glasses and a receding hairline. A final shot showed her in what looked like the American West. Cheryl was standing near a dusty pickup truck, smiling beside a frail, grandmotherly woman in sunglasses. The older woman wasn't smiling and looked uncomfortable.

Tucked in beside the dresser were several large paper rolls, standing on end. I opened one. It was a poster showing Cheryl in a bikini, smiling and holding up a bottle of Asahi beer. All the writing on the poster was in Japanese.

I went into the bathroom.

I saw a pair of jeans kicked in the corner. A white sweater tossed on the countertop. A wet towel on a hook by the shower stall. Beads of water inside the stall. Electric hair-curlers unplugged by the counter. Stuck in the mirror frame, photos of Cheryl standing with another Japanese man on the Malibu pier. This man was in his midthirties, and handsome. In one photograph, he had draped his arm familiarly over her shoulder. I could clearly see the scar on his hand.

"Bingo," I said.

Connor came into the room. "Find something?"

"Our man with the scar."

"Good." Connor studied the picture carefully. I looked back at the clutter of the bathroom. The stuff around the sink. "You know," I said, "something bothers me about this place."

"What's that?"

"I know she hasn't lived here long. And I know everything is rented . . . but still . . . I can't get over the feeling that this place has a contrived look. I can't quite put my finger on why."

Connor smiled. "Very good, Lieutenant. It does have a contrived look. And there's a reason for it."

He handed me a Polaroid photo. It showed the bathroom we were standing in. The jeans kicked in the corner. The towel hanging. The curlers on the counter. But it was taken with one of those ultra-wide-angle cameras that distort everything. The SID teams sometimes used them for evidence.

"Where did you get this?"

"From the trash bin in the hall, by the elevators."

"So it must have been taken earlier tonight."

"Yes. Notice anything different about the room?"

I examined the Polaroid carefully. "No, it looks the same . . . wait a minute. Those pictures stuck in her mirror. They aren't in the Polaroid. Those pictures have been added."

"Exactly." Connor walked back into the bedroom. He picked up one of the framed pictures on the dresser. "Now look at this one," he said. "Miss Austin and a Japanese friend in Shinjuku Station in Tokyo. She was probably drawn to the Kabukichō section—or perhaps she was just shopping. Notice the right-hand edge of the picture. See the narrow strip that's lighter in color?"

"Yes." And I understood what that strip meant: there had been another picture on top of this one. The edge of this picture had stuck out, and was sun-faded. "The overlying picture has been removed."

"Yes," Connor said.

"The apartment has been searched."

"Yes," Connor said. "A very thorough job. They came in earlier tonight, took Polaroids, searched the rooms, and then put things back the way they were. But it's impossible to do that exactly. The Japanese say artlessness is the most difficult art. And these men can't help themselves, they're obsessive. So they leave the picture frames a little too squared-off on the counter, and the perfume bottles a little too carefully cluttered. Everything is a little forced. Your eye can see it even if your brain doesn't register it."

I said, "But why search the room? What pictures did they remove? Her with the killer?"

"That's not clear," Connor said. "Evidently her association with Japan, and with Japanese men, was not objectionable. But there was something they had to get right away, and it can only be—"

Then, from the living room, a tentative voice said, "Lynn? Honey? You here?"

She was silhouetted in the doorway, looking in. Barefooted, wearing shorts and a tank top. I couldn't see her face well, but she was obviously what my old partner Anderson would call a snake charmer.

Connor showed his badge. She said her name was Julia Young. She had a Southern accent, and a slight slur to her speech. Connor turned on the light and we could see her better. She was a beautiful girl. She came into the room hesitantly.

"I heard the music—is she here? Is Cherylynn okay? I know she went to that party tonight."

"I haven't heard anything," Connor said, with a quick glance at me. "Do you know Cherylynn?"

"Well, sure. I live right across the hall, in number eight. Why is everybody in her room?"

"Everybody?"

"Well, you two. And the two Japanese guys."

"When were they here?"

"I don't know. Maybe half an hour ago. Is it something about Cherylynn?"

I said, "Did you get a look at the men, Miss Young?" I was thinking she might have been looking out of the peephole of her door.

"Well, I *guess*. I said hello to them."

"How's that?"

"I know one of them pretty well. Eddie."

"Eddie?"

"Eddie Sakamura. We all know Eddie. Fast Eddie."

I said, "Can you describe him?"

She gave me a funny look. "He's the guy in the pictures—the young guy with the scar on his hand. I thought everybody knew Eddie Sakamura. He's in the newspaper all the time. Charities and stuff. He's a big party guy."

I said, "Do you have any idea how I could find him?"

Connor said, "Eddie Sakamura is part owner of a Polynesian restaurant in Beverly Hills called Bora Bora. He hangs out there."

"That's him," Julia said. "That place is like his office. I can't stand it myself, it's too noisy. But Eddie's just running around, chasing those big blondes. He loves to look up to a girl."

She leaned against a table, and pushed her full brown hair back from her face seductively. She looked at me and gave a little pout. "You two guys partners?"

"Yes," I said.

"He showed me his badge. But you didn't show me yours."

I took out my wallet. She looked at it. "Peter," she said, reading. "My very first boyfriend was named Peter. But he wasn't as handsome as you." She smiled at me.

Connor cleared his throat and said, "Have you been in Cherylynn's apartment before?"

"Well, I *guess*. I live right across the way. But she hasn't been in town much lately. Seems like she's always traveling."

"Traveling where?"

"All over. New York, Washington, Seattle, Chicago . . . all over. She has this boyfriend who travels a lot. She meets him. Actually I think she just meets him when his wife isn't around."

"This boyfriend is married?"

"Well, there's something in the way. You know. Obstructing."

"Do you know who he is?"

"No. She once said he'd never come to her apartment. He's some big important guy. Real rich. They send the jet for her, and off she goes. Whoever he is, he drives Eddie crazy. But Eddie is the jealous type, you know. Got to be *iro otoko* to all the girls. The sexy lover."

Connor said, "Is Cheryl's relationship a secret? With this boyfriend?"

"I don't know. I never thought it was. It's just real intense. She's madly in love with the guy."

"She's madly in love?"

"You can't imagine. I've seen her drop everything to run and meet him. One night she comes over, gives me two tickets to the Springsteen concert, but she's all excited because she's going to *Detroit*. She's got her little carry-on in her hand. She's got her little nice-girl dress on. Because he just called ten minutes ago and said, 'Meet me.' Her face all bright, she looks about five years old. I don't know why she can't figure it out."

"Figure what out?"

"This guy is just using her."

"Why do you say that?"

"Cherylynn is beautiful, and real sophisticated-looking. She's worked all over the world as a model, mostly in Asia. But deep down she's a small-town girl. I mean, Midland is an oil town, there's lots of money, but it's still a small town. And Cherylynn wants the ring on the finger and the kids and the dog in the yard. And this guy isn't going to do it. She hasn't figured it out."

I said, "But you don't know who this man is?"

"No, I don't." A sly look crossed her face. She shifted her body, dropping one shoulder so her breasts thrust forward. "But you're not really here because of some old boyfriend, are you?"

Connor nodded. "Not really, no."

Julia smiled in a knowing way. "It's Eddie, isn't it?"

"Umm," Connor said.

"I knew it," she said. "I knew he'd get in trouble sooner or later. We all talked about it, all the girls here in the Arms." She made a vague gesture. "Because he's just going too fast. Fast Eddie. You wouldn't think he was Japanese. He's so flashy."

Connor said, "He's from Osaka?"

"His father's a big industrialist there, with Daimatsu. He's a nice old guy. When he comes over to visit, sometimes he sees one of the girls on the second floor. And Eddie. Eddie was supposed to get educated here for a few years, then go home to work for the *kaisha*, the company. But he won't go home. He loves it here. Why not? He's got everything. He buys a new Ferrari every time he bangs up the old one. He's got more money than God. He's lived here long enough, he's just like an American. Handsome. Sexy. And with all the drugs. You know, real party animal. What's in Osaka for him?"

I said, "But you said you always knew . . ."

"That he'd get in trouble? Sure. Because of that crazy side. That *edge*." She shrugged. "A lot of them have it. These guys come over from Tokyo, and even if they have a *shōkai*, an introduction, you still have to be careful. They think nothing of dropping ten or twenty thousand in a night. It's like a tip for them. Leave it on the dresser. But then, what they want to do—at least, some of them . . ."

She drifted into silence. Her eyes had a vacant, unfocused look. I didn't say anything, I just waited. Connor was looking at her, nodding sympathetically.

Abruptly, she began to speak again, as if unaware of the pause. "And to them," she said, "their wishes, their desires, it's just as natural as leaving the tip. It's completely natural to them. I mean, I don't mind a little golden shower or whatever, handcuffs, you know. Maybe a little spanking if I like the guy. But I won't let anybody cut me. I don't care how much money. None of those things with knives or swords . . . But they can be . . . A lot of them, they are so polite, so correct, but then they get turned on, they have this . . . this *way* . . ." She broke off, shaking her head. "They're strange people."

Connor glanced at his watch. "Miss Young, you've been very helpful. We may need to speak to you again. Lieutenant Smith will take your phone number—"

"Yes, of course."

I flipped open my pad.

Connor said, "I'm going to have a word with the doorman."

"Shinichi," she said.

Connor left. I took down Julia's number. She licked her lips as she watched me write. Then she said, "You can tell me. Did he kill her?"

"Who?"

"Eddie. Did he kill Cherylynn?"

She was a pretty girl but I could see the excitement in her eyes. She was looking at me with a steady gaze. Her eyes were shining. It was creepy. I said, "Why do you ask?"

"Because. He was always threatening to. Like this afternoon, he threatened her."

I said, "Eddie was here this afternoon?"

"Sure." She shrugged. "He's here all the time. He came to see her this afternoon, real worked up. They put extra soundproofing to the walls in this building when they took it over. But even so, you could hear them scream at each other in her apartment. Him and Cherylynn. She'd have on her Jerry Lee Lewis, the one she played day and night until you just about went crazy, and they'd be screaming and throwing things. He'd always say, 'I'll kill you, I'll kill you, you bitch.' So. Did he?"

"I don't know."

"But she's dead?" Her eyes still shining.

"Yes."

"It had to happen," she said. She seemed completely calm. "We all knew it. It was just a matter of time. If you want, call me. If you need more information."

"Yes. I will." I gave her my card. "And if you think of anything else, you can call me at this number."

She slipped it into the hip pocket of her shorts, twisting her body. "I like talking to you, Peter."

"Yes. Okay."

I walked down the corridor. When I got to the end I looked back. She was standing in her doorway, waving good-bye.

Connor was using the phone in the lobby while the doorman stared sullenly at him, as if he wanted to stop him, but couldn't think of a reason why.

"That's right," Connor was saying. "All the outgoing calls from that phone between eight and ten p.m. That's right." He listened for a moment. "Well, I don't care if your data isn't organized that way, just get it for me. How long will it take? Tomorrow? Don't be ridiculous. What do you think this is? I need it within two hours. I'll call you back. Yes. Fuck you, too." He hung up. "Let's go, *kōhai*."

We walked outside to the car.

I said, "Checking your contacts?"

"Contacts?" He looked puzzled. "Oh. Graham said something to you about my 'contacts.' I don't have any special informants. He just thinks I do."

"He mentioned the Arakawa case."

Connor sighed. "That old thing." We walked toward the car. "You want to know that story? It's simple. Two Japanese nationals get killed. The department puts detectives on the case who can't speak Japanese. Finally, after a week, they give the case to me."

"And what did you do?"

"The Arakawas were staying at the New Otani Hotel. I got the phone records of the calls they made to Japan. I called those numbers, and spoke to some people in Osaka. Then I called Osaka and talked to the police there. Again, in Japanese. They were surprised to hear we didn't know the whole story."

"I see."

"Not quite," Connor said. "Because the police department here was very embarrassed. The press had gone out on a limb, criticizing the department. All sorts of people had sent flowers. There had been a big show of sympathy for what turned out to be gangsters. A lot of people were embarrassed. So the whole thing became my fault. I had done something underhanded to solve the case. Pissed me off, I can tell you."

"That's why you went to Japan?"

"No. That's another story."

We came to the car. I looked back at the Imperial Arms, and saw Julia Young standing at the window, staring down at us. "She's seductive," I said.

"The Japanese call women like that *shirigaru onna*. They say she has a light ass." He opened the car door, and got in. "But she's on drugs. We can't trust anything she told us. Even so, there's starting to be a pattern I don't like." He glanced at his watch, and shook his head. "Damn. We're taking too long. We'd better go to the Palomino, to see Mr. Cole."

I started driving south, toward the airport. Connor sat back in his seat and folded his arms across his chest. He stared at his feet, looking unhappy.

"Why do you say there's a pattern you don't like?"

Connor said, "The wrappers in the waste basket. The Polaroid in the trash. Those things shouldn't have been left behind."

"You said yourself, they're in a hurry."

"Maybe. But you know the Japanese think American police are incompetent. This sloppiness is a sign of their disdain."

"Well, we're not incompetent."

Connor shook his head. "Compared to the Japanese, we *are* incompetent. In Japan, every criminal gets caught. For major crimes, convictions run ninety-nine percent. So any criminal in Japan knows from the outset he is going to get caught. But here, the conviction rate is more like seventeen percent. Not even one in five. So a criminal in the States knows he probably *isn't* going to get caught—and if he's caught, he won't be convicted, thanks to all his legal safe-guards. And you know every study of police effectiveness shows that American detectives either solve the case in the first six hours, or they never solve it at all."

"So what are you saying?"

"I'm saying that a crime occurred here with the expectation that it won't be solved. And I want to solve it, *kōhai*."

Connor was silent for the next ten minutes. He sat very still, with his arms folded and his chin sunk on his chest. His breathing was deep and regular. I might have thought he had fallen asleep, except his eyes were open.

I just drove the car, and listened to him breathe.

Finally, he said: "Ishiguro."

"What about him?"

"If we knew what made Ishiguro behave as he did, we'd understand this case."

"I don't understand."

"It's hard for an American to see him clearly," Connor said. "Because in America, you think a certain amount of error is normal. You expect the plane to be late. You expect the mail to be undelivered. You expect the washing machine to break down. You expect things to go wrong all the time.

"But Japan is different. Everything *works* in Japan. In a Tokyo train station, you can stand at a marked spot on the platform and when the train stops, the doors will open right in front of you. Trains are on time. Bags are not lost. Connections are not missed. Deadlines are met. Things happen as planned. The Japanese are educated, prepared, and moti-vated. They get things done. There's no screwing around."

"Uh-huh . . ."

"And tonight was a very big night for the Nakamoto Corporation. You can be sure they planned everything down to the smallest detail. They have the vegetarian hors d'oeuvres that Madonna likes and the photographer she prefers. Believe me: they're prepared. They have planned for every exigency. You know how they are: they sit around and discuss endless possibilities—what if there's a fire? What if there's an earthquake? A bomb scare? Power failure? Endlessly going over the most unlikely events. It's obsessive, but when the final night arrives, they've thought of everything and they're in complete control. It's very bad form not to be in control. Okay?"

"Okay."

"But there is our friend Ishiguro, the official representative of Nakamoto, standing in front of a dead girl, and he's clearly not in control. He's *yōshiki nō*, doing Western-style confrontation, but he isn't comfortable—I'm sure you noticed the sweat on his lip. And his hand is damp; he keeps wiping it on his trousers. He is *rikutsuppoi*, too argumentative. He's talking too much.

"In short, he's behaving as if he doesn't really know what to do, as if he doesn't even know who this girl is—which he certainly does, since he knows everybody invited to that party—and pretending he doesn't know who killed her. When he almost certainly knows that, too."

The car bounced in a pothole, and jolted back up. "Wait a minute. Ishiguro knows who killed the girl?"

"I'm sure of it. And he's not the only one. At least three people must know who killed her, at this point. Didn't you say you used to be in press relations?"

"Yes. Last year."

"You keep any contacts in TV news?"

"A few," I said. "They might be rusty. Why?"

"I want to look at some tape that was shot tonight."

"Just look? Not subpoena?"

"Right. Just look."

"That shouldn't be a problem," I said. I was thinking I could call Jennifer Lewis at KNBC, or Bob Arthur at KCBS. Probably Bob.

Connor said, "It has to be somebody you can approach personally. Otherwise the stations won't help us. You noticed there were no TV crews at the crime scene tonight. At most crime scenes, you have to fight your way past the cameras just to get to the tape. But tonight, no TV crews, no reporters. Nothing."

I shrugged. "We were on land lines. The press couldn't monitor radio transmissions."

"They were already there," Connor said, "covering the party with Tom Cruise and Madonna. And then a girl gets murdered on the floor above. So where were the TV crews?"

I said, "Captain, I don't buy it."

One of the things I learned as a press officer is that there aren't any conspiracies. The press is too diverse, and in a sense too disorganized. In fact, on the rare occasions when we needed an embargo—like a kidnapping with ransom negotiations in progress—we had a hell of a time getting cooperation. "The paper closes early. The TV crews have to make the eleven o'clock news. They probably went back to edit their stories."

"I disagree. I think the Japanese expressed concern about their *kigyō image*, their company image, and the press cooperated with no coverage. Trust me, *kōhai*: the pressure is being applied."

"I can't believe that."

"Take my word for it," Connor said. "The pressure is on."

Just then, the car phone rang.

"God damn it, Peter," a familiar rough voice said. "What the fuck's going on with that homicide investigation?" It was the chief. It sounded like he had been drinking.

"How do you mean, Chief?"

Connor looked at me, and punched the speaker phone button so he could hear.

The chief said: "You guys harassing the Japanese? We going to have another set of racial allegations against the department here?"

"No sir," I said. "Absolutely not. I don't know what you've heard—"

"I heard that dumb fuck Graham was making insults as usual," the chief said.

"Well, I wouldn't exactly say insults, Chief—"

"Look, Peter. Don't shit me. I already reamed out Fred Hoffmann for sending Graham in the first place. I want that racist turd off the case. We've all got to get along with the Japanese from now on. It's the way the world is. You hearing me, Peter?"

"Yes, sir."

"Now about John Connor. You got him with you, is that right?"

"Yes, sir."

"Why did you bring him into this?"

I thought: why did *I* bring him in? Fred Hoffmann must have decided to say that Connor was my idea, and not his own.

"I'm sorry," I said. "But I—"

"I understand," the chief said. "You probably thought you couldn't handle the case yourself. Wanted some help. But I'm afraid you bought more trouble than help. Because the Japanese don't like Connor. And I got to tell you. I go way back with John. We entered the academy together back in fifty-nine. He's always been a loner and a troublemaker. You know, anybody who goes to live in some foreign country, it's because he can't fit in here at home. I don't want him screwing up this investigation now."

"Chief—"

"This is how I see it, Peter. You got a homicide here, wrap it up and get it over with. Do it quick and do it neat. I'm looking to you and you alone. You hearing me?"

"Yes, sir."

"The connection is good?"

"Yes, sir," I said.

"Wrap it up, Pete," the chief said. "I don't want anybody else calling me on this."

"Yes, sir."

"Finish it by tomorrow latest. That's it." And he hung up. I put the phone back in the cradle.

"Yes," Connor said. "I'd say pressure is being applied."

I drove south on the 405 freeway, toward the airport. It was foggier here. Connor stared out the window.

"In a Japanese organization, you'd never get a call like that. The chief just hung you out to dry. He takes no responsibility—it's all your problem. And he's blaming you for things that have nothing to do with you, like Graham, and me." Connor shook his head. "The Japanese don't do that. The Japanese have a saying: fix the problem, not the blame. In American organizations it's all about *who* fucked up. Whose head will roll. In Japanese organizations it's about *what's* fucked up, and how to fix it. Nobody gets blamed. Their way is better."

Connor was silent, staring out the window. We were driving past Slauson, the Marina freeway a dark curve arcing above us in the fog.

I said, "The chief was in the bag, that's all."

"Yes. And uninformed, as usual. But even so, it sounds like we'd better have this case solved before he gets out of bed tomorrow."

"Can we do that?"

"Yes. If Ishiguro delivers those tapes."

The phone rang again. I answered it.

It was Ishiguro.

I handed the phone to Connor.

I could hear Ishiguro faintly through the receiver. He sounded tense, speaking rapidly. "*A, moshi moshi, Connor-*

san desuka? Keibi no heyani denwa shitan desuga ne. Daremo denain desuyo."

Connor cupped his hand over the phone and translated. "He called the security guard but no one was there."

"*Sorede, chuōkeibishitsu ni renraku shite, hito wo okutte moraimashite, issho ni tēpu o kakunin shite kimashita.*"

"Then he called the main security office and asked them to come down with him to check the tapes."

"*Tēpu wa subete rekōdā no naka ni arimasu. Nakunattemo torikaeraretemo imasen. Subete daijōbu desu.*"

"The tapes are all in the recorders. No tapes are missing or switched." Connor frowned and replied. "*Iya, tēpu wa surikaerarete iru hazu nanda. Tēpu o sagase!*"

"*Dakara, daijōbu nandesu, Connor-san. Dōshiro to iun desuka?*"

"He insists everything is in order."

Connor said, "*Tēpu o sagase!*" To me, he said, "I told him I wanted the damn tapes."

"*Daijōbuda to itterudeshou. Dōshite sonnaini tēpu ni kodawarun desuka?*"

"*Ore niwa wakatte irunda. Tēpu wa nakunatte iru.* I know more than you think, Mr. Ishiguro. *Mōichido iu, tēpu o sagasunda!*"

Connor banged the phone in the cradle, and sat back, snorting angrily. "Bastards. They're taking the position that there are no missing tapes."

"What does that mean?" I said.

"They've decided to play hardball." Connor stared out the window at the traffic, and tapped his teeth with his finger. "They'd never do it unless they felt they had a strong position. An unassailable position. Which means . . ."

Connor drifted off into his private thoughts. I saw his face intermittently reflected in the glass under passing street lamps. Finally he said, "No, no, no," as if he were talking to someone.

"No, what?"

"It can't be Graham." He shook his head. "Graham is too risky—too many ghosts from the past. And it's not me, either. I'm old news. So it must be you, Peter."

I said, "What are you talking about?"

"Something has happened," Connor said, "to make Ishiguro think he has leverage. And I'd guess it's something to do with you."

"Me?"

"Yeah. It's almost certainly something personal. You have any problems in your past?"

"Like what?"

"Any priors, arrests, internal affairs investigations, allegations of questionable conduct like drinking or homosexuality or chasing women? Any drug rehab program, problems with partners, problems with superiors. Anything personal or professional. Anything."

I shrugged. "Jeez, I don't think so."

Connor just waited, looking at me. Finally he said, "They think they have something, Peter."

"I'm divorced. I'm a single parent. I have a daughter, Michelle. She's two years old."

"Yes . . ."

"I lead a quiet life. I take care of my kid. I'm responsible."

"And your wife?"

"My ex-wife is a lawyer in the D.A.'s office."

"When did you get divorced?"

"Two years ago."

"Before the child was born?"

"Just after."

"Why did you get divorced?"

"Christ. Why does anybody get divorced."

Connor said nothing.

"We were only married a year. She was young when we met. Twenty-four. She had these fantasies about things. We met in court. She thought I was a rough, tough detective facing danger every day. She liked that I had a gun. All that. So we had this affair. Then when she got pregnant she didn't want to have an abortion. She wanted to get married instead. It was some romantic idea she had. She didn't really think it through. But the pregnancy was hard, and it was too late to abort, and pretty soon she decided she didn't like living with me because my apartment was small, and I didn't make enough money, and I lived in Culver City instead of Brentwood. And by the time the baby was finally born, it was like she was completely disillusioned. She said she had made a mistake. She wanted to pursue her career. She didn't want to be married to a cop. She didn't want to raise a kid. She said she was sorry, but it was all a mistake. And she left."

Connor was listening with his eyes closed. "Yes . . ."

"I don't see why all this matters. She left two years ago. And after that, I couldn't—I didn't want to work detective hours any more, because now I had to raise the kid, so I took the tests and transferred to Special Services, and I worked the press office. No problems there. Everything went fine. Then last year this Asian liaison job came up, and it paid better. Another couple hundred a month. So I applied for that."

"Uh-huh."

"I mean, I can really use the money. I have extra expenses now, like Michelle's day care. You know what day care costs for two-year-olds? And I have full-time housekeeping, and Lauren doesn't make her child-support payments more than half the time. She says she can't manage on her salary, but she just bought a new BMW, so I don't know. I mean, what am I going to do, take her to court? She works for the fucking D.A."

Connor was silent. Up ahead, I saw the airplanes coming down over the freeway. We were approaching the airport.

"Anyway," I said. "I was glad when the liaison job came along. Because it works out better for the hours, and for the money. And that's how I got to be here. In this car with you. That's it."

"*Kōhai*," he said quietly. "We're in this together. Just tell me. What is the problem?"

"There isn't any problem."

"*Kōhai*."

"There isn't."

"*Kōhai* . . ."

"Hey, John," I said, "let me tell you something. When you apply for Special Services liaison, five different committees go over your record. To get a liaison job, you have to be *clean*. The committees went over my record. And they found nothing substantial."

Connor nodded. "But they found *something*."

"Christ," I said, "I was a detective for five years. You can't work that long without a few complaints. You know that."

"And what were the complaints against you?"

I shook my head. "Nothing. Little stuff. I arrested a guy my first year, he accused me of undue force. That charge was dropped after inquiry. I arrested a woman for armed robbery, she claimed I planted a gram on her. Charge dropped; it was her gram. Murder suspect claimed I beat and kicked him during questioning. But other officers were present at all times. A drunken woman on a domestic violence call later claimed I molested her child. She dropped the charge. Teenage gang leader arrested for murder said I made a homosexual pass at him. Charge withdrawn. That's it."

If you're a cop you know that complaints like these are background noise, like traffic on the street. There's nothing you can do about them. You're in an adversarial environment, accusing people of crimes all the time. They accuse you back. That's just the way it works. The department never pays any attention unless there's a pattern or repetition. If a guy has three or four complaints of undue force over a couple of years, then he gets an inquiry. Or a string of racial complaints, he gets an inquiry. But otherwise, as the assistant chief Jim Olson always says, being a cop is a job for the thick-skinned.

Connor didn't say anything for a long time. He frowned, thinking it over. Finally he said, "What about the divorce? Problems there?"

"Nothing unusual."

"You and your ex are on speaking terms?"

"Yes. We're okay. Not great. But okay."

He was still frowning. Still looking for something. "And you left the detective division two years ago?"

"Yes."

"Why?"

"I already told you."

"You said that you couldn't work the hours."

"That was most of it, yeah."

"That, and what else?"

I shrugged. "After the divorce, I just didn't want to work homicide any more. I felt like—I don't know. Disillusioned. I had this little infant and my wife had moved out. She was going on with her life, dating some hotshot attorney. I was left holding the kid. I just felt flat. I didn't want to be a detective any more."

"You seek counseling at that time? Therapy?"

"No."

"Trouble with drugs or alcohol?"

"No."

"Other women?"

"Some."

"During the marriage?"

I hesitated.

"Farley? In the mayor's office?"

"No. That was later."

"But there *was* somebody during the marriage."

"Yes. But she lives in Phoenix now. Her husband got transferred."

"She was in the department?"

I shrugged.

Connor sat back in his seat. "Okay, *kōhai*," he said. "If this is all there is, you're fine." He looked at me.

"That's all."

"But I have to warn you," he said. "I've been through this kind of thing before, with the Japanese. When the Japanese play hardball, they can make things unpleasant. *Really* unpleasant."

"You trying to scare me?"

"No. Just telling you the way things are."

"Fuck the Japanese," I said. "I've got nothing to hide."

"Fine. Now I think you better call your friends at the network, and tell them we'll be over, after our next stop."

A 747 roared low overhead, its landing lights flaring in the fog. It passed the sputtering neon sign that read GIRLS! GIRLS! ALL NUDE! GIRLS! It was around eleven-thirty when we went inside.

To call the Club Palomino a strip joint was to flatter it. It was a converted bowling alley with cactus and horses painted on the walls. It seemed smaller inside than it appeared from the outside. A woman in a silver tassled G-string who looked close to forty danced listlessly in orange light. She seemed as bored as the customers hunched over tiny pink tables. Topless waitresses moved through the smoky air. The tape-recorded music had a loud hiss.

A guy just inside the door said, "Twelve bucks. Two drink minimum." Connor flipped his badge. The guy said, "Okay, fine."

Connor looked around and said, "I didn't know Japanese came here." I saw three businessmen in blue suits, sitting at a corner table.

"Hardly ever," the bouncer said. "They like the Star Strip downtown. More glitz, more tits. You ask me, those guys got lost from their tour."

Connor nodded, "I'm looking for Ted Cole."

"At the bar. Guy with the glasses."

Ted Cole was sitting at the bar. His windbreaker covered his Nakamoto Security uniform. He stared at us dully when we came up and sat beside him.

The bartender came over. Connor said, "Two Buds."

"No Bud. Asahi okay?"

"Okay."

Connor flipped his badge. Cole shook his head and turned away from us. He looked studiously at the stripper.

"I don't know anything."

Connor said, "About what?"

"About anything. I'm just minding my own business. I'm off duty." He was a little drunk.

Connor said, "When did you get off duty?"

"I got off early tonight."

"Why is that?"

"Stomach trouble. I got an ulcer, it acts up sometimes. So I got off early."

"What time?"

"I got off at eight-fifteen at the latest."

"Do you punch a time clock?"

"No. We don't do that. No time clock."

"And who took over for you?"

"I got relieved."

"By whom?"

"My supervisor."

"Who is that?"

"I don't know him. Japanese guy. Never seen him before."

"He's your supervisor, and you never saw him before?"

"New guy. Japanese. I don't know him. What do you want from me, anyway?"

"Just to ask a few questions," Connor said.

"I got nothing to hide," Cole said.

One of the Japanese men sitting at the table came up to the bar. He stood near us and said to the bartender, "What kind of cigarettes you got?"

"Marlboro," the bartender said.

"What else?"

"Maybe Kools. I have to check. But I know we got Marlboro. You want Marlboro?"

Ted Cole stared at the Japanese man. The Japanese seemed not to notice him as he stood at the bar. "Kent?" the Japanese said. "You got any Kent lights?"

"No. No Kent."

"Okay then, Marlboro," the Japanese man said. "Marl-

boro is okay." He turned and smiled at us. "This is Marlboro country, right?"

"That's right," Connor said.

Cole picked up his beer and sipped it. We were all silent.
The Japanese man beat the bar with his hands, in time to the
music. "Great place," he said. "Lot of atmosphere."

I wondered what he was talking about. This place was a
dump.

The Japanese slid onto the bar stool next to us. Cole
studied his beer bottle as if he'd never seen one before. He
turned it in his hands, making rings on the bar top.

The bartender brought cigarettes, and the Japanese man
tossed a five-dollar bill on the table. "Keep the change." He
tore open the pack, and took out a cigarette. He smiled at us.

Connor took out his lighter to light the man's cigarette.
As the man leaned over the flame, he said, "*Doko kaisha
ittenno?*"

The man blinked. "Sorry?"

"*Wakannē no?*" Connor said. "*Doko kaisha ittenno?*"

The man smiled, and slipped off the bar stool. "*Soro soro
ikanakutewa. Shitsurei shimasu.*" He gave a little wave, and
he went back to his friends across the room.

"*Dewa mata,*" Connor said. He moved around to sit on
the stool where the Japanese man had been sitting.

Cole said, "What was that all about?"

"I just asked him what company he worked for," Connor
said. "But he didn't want to talk. I guess he wanted to get
back to his friends." Connor ran his hands under the bar,
feeling. "Feels clean."

Connor turned back to Cole and said, "Now then, Mr.
Cole. You were telling me that a supervisor took over for
you. At what time was that?"

"Eight-fifteen."

"And you didn't know him?"

"No."

"And before that time, while you were on duty, were you
taping from the video cameras?"

"Sure. The security office always tapes from the cameras."

"And did the supervisor remove the tapes?"

"Remove them? I don't think so. The tapes are still there, as far as I know."

He looked at us in a puzzled way.

"You fellows are interested in the tapes?"

"Yes," Connor said.

"Because I never paid much attention to the tapes. I was interested in the cameras."

"How's that?"

"They were getting the building ready for the big party, and there were lots of last-minute details. But you still had to wonder why they pulled so many security cameras off other parts of the building and put them up on that floor."

I said, "They what?"

"Those cameras weren't on the forty-sixth floor yesterday morning," Cole said. "They were scattered all around the building. Somebody moved them during the day. They're easy to move, you know, because there's no wires attached."

"The cameras have no wires?"

"No. It's all cellular transmission inside the building itself. Built that way. That's why they don't have audio: they can't transmit full bandwidth on cellular. So they just send an image. But they can move those cameras around to suit their purposes. See whatever they want to see. You didn't know that?"

"No," I said.

"I'm surprised nobody told you. It's one of the features of the building they're most proud of." Cole drank his beer. "Only question I have is why somebody would take five cameras and install them on the floor *above* the party. 'Cause there's no security reason. You can lock off the elevators above a certain floor. So for security, you'd want your cameras on the floors below the party. Not above."

"But the elevators weren't locked off."

"No. I thought that was kind of unusual, myself." He looked at the Japanese across the room. "I got to be going soon," he said.

"Well," Connor said. "You've been very helpful, Mr. Cole. We may want to question you again—"

"I'll write down my phone number for you," Cole said, scribbling on a bar napkin.

"And your address?"

"Yeah, right. But actually, I'm going out of town for a few days. My mother's been feeling sick, and she asked me to take her down there to Mexico for a few days. Probably go this weekend."

"Long trip?"

"Week or so. I got vacation days coming up, it seems like a good time to take it."

"Sure," Connor said. "I can see how it would. Thanks again for your help." He shook hands with Cole, and punched him lightly on the shoulder. "And you take care of *your* health."

"Oh, I will."

"Stop drinking, and have a safe drive home." He paused. "Or wherever you may decide to go tonight, instead."

Cole nodded. "I think you're right. That's not a bad idea."

"I know I'm right."

Cole shook my hand. Connor was heading out the door. Cole said, "I don't know why you guys are bothering."

"With the tapes?"

"With the Japanese. What can you do? They're ahead of us every step of the way. And they have the big guys in their pocket. We can't beat 'em now. You two guys'll never beat 'em. They're just too good."

Outside, beneath the crackling neon sign, Connor said, "Come on, time is wasting."

We got in the car. He handed me the bar napkin. On it was scrawled in block letters:

THEY STOLE THE TAPES

"Let's get going," Connor said.

I started the car.

The eleven o'clock news was finished for the night, and the newsroom was nearly deserted. Connor and I went down the hall to the sound stage where the *Action News* set was still lit up.

On the set, the evening broadcast was being replayed with the sound off. The anchorman pointed to the monitor. "I'm not stupid, Bobby. I watch these things. She did the lead-in and the wrap-up the last three nights." He sat back in his chair and crossed his arms. "I'm waiting to hear what you have to say, Bobby."

My friend Bob Arthur, the heavyset, tired producer of the eleven o'clock news, sipped a tumbler of straight scotch as big as his fist. He said, "Jim, it just worked out that way."

"Worked out that way my ass," the anchorman said.

The anchorwoman was a gorgeous redhead with a killer figure. She was taking a long time to shuffle through her notes, making sure she stayed to overhear the conversation between Bob and her coanchor.

"Look," the anchorman said. "It's in my contract. Half the lead-ins and half the wraps. It's contractual."

"But Jim," the producer said. "The lead tonight was Paris fashions and the Nakamoto party. That's human interest stuff."

"It should have been the serial killer."

Bob sighed. "His arraignment was postponed. Anyway, the public is tired of serial killers."

The anchorman looked incredulous. "The public is tired of serial killers? Now, where'd you get that?"

"You can read it yourself in the focus groups, Jim. Serial

killers are overexposed. Our audience is worried about the economy. They don't want any more serial killers."

"Our audience is worried about the economy so we lead off with Nakamoto and Paris fashions?"

"That's right, Jim," Bob Arthur said. "In hard times, you do star parties. That's what people want to see: fashion and fantasy."

The anchor looked sullen. "I'm a journalist, I'm here to do hard news, not fashion."

"Right, Jim," the producer said. "That's why Liz did the intros tonight. We want to keep your image hard news."

"When Teddy Roosevelt led this country out of the Great Depression, he didn't do it with fashion and fantasy."

"Franklin Roosevelt."

"Whatever. You know what I'm saying. If people are worried, let's *do* the economy. Let's *do* the balance of payments or whatever it is."

"Right, Jim. But this is the eleven o'clock news in the local market, and people don't want to hear—"

"And that's what's wrong with America," the anchorman pronounced, stabbing the air with his finger. "People don't want to hear the real news."

"Right, Jim. You're absolutely right." He put his arm over the anchorman's shoulder. "Get some rest, okay? We'll talk tomorrow."

That seemed to be a signal of some kind, because the anchorwoman finished with her notes and strode off.

"I'm a journalist," the anchor said. "I just want to do the job I was trained for."

"Right, Jim. More tomorrow. Have a good night."

"Stupid dickhead," Bob Arthur said, leading us down a corridor. "Teddy Roosevelt. Jesus. They're not journalists. They're actors. And they count their lines, like all actors." He sighed, and took another drink of scotch. "Now tell me again, what do you guys want to see?"

"Tape from the Nakamoto opening."

"You mean the air tapes? The story we ran tonight?"

"No, we want to see the original footage from the camera."

"The field tapes. Jeez. I hope we still have them. They may have been bulked."

"Bulked?"

"Bulk degaussed. Erased. We shoot forty cassettes a day here. Most of them get erased right away. We used to save field tapes for a week, but we're cutting costs, you know."

On one side of the newsroom were shelves of stacked Betamax cartridges. Bob ran his finger along the boxes. "Nakamoto . . . Nakamoto . . . No, I don't see them." A woman went past. "Cindy, is Rick still here?"

"No, he's gone home. You need something?"

"The Nakamoto field tapes. They aren't on the shelf."

"Check Don's room. He cut it."

"Okay." Bob led us across the newsroom to the editing bays on the far side. He opened a door, and we entered a small, messy room with two monitors, several tape decks, and an editing console. Tapes in boxes were scattered around the floor. Bob rummaged through them. "Okay, you guys are in luck. Camera originals. There's a lot of it. I'll get Jenny to run you through them. She's our best spotter. She knows everybody." He stuck his head out the door. "Jenny? Jenny!"

"Okay, let's see," Jenny Gonzales said, a few minutes later. She was a bespectacled, heavyset woman in her forties. She scanned the editor's notes and frowned. "It doesn't matter how many times I tell them, they just will not put things in proper . . . Finally. Here we are. Four tapes. Two limo driveups. Two roving inside, at the party. What do you want to see?"

Connor said, "Start with the driveups." He glanced at his watch. "Is there any way to do this fast? We're in a hurry."

"Fast as you want. I'm used to it. Let's see it at high speed."

She hit a button. At high speed, we saw the limousines pulling up, the doors jumping open, the people getting out, jerkily walking away.

"Looking for anyone in particular? Because I see some-body marked footages for celebrities during the edit."

"We're not looking for a celebrity," I said.

"Too bad. It's probably all we shot." We watched the tape. Jenny said, "There's Senator Kennedy. He's lost some weight, hasn't he. Oops, gone. And Senator Morton. Look-ing very fit. No surprise. That creepy assistant of his. He makes my teeth shiver. Senator Rowe, without his wife, as usual. There's Tom Hanks. I don't know this Japanese guy."

Connor said, "Hiroshi Masukawa, vice-president of Mit-sui."

"There you go. Senator Chalmers, hair transplant look-ing good. Congressman Levine. Congressman Daniels. Sober for a change. You know, I'm surprised Nakamoto got so many of these Washington people to attend."

"Why do you say that?"

"Well, when you get down to it, it's just the opening of some new building. An ordinary corporate bash. It's on the West Coast. And Nakamoto is pretty controversial right at the moment. Barbra Streisand. I don't know who the guy is with her."

"Nakamoto is controversial? Why?"

"Because of the MicroCon sale."

I said, "What's MicroCon?"

"MicroCon is an American company that makes com-puter equipment. A Japanese company named Akai Ceram-ics is trying to buy it. There's opposition to the sale in Congress, because of worries about America losing technol-ogy to Japan."

I said, "And what does this have to do with Nakamoto?"

"Nakamoto's the parent company of Akai." The first tape finished, and popped out. "Nothing there you wanted?"

"No. Let's go on."

"Right." She slid the second tape in. "Anyway, I'm sur-prised how many of these senators and congressmen felt it was acceptable to show up here tonight. Okay, here we go. More driveups. Roger Hillerman, under secretary of state for Pacific affairs. That's his assistant with him. Kenichi Aikou, consul general of Japan, here in L.A. Richard Meier, architect. Works for Getty. Don't know her. Some Japanese . . ."

Connor said, "Hisashi Koyama, vice-president of Honda U.S."

"Oh, yeah," Jenny said. "He's been here about three years now. Probably going home soon. That's Edna Morris, she heads the U.S. delegation to the GATT talks. You know, General Agreement on Tariffs and Trade. I can't believe she showed up here, it's an obvious conflict of interest. But there she is, all smiling and relaxed. Chuck Norris. Eddie Sakamura. Sort of a local playboy. Don't know the girl with him. Tom Cruise, with his Australian wife. And Madonna, of course."

On the accelerated tape, the strobes flashed almost continuously as Madonna stepped from her limousine and preened. "Want to slow it down? You interested in this?"

Connor said, "Not tonight."

"Well, we probably have a lot on her," Jenny said. She pushed the very high-speed fast-forward and the image streaked gray. When she punched back, Madonna was wiggling toward the elevator, leaning on the arm of a slender Hispanic boy with a mustache. The image blurred as the camera swung back toward the street. Then it stabilized again.

"There's Daniel Okimoto. Expert on Japanese industrial policy. That's Arnold, with Maria. And behind them is Steve Martin, with Arata Isozaki, the architect who designed the Museum—"

Connor said, "Wait."

She punched the console button. The picture froze. Jenny seemed surprised. "You're interested in Isozaki?"

"No. Back up, please."

The tape ran backward, the frames flicking and blurring as the camera panned off Steve Martin, and went back to record the next arrival from the limousines. But for a moment in the pan, the camera swung past a group of people who had already gotten out of their limousines, and were walking up the carpeted sidewalk. .

Connor said, "There."

The image froze. Slightly blurred, I saw a tall blonde in a black cocktail dress walking forward alongside a handsome man in a dark suit.

"Huh," Jenny said. "You interested in him, or her?"

"Her."

"Let me think," Jenny said, frowning. "I've seen her at parties with the Washington types for about nine months now. She's this year's Kelly Emberg. The athletic modelly kind. But sophisticated, sort of a Tatiana look-alike. Her name is . . . Austin. Cindy Austin, Carrie Austin . . . Cheryl Austin. That's it."

I said, "You know anything else about her?"

Jenny shook her head. "Listen, I think getting a name is pretty good. These girls show up all the time. You see a new one everywhere for six months, a year, and then they're gone. God knows where they go. Who can keep track of them?"

"And the man with her?"

"Richard Levitt. Plastic surgeon. Does a lot of big stars."

"What's he doing here?"

She shrugged. "He's around. Like a lot of these guys, he's a companion to the stars in their time of need. If his patients are getting divorced or whatever, he escorts the woman. When he's not taking out clients, he takes out models like her. They certainly look good together."

On the monitor, Cheryl and her escort walked toward us in intermittent jerks: one frame every thirty seconds. Stepping slow. I noticed they never looked at each other. She seemed tense, expectant.

Jenny Gonzales said, "So. Plastic surgeon and a model. Can I ask what's the big deal about these two? Because at an evening like this, they're just, you know, party favors."

Connor said, "She was killed tonight."

"Oh, *she's* the one? Interesting."

I said, "You've heard about the murder?"

"Oh, sure."

"Was it on the news?"

"No, didn't make the eleven o'clock," Jenny said. "And it probably won't be on tomorrow. I can't see it myself. It's not really a story."

"Why is that?" I asked, glancing at Connor.

"Well, what's the peg?"

"I don't follow you."

"Nakamoto would say, it's only news because it happened at their opening. They'd take the position that any reporting of it is a smear on them. But in a way they're right. I mean, if this girl got killed on the freeway, it wouldn't make the news. If she got killed in a convenience store robbery, it wouldn't make the news. We have two or three of those every night. So the fact that she gets killed at a party . . . who cares? It's still not news. She's young and pretty, but she's not special. It's not as if she has a series or anything."

Connor glanced at his watch. "Shall we look at the other tapes?"

"The footage from the party? Sure. You looking for this particular girl?"

"Right."

"Okay, here we go." Jenny put in the third tape.

We saw scenes from the party on the forty-fifth floor: the swing band, people dancing beneath the hanging decorations. We strained for a glimpse of the girl in the crowd. Jenny said, "In Japan, we wouldn't have to do this by eye. The Japanese have pretty sophisticated video-recognition software now. They have a program where you identify an image, say a face, and it'll automatically search tape for you, and find every instance of that face. Find it in a crowd, or wherever it appears. Has the ability to see a single view of a three-dimensional object, and then to recognize the same object in other views. It's supposed to be pretty nifty. But slow."

"I'm surprised the station hasn't got it."

"Oh, it's not for sale here. The most advanced Japanese video equipment isn't available in this country. They keep us three to five years behind. Which is their privilege. It's their technology, they can do what they want. But it'd sure be useful in a case like this."

The party images were streaming past, a frenetic blur.

Suddenly, she locked the image.

"There. Background camera left. Your Austin girl's talking to Eddie Sakamura. Of course he'd know her. Sakamura knows all the models. Normal speed here?"

"Please," Connor said, staring at the screen.

The camera made a slow pan around the room. Cheryl Austin remained in view for most of the shot. Laughing with Eddie Sakamura, throwing her head back, resting her hand on his arm, happy to be with him. Eddie clowned for her, his face mobile. He seemed to enjoy making her laugh. But from time to time, her eyes flicked away, glancing around the room. As if she was waiting for something to happen. Or for someone to arrive.

At one point, Sakamura became aware he did not have her full attention. He grabbed her arm and pulled her roughly toward him. She turned her face away from him. He leaned close to her and said something angrily. Then a bald man stepped forward, very close to the camera. The light flared on his face, washing out his features, and his head blocked our view of Eddie and the girl. Then the camera panned left, and we lost them.

"Damn."

"Again?" Jenny backed it up, and we ran it once more.

I said, "Eddie's obviously not happy with her."

"I'd say."

Connor frowned. "It's so difficult to know what we are seeing. Do you have sound for this?"

Jenny said, "Sure, but it's probably walla." She punched buttons and ran it again. The track was continuous cocktail party din. Only for brief moments did we hear an isolated phrase.

At one point, Cheryl Austin looked at Eddie Sakamura and said, ". . . can't help if it's important to you I get . . ."

His reply to her was garbled, but later, he said clearly

to her, "Don't understand . . . all about the Saturday meeting . . ."

And in the last few seconds of the pan, when he pulled her to him, he snarled a phrase like ". . . be a fool . . . no cheapie . . ."

I said, "Did he say 'No cheapie'? "

"Something like that," Connor said.

Jenny said, "Want to run it again?"

"No," Connor said. "There's nothing more to be learned here. Go forward."

"Right," Jenny said.

The image accelerated, the party-goers becoming frenetic, laughing and raising glasses for quick sips. And then I said, "Wait."

Back to normal speed. A blond woman in an Armani silk suit shaking hands with the bald-headed man we had seen a few moments before.

"What is it?" Jenny said, looking at me.

"That's his wife," Connor said.

The woman leaned forward to kiss the bald man lightly on the mouth. Then she stepped back and made some comment about the suit he was wearing.

"She's a lawyer in the D.A.'s office," Jenny said. "Lauren Davis. She's assisted on a couple of big cases. The Sunset Strangler, the Kellerman shooting. She's very ambitious. Smart and well connected. They say she has a future if she stays in the office. It must be true, because Wyland doesn't ever let her get air time. As you see, she makes a good appearance, but he keeps her away from the microphones. The bald guy she's talking to is John McKenna, with Regis McKenna in San Francisco. The company that does the publicity for most high-tech firms."

I said, "We can go forward."

Jenny pushed the button. "She really your wife, or is your partner kidding?"

"No, she's really my wife. Was."

"You're divorced now?"

"Yeah."

Jenny looked at me, and started to say something. Then

she decided not to, and looked back at the screen. On the monitor, the party continued at high speed.

I found myself thinking of Lauren. When I knew her, she was bright and ambitious, but she really didn't understand very much. She had grown up privileged, she had gone to Ivy League schools, and had the privileged person's deep belief that whatever she happened to think was probably true. Certainly good enough to live by. Nothing needed to be checked against reality.

She was young, that was part of it. She was still feeling the world, learning how it worked. She was enthusiastic, and she could be impassioned in expounding her beliefs. But of course her beliefs were always changing, depending on whom she had talked to last. She was very impressionable. She tried on ideas the way some women try on hats. She was always informed on the latest trend. I found it youthful and charming for a while, until it began to annoy me.

Because she didn't have any core, any real substance. She was like a television set: she just played the latest show. Whatever it was. She never questioned it.

In the end, Lauren's great talent was to conform. She was expert at watching the TV, the newspaper, the boss—whatever she saw as the source of authority—and figuring out what direction the winds were blowing. And positioning herself so she was where she ought to be. I wasn't surprised she was getting ahead. Her values, like her clothes, were always smart and up-to-date—

". . . to you, Lieutenant, but it's getting late . . . Lieutenant?"

I blinked, and came back. Jenny was talking to me. She pointed to the screen, where a frozen image showed Cheryl Austin in her black dress, standing with two older men in suits.

I looked over at Connor, but he had turned away, and was talking on the telephone.

"Lieutenant? This of interest to you?"

"Yes, sure. Who are they?"

Jenny started the tape. It ran at normal speed.

"Senator John Morton and Senator Stephen Rowe.

They're both on the Senate Finance Committee. The one that's been having hearings about this MicroCon sale."

On the screen, Cheryl laughed and nodded. In motion, she was remarkably beautiful, an interesting mixture of innocence and sexuality. At moments, her face appeared knowing and almost hard. She appeared to know both men, but not well. She did not come close to either of them, or touch them except to shake hands. For their part, the senators seemed acutely aware of the camera, and maintained a friendly, if somewhat formal demeanor.

"Our country's going to hell, and on a Thursday night, United States senators are standing around chatting with models," Jenny said. "No wonder we're in trouble. And these are important guys. They're talking about Morton as a presidential candidate in the next election."

I said, "What do you know about them personally?"

"They're both married. Well. Rowe's semi-separated. His wife stays home in Virginia. He gets around. Tends to drink too much."

I looked at Rowe on the monitor. He was the same man who had gotten on the elevator with us earlier in the evening. And he had been drunk then, almost falling down. But he wasn't drunk now.

"And Morton?"

"Supposedly he's Mr. Clean. Ex-athlete, fitness nut. Eats health food. Family man. Morton's big area is science and technology. The environment. American competitiveness, American values. All that. But he can't be that clean, I've heard he has a young girlfriend."

"Is that right?"

She shrugged. "The story is, his staffers are trying to break it off. But who knows what's true."

The tape ejected and Jenny pushed in the next one. "This is the last, fellas."

Connor hung up the phone and said, "Forget the tape." He stood. "We've got to go, *kōhai*."

"Why?"

"I've been talking to the phone company about the calls

made from the pay phone in the lobby of the Nakamoto building between eight and ten."

"And?"

"No calls were made during those hours."

I knew that Connor thought that someone had gone out of the security room and called from the pay phone—Cole, or one of the Japanese. Now his hopes of following a promising lead by tracing the call were dashed. "That's too bad," I said.

"Too bad?" Connor said, surprised. "It's extremely helpful. It narrows things down considerably. Miss Gonzales, do you have any tapes of people leaving the party?"

"Leaving? No. Once the guests arrived, all the crews went upstairs to shoot the actual party. Then they brought the tape back here to make the deadline, while the party was still going on."

"Fine. Then I believe we're finished here. Thanks for your help. Your knowledge is remarkable. *Kōhai*, let's go."

Driving again. This time to an address in Beverly Hills. By now it was after one in the morning, and I was tired. I said, "Why does the pay phone in the lobby matter so much?"

"Because," Connor said, "our whole conception of this case revolves around whether someone made a call from that phone, or not. The real question now is, which company in Japan has locked horns with Nakamoto?"

"Which company in Japan?" I said.

"Yes. It is clearly a corporation belonging to a different *keiretsu*," Connor said.

I said, "*Keiretsu*?"

"The Japanese structure their businesses in large organizations they call *keiretsu*. There are six major ones in Japan, and they're huge. For example, the Mitsubishi *keiretsu* consists of seven hundred separate companies that work together, or have interrelated financing, or interrelated agreements of various sorts. Big structures like that don't exist in America because they violate our antitrust laws. But they are the norm in Japan. We tend to think of corporations as standing alone. To see it the Japanese way, you'd have to imagine, say, an association of IBM and Citibank and Ford and Exxon, all having secret agreements among themselves to cooperate, and to share financing or research. That means a Japanese corporation never stands alone — it's always acting in partnership with hundreds of other companies. And in competition with the companies of other *keiretsu*.

"So when you think about what Nakamoto Corporation

is doing, you have to ask what the Nakamoto *keiretsu* is doing, back in Japan. And what companies in other *keiretsu* oppose it. Because this murder is embarrassing to Nakamoto. It could even be seen as an attack against Nakamoto."

"An attack?"

"Think about it. Nakamoto plans a great, star-studded opening night for their building. They want it to go perfectly. For some reason, a guest at the party gets strangled. And the question is—who called it in?"

"Who reported the murder?"

"Right. Because after all, Nakamoto controls that environment completely: it's their party, their building. And it would be a simple matter for them to wait until eleven o'clock, after the party was over and the guests had left, to report the murder. If I were preoccupied with appearances, with the nuances of public face, that's the way I'd do it. Because anything else is potentially dangerous to the corporate image of Nakamoto."

"Okay."

"But the report wasn't delayed," Connor said. "On the contrary, somebody called it in at eight thirty-two, just as the party was getting under way. Thus putting the whole evening at risk. And our question has always been: who called it in?"

I said, "You told Ishiguro to find the person who called. And he hasn't done it yet."

"Correct. Because he can't."

"He doesn't know who called it in?"

"Correct."

"You don't think anybody from the Nakamoto Corporation made the call?"

"Correct."

"An enemy of Nakamoto called?"

"Almost certainly."

I said, "So how do we find out who called the report in?"

Connor laughed. "That's why I checked the lobby phone. It's crucial to that question."

"Why is it crucial?"

"Suppose you work for a competing corporation, and you want to know what's going on inside Nakamoto. You can't find out, because Japanese corporations hire their executives for life. The executives feel they are part of a family. And they'd never betray their own family. So Nakamoto Corporation presents an impenetrable mask to the rest of the world, which makes even the smallest details meaningful: which executives are in town from Japan, who is meeting with whom, comings and goings, and so on. And you might be able to learn those details, if you strike up a relationship with an American security guard who sits in front of monitors all day. Particularly if that guard has been subjected to Japanese prejudice against blacks."

"Go on," I said.

"The Japanese often try to bribe local security officers from rival firms. The Japanese are honorable people, but their tradition allows such behavior. All's fair in love and war, and the Japanese see business as war. Bribery is fine, if you can manage it."

"Okay."

"Now, in the first few seconds after the murder, we can be certain of only two people who knew a girl had been killed. One is the killer himself. The other is the security guard, Ted Cole, who watched it on the monitors."

"Wait a minute. Ted Cole watched it on the monitors? He knows who the killer is?"

"Obviously."

"He said he left at eight-fifteen."

"He was lying."

"But if you knew that, then why didn't we—"

"He'll never tell *us*," Connor said. "The same way Phillips won't tell us. That's why I didn't arrest Cole, bring him down for questioning. In the end it would be a waste of time—and time is of the essence here. We know he won't tell us. My question is, *did he tell anyone else*?"

I began to see what he was driving at. "You mean, did he walk out of the security office to the lobby pay phone, and call somebody to tell them that a murder had occurred?"

"Correct. Because he wouldn't use the phone in his office.

He'd use the pay phone, and call somebody—an enemy of Nakamoto, a competing corporation. Somebody."

I said, "But now we know that no calls were made from that phone."

"Correct," Connor said.

"So your whole line of reasoning collapses."

"Not at all. It is clarified. If Cole didn't notify anybody, then who phoned in the murder? Clearly, the source can only be the murderer himself."

I felt a chill.

"He called it in to embarrass Nakamoto?"

"Presumably," Connor said.

"Then where did he call from?"

"That's not clear yet. I assume from somewhere inside the building. And there are a few other confusing details that we have not begun to consider."

"Such as?"

The car phone rang. Connor answered it, and handed the receiver to me. "It's for you."

"No, no," Mrs. Ascenio said. "The baby is fine. I checked on her a few minutes ago. She is fine. Lieutenant, I wanted you to know Mrs. Davis called." That was how she referred to my ex-wife.

"When?"

"I think ten minutes ago."

"Did she leave a number?"

"No. She say she can't be reached tonight. But she want you to know: something has come up, and maybe she go out of town. So she say maybe she don't take the baby this weekend."

I sighed. "Okay."

"She say she call you tomorrow and let you know for sure."

"Okay."

I wasn't surprised. It was typical Lauren. Last-minute changes. You could never make plans involving Lauren because she was always changing her mind. Probably this latest change meant that she had a new boyfriend and she might go away with him. She wouldn't know until tomorrow.

I used to think all this unpredictability was bad for Michelle, that it would make her insecure. But kids are practical. Michelle seems to understand that's the way her mother is, and she doesn't get upset.

I'm the one who gets upset.

Mrs. Ascenio said, "You coming back soon, Lieutenant?"

"No. It looks like I'll be out all night. Can you stay?"

"Yes, but I have to leave by nine in the morning. You want I pull out the couch?"

I had a couch bed in the living room. She used it when she stayed over. "Yes, sure."

"Okay, good-bye, Lieutenant."

"Good-bye, Mrs. Ascenio."

Connor said, "Anything wrong?" I was surprised to hear tension in his voice.

"No. Just my ex pulling her usual shit. She's not sure she'll take the baby this weekend. Why?"

Connor shrugged. "Just asking."

I didn't think that was all there was to it. I said, "What did you mean earlier, when you said that this case could turn ugly?"

"It may not," Connor said. "Our best solution is to wrap it up in the next few hours. And I think we can. Here's the restaurant up ahead on the left."

I saw the neon sign. Bora Bora.

"This is the restaurant owned by Sakamura?"

"Yes. Actually he's just a part owner. Don't let the valet take the car. Park it in the red. We may need to leave quickly."

The Bora Bora was this week's hot L.A. restaurant. The decor was a jumble of Polynesian masks and shields. Lime green wooden outriggers jutted out over the bar like teeth. Above the open kitchen, a Prince video played ghostlike on an enormous five-meter screen. The menu was Pacific Rim;

the noise deafening; the clientele movie-industry hopeful. Everyone was dressed in black.

Connor smiled. "It looks like Trader Vic's after a bomb went off, doesn't it? Stop staring. Don't they let you out enough?"

"No, they don't," I said. Connor turned to speak to the Eurasian hostess. I looked at the bar, where two women kissed briefly on the lips. Farther down, a Japanese man in a leather bomber jacket had his arm around a huge blonde. They were both listening to a man with thinning hair and a pugnacious manner whom I recognized as the director of—

"Come on," Connor said to me. "Let's go."

"What?"

"Eddie's not here."

"Where is he?"

"At a party in the hills. Let's go."

The address was on a winding road in the hills above Sunset Boulevard. We would have had a good view of the city up here, but the mist had closed in. As we approached, the street was lined on both sides with luxury cars: mostly Lexus sedans, with a few Mercedes convertibles and Bentleys. The parking attendants looked surprised as we pulled up in our Chevy sedan, and headed up to the house.

Like other residences on the street, the house was surrounded by a three-meter wall, the driveway closed off with a remote-controlled steel gate. There was a security camera mounted above the gate, and another at the path leading up to the house itself. A private security guard stood by the path and checked our badges.

I said, "Whose house is this?"

Ten years ago, the only people in Los Angeles who maintained such elaborate security were either Mafioso, or stars like Stallone whose violent roles attracted violent attention. But lately it seemed everybody in wealthy residential areas had security. It was expected, almost fashionable. We walked up steps through a cactus garden toward the house, which was modern, concrete, and fortresslike. Loud music played.

"This house belongs to the man who owns Maxim Noir." He must have seen my blank look. "It's an expensive clothing store famous for its snotty salespeople. Jack Nicholson and Cher shop there."

"Jack Nicholson and Cher," I said, shaking my head. "How do you know about it?"

"Many Japanese shop at Maxim Noir now. It's like most expensive American stores—it'd go out of business without visitors from Tokyo. It's dependent on the Japanese."

As we approached the front door a large man in a sport coat appeared. He had a clipboard with names. "I'm sorry. It's by invitation only, gentlemen."

Connor flashed his badge. "We'd like to speak to one of your guests," he said.

"Which guest is that, sir?"

"Mr. Sakamura." .

He didn't look happy. "Wait here, please."

From the entryway, we could see into the living room. It was crowded with party-goers, who at a quick glance seemed to be many of the same people who had been at the Nakamoto reception. As in the restaurant, almost everyone was wearing black. But the room itself caught my attention: it was stark white, entirely unadorned. No pictures on the wall. No furniture. Just bare white walls and a bare carpet. The guests looked uncomfortable. They were holding cocktail napkins and drinks, looking around for someplace to put them.

A couple passed us on their way to the dining room. "Rod always knows what to do," she said.

"Yes," he said. "So elegantly minimalist. The *detail* in executing that room. I don't know how he ever got that paint job. It's abso*lutely* perfect. Not a brush stroke, not a blemish. A perfect surface."

"Well, it has to be," she said. "It's integral to his whole conception."

"It's really quite daring," the man said.

"Daring?" I said. "What are they talking about? It's just an empty room."

Connor smiled. "I call it *faux zen*. Style without substance."

I scanned the crowd.

"Senator Morton's here." He was standing in the corner, holding forth. Looking very much like a presidential candidate.

"So he is."

The guard hadn't returned, so we stepped a few feet into the room. As I approached Senator Morton, I heard him say, "Yes, I can tell you exactly why I'm disturbed about the extent of Japanese ownership of American industry. If we lose the ability to make our own products, we lose control over our destiny. It's that simple. For example, back in 1987 we learned that Toshiba sold the Russians critical technology that allowed the Soviets to silence their submarine propellers. Russian nuclear subs now sit right off the coast and we can't track them, because they got technology from Japan. Congress was furious, and the American people were up in arms. And rightly so, it was outrageous. Congress planned economic retaliation against Toshiba. But the lobbyists for American companies pleaded their case for them, because American companies like Hewlett-Packard and Compaq were dependent on Toshiba for computer parts. They couldn't stand a boycott because they had no other source of supply. The fact was, we couldn't afford to retaliate. They could sell vital technology to our enemy, and there wasn't a damned thing we could do about it. That's the problem. We're now dependent on Japan—and I believe America shouldn't be dependent on any nation."

Somebody asked a question, and Morton nodded. "Yes, it's true that our industry is not doing well. Real wages in this country are now at 1962 levels. The purchasing power of American workers is back where it was thirty-odd years ago. And that matters, even to the well-to-do folks that I see in this room, because it means American consumers don't have the money to see movies, or buy cars, or clothing, or whatever you people have to sell. The truth is, our nation is sliding badly."

A woman asked another question I couldn't hear, and Morton said, "Yes, I said 1962 levels. I know it's hard to believe, but think back to the fifties, when American workers could own a house, raise a family, and send the kids to college, all on a single paycheck. Now both parents work and most people still can't afford a house. The dollar buys less, everything is more expensive. People struggle just to hold on to what they have. They can't get ahead."

I found myself nodding as I listened. About a month before, I had gone looking for a house, hoping to get a backyard for Michelle. But housing prices were just impossible in L.A. I was never going to be able to afford one, unless I remarried. Maybe not even then, considering—

I felt a sharp jab in the ribs. I turned around and saw the doorman. He jerked his head toward the front door. "Back, fella."

I was angry. I glanced at Connor, but he just quietly moved back to the entrance.

In the entryway, the doorman said, "I checked. There's no Mr. Sakamura here."

"Mr. Sakamura," Connor said, "is the Japanese gentleman standing at the back of the room, to your right. Talking to the redhead."

The doorman shook his head. "I'm sorry, fellas. Unless you have a search warrant, I'll have to ask you to leave."

"There isn't a problem here," Connor said. "Mr. Sakamura is a friend of mine. I know he'd like to talk to me."

"I'm sorry. Do you have a search warrant?"

"No," Connor said.

"Then you're trespassing. And I'm asking you to leave." Connor just stood there.

The doorman stepped back and planted his feet wide. He said, "I think you should know I'm a black belt."

"Are you really?" Connor said.

"So is Jeff," the doorman said, as a second man appeared.

"Jeff," Connor said. "Are you the one who'll be driving your friend here to the hospital?"

Jeff laughed meanly. "Hey. You know, I like humor. It's funny. Okay, Mr. Wise Guy. You're in the wrong place. You've had it explained. Move out. *Now*." He poked Connor in the chest with a stubby finger.

Connor said quietly, "That's assault."

Jeff said, "Hey. Fuck you, buddy. I told you you're in the wrong place—"

Connor did something very fast, and Jeff was suddenly down on the floor, moaning in pain. Jeff rolled away, coming to rest against a pair of black trousers. Looking up, I saw that the man wearing the trousers was dressed entirely in black: black shirt, black tie, black satin jacket. He had white hair and a dramatic Hollywood manner. "I'm Rod Dwyer. This is my home. What seems to be the problem?"

Connor introduced us politely and showed his badge. "We're here on official business. We asked to speak to one of your guests, Mr. Sakamura, who is the man standing over there in the corner."

"And this man?" Dwyer asked, pointing to Jeff, who was gasping and coughing on the floor.

Connor said calmly, "He assaulted me."

"I didn't fucking assault him!" Jeff said, sitting up on his elbow, coughing.

Dwyer said, "Did you *touch* him?"

Jeff was silent, glowering.

Dwyer turned back to us. "I'm sorry this happened. These men are new. I don't know what they were thinking of. Can I get you a drink?"

"Thanks, we're on duty," Connor said.

"Let me ask Mr. Sakamura to come over and talk to you. Your name again?"

"Connor."

Dwyer walked away. The first man helped Jeff to his feet. As Jeff limped away, he muttered, "Fucking assholes."

I said, "Remember when police were respected?"

But Connor was shaking his head, looking down at the floor. "I am very ashamed," he said.

"Why?"

He wouldn't explain further.

"Hey, John! John Connor! *Hisashiburi dana!* Long time no see! How they hanging, guy? Hey!" He punched Connor in the shoulder.

Up close, Eddie Sakamura wasn't so handsome. His complexion was gray, with pock-marked skin, and he smelled like day-old scotch. His movements were edgy, hyperactive, and he spoke quickly. Fast Eddie was not a man at peace.

Connor said, "I'm pretty good, Eddie. How about you? How you doing?"

"Hey, can't complain, Captain. One or two things only. Got a five-oh-one, drunk driving, try to beat that, but you know, with my record, it's getting hard. Hey! Life goes on! What're you doing here? Pretty wild place, huh? Latest thing: no furniture! Rod sets new style. Great! Nobody can sit down any more!" He laughed. "New style! Great!"

I had the feeling he was on drugs. He was too manic. I got a good look at the scar on his left hand. It was purple-red, roughly four centimeters by three. It appeared to be an old burn.

Connor lowered his voice and said, "Actually, Eddie, we're here about the *yakkaigoto* at Nakamoto tonight."

"Ah, yes," Eddie said, lowering his voice, too. "No surprise she came to a bad end. That's one *henntai*."

"She was perverted? Why do you say that?"

Eddie said, "Want to step outside? Like to smoke cigarette and Rod doesn't allow smoking in the house."

"Okay, Eddie."

We went outside and stood by the edge of the cactus garden. Eddie lit a Mild Seven Menthol. "Hey, Captain, I don't know what you heard already so far. But that girl. She fucked some of the people in there. She fucked Rod. Some of the other people. So. We can talk easier out here, okay with you?"

"Sure."

"I know that girl real well. Real well. You know I'm *hipparidako*, hey? I can't help it. Popular guy! She's all over me. All the time."

"I know that, Eddie. But you say she had problems?"

"Big problems, amigo. Grande problemos. I tell you. She was a sick girl, this girl. She got off on pain."

"World's full of 'em, Eddie."

He sucked on his cigarette. "Hey, no," he said. "I'm talking something else. I'm talking, how she gets off. When you hurt her real bad she comes. She's always asking, more, more. Do it more. Squeeze harder."

Connor said, "Her neck?"

"Yeah. Her neck. Right. Squeeze her neck. Yeah. You heard? And sometimes a plastic bag. You know, dry-cleaning bag? Put it over her head and clamp it, hold it around her neck while you fuck her and she sucks the plastic against her mouth and turns blue in the face. Claws at your back. Gasp and wheeze. Christ Almighty. Don't care for that, myself. But I'm telling you, this girl has a pussy. I mean she gets off, it's wild ride. You remember afterwards. I'm telling you. But for me, too much. Always on the edge, you know? Always a risk. Always pushing the edge. Maybe this time. Maybe this is the last time. You know what I'm saying?" He flicked his cigarette away. It sputtered among the cactus thorns. "Sometimes it's exciting. Like Russian roulette. Then I couldn't take it, Captain. Seriously. I couldn't. And you know me, I like a wild time."

I decided that Eddie Sakamura gave me the creeps. I tried to make notes while he talked, but his words were tumbling out, and I couldn't keep up. He lit another cigarette, his hands shaking. He kept talking fast, swinging the glowing tip in the air for emphasis.

"And I mean, this girl, it's a *problem*," Eddie said. "Okay, pretty girl. She's pretty. But sometimes she can't go out, looks too bad. Sometimes, she needs lot of makeup, because neck is sensitive skin, man. And hers is bruised. Ring around the collar. Bad. You saw that, maybe. You see her dead, Captain?"

"Yeah, I saw her."

"So then . . ." he hesitated. He seemed to step back, reconsider something. He flicked ash from the cigarette. "So. Was she strangled, or what?"

"Yes, Eddie. She was strangled."

He inhaled. "Yeah. Figures."

"Did you see her, Eddie?"

"Me? No. What are you talking about? How could I see her, Captain?" He exhaled, blowing smoke into the night.

"Eddie. Look at me."

Eddie turned toward Connor.

"Look in my eyes. Now tell me. Did you see the body?"

"No. Captain, come on." Eddie gave a nervous little

laugh, and looked away. He flicked the cigarette so it tumbled in the air, dripping sparks. "What is this? Third degree? No. I didn't see the body."

"Eddie."

"I swear to you, Captain."

"Eddie. How are you involved in this?"

"Me? Shit. Not me, Captain. I know the girl, sure. I see her sometimes. I fuck her, sure. What the hell. She's little weird, but she's fun. A fun girl. Great pussy. That's it, man. That's all of it." He looked around, lit another cigarette. "This's a nice cactus garden, huh? Xeriscape, they call it. It's the latest thing. Los Angeles goes back to desert life. It's *hayatterunosa*: very fashionable."

"Eddie."

"Come on, Captain. Give me break here. We know each other long time."

"Sure, Eddie. But I have some problems. What about the security tapes?"

Eddie looked blank, innocent. "Security tapes?"

"A man with a scar on his hand and a tie with triangles on it came into the Nakamoto security office and took the security videotapes."

"*Fuck*. What security office? What're you doing, Captain?"

"Eddie."

"Who said that to you? That's not *true*, man. Take the security tapes? I never did thing like that. What're you, crazy?" He twisted his tie, looked at the label. "This is Polo tie, Captain. Ralph Lauren. Polo. Lot of these ties, bet you."

"Eddie. What about the Imperial Arms?"

"What about it?"

"You go there tonight?"

"No."

"You clean up Cheryl's room?"

"*What*?" Eddie appeared shocked. "*What?* No. Clean up her room? Where you getting all this shit, Captain?"

"The girl across the hall . . . Julia Young," Connor said.

"She told us she saw you tonight, with another man. In Cheryl's room at the Imperial Arms."

Eddie threw his arms in the air. "Jesus. Captain. You listen. That girl wouldn't know, she saw me last night or last month, man. That girl is a fucking hophead. You look between her toes you find the marks. You look under her tongue. Look on her pussylips. You find 'em. That's a dream girl, man. She doesn't know when things happen. *Man*. You come here, give me this. I don't like this." Eddie tossed his cigarette away, and immediately lit another. "I don't like this one bit. You don't see what's going on?"

"No," Connor said. "Tell me, Eddie. What's going on?"

"This shit's not true, man. None of this true." He puffed rapidly. "You know what this is about? It's not about some fucking girl, man. It's about Saturday meetings. The *Doyou kai, Connor-san*. The secret meetings. That's what it's about."

Connor snapped, "*Sonna bakana*."

"No *bakana, Connor-san*. Not bullshit."

"What does a girl from Texas know about *Doyou kai*?"

"She knows something. *Hontō nanda*. And she likes to cause trouble, this girl. She likes to make turmoil."

"Eddie, I think maybe you better come in with us."

"Fine. Perfect. You do their job for them. For the *kuromaku*." He spun to Connor. "Shit, Captain. Come on. You know how it works. This girl killed at Nakamoto. You know my family, my father, is Daimatsu. Now in Osaka they will read that a girl is killed at Nakamoto and I am arrested in connection. His son."

"Detained."

"Detained. Whatever. You know what that will mean. *Taihennakoto ni naru zo*. My father resign, his company must make apologies to Nakamoto. Perhaps reparations. Give some advantage in business. It is powerful *ōsawagi ni naruzo*. You will do this, if you take me into your custody." He flicked his cigarette away. "Hey. You think I did this murder, you arrest me. Fine. But you are just covering your ass, you maybe do a lot of damage to me. Captain: you know this."

Connor said nothing for a long time. There was a long silence. They walked around the garden, in circles.

Finally, Eddie said, "*Na, Connor-san. Tanomuyo ...*" His voice sounded pleading. It seemed like he was asking for a break.

Connor sighed. "You got your passport, Eddie?"

"Yeah, sure. Always."

"Let's have it."

"Yeah, sure. Okay, Captain. Here goes."

Connor glanced at it, handed it to me. I slipped it in my pocket.

"Okay, Eddie. But this better not be *murina koto*. Or you'll be declared persona non grata, Eddie. And I will personally put you on the next plane for Osaka. *Wakattaka*?"

"Captain, you protect the honor of my family. *On ni kiru yo*." And he bowed formally, both hands at his sides.

Connor bowed back.

I just stared. I couldn't believe what I was seeing. Connor was going to let him go. I thought he was crazy to allow it.

I handed Eddie my business card and gave my usual speech about how he could call me later if he thought of anything. Eddie shrugged and slipped the card into his shirt pocket, as he lit another cigarette. I didn't count: he was dealing with Connor.

Eddie started back toward the house, paused. "I have this redhead here, very interesting," he said. "When I leave the party, I go to my house in the hills. You need me, I will be there. Good night, Captain. Good night, Lieutenant."

"Good night, Eddie."

We went back down the steps.

"I hope you know what you are doing," I said.

"So do I," Connor said.

"'Cause he seems guilty as hell to me."

"Maybe."

"If you ask me, it'd be better to take him in. Safer."

"Maybe."

"Want to go back and get him?"

"No." He shook his head. "My *dai rokkan* says no."

I knew that word: it meant sixth sense. The Japanese were big on intuition. I said, "Yeah, well, I hope you're right."

We continued down the steps in the darkness.

"Anyway," Connor said. "I owe him."

"For what?"

"There was a time, a few years ago, when I needed some information. You remember the *fugu* poisoning business? No? Well anyway, no one in the community would tell me. They stonewalled me. And I needed to know. It was . . . it was important. Eddie told me. He was scared to do it, because he didn't want anyone to know. But he did it. I probably owe my life to him."

We came to the bottom of the stairs.

"And did he remind you of that?"

"He would never remind me. It is my job to remember."

I said, "That's fine, Captain. All that obligation stuff is fine and noble. And I'm all for interracial harmony. But meanwhile, it's possible that he killed her, stole the tapes, and cleaned up the apartment. Eddie Sakamura looks like a blown-out speedball to me. He acts like a suspect. And we're just walking away. Letting him go."

"Right."

We kept walking. I thought it over and got more worried. I said, "You know, officially this is my investigation."

"Officially, it's Graham's investigation."

"Yeah, okay. But we're going to look stupid if it turns out he did it."

Connor sighed, as if he was losing patience. "Okay. Let's go over it the way you think it might have happened. Eddie kills the girl, right?"

"Right."

"He can see her any time but he decides to fuck her on the boardroom table, and he kills her. Then he goes down to the lobby, and pretends to be a Nakamoto executive—even though the last thing Eddie Sakamura looks like is an executive. But let's say he passes himself off. He manages to dismiss the guard. He takes the tapes. He walks out just as Phillips comes in. Then he goes to Cheryl's apartment to clean that up, but somehow he adds a picture of himself, stuck in Cheryl's mirror. Next he stops by the Bora Bora and tells everybody he's going to a party in Hollywood. Where we find him, in a room without furniture, calmly chatting up a redhead. Is that how the evening lays out to you?"

I said nothing. It didn't make much sense, when he put it that way. On the other hand . . .

"I just hope he didn't do it."

"So do I."

We came down to the street level. The valet ran to get our car.

"You know," I said, "the blunt way he talks about things, like putting the bag over her head, it's creepy."

"Oh, that doesn't mean anything," Connor said. "Remember, Japan has never accepted Freud or Christianity. They've never been guilty or embarrassed about sex. No problem with homosexuality, no problem with kinky sex. Just matter-of-fact. Some people like it a certain way, so some people do it that way, what the hell. The Japanese can't understand why we get so worked up about a straight-forward bodily function. They think we're a little screwed up on the subject of sex. And they have a point." Connor glanced at his watch.

A security car pulled up. The uniformed guard leaned out. "Hey, is there a problem at the party up there?"

"Like what?"

"Couple of guys get in a fight? Some kind of fight? We had a report phoned in."

"I don't know," Connor said. "Maybe you better go up and check."

The guard climbed out of his car, hefted a big gut, and started up the stairs. Connor looked back at the high walls. "You know we have more private security than police, now? Everyone's building walls and hiring guards. But in Japan, you can walk into a park at midnight and sit on a bench and nothing will happen to you. You're completely safe, day or night. You can go anywhere. You won't be robbed or beaten or killed. You're not always looking behind you, not always worrying. You don't need walls or bodyguards. Your safety is the safety of the whole society. You're free. It's a wonderful feeling. Here, everybody has to lock themselves up. Lock the door. Lock the car. People who spend their whole lives locked up are in prison. It's crazy. It kills the spirit. But it's been so long now that Americans have forgotten what it's like to really feel *safe*. Anyway. Here's our car. Let's get down to the division."

We had started driving down the street when the DHD operator called. "Lieutenant Smith," she said, "we have a request for Special Services."

"I'm pretty busy," I said. "Can the backup take it?"

"Lieutenant Smith, we have patrol officers requesting Special Services for a vee dig in area nineteen."

She was telling me there was a problem with a visiting dignitary. "I understand," I said, "but I've already rolled out on a case. Give it to the backup."

"But this is on Sunset Plaza Drive," she said. "Aren't you located—"

"Yes," I said. Now I understood why she was insistent. The call was only a few blocks away. "Okay," I said. "What's the problem?"

"It's a vee dig DUI. Reported in as G-level plus one. Last name is Rowe."

"Okay," I said. "We're going." I hung up the phone, and turned the car around.

"Interesting," Connor said. "G-level plus one is American government?"

"Yes," I said.

"It's Senator Rowe?"

"Sounds like it," I said. "Driving under the influence."

The black Lincoln sedan had come to a stop on the lawn of a house along the steep part of Sunset Plaza Drive. Two black and whites were pulled up at the curb, red lights flashing. Up on the lawn, a half-dozen people were standing beside the Lincoln. A man in his bathrobe, arms folded across his chest. A couple of girls in short glittery sequin dresses, a very handsome blond man about forty in a tuxedo, and a younger man in a blue suit, whom I recognized as the young man who had gotten on the elevator with Senator Rowe earlier.

The patrolmen had the video camera out, shining the bright light on Senator Rowe. He was propping himself up against the front fender of the Lincoln, holding his arm up to cover his face against the light. He was swearing loudly as Connor and I walked up.

The man in the bathrobe came toward us and said, "I want to know who's going to pay for this."

"Just a minute, sir." I kept walking.

"He can't just ruin my lawn like this. It has to be paid for."

"Just give me a minute, sir."

"Scared the hell out of my wife, too, and she has cancer."

I said, "Sir, please give me a minute, and then I'll talk to you."

"Cancer of the *ear*," he said emphatically. "The *ear*."

"Yes, sir. All right, sir." I continued toward the Lincoln, and the bright light.

As I passed the aide, he fell into step beside me and said, "I can explain everything, Detective." He was about thirty, with the bland good looks of a congressional staffer. "I'm sure I can resolve everything."

"Just a minute," I said. "Let me talk to the senator."

"The senator's not feeling well," the aide said. "He's very tired." He stepped in front of me. I just walked around him. He hurried to catch up. "It's jet lag, that's the problem. The senator has jet lag."

"I have to talk to him," I said, stepping into the bright light. Rowe was still holding up his arm. I said, "Senator Rowe?"

"Turn that fucking thing *off*, for fuck's sake," Rowe said. He was heavily intoxicated; his speech so slurred it was difficult to understand him.

"Senator Rowe," I said, "I'm afraid I'll have to ask you to—"

"Fuck you and the horse you rode in on."

"Senator Rowe," I said.

"Turn that fucking camera off."

I looked back to the patrolman and signaled to him. He reluctantly turned the camera off. The light went out.

"Jesus *Christ*," Rowe said, finally dropping his arm. He looked at me with bleary eyes. "What the fuck is going on here."

I introduced myself.

"Then why don't you *do* something about this *fucking zoo*," Rowe said. "I'm just driving to my *fucking hotel*."

"I understand that, Senator."

"Don't know . . ." He waved his hand, a sloppy gesture. "What the fucking *problem* is around here."

"Senator, you were driving this car?"

"Fuck. Driving." He turned away. "Jerry? Explain it to them. Christ's sake."

The aide came up immediately. "I'm sorry about all this," he said smoothly. "The senator isn't feeling at all well. We just came back from Tokyo yesterday evening. Jet lag. He's not himself. He's tired."

"Who was driving the car?" I said.

"I was," the aide said. "Absolutely."

One of the girls giggled.

"No, he wasn't," the man in the bathrobe shouted, from the other side of the car. "*He* was driving it. And he couldn't get out of the car without falling down."

"Christ, fucking zoo," Senator Rowe said, rubbing his head.

"Detective," the aide said, "I was driving the car and these two women here will testify that I was." He gestured to the girls in party dresses. Giving them a look.

"That's a goddamn lie," the man in the bathrobe said.

"No, that's correct," the handsome man in the tuxedo said, speaking for the first time. He had a suntan and a relaxed manner, like he was used to having his orders obeyed. Probably a Wall Street guy. He didn't introduce himself.

"I was driving the car," the aide said.

"All gone to shit," Rowe muttered. "Want to go to my hotel."

"Was anyone hurt here?" I said.

"Nobody was hurt," the aide said. "Everybody is fine."

I asked the patrolmen behind me, "You got a one-ten to file?" That was the report of property damage for vehicular accident.

"We don't need to," a patrolman said to me. "Single car, and the amount doesn't qualify." You only had to fill it out if the damage was more than two hundred dollars. "All we got is a five-oh-one. If you want to run with that."

I didn't. One of the things you learned about in Special Services was SAR, situational appropriate response. SAR meant that in the case of elected officials and celebrities, you let it go unless somebody was going to press charges. In practice, that meant that you didn't make an arrest short of a felony.

I said to the aide, "You get the property owner's name and address, so you can deal with the damage to the lawn."

"He already got my name and address," the man in the bathrobe said. "But I want to know what's going to be *done*."

"I told him we'd repair any damage," the aide said. "I assured him we would. He seems to be—"

"Damn it, look: her planting is *ruined*. And she has *cancer* of the *ear*."

"Just a minute, sir." I said to the aide, "Who's going to drive the car now?"

"I am," the aide said.

"He is," Senator Rowe said, nodding. "Jerry. Drive the car."

I said to the aide, "All right. I want you to take a breatholyzer—"

"Sure, yes—"

"And I want to see your driver's license."

"Of course."

The aide blew into the breatholyzer and handed me his driver's license. It was a Texas license. Gerrold D. Hardin, thirty-four years old. Address in Austin, Texas. I wrote down the details, and gave it back.

"All right, Mr. Hardin. I'm going to release the senator into your custody tonight."

"Thank you, Lieutenant. I appreciate it."

The man in the bathrobe said, "You're going to *let him go*?"

"Just a minute, sir." I said to Hardin, "I want you to give this man your business card, and stay in contact with him. I expect the damage to his yard to be resolved to his satisfaction."

"Absolutely. Of course. Yes." Hardin reached into his pocket for a card. He brought out something white in his hand, like a handkerchief. He stuffed it hastily back in his pocket, and then walked over to give his card to the man in the bathrobe.

"You're going to have to replace all her begonias."

"Fine, sir," Hardin said.

"*All* of 'em."

"Yes. That's fine, sir."

Senator Rowe pushed off the front fender, standing unsteadily in the night. "Fucking begonias," he said. "Christ, what a fucking night this is. You got a wife?"

"No," I said.

"I do," Rowe said. "Fucking begonias. Fuck."

"This way, Senator," Hardin said. He helped Rowe into the passenger seat. The girls climbed into the back seat, on either side of the handsome Wall Street guy. Hardin got behind the wheel and asked Rowe for the keys. I looked away to watch the black and whites as they pulled away from the curb. When I turned back, Hardin rolled down the window and looked at me. "Thank you for this."

"Drive safely, Mr. Hardin," I said.

He backed the car off the lawn, driving over a flower bed.

"*And* the irises," the man in the bathrobe shouted, as the car pulled away down the road. He looked at me. "I'm telling you, the other man was driving, and he was drunk."

I said, "Here's my card. If things don't turn out right, call me."

He looked at the card, shaking his head, and went back into his house. Connor and I got back into the car. We drove down the hill.

Connor said, "You got information on the aide?"

"Yes," I said.

"What was in his pocket?"

"I'd say it was a pair of women's panties."

"So would I," Connor said.

Of course there was nothing we could do. Personally, I would have liked to spin the smug bastard around, push him up against the car and search him, right there. But we both knew our hands were tied: we had no probable cause to search Hardin, or to arrest him. He was a young man driving with two young women in the back seat, either of whom might be without her panties, and a drunken United States senator in the front seat. The only sensible thing to do was to let them all go.

But it seemed like an evening of letting people go.

The phone rang. I pushed the speaker button. "Lieutenant Smith."

"Hey, buddy." It was Graham. "I'm over here at the morgue, and guess what? I have some Japanese bugging me to attend the autopsy. Wants to sit in and observe, if you can believe that shit. He's all bent out of shape because we started the autopsy without him. But the lab work is starting to come back. It is not looking good for Nippon Central. I'd say we have a Japanese perp. So: you coming here or what?"

I looked at Connor. He nodded.

"We're heading there now," I said.

The fastest way to the morgue was through the emergency room at County General Hospital. As we went through, a black man covered in blood was sitting up on his gurney, screaming "Kill the pope! Kill the pope! Fuck him!" in a drug-crazed frenzy. A half-dozen attendants were trying to push him down. He had gunshot wounds in his shoulder and hand. The floors and walls of the emergency room were spattered with blood. An orderly went down the hall, cleaning it up with a mop. The hallways were lined with black and Hispanic people. Some of them held children in their laps. Everyone looked away from the bloody mop. From somewhere down the corridor, we heard more screams.

We got onto the elevator. It was quiet.

Connor said, "A homicide every twenty minutes. A rape every seven minutes. A child murdered every four hours. No other country tolerates these levels of violence."

The doors opened. Compared to the emergency room, the basement corridors of the county morgue were positively tranquil. There was a strong odor of formaldehyde. We went to the desk, where the thin, angular deaner, Harry Landon, was bent over some papers, eating a ham sandwich. He didn't look up. "Hey, guys."

"Hey, Harry."

"What you here for? Austin prep?"

"Yeah."

"They started about half an hour ago. Guess there's a big rush on her, huh?"

"How's that?"

"The chief called Dr. Tim out of bed and told him to do it pronto. Pissed him off pretty good. You know how particular Dr. Tim is." The deaner smiled. "And they called in a lot of lab people, too. Who ever heard of pushing a full workup in the middle of the night? I mean, you know what this is going to cost in overtime?"

I said, "And what about Graham?"

"He's around here someplace. He had some Japanese guy chasing after him. Dogging him like a shadow. Then every half hour, the Japanese asks me can he use the phone, and he makes a call. Speaks Japanese a while. Then he goes back to bothering Graham. He says he wants to see the autopsy, if you can believe that. Keeps pushing, pushing. But anyway, the Japanese makes his last call about ten minutes ago, and suddenly a big change comes over him. I was here at the desk. I saw it on his face. He goes *mojo mojo* like he can't believe his ears. And then he *runs* out of here. I mean it: *runs*."

"And where's the autopsy?"

"Room two."

"Thanks, Harry."

"Close the *door*."

"Hi, Tim," I said, as we came into the autopsy room. Tim Yoshimura, known to everyone as Dr. Tim, was leaning over the stainless-steel table. Even though it was one-forty in the morning, he was as usual immaculate. Everything was in place. His hair was neatly combed. His tie was perfectly knotted. The pens were lined up in the pocket of his starched lab coat.

"Did you *hear* me?"

"I'm closing it, Tim." The door had a pneumatic self-closing mechanism, but apparently that wasn't fast enough for Dr. Tim.

"It's only because I don't want that Japanese individual looking in."

"He's gone, Tim."

"Oh, is he? But he may be back. He's been unbelievably persistent and irritating. The Japanese can be a real pain in the ass."

I said, "Sounds funny coming from you, Tim."

"Oh, I'm not Japanese," he said seriously. "I'm Japanese-American, which means in their eyes I'm *gaijin*. If I go to

Japan, they treat me like any other foreigner. It doesn't matter how I look, I was born in Torrance—and that's the end of it." He glanced over his shoulder. "Who's that with you? Not John Connor? Haven't seen you in ages, John."

"Hi, Tim." Connor and I approached the table. I could see the dissection was already well advanced, that the Y-shaped incision had been made, and the first organs removed and placed neatly on stainless steel trays.

"Now maybe *somebody* can tell me, what is the big deal about this case?" Tim said. "Graham is so pissed off he won't say anything. He went next door to the lab to see the first of the results. But I still want to know why I got called out of bed to do this one. Mark's on duty, but he is apparently not senior enough to do it. And of course the M.E. is out of town at a conference in San Francisco. Now that he has that new girlfriend he is always out of town. So I get called. I can't remember the last time I got called out of bed."

"You can't?" I said. Dr. Tim was precise in all ways, including his memory.

"The last time was January three years ago. But that was to *cover*. Most of the staff was out with the flu, and the cases were backing up. Finally one night we ran out of lockers. They had these bodies lying around on the floor in bags. Stacked up in piles. Something had to be done. The smell was terrible. But no, I can't remember being called out just because a case was politically *tense*. Like this one."

Connor said, "We're not sure why it is tense, either."

"Maybe you better find out. Because there's a lot of pressure here. The M.E. calls me from San Francisco, and he keeps saying, 'Do it now, do it tonight, and get it done.' I say, 'Okay, Bill.' Then he says, 'Listen, Tim. Do this one right. Go slow, take lots of pictures and lots of notes. Document your ass off. Shoot with two cameras. Because I got a feeling that anybody who has anything to do with this case could get into deep shit.' So. It's natural to wonder what the big deal is."

Connor said, "What time was that call to you?"

"About ten-thirty, eleven."

"The M.E. say who called him?"

"No. But it's usually only one of two people: the chief of police or the mayor."

Tim looked at the liver, pulling apart the lobes, then placed it on a steel tray. The assistant was taking flash pictures of each organ and then setting it aside.

"So? What've you found?"

"Frankly, the most interesting findings so far are external," Dr. Tim said. "She had heavy makeup on her neck, to cover a pattern of multiple contusions. Bruises of different ages. Without a spectroscopic curve for the hemoglobin breakdown products at the bruise sites, I'd still say these bruises are of variable age, up to two weeks old. Perhaps older. Consistent with a pattern of repeated, chronic cervical trauma. I don't think there's any question: we're looking at a case of sexual asphyxia."

"She's a gasper?"

"Yeah. She is."

Kelly thought so. For once Kelly was right.

"It's more common in men, but it is certainly reported in women. The syndrome is the individual is sexually aroused only by the hypoxia of near-strangulation. These individuals ask their sexual partners to strangle them, or put a plastic bag over their head. When they're alone, they sometimes tie a cord around their neck, and hang themselves while they masturbate. Since the effect requires that they are strangled almost to the point of passing out, it's easy to make a mistake and go too far. They do, all the time."

"And in this case?"

Tim shrugged. "Well. She has physical findings consistent with a sexual asphyxia syndrome of long standing. And she has ejaculate in her vagina and abrasions on her external vaginal labia, consistent with a forced sexual episode on the same night of her death."

Connor said, "You're sure the vaginal abrasions occurred before death?"

"Oh, yes. They are definitely antemortem injuries. There's no question she had forced sex sometime before she died."

"Are you saying she was raped?"

"No. I wouldn't go that far. As you see, the abrasions are not severe, and there are no associated injuries to other parts of her body. In fact, there are no signs of physical struggle at all. So I would consider the findings consistent with premature vaginal entry with insufficient lubrication of the external labia."

I said, "You're saying she wasn't wet."

Tim looked pained. "Well. In crude layman's terms."

"How long before death did these abrasions occur?"

"It could be as much as an hour or two. It wasn't near the actual time of death. You can tell that from the extravasation and swelling of the affected areas. If death occurs soon after the injury, blood flow stops, and therefore the swelling is limited or absent. In this case, as you see, swelling is quite pronounced."

"And the sperm?"

"Samples have gone to the lab. Along with all her usual fluids." He shrugged. "Have to wait and see. Now, are you two going to fill me in? Because it looks to me like this little girl was going to get in trouble, sooner or later. I mean, she's *cute*, but she's screwed up. So . . . what is the big deal? Why am I out of bed in the middle of the night to do a careful, documented post on some little gasper?"

I said, "Beats me."

"Come on. Fair is fair," Dr. Tim said. "I showed you mine, now you show me yours."

"Why, Tim," Connor said. "You made a joke."

"Fuck you," Tim said. "You guys owe me. Come on."

"I'm afraid Peter is telling you the truth," Connor said. "All we know is that this murder occurred at the time of a big public Japanese reception, and they are eager to get it cleared up right away."

"That makes sense," Tim said. "The last time the shit hit the fan around here, it was because of that thing involving the Japanese consulate. Remember, the Takashima kidnapping case? Maybe you don't remember: it never made the papers. The Japanese managed to keep it *very* quiet. But anyway, a guard was killed under odd circumstances, and for two days, they put a hell of a pressure on our office. I was amazed what they could do. We had Senator Rowe calling us in person, telling us what to do. The governor calling in person. Everybody calling us. You'd think it was the president's kid. I mean, these people have *influence*."

"Of course they do. They've paid handsomely for it," Graham said, coming into the room.

"Close the *door*," Tim said.

"But this time, all their fucking influence won't help," Graham said. "Because this time, we have them by the short and curlies. We have a murder: and based on the lab results so far, we can say without question that the murderer was Japanese."

The pathology lab next door was a large room lit by even banks of fluorescent lights. Rows of microscopes, neatly laid out. But late at night, only two technicians were working in the big space. And Graham was standing beside them, gloating.

"Look for yourself. Pubic hair comb-through reveals male pubic hair, moderate curl, ovoid cross section, almost certainly Asian in origin. The first semen analysis is blood type: AB, relatively rare among Caucasians, but much more common among Asians. The first analysis of protein in the seminal fluid comes up negative for the genetic marker for . . . what's it called?"

"Ethanol dehydrogenase," the technician said.

"Right. Ethanol dehydrogenase. It's an enzyme. Missing in Japanese. And missing in this seminal fluid. And there's the Diego factor, which is a blood-group protein. So. We have more tests coming, but it seems clear that this girl had forced sex with a Japanese man before she was killed by him."

"It's clear you've found evidence of Japanese semen in her vagina," Connor said. "That's all."

"Christ," Graham said. "Japanese semen, Japanese pubic hair, Japanese blood factors. We are talking a Japanese perp here."

He had set out some pictures from the crime scene, showing Cheryl lying on the boardroom table. He started to pace back and forth in front of them.

"I know where you guys have been, and I know you've been wasting your time," Graham said. "You went for videotapes: but they're gone, right? Then you went to her apartment: but it was cleaned up before you ever got there. Which is exactly what you'd expect if the perp is Japanese. It lays right out, plain as can be."

Graham pointed to the pictures. "There's our girl. Cheryl Austin from Texas. She's cute. Fresh. Good figure. She's an actress, sort of. She does a few commercials. Maybe a Nissan commercial. Whatever. She meets some people. Makes some contacts. Gets on some lists. You with me?"

"Yes," I said to Graham. Connor was staring intently at the pictures.

"One way or another, our Cheryl's doing well enough to be wearing a black Yamamoto gown when she gets invited to the grand opening of the Nakamoto Tower. She comes with some guy, maybe a friend or a hairdresser. A beard. Maybe she knows other people at the party, and maybe not. But in the course of the evening, somebody big and powerful suggests they slip away for a while. She agrees to go upstairs. Why not? This girl likes adventure. She likes danger. She's cruising for a bruising. So she goes upstairs—maybe with the other guy, maybe separately. But anyway, they meet upstairs, and they look around for a place to do it. A place that's exciting. And they decide—him, probably, *he* decides—to do it right on the fucking boardroom table. So they start doing it, they're whanging away but things get out of hand. Her loverboy gets a little too worked up, or else he's kinky, and . . . he squeezes her neck a little too hard. And she's dead. You with me so far?"

"Yes . . ."

"So now loverboy has a problem. He's come upstairs to fuck a girl, but unfortunately he's killed her. So what does he do? What *can* he do? He goes back down, rejoins the party, and since he is a big samurai cocksman, he tells one of his underlings that he has this little problem. He has unfortunately snuffed out the life of a local whore. Very inconvenient for his busy schedule. So the underlings run around and clean up the boss's mess. They clean up incriminating evidence from the floor upstairs. They remove the videotapes. They go to her apartment and remove evidence there. Which is all fine, except it takes time. So somebody has to stall the police. And that's where their smoothie suckass lawyer Ishiguro comes in. He delays us a good hour and a half. So. How does that sound?"

There was a silence when he had finished. I waited for Connor to speak.

"Well," Connor said, at last. "My hat is off to you, Tom. That sequence of events sounds correct in many respects."

"You're damned right it does." Graham puffed up. "Damn fucking right."

The telephone rang. The lab technician said, "Is there a Captain Connor here?"

Connor went to answer the phone. Graham said to me, "I'm telling you. A Jap killed this girl, and we are going to find him and fucking flay him. *Flay* him."

I said, "Why do you have it in for them, anyway?"

Graham gave me a sullen look. He said, "What are you talking about?"

"I'm talking about how you hate the Japanese."

"Hey, listen," Graham said. "Let's get something straight, Petey-san. I don't hate anybody. I do my job. Black man, white man, Japanese man, it makes no difference to me."

"Okay, Tom." It was late at night. I didn't want to argue.

"No, hell. You fucking think I'm prejudiced."

"Let's just drop it, Tom."

"No, hell. We're not going to drop it. Not now. Let me tell you something, Petey-san. You got yourself this fucking liaison job, isn't that right?"

"That's right, Tom."

"And how come you applied for it? Because of your great love of Japanese culture?"

"Well, at the time, I was working in the press office—"

"No, no, cut the shit. You applied for it," Graham said, "because there was an extra stipend, isn't that right? Two, three thousand a year. An educational stipend. It comes into the department from the Japan-America Amity Foundation. And the department allows it as an educational stipend, paid to members of the force so that they can further their education in Japanese language and culture. So. How're those studies going, Petey-san?"

"I'm studying."

"How often?"

"One night a week."

"One night a week. And if you miss classes, do you lose your stipend?"

"No."

"Fucking right you don't. In fact, it doesn't make any difference if you go to classes at all. The fact is, buddy, you got yourself a bribe. You got three thousand dollars in your pocket and it comes right from the land of the rising sun. Of course, it's not that much. Nobody can buy you for three grand, right? Of course not."

"Hey, Tom—"

"But the thing is, they aren't buying you. They're just *influencing* you. They just want you to think twice. To tend to look favorably upon them. And why not? It's human nature. They've made your life a little better. They contribute to your well-being. Your family. Your little girl. They scratch your back, so why shouldn't you scratch theirs? Isn't that about it, Petey-san?"

"No, it isn't," I said. I was getting angry.

"Yes, it is," Graham said. "Because that's how influence works. It's deniable. You say it isn't there. You tell yourself it isn't there—but it is. The only way you can be clean is to be *clean*, man. If you got no stake in it, if you got no income from it, then you can talk. Otherwise, man, they pay you and I say, they *own* you."

"Just a fucking minute—"

"So don't you talk to me about *hating*, man. This country is in a war and some people understand it, and some other people are siding with the enemy. Just like in World War II, some people were paid by Germany to promote Nazi propaganda. New York newspapers published editorials right out of the mouth of Adolf Hitler. Sometimes the people didn't even know it. But they did it. That's how it is in a war, man. And *you* are a fucking collaborator."

I was grateful when, at that moment, Connor came back

to where we were standing. Graham and I were about to square off when Connor said calmly, "Now, just so I understand, Tom. According to your scenario, after the girl was murdered, what happened to the tapes?"

"Oh, hell, those tapes are *gone*," Graham said. "You're never going to see those tapes again."

"Well, it's interesting. Because that call was the division headquarters. It seems Mr. Ishiguro is there. And he's brought a box of videotapes with him, for me to look at."

Connor and I drove over. Graham took his own car. I said, "Why did you say the Japanese would never touch Graham?"

"Graham's uncle," Connor said. "He was a prisoner of war during World War II. He was taken to Tokyo, where he disappeared. Graham's father went over after the war to find out what happened to him. There were unpleasant questions about what happened. You probably know that some American servicemen were killed in terminal medical experiments in Japan. There were stories about the Japanese feeding their livers to subordinates as a joke, things like that."

"No, I didn't know," I said.

"I think everybody would prefer to forget that time," Connor said, "and move on. And probably correctly. It's a different country now. What was Graham going on about?"

"My stipend as a liaison officer."

Connor said, "You told me it was fifty a week."

"It's a little more than that."

"How much more?"

"About a hundred dollars a week. Fifty-five hundred a year. But that's to cover classes, and books, and commuting expenses, baby-sitters, everything."

"So you get five grand," Connor said. "So what?"

"Graham was saying I was influenced by it. That the Japanese had bought me."

Connor said, "Well, they certainly try to do that. And they're extremely subtle."

"They tried it with you?"

"Oh, sure." He paused. "And often I accepted. Giving gifts to ensure that you will be seen favorably is something the Japanese do by instinct. And it's not so different from what we do, when we invite the boss over for dinner. Goodwill is goodwill. But we don't invite the boss over for dinner when we're up for a promotion. The proper thing to do is to invite the boss early in the relationship, when nothing is at stake. Then it's just goodwill. The same with the Japanese. They believe you should give the gift early, because then it is not a bribe. It is a gift. A way of making a relationship with you before there is any pressure on the relationship."

"And you think that's okay?"

"I think it's the way the world works."

"Do you think it's corrupting?"

Connor looked at me and said, "Do you?"

I took a long time to answer. "Yes. I think maybe so."

He started to laugh. "Well, that's a relief," he said. "Because otherwise, the Japanese would have wasted all their money on you."

"What's so funny?"

"Your confusion, *kōhai*."

"Graham thinks it's a war."

Connor said, "Well, that's true. We are definitely at war with Japan. But let's see what surprises Mr. Ishiguro has for us in the latest skirmish."

As usual, the fifth-floor anteroom of the downtown detective division was busy, even at two o'clock in the morning. Detectives moved among the beat-up prostitutes and twitching druggies brought in for questioning; in the corner a man in a checked sport coat was shouting, "I said, shut the fuck *up*!" over and over to a female officer with a clipboard.

In all the swirl and noise, Masao Ishiguro looked distinctly out of place. Wearing his blue pinstripe suit, he sat in the corner with his head bowed and his knees pressed together. He had a cardboard box balanced on his knees.

When he saw us, he jumped to his feet. He bowed deeply, placing his hands flat on his thighs, a sign of additional respect. He held the bow for several seconds. Then he immediately bowed again, and this time he waited, bent over, staring at the floor, until Connor spoke to him in Japanese. Ishiguro's reply, also in Japanese, was quiet and deferential. He kept looking at the floor.

Tom Graham pulled me over by the water cooler. "Holy Christ," he said. "It looks like we got a fucking *confession* happening here."

"Yeah, maybe," I said. I wasn't convinced. I'd seen Ishiguro change his demeanor before.

I watched Connor as he talked to Ishiguro. The Japanese man remained hangdog. He kept looking at the floor.

"I never would have figured him," Graham said. "Not in a million years. Never him."

"How is that?"

"Are you kidding? To kill the girl, and then to stay in the

137

room, and order us around. What fucking nerves of steel. But look at him now: Christ, he's almost *crying*."

It was true: tears seemed to be welling up in Ishiguro's eyes. Connor took the box and turned away, crossing the room to us. He gave me the box. "Deal with this. I'm going to take a statement from Ishiguro."

"So," Graham said. "Did he confess?"

"To what?"

"The murder."

"Hell, no," Connor said. "What makes you think that?"

"Well, he's over there bowing and scraping—"

"That's just *sumimasen*," Connor said. "I wouldn't take it too seriously."

"He's practically crying," Graham said.

"Only because he thinks it'll help him."

"He didn't confess?"

"No. But he discovered that the tapes had been removed, after all. That means he made a serious mistake, with his public blustering in front of the mayor. Now he could be accused of concealing evidence. He could be disbarred. His corporation could be disgraced. Ishiguro is in big trouble, and he knows it."

I said, "And that's why he's so humble?"

"Yes. In Japan, if you screw up, the best thing is to go to the authorities and make a big show of how sorry you are, and how bad you feel, and how you will never do it again. It's pro forma, but the authorities will be impressed by how you've learned your lesson. That's *sumimasen*: apology without end. It's the Japanese version of throwing yourself on the mercy of the court. It's understood to be the best way to get leniency. And that's all Ishiguro is doing."

"You mean it's an act," Graham said, his eyes hardening.

"Yes and no. It's difficult to explain. Look. Review the tapes. Ishiguro says he brought one of the VCRs, because the tapes are recorded in an unusual format, and he was afraid we wouldn't be able to play them. Okay?"

I opened the cardboard box. I saw twenty small eight-millimeter cartridges, like audio cassette cartridges. And I saw a small box, the size of a Walkman, which was the VCR. It had cables to hook to a TV.

"Okay," I said. "Let's have a look."

The first of the tapes that showed the forty-sixth floor was a view from the atrium camera, high up, looking down. The tape showed people working on the floor, in what looked like an ordinary office day. We fast-forwarded through that. Shadows of sunlight coming through the windows swung in hot arcs across the floor, and then disappeared. Gradually, the light on the floor softened and dimmed, as daylight came to an end. One by one, desk lights came on. The workers moved more slowly now. Eventually they began to depart, leaving their desks one by one. As the population thinned, we noticed something else. Now the camera moved occasionally, panning one or another of the workers as they passed beneath. Yet at other times, the camera would not pan. Eventually we realized the camera must be equipped for automatic focusing and tracking. If there was a lot of movement in the frame—several people going in different directions—then the camera did not move. But if the frame was mostly empty, the camera would fix on a single person walking through, and track him.

"Funny system," Graham said.

"It probably makes sense for a security camera," I said. "They'd be much more concerned about a single person on the floor than a crowd."

As we watched, the night lights came on. The desks were all empty. Now the tape began to flicker rapidly, almost like a strobe.

"Something wrong with this tape?" Graham said, suspiciously. "They fucked around with it?"

"I don't know. No, wait. It's not that. Look at the clock."

On the far wall, we could see the office clock. The minute hands were sweeping smoothly from seven-thirty toward eight o'clock.

"It's time lapse," I said.

"What is it, taking snapshots?"

I nodded. "Probably, when the system doesn't detect anybody for a while, it begins to take single frames every ten or twenty seconds, until—"

"Hey. What's that?"

The flickering had stopped. The camera had begun to pan to the right, across the deserted floor. But there was nobody in the frame. Just empty desks, and occasional night lights, which flared in the video.

"Maybe they have a wide sensor," I said. "That looks beyond the borders of the image itself. Either that, or it's being moved manually. By a guard, somewhere. Maybe down in the security room."

The panning image came to rest on the elevator doors. The doors were at the far right, in deep shadow, beneath a kind of ceiling overhang that blocked our view.

"Jeez, dark under there. Is someone there?"

"I can't see anything," I said.

The image began to swim in and out of focus.

"What's happening now?" Graham said.

"Looks like the automatic focus is having trouble. Maybe it can't decide what to focus on. Maybe the overhang is bothering the logic circuits. My video camera at home does the same thing. The focus gets screwed up when it can't tell what I am shooting."

"So is the camera trying to focus on something? Because I can't see anything. It just looks black under there."

"No, look. There's someone there. You can see pale legs. Very faint."

"Christ," Graham said, "that's our girl. Standing by the elevator. No, wait. Now she's moving."

A moment later, Cheryl Austin stepped from beneath the ceiling overhang, and we saw her clearly for the first time.

She was beautiful and assured. She moved unhesitatingly into the room. She was direct, purposeful in her movements, with none of the awkward, shuffling sloppiness of the young.

"Jesus, she's good-looking," Graham said.

Cheryl Austin was tall and slender; her short blond hair

made her seem even taller. Her carriage was erect. She turned slowly, surveying the room as if she owned it.

"I can't believe we're seeing this," Graham said.

I knew what he meant. This was a girl who had been killed just a few hours before. Now we were seeing her on a video-tape, walking around just minutes before her death.

On the monitor, Cheryl picked up a paperweight on one of the desks, turned it in her hand, put it back. She opened her purse, closed it again. She glanced at her watch.

"Starting to fidget."

"She doesn't like to be kept waiting," Graham said. "And I bet she doesn't have much practice at it, either. Not a girl like that."

She began to tap on the desk with her fingers in a distinct rhythm. It seemed familiar to me. She bobbed her head to the rhythm. Graham squinted at the screen, "Is she talking? Is she saying something?"

"It looks like it," I said. We could barely see her mouth moving. And then I suddenly put it together, her move-ments, everything. I realized I could sync her lips. "I chew my nails and I twiddle my thumbs. I'm real nervous but it sure is fun. Oh baby, you drive me crazy . . ."

"Jesus," Graham said. "You're right. How'd you know that?"

"Goodness, gracious, great balls of—"

Cheryl stopped singing. She turned toward the elevators.

"Ah. Here we go."

Cheryl walked toward the elevators. Just as she stepped beneath the overhang, she threw her arms around the man who had arrived. They embraced and kissed warmly. But the man remained beneath the overhang. We could see his arms around Cheryl, but we could not see his face.

"Shit," Graham said.

"Don't worry," I said. "We'll see him in a minute. If not this camera, another camera. But I think we can say this is not somebody she just met. This is somebody she already knows."

"Not unless she's *real* friendly. Yeah, look. This guy isn't wasting any time."

The man's hands slid up the black dress, raising her skirt. He squeezed her buttocks. Cheryl Austin pressed against his body. Their clinch was intense, passionate. Together they moved deeper into the room, turning slowly. Now the man's back was to us. Her skirt was bunched around her waist. She reached down to rub his crotch. The couple half walked, half stumbled to the nearest desk. The man bent her back against the desk and suddenly she protested, pushing him away.

"Ah, ah. Not so fast," Graham said. "Our girl has standards, after all."

I wondered if that was it. Cheryl seemed to have led him on, then changed her mind. I noticed that she had changed moods almost instantaneously. It made me wonder if she had been acting all along, if her passion was faked. Certainly the man did not seem particularly surprised by her sudden change. Sitting up on the desk, she kept pushing at him, almost angrily. The man stepped away. His back was still to us. We couldn't see his face. As soon as he had stepped back, she changed again: smiling, kittenish now. With slow movements, she got off the desk and adjusted her skirt, twisting her body provocatively as she looked around. We could see his ear and the side of his face, just enough to see that his jaw was moving. He was talking to her. She smiled at him, and came forward, slid her arms around his neck. Then they began kissing again, their hands moving over each other. Walking slowly through the office, toward the conference room.

"So. Did she choose the conference room?"

"Hard to say."

"Shit, I still can't see his face."

By now they were near the center of the room, and the camera was shooting almost directly down. All we saw was the top of his head.

I said, "Does he look Japanese to you?"

"Fuck. Who can tell. How many other cameras were in that room?"

"Four others."

"Well. His face can't be blocked in all four. We'll nail his ass."

I said, "You know, Tom, this guy looks pretty big. He looks taller than she is. And she was a tall girl."

"Who can tell, in this angle? I can't tell anything except he has a suit on. Okay. There they go, toward the conference room."

As they approached the room, she suddenly began to struggle.

"Oops," Graham said. "She's unhappy again. Moody young thing, isn't she?"

The man gripped her tightly and she spun, trying to twist free. He half carried her, half dragged her to the room. At the doorway, she spun a final time, grabbed the door frame, struggling.

"She lose the purse there?"

"Probably. I can't see clearly."

The conference room was located directly opposite the camera, so we had a view of the entire room. But the interior of the conference room was very dark, so the two people were silhouetted against the lights of the skyscrapers through the outer glass windows. The man lifted her up in his arms and set her down on the table, rolled her onto her back. She became passive, liquid, as he slid her skirt up her hips. She seemed to be accepting, moving to meet him, and then he made a quick movement between their bodies, and suddenly something flew away.

"There go the panties."

It looked as if they landed on the floor. But it was hard to tell for sure. If they were panties, they were black, or some other dark color. So much, I thought, for Senator Rowe.

"The panties were gone by the time we got there," Graham said, staring at the monitor. "Fucking withholding of evidence, pure and simple." He rubbed his hands together. "You got any Nakamoto stock, buddy, I'd sell it. 'Cause it isn't going to be worth shit by tomorrow afternoon."

On the screen, she was still welcoming him, and he was fumbling with his zipper, when suddenly she tried to sit up, and slapped him hard on the face.

Graham said, "There we go. A little *spice*."

The man grabbed her hands, and tried to kiss her, but she resisted him, turning her face away. He pushed her back on the table. He leaned his weight on her body, holding her there. Her bare legs kicked and churned.

The two silhouettes merged and separated. It was difficult to determine exactly what was happening. It looked as if Cheryl kept trying to sit up, and the man kept shoving her back. He held her down, one hand on her upper chest, while her legs kicked at him, and her body twisted on the table. He still held her on the table, but the whole scene was more arduous than arousing. As it continued, I had trouble with the image I was seeing. Was this a genuine rape? Or was she play-acting? After all, she kept kicking and struggling, but she wasn't succeeding in pushing him away. The man might be stronger than she was, but I had the feeling that she could have kicked him back if she had really wanted to. And sometimes it looked as if her arms were locked around his neck, instead of trying to push him away. But it was difficult to know for sure when we were seeing—

"Uh-oh. Trouble."

The man stopped his rhythmic pumping. Beneath him, Cheryl went limp. Her arms slid away from his shoulders, dropped back on the table. Her legs fell slack on either side of him.

Graham said, "Is that it? Did it just happen?"

"I can't tell."

The man patted her cheek, then shook her more vigorously. He seemed to be talking to her. He remained there for a while, maybe thirty seconds, and then he slipped away from her body. She stayed on the table. He walked around her. He was moving slowly, as if he could not believe it.

Then he looked off to the left, as if he had heard a sound. He stood frozen for a moment, and then he seemed to make up his mind. He went into action, moving around the room, looking in a methodical way. He picked up something from the floor.

"The panties."

"He took 'em himself," Graham said. "Shit."

Now the man moved around the girl, and bent briefly over her body on the far side.

"What's he doing there?"

"I don't know. I can't see."

"Shit."

The man straightened and moved away from the conference room, back into the atrium. He was no longer silhouetted. There was a chance we could identify him. But he was looking back into the conference room. Back at the dead girl.

"Hey, buddy," Graham said, talking to the image on the monitor. "Look over here, buddy. Come on. Just for a minute."

On the screen, the man continued to look at the dead girl as he took several more steps into the atrium. Then he began to walk quickly away to the left.

"He's not going back to the elevators," I said.

"No. But I can't see his *face*."

"Where is he going?"

"There's a stairwell at the far end," Graham said. "Fire exit."

"Why is he going there, instead of the elevator?"

"Who knows? I just want to see his face. Just once."

But now the man was to the far left of our camera, and even though he was no longer turned away, we could see only his left ear and cheekbone. He walked quickly. Soon he would be gone from our view, beneath the ceiling overhang at the far end of the room.

"Ah, shit. This angle's no good. Let's look at another tape."

"Just a minute," I said.

Our man was moving toward a dark passageway that must lead to the staircase. But as he went, he passed a decorative gilt-frame mirror hanging on the wall, right by the passage. He passed it just as he went under the overhang, into final darkness.

"There!"

"How do you stop this thing?"

I was pressing buttons on the player frantically. I finally

found the one that stopped it. We went back. Then forward again.

Again, the man moved purposefully toward the dark passage, with long, quick strides. He moved past the mirror, and for an instant—a single video frame—we could see his face reflected in the mirror—see it clearly—and I pressed the button to freeze the frame—

"Bingo," I said.

"A fucking Jap," Graham said. "Just like I told you."

Frozen in the mirror was the face of the killer as he strode toward the stairwell. I had no trouble recognizing the tense features of Eddie Sakamura.

"This one is mine," Graham said. "It's my case. I'm going to go bring the bastard in."

"Sure," Connor said.

"I mean," Graham said, "I'd rather go alone."

"Of course," Connor said. "It's your case, Tom. Do whatever you think best."

Connor wrote down Eddie Sakamura's address for him.

"It's not that I don't appreciate your help," Graham said. "But I'd rather handle it myself. Now, just so I have my facts straight: you guys talked to this guy earlier tonight, and you didn't bring him in?"

"That's right."

"Well, don't worry about it," Graham said. "I'll bury that in the report. It won't come back to you, I promise you." Graham was in a magnanimous mood, pleased at the prospect of arresting Sakamura. He glanced at his watch. "Fucking A. Less than six hours since the original call, and we already have the murderer. Not bad."

"We don't have the murderer quite yet," Connor said. "I'd bring him in right away, if I were you."

"I'm leaving now," Graham said.

"Oh, and Tom," Connor said, as Graham headed toward the door. "Eddie Sakamura is a strange guy, but he's not known to be violent. I doubt very much that he's armed. He probably doesn't even own a gun. He went home from the party with a redhead. He's probably in bed with her now. I think it would be advisable to bring him in alive."

"Hey," Graham said. "What is it with you two?"

"Just a suggestion," Connor said.

147

"You really think I'm going to shoot this little shithead?"

"You'll go out there with a couple of black and whites for backup, won't you?" Connor said. "The patrolmen might be excitable. I'm just giving you the background."

"Hey. Thanks for your fucking support," Graham said, and he left. He was so broad, he had to turn slightly sideways to go through the door.

I watched him go. "Why are you letting him do this alone?"

Connor shrugged. "It's his case."

"But you've been aggressive all night in pursuing his case. Why stop now?"

Connor said. "Let Graham have the glory. After all, what has it got to do with us? I'm a cop on extended leave. And you're just a corrupt liaison officer." He pointed to the videotape. "You want to run that for me, before you give me a ride home?"

"Sure." I rewound the tape.

"I was thinking we could get a cup of coffee, too," Connor said. "They make a good one in the SID labs. At least, they used to."

I said, "You want me to get coffee while you look at the tape?"

"That would be nice, *kōhai*," Connor said.

"Sure." I started the tape for him, and turned to leave.

"Oh, and *kōhai*. While you're down there, ask the night duty officer what facilities the department has for videotapes. Because all these need to be duplicated. And we may need hard copies of individual frames. Especially if there's trouble about Sakamura's arrest as Japan-bashing by the department. We may need to release a picture. To defend ourselves."

It was a good point. "Okay," I said. "I'll check."

"And I take mine black with one sugar." He turned to look at the monitor.

The scientific investigation division, or SID, was in the basement of Parker Center. It was after two in the morning when I got there, and most of the sections were closed down.

SID was pretty much a nine-to-five operation. Of course, the teams worked at night collecting evidence from crime scenes, but the evidence was then stored in lockers, either downtown or at one of the divisions, until the next morning.

I went to the coffee machine, in the little cafeteria next to Latent Prints. All around the room were signs reading DID YOU WASH YOUR HANDS? THIS MEANS YOU and DON'T EXPOSE FELLOW OFFICERS TO RISK. WASH YOUR HANDS. The reason was that the SID teams used poisons, especially Criminalistics. There was so much mercury, arsenic, and chromium floating around that in the old days, officers had sometimes gotten sick by drinking from a Styrofoam cup that another lab worker had merely touched.

But these days people were more careful; I got two cups of coffee and went back to the night-duty desk. Jackie Levine was on duty, with her feet up on the desk. She was a heavyset woman wearing toreador pants and an orange wig. Despite her bizarre appearance, she was widely acknowledged to be the best print lifter in the department. She was reading *Modern Bride* magazine. I said, "You going to do it again, Jackie?"

"Hell, no," she said. "My daughter."

"Who's she marrying?"

"Let's talk about something happy," she said. "One of those coffees for me?"

"Sorry," I said. "But I have a question for you. Who handles videotape evidence here?"

"Videotape evidence?"

"Like tape from surveillance cameras. Who analyzes it, makes hard copies, all that?"

"Well, we don't get much call for that," Jackie said. "Electronics used to do it here, but I think they gave it up. Nowadays, video either goes to Valley or Medlar Hall." She sat forward, thumbed through a directory. "If you want, you can talk to Bill Harrelson over at Medlar. But if it's anything special, I think we farm it out to JPL or the Advanced Imaging Lab at U.S.C. You want the contact numbers, or you want to go through Harrelson?"

Something in her tone told me what to do. "Maybe I'll take the contact numbers."

"Yeah, I would."

I wrote the numbers down and went back up to the division. Connor had finished the tape and was running it back and forth at the point where Sakamura's face appeared in the mirror.

"Well?" I said.

"That's Eddie, all right." He appeared calm, almost indifferent. He took the coffee from me and sipped it. "Terrible."

"Yeah, I know."

"It used to be better." Connor set the cup aside, turned off the video recorder, stood, and stretched. "Well, I think we've done a good evening's work. What do you say we get some sleep? I have a big golf game in the morning at Sunset Hills."

"Okay," I said. I packed the tapes back in the cardboard box, and set the VCR carefully in the box, too.

Connor said, "What're you going to do with those tapes?"

"I'll put 'em in the evidence locker."

Connor said, "These are the originals. And we don't have duplicates."

"I know, but I can't get dupes made until tomorrow."

"Exactly my point. Why don't you keep them with you?"

"Take them home?" There were all sorts of departmental injunctions about taking evidence home. It was against the rules, to put it mildly.

He shrugged. "I wouldn't leave this to chance. Take the tapes with you, and then you can arrange the duplication yourself, tomorrow."

I stuck them under my arm. I said, "You don't think anybody at the department would—"

"Of course not," Connor said. "But this evidence is crucial and we wouldn't want anybody to walk by the evidence locker with a big magnet while we were asleep, would we?"

So in the end I took the tapes. As we went out the door, we passed Ishiguro, still sitting there, contrite. Connor said something quickly to him in Japanese. Ishiguro jumped to his feet, bowed quickly, and scurried out of the office.

"Is he really so scared?"

"Yes," Connor said.

Ishiguro moved quickly down the hall ahead of us, head bent low. He seemed almost a caricature of a mousy, frightened man.

"Why?" I said. "He's lived here long enough to know that any case we might have against him for withholding evidence is not strong. And we have even less of a case against Nakamoto."

"That's not the point," Connor said. "He's not worried about legalities. He's worried about scandal. Because that's what would happen if we were in Japan."

We came around the corner. Ishiguro was standing by the banks of elevators, waiting. We waited, too. There was an awkward moment. The first elevator came, and Ishiguro stepped away for us to get on. The doors closed on him bowing to us in the lobby. The elevator started down.

Connor said, "In Japan, he and his company could be finished forever."

"Why?"

"Because in Japan, scandal is the most common way of revising the pecking order. Of getting rid of a powerful opponent. It's a routine procedure over there. You uncover a vulnerability, and you leak it to the press, or to government investigators. A scandal inevitably follows, and the person or organization is ruined. That's how the Recruit scandal brought down Takeshita as prime minister. Or the financial scandals brought down Prime Minister Tanaka in the seventies. It's the same way the Japanese screwed General Electric a couple of years ago."

"They screwed General Electric?"

"In the Yokogawa scandal. You heard of it? No? Well, it's classic Japanese maneuvering. A few years ago, General Electric made the best scanning equipment in the world for hospitals. GE formed a subsidiary, Yokogawa Medical, to market this equipment in Japan. And GE did business the Japanese way: cutting costs below competitors to get market share, providing excellent service and support, entertaining customers—giving potential buyers air tickets and traveler's checks. We'd call it bribes, but it's standard business procedure in Japan. Yokogawa quickly became the market leader, ahead of Japanese companies like Toshiba. The Japanese companies didn't like that and complained about unfairness. And one day government agents raided Yokogawa's offices and found evidence of the bribes. They arrested several Yokogawa employees, and blackened the company name in scandal. It didn't hurt GE sales in Japan very much. It didn't matter that other Japanese companies also offer bribes. For some reason, it was the non-Japanese company that got caught. Amazing, how that happens."

I said, "Is it really that bad?"

"The Japanese can be tough," Connor said. "They say 'business is war,' and they mean it. You know how Japan is always telling us that their markets are open. Well, in the old days, if a Japanese bought an American car, he got audited by the government. So pretty soon, nobody bought an American car. The officials shrug: what can they do? Their market is open: they can't help it if nobody wants an American car. The obstructions are endless. Every imported car has to be individually tested on the dock to make sure it complies with exhaust-emission laws. Foreign drugs can only be tested in Japanese laboratories on Japanese nationals. Foreign skis were once banned because Japanese snow was said to be wetter than European and American snow. That's the way they treat other countries, so it's not surprising they worry about getting a taste of their own medicine."

"Then Ishiguro is waiting for some scandal? Because that's what would happen in Japan?"

"Yes. He's afraid that Nakamoto will be finished in a single stroke. But I doubt that it will. Chances are, it'll be business as usual in Los Angeles tomorrow."

I drove Connor back to his apartment. As he climbed out of the car I said, "Well, it's been interesting, Captain. Thanks for spending the time with me."

"You're welcome," Connor said. "Call me any time, if you need help in the future."

"I hope your golf game isn't too early tomorrow."

"Actually, it's at seven, but at my age I don't need much sleep. I'll be playing at the Sunset Hills."

"Isn't it a Japanese course?" The purchase of the Sunset Hills Country Club was one of the more recent outrages in L.A. The West Los Angeles golf course was bought for a huge cash price: two hundred million dollars in 1990. At the time, the new Japanese owners said no changes would be made. But now, the American membership was slowly being reduced by a simple procedure: whenever an American retired, his place was offered to a Japanese. Sunset Hills memberships were sold in Tokyo for a million dollars each, where they were considered a bargain; there was a long waiting list.

"Well," Connor said, "I'm playing with some Japanese."

"You do that often?"

"The Japanese are avid golfers, as you know. I try to play twice a week. Sometimes you hear things of interest. Good night, *kōhai*."

"Good night, Captain."

I drove home.

I was pulling onto the Santa Monica freeway when the phone rang. It was the DHD operator. "Lieutenant, we have a Special Services call. Officers in the field request assistance of the liaison."

I sighed. "Okay." She gave me the mobile number.

"Hey, buddy."

It was Graham. I said, "Hi, Tom."

"You alone yet?"

"Yeah. I'm heading home. Why?"

"I was thinking," Graham said. "Maybe we should have the Japanese liaison on hand for this bust."

"I thought you wanted to do it alone."

"Yeah, well, maybe you want to come over and help out with this bust. Just so everything is done by the book."

I said, "Is this a CYA?" I meant cover your ass.

"Hey. You going to help me out, or not?"

"Sure, Tom. I'm on my way."

"We'll wait for you."

⬣ Eddie Sakamura lived in a small house on one of those narrow twisting streets high in the Hollywood hills above the 101 freeway. It was 2:45 a.m. when I came around a curve and saw the two black and whites with their lights off, and Graham's tan sedan, parked to one side. Graham was standing with the patrolmen, smoking a cigarette. I had to go back a dozen meters to find a place to park. Then I walked over to them.

We looked up at Eddie's house, built over a garage at street level. It was one of those two-bedroom white stucco houses from the 1940s. The lights were on, and we heard Frank Sinatra singing. Graham said, "He's not alone. He's got some broads up there."

I said, "How do you want to handle it?"

Graham said, "We leave the boys here. I told 'em no shooting, don't worry. You and I go up and make the bust."

Steep stairs ran up from the garage to the house.

"Okay. You take the front and I'll take the back?"

"Hell, no," Graham said. "I want you with me, buddy. He's not dangerous, right?"

I saw the silhouette of a woman pass one of the windows. She looked naked. "Shouldn't be," I said.

"Okay then, let's do it."

We started up the stairs single file. Frank Sinatra was singing "My Way." We heard the laughter of women. It sounded like more than one. "Christ, I hope they got some fucking drugs out."

I thought the chances of that were pretty good. We

reached the top of the stairs, ducking to avoid being seen through the windows.

The front door was Spanish, heavy and solid. Graham paused. I moved a few steps toward the back of the house, where I saw the greenish glow of pool lights. There was probably a back door going out to the pool. I was trying to see where it was.

Graham tapped my shoulder. I came back. He gently turned the handle of the front door. It was unlocked. Graham took out his revolver and looked at me. I took out my gun.

He paused, held up three fingers. Count of three.

Graham kicked the front door open and went in low, shouting "Hold it, police! Hold it right there!" Before I got into the living room, I could hear the women screaming.

There were two of them, completely naked, running around the room and shrieking at the top of their lungs, "Eddie! Eddie!" Eddie wasn't there. Graham was shouting, "Where is he? Where is Eddie Sakamura?" The redhead grabbed a pillow from the couch to cover herself, and screamed, "Get out of here, you fucker!" and then she threw the pillow at Graham. The other girl, a blonde, ran squealing into the bedroom. We followed her, and the redhead threw another pillow at us.

In the bedroom, the blonde fell on the floor and howled in pain. Graham leaned over her with his gun. "Don't shoot me!" she cried. "I didn't do anything!"

Graham grabbed her by the ankle. There was all this twisting bare flesh. The girl was hysterical. "Where is Eddie?" Graham said. "Where is he?"

"*In a meeting!*" the girl squealed.

"Where?"

"*In a meeting!*" And flailing around, she kicked Graham in the nuts with her other leg.

"Aw, Christ," Graham said, letting the girl go. He coughed and sat down hard. I went back to the living room. The redhead had her high heels on but nothing else.

I said, "Where is he?"

"You bastards," she said. "You fucking bastards."

I went past her toward a door at the far end of the room. It was locked. The redhead ran up and began to hit me on the back with her fists. "Leave him alone! Leave him alone!" I was trying to open the locked door while she pounded on me. I thought I heard voices from the other side of the door.

In the next moment Graham's big bulk slammed into the door and the wood splintered. The door opened. I saw the kitchen, lit by the green light of the pool outside. The room was empty. The back door was open.

"*Shit.*"

By now the redhead had jumped on my back, and locked her legs around my waist. She was pulling my hair, screaming obscenities. I spun around in circles, trying to throw her off me. It was one of those strange moments where in the middle of all the chaos I was thinking, *be careful, don't hurt her*, because it would look bad for a pretty young girl to end up with a broken arm or cracked ribs, it would mean police brutality even though right now she was tearing my hair out by the roots. She bit my ear and I felt pain. I slammed myself back against the wall, and I heard her grunt as the breath was knocked out of her. She let go.

Out the window, I saw a dark figure running down the stairs. Graham saw it, too.

"Fuck," he said. He ran. I ran, too. But the girl must have tripped me because I fell over, landing hard. When I got to my feet I heard the sirens of the black and whites and their engines starting up.

Then I was back outside, running down the steps. I was maybe ten meters behind Graham, about thirty feet, when Eddie's Ferrari backed out of the garage, ground the gears, and roared down the street.

The black and whites immediately took up pursuit. Graham ran for his sedan. He had pulled out to follow while I was still running for my own car, parked farther down the road. As his car flashed past me, I could see his face, grim and angry.

I got into my car and followed.

* * *

You can't drive fast in the hills and talk on the phone. I didn't even try. I estimated I was half a kilometer behind Graham, and he was some distance behind the two patrol cars. When I got to the bottom of the hill, the 101 overpass, I saw the flashing lights going down the freeway. I had to back up and pull around to the entrance below Mulholland, and then I joined traffic heading south.

When the traffic began to slow up, I stuck my flasher on the roof, and pulled into the right-hand breakdown lane.

I got to the concrete embankment about thirty seconds after the Ferrari hit it flat out at a hundred and sixty kilometers an hour. I guess the gas tank had exploded on impact, and the flames were jumping fifteen meters into the air. The heat was tremendous. It looked like the trees up on the hill might catch on fire. You couldn't get anywhere near the twisted wreck of the car.

The first of the fire trucks pulled up, with three more black and whites. There were sirens and flashing lights everywhere.

I backed up my car to make room for the trucks, then walked over to Graham. He smoked a cigarette as the firemen began to spray the wreck with foam.

"Christ," Graham said. "What a fucking cockup."

"Why didn't the backup patrolmen stop him when he was in the garage?"

"Because," Graham said, "I told them not to shoot at him. And we weren't there. They were trying to decide what to do when the guy drove away." He shook his head. "This is going to look like shit in the report."

I said, "Still, it's probably better you didn't shoot him."

"Maybe." He ground out his cigarette.

By now, the firemen had gotten the fire out. The Ferrari was a smoking hulk crumpled against the concrete. There was a harsh smell in the air.

"Well," Graham said. "No point staying around here. I'll go back up to the house. See if those girls are still there."

"You need me for anything else?"

"No. You might as well go. Tomorrow is another day. Shit, it'll be paperwork until we drop." He looked at me. He hesitated. "We in sync about this? About what happened?"

"Hell, yes," I said.

"No way to handle it differently," he said. "Far as I can see."

"No," I said. "Just one of those things."

"Okay, buddy. See you tomorrow."

"Good night, Tom."

We got into our cars.

I drove home.

Mrs. Ascenio was snoring loudly on the sofa. It was three forty-five in the morning. I tiptoed past her and looked in Michelle's room. My daughter lay on her back, her covers tossed aside, her arms flung over her head. Her feet stuck through the bars of the crib. I tucked the covers around her and went into my own room.

The television was still on. I turned it off. I pulled off my tie and sat down on the bed to remove my shoes. I suddenly realized how tired I was. I took off my coat and trousers and threw them onto the television set. I lay down on my back and thought I should take off my shirt. It felt sweaty and grimy on my body. I closed my eyes for a moment and let my head sink back into the pillow. Then I felt a pinching, and something tugging at my eyelids. I heard a chirping sound and thought in a moment of horror that birds were pecking at my eyes.

I heard a voice saying, "Open your eyes, Daddy. Open your eyes." And I realized that it was my daughter, trying to pull my eyelids up with small fingers.

"Yuuuh," I said. I glimpsed daylight, rolled away, and buried my face in the pillow.

"Daddy? Open your eyes. Open your eyes, Daddy."

I said, "Daddy was out late last night. Daddy is tired."

She paid no attention. "Daddy, open your eyes. Open your eyes. Daddy? Open your eyes, Daddy."

I knew that she would continue saying the same thing, over and over, until I lost my mind, or opened my eyes. I rolled onto my back and coughed. "Daddy is still tired, Shelly. Go see what Mrs. Ascenio is doing."

"Daddy, open your eyes."

"Can't you let Daddy sleep a while? Daddy wants to sleep a little longer this morning."

"It's morning now, Daddy. Open your eyes. Open your eyes."

I opened my eyes. She was right.

It was morning.

What the hell.

SECOND DAY

SECOND DAY

"Eat your pancakes."

"I don't want any more."

"Just one more bite, Shelly." Sunlight streamed through the kitchen window. I yawned. It was seven o'clock in the morning.

"Is Mommy coming today?"

"Don't change the subject. Come on, Shel. One more bite. Please?"

We were sitting at her kid-size table in the corner of the kitchen. Sometimes I can get her to eat at the little table when she won't eat at the big table. But I wasn't having much luck today. Michelle stared at me.

"Is Mommy coming?"

"I think so. I'm not sure." I didn't want to disappoint her. "We're waiting to hear."

"Is Mommy going out of town again?"

I said, "Maybe." I wondered what "going out of town" meant to a two-year-old, what sort of image she would have of it.

"Is she going with Uncle Rick?"

Who is Uncle Rick? I held the fork in front of her face. "I don't know, Shel. Come on, open up. One more bite."

"He has a new car," Michelle said, nodding solemnly, the way she did whenever she was informing me of important news.

"Is that right?"

"Uh-huh. Black one."

"I see. What kind of car is it?"

"Sades."

165

"A Sades?"

"No. *Sades*."

"You mean Mercedes?"

"Uh-huh. Black one."

"That's nice," I said.

"When is Mommy coming?"

"One more bite, Shel."

She opened her mouth, and I moved the fork toward her. At the last moment she turned her head aside, pursing her lips. "No, Daddy."

"All right," I said. "I give up."

"I'm not hungry, Daddy."

"I can see that."

Mrs. Ascenio was cleaning up the kitchen before she went back to her own apartment. There was another fifteen minutes before my housekeeper Elaine came to take Michelle to day care. I still had to get her dressed. I was putting her pancakes in the sink when the phone rang. It was Ellen Farley, the mayor's press aide.

"Are you watching?"

"Watching what?"

"The news. Channel seven. They're doing the car crash right now."

"They are?"

"Call me back," she said.

I went into the bedroom and turned on the television. A voice was saying, "—reported a high-speed chase on the Hollywood freeway southbound, which ended when the suspect drove his Ferrari sportscar into the Vine Street overpass, not far from the Hollywood Bowl. Observers say the car hit the concrete embankment at more than a hundred miles an hour, instantly bursting into flames. Fire trucks were called to the scene but there were no survivors. The driver's body was so badly burned that his glasses melted. The officer in charge of the pursuit, Detective Thomas Graham, said that the driver, Mr. Edward Sakamura, was wanted in connection with the alleged murder of a woman at a downtown location. But today, friends of Mr. Sakamura expressed disbelief at this charge, and claimed that police strong-arm tactics panicked the suspect and caused him to flee. There are complaints that the incident was racially motivated. It is not clear whether police intended to charge Mr. Sakamura with the murder, and observers noted that this was the third high-speed pursuit on the 101 freeway in the last two weeks. Questions of police judgment in these pursuits have arisen after a Compton woman was killed in a high-speed pursuit last January. Neither Detective Graham nor his assistant Lieutenant Peter Smith was available to be interviewed, and we are waiting to hear if the officers will be disciplined or suspended by the department."

Jesus.

"Daddy . . ."

"Just a minute, Shel."

The image showed the crumpled, smoking wreckage being loaded onto a flatbed truck for removal from the side of the highway. There was a black smear on the concrete where the car had struck the wall.

The station cut back to the studio, where the anchorwoman faced the camera and said, "In other developments, KNBC has learned that two police officers interviewed Mr. Sakamura earlier in the evening in connection with the case, but did not arrest him at that time. Captain John Connor and Lieutenant Smith may face disciplinary review by the department, with questions being raised of possible procedural violations. However, the good news is there are no longer delays for traffic moving southbound on the 101. Now over to you, Bob."

I stared numbly at the TV. *Disciplinary review?*

The phone rang. It was Ellen Farley again. "You get all that?"

"Yeah, I did. I can't believe it. What's it about, Ellen?"

"None of this is coming from the mayor's office, if that's what you're asking. But the Japanese community has been unhappy with Graham before. They think he's a racist. It looks like he played right into their hands."

"I was there. Graham acted correctly."

"Yeah, I know you were there, Pete. Frankly, it's unfortunate. I don't want to see you tarred by the same brush."

I said, "Graham acted correctly."

"Are you listening, Pete?"

"What about this suspension and disciplinary review?"

"That's the first I heard of it," Ellen said. "But that would be internally generated. It's coming from your own department. By the way, is it true? Did you and Connor see Sakamura last night?"

"Yes."

"And you didn't arrest him?"

"No. We didn't have probable cause to arrest him when we talked to him. Later on, we did."

Ellen said, "Do you really think he could have done this murder?"

"I know he did. We have it on tape."

"On tape? Are you serious?"

"Yeah. We have the murder on videotape from one of the Nakamoto security cameras."

She was silent for a while. I said, "Ellen?"

"Look," Ellen said. "Off the record, okay?"

"Sure."

"I don't know what's going on here, Pete. There's more than I understand."

"Why didn't you tell me who the girl was, last night?"

"I'm sorry about that. I had a lot to take care of."

"Ellen."

A silence. Then: "Pete, this girl got around. She knew a lot of people."

"Did she know the mayor?"

Silence.

"How well did she know him?"

"Listen," Ellen said. "Let's just say she was a pretty girl and she knew a lot of people in this town. Personally, I thought she was unbalanced, but she was good-looking and she had a hell of an effect on men. You had to see it to believe it. Now there's a lot of irons in the fire. You saw the *Times* today?"

"No."

"Take a look. If you ask me, you want to be very correct,

the next couple of days. Dot your *i*'s and cross your *t*'s. Do everything by the book. And watch your back, okay?"

"Okay. Thanks, Ellen."

"Don't thank me. I didn't call." Then her voice got softer. "Take care of yourself, Peter."

I heard a dial tone.

"Daddy?"

"Just a minute, Shel."

"Can I watch cartoons?"

"Sure, honey."

I found her a station with some cartoons and walked into the living room. I opened the front door and picked up the *Times* from the mat. It took me a while to find the story on the last page of the Metro section.

CHARGES OF POLICE RACISM
CLOUD JAPANESE FETE

I skimmed the first paragraph. Japanese officials of the Nakamoto corporation complained about "callous and insensitive" police behavior, which they said detracted from a star-studded opening night at their new skyscraper on Figueroa. At least one Nakamoto official expressed the view that the police actions were "racially motivated." A spokesperson said: "We do not believe the Los Angeles Police Department would behave in this fashion if a Japanese corporation were not involved. We feel strongly that the actions of the police reflect a double standard for treatment of Japanese at the hands of American officials." Mr. Hiroshi Ogura, chairman of the board of Nakamoto, was present at the party, which drew such celebrities as Madonna and Tom Cruise, but he could not be reached for comment on the incident. A spokesman said, "Mr. Ogura is deeply disturbed that official hostility should mar this gathering. He very much regrets the unpleasantness that occurred."

According to observers, Mayor Thomas sent a staff member to deal with the police, but with little result. The police did not modify their behavior, despite the presence of the special Japanese liaison officer, Lieutenant Peter Smith, whose job is to defuse racially sensitive situations. . . .

And so on.

You had to read four paragraphs before you discovered that a murder had occurred. That particular detail seemed to be almost irrelevant.

I looked back at the lead. The story was from the City News Service, which meant there was no byline.

I felt angry enough to call my old contact at the *Times,* Kenny Shubik. Ken was the leading Metro reporter. He had been at the paper forever, and he knew everything that was going on. Since it was still eight in the morning, I called him at home.

"Ken. Pete Smith."

"Oh, hi," he said. "Glad you got my message."

In the background, I heard what sounded like a teenage girl: "Oh, *come on,* Dad. Why can't I go?"

Ken said, "Jennifer, let me talk here for a minute."

"What message?" I said.

Ken said, "I called you last night, because I thought you ought to know right away. He's obviously working off a tip. But do you have any idea what's behind it?"

"Behind what?" I said. I didn't know what he was talking about. "I'm sorry, Ken, I didn't get your message."

"Really?" he said. "I called you about eleven-thirty last night. The DHD dispatcher said you had rolled out on a case but you had a car phone. I told her it was important, and for you to call me at home if necessary. Because I felt sure you'd want to know."

In the background, the girl said, "Dad, *come on,* I have to decide what to *wear.*"

"Jennifer, damn it," he said. "Chill out." To me he said, "You have a daughter, don't you?"

"Yeah," I said. "But she's only two."

"Just wait," Ken said. "Look, Pete. You really didn't get my message?"

"No," I said. "I'm calling about something else: the story in this morning's paper."

"What story?"

"The Nakamoto coverage on page eight. The one about 'callous and racist police' at the opening."

"Jeez, I didn't think we had a Nakamoto story yesterday. I know Jodie was doing the party, but that won't run until tomorrow. You know, Japan draws the glitterati. Jeff didn't have anything on the scheds in Metro yesterday."

Jeff was the Metro editor. I said, "There's a story in the paper this morning about the murder."

"What murder?" he said. His voice sounded odd.

"There was a murder at Nakamoto last night. About eight-thirty. One of the guests was killed."

Ken was silent at the other end of the line. Putting things together. Finally he said, "Were you involved?"

"Homicide called me in as Japanese liaison."

"Hmmm," Ken said. "Listen. Let me get to my desk and see what I can find out. Let's talk in an hour. And give me your numbers so I can call you direct."

"Okay."

He cleared his throat. "Listen, Pete," he said. "Just between us. Do you have any problems?"

"Like what?"

"Like a morals problem, or a problem with your bank account. Discrepancy about reported income . . . anything I should know about? As your friend?"

"No," I said.

"I don't need the details. But if there's something that isn't quite right. . . . "

"Nothing, Ken."

" 'Cause if I have to go to bat for you, I don't want to discover I have stepped in shit."

"Ken. What's going on?"

"I don't want to go into detail right now. But offhand I would say somebody is trying to fuck you in the ass," Ken said.

The girl said, "*Dad*dy, that's dis*gust*ing."

"Well, you're not supposed to be listening. Pete?"

"Yeah," I said. "I'm here."

"Call me in an hour," Ken said.

"You're a pal," I said. "I owe you."

"Fucking right you do," Ken said.

He hung up.

I looked around the apartment. Everything still looked the same. Morning sunlight was still streaming into the room. Michelle was sitting in her favorite chair, watching cartoons and sucking her thumb. But somehow everything felt different. It was creepy. It was like the world had tilted.

But I had things to do. It was also getting late; I had to get her dressed before Elaine came to take her to day care. I told her that. She started to cry. So I turned off the television set, and she threw herself on the floor and began to kick and scream. "No, Daddy! Car*toons*, Daddy!"

I picked her up and slung her underarm to the bedroom to get her changed. She was screaming at the top of her lungs. The phone rang again. This time it was the division dispatcher.

"Morning, Lieutenant. I have your uncleared messages."

"Let me get a pencil," I said. I put Michelle down. She cried even louder. I said, "Can you go pick out which shoes you want to wear today?"

"Sounds like you got a murder there," the dispatcher said.

"She doesn't want to get dressed for school."

Michelle was tugging at my leg. "No, Daddy. No school, Daddy."

"Yes, school," I said firmly. She bawled. "Go ahead," I said to the dispatcher.

"Okay, eleven forty-one last night, you had a call from a Ken Subotik or Subotnick, *L.A. Times,* he said please call him. Message reads 'The Weasel is checking up on you.' He said you would know what that meant. You can call him at home. You have the number?"

"Yes."

"Okay. One forty-two a.m. this morning, you had a call from a Mr. Eddie Saka—looks like Sakamura. He said it's urgent, please call him at home, 555-8434. It's about the missing tape. Okay?"

Shit.

I said, "What time was that call?"

"One forty-two a.m. The call was forwarded to County General and I guess their switchboard couldn't locate you. You were at the morgue or something?"

"Yeah."

"Sorry, Lieutenant, but once you're out of your car, we have to go through intermediates."

"Okay. Anything else?"

"Then at six forty-three a.m., Captain Connor left a beeper number for you to call. He said he's playing golf this morning."

"Okay."

"And at seven-ten, we had a call from Robert Woodson, who is with Senator Morton's office. Senator Morton wants to meet you and Captain Connor at one o'clock today at the Los Angeles Country Club. He asked that you call and confirm that you will attend the meeting with the senator. I tried to reach you but your phone was busy. Will you call the senator?"

I said I would call the senator. I told the dispatcher to page Connor for me at the golf course, and have him call me in the car.

I heard the front door unlock. Elaine came in. "Good morning," she said.

"I'm afraid Shelly isn't dressed yet."

"That's okay," she said. "I'll do it. What time is Mrs. Davis coming to pick her up?"

"We're waiting to hear."

Elaine had been through this routine many times before. "Come on, Michelle. Let's pick your clothes for today. Time to get ready for school."

I looked at my watch, and was on my way to get another cup of coffee when the phone rang. "Lieutenant Peter Smith, please."

It was the assistant chief, Jim Olson.

* * *

"Hi, Jim."

"Morning, Pete." He sounded friendly. But Jim Olson never called anybody before ten o'clock in the morning unless there was a big problem. Olson said, "Looks like we got ourselves a rattlesnake by the tail. You see the papers today?"

"Yeah, I did."

"You happen to catch the morning news?"

"Some of it."

"The chief's been calling me for damage control. I wanted to get where you stand before I make a recommendation. Okay?"

"Okay."

"I just got off the phone with Tom Graham. He admits last night was a prime screwup. Nobody is covered in glory."

"I'm afraid not."

"Couple of naked broads impeded two able-bodied police officers and prevented apprehension of the suspect? Is that about it?"

It sounded ridiculous. I said, "You had to be there, Jim."

"Uh-huh," he said. "Well, one good thing so far. I've been checking if correct pursuit procedures were followed. Apparently they were. We have recordings off the computers, and we have voice recordings off the radio, and it's all strictly by the book. Thank God. Nobody even swears. We can release those records to the media if this thing gets any worse. So we're covered there. But it's very unfortunate that Sakamura is dead."

"Yes."

"Graham went back to get the girls, but the house was deserted. The girls were gone."

"I see."

"In all the rush, nobody got the names of the girls?"

"No, I'm afraid not."

"That means we have no witnesses to the events in the house. So we're a little vulnerable."

"Uh-huh."

"They're cutting Sakamura's body out of the wreck this morning to ship what's left to the morgue. Graham tells me as far as he's concerned, the case is wrapped up. I gather there are videotapes that show Sakamura killed the girl. Graham says he is ready to file his concluding five-seven-nine report. Is that how you see it? The case closed?"

"I guess so, Chief. Sure."

"Then we can shut this fucker down," the chief said. "The Japanese community finds the Nakamoto inquiry irritating and offensive. They don't want it to continue any longer than necessary. So if we can call it a day, it would help."

"It's okay with me," I said. "Let's call it a day."

"Well that's good, Pete," the chief said. "I'm going to speak to the chief, see if we can head off any disciplinary action."

"Thanks, Jim."

"Try not to worry. Myself, I don't see a disciplinary issue. As long as we have videos that show Sakamura did it."

"Yeah, we do."

"About those videos," he said. "I've had Marty looking in the evidence locker. He can't seem to find 'em."

I took a deep breath and said, "No, I have them."

"You didn't log them in the evidence locker last night?"

"No. I wanted to get copies made."

He coughed. "Pete. It'd be better if you had followed procedure on that."

"I wanted to get copies made," I said.

"Tell you what," Jim said, "get your copies made, and get the originals onto my desk by ten o'clock. Okay?"

"Okay."

"It can take that long to locate the material from the evidence locker. You know how it is."

He was saying he would cover for me. "Thanks, Jim."

"Don't thank me, because I didn't do anything," he said. "Far as I know, procedure has been followed."

"Right."

"But just between you and me: get it done right away. I can hold the fort for a couple of hours. But something's going on down here. I don't know exactly where it's coming from. So don't push it, okay?"

"Okay, Jim. I'm on my way now."

I hung up the phone, and went to get copies made.

Pasadena looked like a city at the bottom of a glass of sour milk. The Jet Propulsion Laboratory, on the outskirts of town, was nestled in the foothills near the Rose Bowl. But even at eight-thirty in the morning, you couldn't see the mountains through the yellow-white haze.

I tucked the box of tapes under my arm, showed my badge, signed the guard's clipboard, and swore I was an American citizen. The guard sent me to the main building, across an inner courtyard.

For decades, the Jet Propulsion Laboratory had served as the command center for American spacecraft that photographed Jupiter and the rings of Saturn, and sent pictures back to earth as video images. JPL was the place where modern video-image processing had been invented. If anybody could copy these tapes, they could.

Mary Jane Kelleher, the press secretary, took me up to the third floor. We walked down a lime green corridor, past several doors that opened into empty offices. I mentioned it.

"It's true," she said, nodding. "We've been losing some good people, Peter."

"Where are they going?" I said.

"Mostly to industry. We always lost a few to IBM in Armonk, or Bell Labs in New Jersey. But those labs don't have the best equipment or funding any more. Now it's the Japanese research labs like Hitachi in Long Beach, Sanyo in Torrance, Canon in Inglewood. They're hiring a lot of American researchers now."

"Is JPL concerned about it?"

"Sure," she said. "Everybody knows the best way to

177

transfer technology is inside somebody's head. But what can you do?" She shrugged. "Researchers want to do research. And America doesn't do so much R and D any more. Budgets are tighter. So it's better to work for the Japanese. They pay well, and they genuinely respect research. If you need a piece of equipment, you get it. Anyway, that's what my friends tell me. Here we are."

She took me into a laboratory crammed with video equipment. Black boxes stacked on metal shelves and on metal tables; cables snaking across the floor; a variety of monitors and display screens. In the center of all this was a bearded man in his midthirties named Kevin Howzer. He had an image on his monitor of a gear mechanism, in shifting rainbow colors. The desk was littered with Coke cans and candy wrappers; he had been up all night, working.

"Kevin, this is Lieutenant Smith from the L.A.P.D. He's got some unusual videotapes he needs copied."

"Just copied?" Howzer sounded disappointed. "You don't want anything *done* to them?"

"No, Kevin," she said. "He doesn't."

"No problem."

I showed Howzer one of the cassettes. He turned it over in his hand, and shrugged. "Looks like a standard eight-millimeter cart. What's on it?"

"High-definition Japanese TV."

"You mean it's an HD signal?"

"I guess so."

"Shouldn't be a problem. You got a playback I can use?"

"Yes." I took the playback machine out of the box and handed it to him.

"Jeez, they make things nice, don't they? Beautiful unit." Kevin examined the controls in front. "Yeah, that's high-definition all right. I can handle it." He turned the box around and peered at the plugs on the back. Then he frowned. He swung his desk light over and opened the plastic flap on the cassette, exposing the tape. It had a faint silver tinge. "Huh. Do these tapes involve anything legal?"

"Actually, they do."

He handed it back to me. "Sorry. I can't copy it."

"Why not?"

"See the silver color? That's evaporated metal tape. Very high density. I'll bet the format has real-time compression and decompression coming out of the box. I can't make you a copy, because I can't match the formats, which means I can't lay down the signal in an equivalent way that is guaranteed readable. I can make you a copy, but I can't be sure the copy is exact because I can't match formats. So if you have any legal issues—and I assume you do—you're going to have to take it somewhere else to get it copied."

"Like where?"

"This could be the new proprietary D-four format. If it is, the only place that can copy it is Hamaguchi."

"Hamaguchi?"

"The research lab in Glendale, owned by Kawakami Industries. They have every piece of video equipment known to man over there."

I said, "Do you think they'd help me?"

"To make copies? Sure. I know one of the lab directors, Jim Donaldson. I can call over there for you, if you like."

"That would be great."

"No problem."

◆ Hamaguchi Research Institute was a featureless, mirrored glass building in an industrial park in north Glendale. I carried my box into the lobby. Behind the sleek reception desk I could see an atrium in the center of the building, and smoked-glass-walled laboratories on all sides.

I asked for Dr. Jim Donaldson and took a seat in the lobby. While I was waiting, two men in suits came in, nodded familiarly to the receptionist, and sat on the couch near me. Ignoring me, they spread out glossy brochures on the coffee table.

"See here," one of them said, "this is what I was talking about. This is the shot we end with. This one closes."

I glanced over, saw a view of wildflowers and snow-capped mountains. The first man tapped the photos.

"I mean, that's the Rockies, my friend. It's real Americana. Trust me, that's what sells them. And it's a hell of a parcel."

"How big did you say it is?"

"It's a hundred and thirty thousand acres. The biggest remaining piece of Montana that's still available. Twenty by ten kilometers of prime ranch acreage fronting on the Rockies. It's the size of a national park. It's got grandeur. It's got dimension, scope. It's very high quality. Perfect for a Japanese consortium."

"And they talked price?"

"Not yet. But the ranchers, you know, they're in a tough situation. It's legal now for foreigners to export beef to Tokyo, and beef in Japan is something like twenty, twenty-two dollars a kilo. But nobody in Japan will buy American

180

beef. If Americans send beef, it will rot on the docks. But if they sell their ranch to the Japanese, then the beef can be exported. Because the Japanese will buy from a Japanese-owned ranch. The Japanese will do business with other Japanese. And ranches all around Montana and Wyoming have been sold. The remaining ranchers see Japanese cowboys riding on the range. They see the other ranches putting in improvements, rebuilding barns, adding modern equipment, all that. Because the other ranches can get high prices in Japan. So the American owners, they're not stupid. They see the writing on the wall. They know they can't compete. So they sell."

"But then what do the Americans do?"

"Stay and work for the Japanese. It's not a problem. The Japanese need someone to teach them how to ranch. And everybody on the ranch gets a raise. The Japanese are sensitive to American feelings. They're sensitive people."

The second man said, "I know, but I don't like it. I don't like the whole thing."

"That's fine, Ted. What do you want to do, write your congressman? They're all working for the Japanese, anyway. Hell, the Japanese are running these ranches with American government subsidies." The first man twisted a gold chain at his wrist. He leaned close to his companion. "Look, Ted. Let's not get all moral here. Because I can't afford it. And neither can you. We are talking a four-percent overall and a five-year payout on a seven hundred mil purchase. Let's make sure we keep that in sight, okay? You personally are looking at two point four million in the first year alone. And it's a five-year payout. Right?"

"I know. It just bothers me."

"Well, Ted. I don't think you'll be bothered when this deal closes. But there's a couple of details we need to handle . . ." At that point, they seemed to realize I was listening. They stood up and moved out of earshot. I heard the first man say something about "assurances that the State of Montana favors and approves . . ." and the second man was nodding, slowly. The first man punched him in the shoulder, cheering him up.

"Lieutenant Smith?"

A woman was standing beside my chair. "Yes?"

"I'm Kristen, Dr. Donaldson's assistant. Kevin over at JPL called about you. Something about tapes you need help with?"

"Yes. I need them copied."

"I'm sorry I wasn't here to take Kevin's call. One of the secretaries took it, and she didn't really understand the situation."

"How's that?"

"Unfortunately, Dr. Donaldson isn't here right now. He's making a speech this morning."

"I see."

"And that makes it difficult for us. With him not in the lab."

"I just want to copy some tapes. Perhaps someone else in the lab can help me," I said.

"Ordinarily yes, but I'm afraid it's impossible today."

It was the Japanese wall. Very polite, but a wall. I sighed. It was probably unrealistic to imagine a Japanese research company would help me. Even with something as neutral as copying tapes.

"I understand."

"Nobody's in the lab this morning at all. They were all working late on a rush project last night, and I guess they were here to all hours. So everybody's late coming in today. That's what the other secretary didn't understand. People are coming in late. So. I don't know what to tell you."

I made one last attempt. "As you know, my boss is the chief of police. This is the second place I've stopped at already this morning. He's really riding me to get this duplicated right away."

"I'd love to help you. I know Dr. Donaldson would be happy to. We've done special work for the police before. And I'm sure we can duplicate whatever material you have. Maybe later today. Or if you'd care to leave it with us . . ."

"I'm afraid I can't do that."

"Okay. Sure. I understand. Well, I'm sorry, Lieutenant.

Perhaps you can come back later in the day?" She gave a little shrug.

I said, "Probably not. I guess it's just my bad luck that everybody had to work last night."

"Yes. It's a pretty unusual situation."

"What was it, something came up? Research problem?"

"I really don't know. We have so much video capability on site, occasionally we get a rush request for something unusual. A TV commercial that needs a special effect, or something like that. We worked on that new Michael Jackson video for Sony. Or somebody needs to restore tape that has been ruined. You know, rebuild the signal. But I don't know what came up last night. Except it must have been a lot of work. Something like twenty tapes to be worked on. And a real rush. I hear they didn't finish until after midnight."

I thought: *It can't be.*

I was trying to think what Connor would do, how he would handle it. I decided it was worth a stab in the dark. I said, "Well, I'm sure Nakamoto is grateful for all your hard work."

"Oh, they are. Because it turned out real well for them. They were happy."

I said, "You mentioned that Mr. Donaldson was giving a speech—"

"*Dr.* Donaldson, yes—"

"Where is he doing that?"

"At a corporate-training seminar at the Bonaventure Hotel. Management techniques in research. He must be pretty tired this morning. But he's always a good speaker."

"Thanks." I gave her my card. "You've been very helpful, and if there is ever anything you think of, or want to tell me, call me."

"Okay." She glanced at my card. "Thank you."

I turned to go. As I was leaving, an American in his late twenties, wearing an Armani suit and the smug look of an M.B.A. who reads the fashion magazines, came down and said to the other two men, "Gentlemen? Mr. Nakagawa will see you now."

The men leapt up, grabbing their glossy brochures and pictures, and followed the assistant as he walked in calm measured strides toward the elevator.

I went back outside, into the smog.

The sign in the hallway read WORKING TOGETHER: JAPANESE AND AMERICAN MANAGEMENT STYLES. Inside the conference room, I saw one of those twilight business seminars where men and women sit at long tables covered in gray cloth, taking notes in semigloom as a lecturer drones on at the podium.

While I was standing there, in front of a table with the name tags of latecomers, a bespectacled woman came over to me and said, "Have you registered? Did you get your packet?"

I turned slightly and flashed my badge. I said, "I would like to speak to Dr. Donaldson."

"He's our next speaker. He's on in seven or eight minutes. Can someone else help you?"

"It'll just take a moment."

She hesitated. "But there's so little time before he speaks . . ."

"Then you better get going."

She looked as if I had slapped her. I don't know what she expected. I was a police officer and I'd asked to speak to somebody. Did she think it was negotiable? I felt irritable, remembering the young fashion plate in the Armani suit. Walking in measured steps, like a person of weight and importance, as he led the real estate salesmen away. Why did that kid think he was important? He might have an M.B.A., but he was still just answering the door for his Japanese boss.

Now, I watched the woman circle the conference room, moving toward the dais where four men waited to speak.

The business audience was still taking notes as the sandy-haired man at the podium said, "There *is* a place for the foreigner in a Japanese corporation. Not at the top, of course, perhaps not even in the upper echelons. But there is certainly a place. You must realize that the place you hold as a foreigner in a Japanese corporation is an important one, that you are respected, and that you have a job to do. As a foreigner, you will have some special obstacles to overcome, but you can do that. You can succeed if you remember to *know your place*."

I looked at the businessmen in their suits with their heads bowed, taking notes. I wondered what they were writing. Know your place?

The speaker continued: "Many times you hear executives say, 'I have no place in a Japanese corporation, and I had to quit.' Or you will hear people say, 'They didn't listen to me, I had no chance to get my ideas implemented, no chance for advancement.' Those people didn't understand the role of a foreigner in Japanese society. They were not able to fit in, and so they had to leave. But that is *their* problem. The Japanese are perfectly ready to accept Americans and other foreigners in their companies. Indeed, they are eager to have them. And you will be accepted: so long as you remember your place."

A woman raised her hand and said, "What about prejudice against women in Japanese corporations?"

"There is no prejudice against women," the speaker said.

"I've heard that women can't advance."

"That is simply not true."

"Then why all the lawsuits? Sumitomo Corp. just settled a big antidiscrimination suit. I read one-third of Japanese corporations have had suits brought by American employees. What about that?"

"It is perfectly understandable," the speaker said. "Any time a foreign corporation begins to do business in a new country, it is likely to make mistakes while it gets used to the habits and patterns of the country. When American corporations first went multinational in Europe in the fifties and sixties, they encountered difficulties in the countries they entered, and there were lawsuits then. So it is not remarkable that Japanese corporations also have some period of adjustment coming into America. It is necessary to be patient."

A man said with a laugh, "Is there ever a time when it's *not* necessary to be patient with Japan?" But he sounded rueful, not angry.

The others in the room continued to make notes.

"Officer? I'm Jim Donaldson. What is this about?"

I turned. Dr. Donaldson was a tall, thin man with glasses and a precise, almost prissy air. He was dressed in collegiate style, a tweed sport coat and a red tie. But he had the nerd pack of pens peeking out of his shirt pocket. I guessed he was an engineer.

"I just had a couple of questions about the Nakamoto tapes."

"The Nakamoto tapes?"

"The ones in your laboratory last night."

"My laboratory? Mr., ah—"

"Smith, Lieutenant Smith." I gave him my card.

"Lieutenant, I'm sorry, but I don't know what you're talking about. Tapes in my lab last night?"

"Kristen, your secretary, said everybody in the lab was working late on some tapes."

"Yes. That's true. Most of my staff."

"And the tapes came from Nakamoto."

"From *Nakamoto*?" He shook his head. "Who told you that?"

"She did."

"I assure you, Lieutenant, the tapes were not from Nakamoto."

"I heard there were twenty tapes."

"Yes, at least twenty. I'm not sure of the exact number. But they were from McCann-Erickson. An ad campaign for Asahi beer. We had to do a logo transformation on every ad in the campaign. Now that Asahi beer is the number one beer in America."

"But the question of Nakamoto—"

"Lieutenant," he said impatiently, glancing at the podium, "let me explain something. I work for Hamaguchi Research Labs. Hamaguchi is owned by Kawakami Industries. A competitor of Nakamoto. Competition among the Japanese corporations is very intense. *Very* intense. Take my word for it: my lab didn't do any work on any Nakamoto tapes last night. Such a thing would never happen, under any circumstances. If my secretary said it did, she's mistaken. It's absolutely out of the realm of possibility. Now, I have to give a speech. Is there anything else?"

"No," I said. "Thanks."

There was scattered applause as the speaker on the podium finished. I turned and left the room.

I was driving away from the Bonaventure when Connor called in from the golf course. He sounded annoyed. "I got your page. I had to interrupt my game. This better be good."

I told him about the one o'clock appointment with Senator Morton.

"All right," he said. "Pick me up here at ten-thirty. Anything else?"

I told him about my trips to JPL and Hamaguchi, then my conversation with Donaldson.

Connor sighed. "That was a waste of time."

"Why?"

"Because Hamaguchi is funded by Kawakami, and they're in competition with Nakamoto. There is no way they would do anything to help Nakamoto."

"That's what Donaldson told me," I said.

"Where are you going now?"

"To the U.S.C. video labs. I'm still trying to get the tapes copied."

Connor paused. "Anything else I should know?"

"No."

"Fine. See you at ten-thirty."

"Why so early?"

"Ten-thirty," he said, and hung up.

* * *

As soon as I hung up, the phone rang. "You were supposed to call me." It was Ken Shubik at the *Times*. He sounded sulky.

"Sorry. I got tied up. Can we talk now?"

"Sure."

"You got information for me?"

"Listen." He paused. "Are you anywhere around here?"

"About five blocks from you."

"Then come by for a cup of coffee."

"You don't want to talk on the phone?"

"Well . . ."

"Come on, Ken. You always want to talk on the phone." Shubik was like all the *Times* reporters, he sat at his desk in front of his computer and wore a headset and talked on the phone all day long. It was his preferred way of doing things. He had all his stuff in front of him, he could type his notes into the computer as he talked. When I was a press officer, my office had been at police headquarters in Parker Center, two blocks from the Times building. And still a reporter like Ken would rather talk to me on the phone than see me in person.

"Come on by, Pete."

That was clear enough.

Ken didn't want to talk on the phone.

"Okay, fine," I said. "See you in ten minutes."

The *Los Angeles Times* is the most profitable newspaper in America. The newsroom takes up one entire floor of the Times building, and thus is the area of a city block. The space has been skillfully subdivided, so you are never confronted by how large it actually is, and how many hundreds of people work there. But still it seems you walk for days past reporters sitting at clusters of modular workstations, with their glowing computer screens, their blinking telephones, and their tacked-up pictures of the kids.

Ken's workstation was in Metro, on the east side of the building. I found him standing by his desk, pacing. Waiting for me. He took me by the elbow.

"Coffee," he said. "Let's get coffee."

"What is it?" I said. "You don't want to be seen with me?"

"No. Shit. I want to avoid the Weasel. He's down hustling that new girl on Foreign. She doesn't know any better yet." Ken nodded toward the far end of the newsroom. There, by the windows, I saw the familiar figure of Willy Wilhelm, known to everyone as Weasel Wilhelm. Willy's narrow, ferretlike face was at this moment composed into a mask of smiling attentiveness as he joked with a blond girl sitting before a terminal.

"Very cute."

"Yeah. A little big in the rear. She's Dutch," Ken said. "She's only been here a week. She hasn't heard about him."

Most organizations had a person like the Weasel: somebody who is more ambitious than scrupulous, somebody who finds a way to make himself useful to the powers that be, while being roundly hated by everyone else. That was the case with Weasel Wilhelm.

Like most dishonest people, the Weasel believed the worst about everybody. He could always be counted on to portray events in their most unflattering light, insisting that anything less was a cover-up. He had a nose for human weakness and a taste for melodrama. He cared nothing for the truth of any situation, and he considered a balanced appraisal weak. As far as the Weasel was concerned, the underlying truth was always strong stuff. And that was what he dealt in.

The other reporters at the *Times* despised him.

Ken and I went into the central hallway. I followed him toward the coffee machines, but he led me into the library. In the middle of the floor, the *Times* had a library that was larger and better equipped than many college facilities.

"So, what is it about Wilhelm?" I said.

"He was in here last night," Ken said. "I came by after the theater to pick up some notes I needed for a morning interview I was doing from home. And I saw the Weasel in the library. Maybe eleven o'clock at night. You know how ambitious the little turd is. I could see it in his face. He had the scent of blood. So naturally, you want to know about what."

"Naturally," I said. The Weasel was an accomplished backstabber. A year earlier, he had managed to get the editor of the Sunday Calendar fired. Only at the last minute did he fail to land the job himself.

Ken said, "So I whisper to Lilly, the night librarian. 'What is it? What's the Weasel up to?' She says, 'He's checking police reports on some cop.' So that's a relief, I think. But then I begin to wonder. I mean, I'm still the senior Metro reporter. I still do a story out of Parker Center a couple of times a month. What does he know that I don't? For all I know, this should be my story. So I say to Lilly, what's the name of this cop?"

"Let me guess," I said.

"That's right," Ken said. "Peter J. Smith."

"What time was this?"

"About eleven."

"Great," I said.

"I thought you'd want to know," Ken said.

"I do."

"So I said to Lilly—this is last night—I said, 'Lilly, what kind of stuff is he pulling?' And he's pulling everything, all the old clips from the morgue, and apparently he's got a source inside Parker who's going to leak him internal affairs records. Some kind of a hearing about child molestation. Charge brought a couple of years ago."

"Ah, shit," I said.

"That true?" Ken said.

"There was a hearing," I said. "But it was bullshit."

Ken looked at me. "Fill me in."

"It was three years back," I said. "I was still working detective. My partner and I answered a domestic violence call in Ladera Heights. Hispanic couple, fighting. Both very drunk. Woman wants me to arrest her husband, and when I refuse to, says he's sexually abusing her baby. I go look at the baby. The baby looks okay. I still refuse to arrest the husband. The woman is pissed. The next day she comes in and accuses *me* of sexual molestation. There's a preliminary hearing. Charges dismissed as without merit."

"Okay," Ken said. "Now, you got any travel that's questionable?"

I frowned. "Travel?"

"The Weasel was trying to locate travel records last night. Airplane trips, junkets, padded expenses . . ."

I shook my head. "It doesn't ring a bell."

"Yeah, I figured he must be wrong about that one. You're a single parent, you're not going on any junkets."

"No way."

"Good."

We were walking deeper into the library. We came to a corner where we could see out to the Metro section of the newsroom through glass walls. I saw the Weasel still talking to the girl, chatting her up. I said, "What I don't understand, Ken, is why me? I mean, I got no heat on me at all.

No controversy. I haven't been a working detective for three years. I'm not even a press officer any more. I'm liaison. I mean, what I do is political. So why is a *Times* reporter gunning for me?"

"At eleven o'clock on a Thursday night, you mean?" Ken said. He was staring at me like I was an idiot. Like there was drool coming down my chin.

I said, "You think the Japanese are doing this?"

"I think the Weasel does jobs for people. He is a scumbag for hire. He does jobs for the studios, record companies, brokerage houses, even the realtors. He's a *consultant*. The Weasel now drives a Mercedes 500SL, you know."

"Oh, yeah?"

"Pretty good on a reporter's salary, wouldn't you say?"

"Yeah, I would."

"So. You got on the wrong side of somebody? You do that last night?"

"Maybe."

"Because somebody called the Weasel to track you down."

I said, "I can't believe this."

"Believe it," Ken said. "The only thing that worries me is the Weasel's source inside Parker Center. Somebody in the department's leaking him internal affairs stuff. You okay inside your own department?"

"As far as I know."

"Good. Because the Weasel is up to his usual tricks. This morning I talked to Roger Bascomb, our in-house counsel."

"And?"

"Guess who called him all hot and bothered with a question last night? The Weasel. And you want to guess what the question was?"

I said nothing.

"The question was, does serving as a police press-officer make an individual a public personality? As in, a public personality who can't sue for libel?"

I said, "Jesus."

"Right."

"And the answer?"

"Who cares about the answer? You know how this works. All the Weasel has to do is call a few people and say, 'Hi, this is Bill Wilhelm over here at the *L.A. Times*. We're going with a story tomorrow that says Lieutenant Peter Smith is a child molester, do you have any comment on that?' A few well-placed calls, and the story doesn't even have to run. The editors can kill it but the damage is already done."

I said nothing. I knew what Ken was telling me was true. I had seen it happen more than once.

I said, "What can I do?"

Ken laughed. "You could arrange one of your famous incidents of L.A. police brutality."

"That's not funny."

"Nobody at this paper would cover it, I can promise you that. You could fucking kill him. And if somebody made a home video? Hey, people here would *pay* to see it on video."

"Ken."

Ken sighed. "I can dream. Okay. There's one thing. Last year, after Wilhelm was involved in the, ah, change of management over in Calendar, I got an anonymous package in the mail. So did a few other people. Nobody did anything about it at the time. It's pretty dirty pool. You interested?"

"Yeah."

Ken took a small manila envelope from the inside pocket of his sport coat. It had one of those strings that you wrap back and forth to close it. Inside was a series of photos, printed in a strip. It showed Willy Wilhelm engaged in an intimate act with a dark-haired man. His head buried in his lap.

"You can't see the Weasel's face too well in all the angles," Ken said. "But it's him, all right. Action snap of the reporter entertaining his source. Having a drink with him, so to speak."

"Who is the guy?"

"It took us a while. His name is Barry Borman. He's the regional head of sales for Kaisei Electronics in southern California."

"What can I do with this?"

"Give me your card," Ken said. "I'll clip it to the envelope, and have it delivered to the Weasel."

I shook my head. "I don't think so."

"It'd sure make him think twice."

"No," I said. "It's not for me."

Ken shrugged. "Yeah. It might not work, anyway. Even if we squeeze the Weasel's nuts, the Japanese probably have other ways. I still haven't been able to find out how that story ran last night. All I hear is, 'Orders from the top, orders from the top.' Whatever that means. It could mean anything."

"Somebody must have written it."

"I tell you, I can't find out. But you know, the Japanese have a powerful influence at the paper. It's more than just the ads they take. It's more than their relentless PR machine drumming out of Washington, or the local lobbying and the campaign contributions to political figures and organizations. It's the sum of all those things and more. And it's starting to be insidious. I mean, you can be sitting around in a staff meeting discussing some article that we might run, and you suddenly realize, nobody wants to *offend* them. It isn't a question of whether a story is right or wrong, news or not news. And it isn't a one-to-one equation, like 'We can't say that or they'll pull their ads.' It's more subtle than that. Sometimes I look at my editors, and I can tell they won't go with certain stories because they are afraid. They don't even know what they are afraid of. They're just afraid."

"So much for a free press."

"Hey," Ken said. "This is not the time for sophomore bullshit. You know how it works. The American press reports the prevailing opinion. The prevailing opinion is the opinion of the group in power. The Japanese are now in power. The press reports the prevailing opinion as usual. No surprises. Just take care."

"I will."

"And don't hesitate to call, if you decide you want to arrange mail service."

* * *

I wanted to talk to Connor. I was beginning to understand why Connor had been worried, and why he had wanted to conclude the investigation quickly. Because a well-mounted campaign of innuendo is a fearsome thing. A skillful practitioner—and the Weasel was skillful—would arrange it so that a new story came out, day after day, even when nothing happened. You got headlines like GRAND JURY UNDECIDED ON POLICEMAN'S GUILT when in fact the grand jury hadn't met yet. But people saw the headlines, day after day, and drew their own conclusions.

The truth was, there was always a way to spin it. At the end of the innuendo campaign, if your subject was found blameless, you could still mount a headline like GRAND JURY FAILS TO FIND POLICEMAN GUILTY or DISTRICT ATTORNEY UNWILLING TO PROSECUTE ACCUSED COP. Headlines like that were as bad as a conviction.

And there was no way to bounce back from weeks of negative press. Everybody remembered the accusation. Nobody remembered the exoneration. That was human nature. Once you were accused, it was tough to get back to normal.

It was getting creepy, and I had a lot of bad feelings. I was a little preoccupied, pulling into the parking lot next to the physics department at U.S.C., when the phone rang again. It was assistant chief Olson.

"Peter."

"Yes, sir."

"It's almost ten o'clock. I thought you'd be down here putting the tapes on my desk. You promised them to me."

"I've been having trouble getting the tapes copied."

"Is that what you've been doing?"

"Sure. Why?"

"Because from the calls I get, it sounds like you aren't dropping this investigation," Jim Olson said. "In the last hour, you've been out asking questions at a Japanese research institute. Then you've interrogated a scientist who works for a Japanese research institute. You're hanging around some Japanese seminar. Let's get it straight, Peter. Is the investigation over, or not?"

"It's over," I said. "I'm just trying to get the tapes copied."

"Make sure that's all it is," he said.

"Right, Jim."

"For the good of the whole department—and the individuals in it—I want this thing behind us."

"Right, Jim."

"I don't want to lose control of this situation."

"I understand."

"I hope you do," he said. "Get the copies made, and get your ass down here." And he hung up.

I parked the car, and went into the physics building.

I waited at the top of the lecture hall while Phillip Sanders finished his lecture. He stood in front of a blackboard covered with complex formulas. There were about thirty students in the room, most of them seated down near the front. I could see the backs of their heads.

Dr. Sanders was about forty years old, one of those energetic types, in constant motion, pacing back and forth, tapping the equations on the blackboard in short emphatic jabs with his chalk as he pointed to the "signal covariant ratio determination" and the "factorial delta bandwidth noise." I couldn't even guess what subject he was teaching. Finally I concluded it must be electrical engineering.

When the bell rang on the hour, the class stood and packed up their bags. I was startled: nearly everyone in the class was Asian, both men and women. Those that weren't Oriental were Indian or Pakistani. Out of thirty students only three were white.

"That's right," Sanders said to me later, as we walked down the hallway toward his laboratory. "A class like Physics 101 doesn't attract Americans. It's been that way for years. Industry can't find them, either. We would be up shit creek if we didn't have the Orientals and Indians who come here to get doctorates in math and engineering, and then work for American companies."

We continued down some stairs, and turned left. We were in a basement passageway. Sanders walked quickly.

"But the trouble is, it's changing," he continued. "My Asian students are starting to go home. Koreans are going back to Korea. Taiwanese the same. Even Indians are returning home. The standard of living is going up in their countries, and there's more opportunity back home now. Some of these foreign countries have large numbers of well-trained people." He led me briskly down a flight of stairs. "Do you know what city has the highest number of Ph.D.'s per capita in the world?"

"Boston?"

"Seoul, Korea. Think about *that* as we rocket into the twenty-first century."

Now we were going down another corridor. Then briefly outside, into sunlight, down a covered walkway, and back into another building. Sanders kept glancing back over his shoulder, as if he was afraid of losing me. But he never stopped talking.

"And with foreign students going home, we don't have enough engineers to do American research. To create new American technology. It's a simple balance sheet. Not enough trained people. Even big companies like IBM are starting to have trouble. Trained people simply don't exist. Watch the door."

The door swung back toward me. I went through. I said, "But if there are all these high-tech job opportunities, won't they begin to attract students?"

"Not like investment banking. Or law." Sanders laughed. "America may lack engineers and scientists, but we lead the world in the production of lawyers. America has half the lawyers in the entire world. Think of that." He shook his head.

"We have four percent of the world population. We have eighteen percent of the world economy. But we have fifty percent of the lawyers. And thirty-five thousand more every year, pouring out of the schools. That's where our productivity's directed. That's where our national focus is. Half our TV shows are about lawyers. America has become Land of Lawyers. Everybody suing. Everybody disputing. Everybody in court. After all, three quarters of a million American lawyers have to do *something*. They have to make their three hundred thousand a year. Other countries think we're crazy."

He unlocked a door. I saw a sign that said ADVANCED IMAGING LABORATORY in hand-painted lettering, and an arrow. Sanders led me down a long basement hallway.

"Even our brightest kids are badly educated. The best American kids now rank twelfth in the world, after the industrialized countries of Asia and Europe. And that's our top students. At the bottom, it's worse. One-third of high school graduates can't read a bus schedule. They're illiterate."

We came to the end of the hallway, and turned right. "And the kids I see are lazy. Nobody wants to work. I teach physics. It takes years to master. But all the kids want to dress like Charlie Sheen and make a million dollars before they're twenty-eight. The only way you can make that kind of money is in law, investment banking, Wall Street. Places where the game is paper profits, something for nothing. But that's what the kids want to do, these days."

"Maybe at U.S.C."

"Trust me. Everywhere. They all watch television."

He swung another door open. Still another corridor. This one smelled moldy, damp.

"I know, I know. I'm old-fashioned," Sanders said. "I still believe that every human being stands for something. You stand for something. I stand for something. Just being on this planet, wearing the clothes we wear, doing the work we do, we each stand for something. And in this little corner of the world," he said, "we stand for cutting the crap. We analyze network news and see where they have been fucking around with the tape. We analyze TV commercials and show where the tricks are—"

Sanders suddenly stopped.

"What's the matter?"

"Wasn't there someone else?" he said. "Didn't you come here with someone else?"

"No. Just me."

"Oh, good." Sanders continued on at his same breakneck pace. "I always worry about losing people down here. Ah, okay. Here we are. The lab. Good. This door is just where I left it."

With a flourish, he threw the door open. I stared at the room, shocked.

"I know it doesn't look like much," Sanders said.

That, I thought, was a serious understatement.

I was looking at a basement space with rusty pipes and fittings hanging down from the ceiling. The green linoleum on the floor curled up in several places to expose concrete beneath. Arranged around the room were battered wooden tables, each heaped with equipment, and drooping wires down the sides. At each table, a student sat facing monitors. In several places, water plinked into buckets on the floor. Sanders said, "The only space we could get was here in the basement, and we don't have the money to put in little amenities like a ceiling. Never mind, doesn't matter. Just watch your head."

He moved forward into the room. I am about a hundred and eighty centimeters tall, not quite six feet, and I had to crouch to enter the room. From somewhere in the ceiling above, I heard a harsh rasping sizzle.

"Skaters," Sanders explained.

"Sorry?"

"We're underneath the ice rink. You get used to it. Actually, it's not bad now. When they have hockey practice in the afternoon, then it's a bit noisy."

We moved deeper into the room. I felt like I was in a submarine. I glanced at the students at their workstations. They were all intent on their work; nobody looked up as we passed. Sanders said, "What kind of tape do you want to duplicate?"

"Eight-millimeter Japanese. Security tape. It might be difficult."

"Difficult? I doubt that very much," Sanders said. "You know, back in my youth, I wrote most of the early video image-enhancement algorithms. You know, despeckling and inversion and edge tracing. That stuff. The Sanders algorithms were the ones everybody used. I was a graduate student at Cal Tech then. I worked at JPL in my spare time. No, no, we can do it."

I handed him a tape. He looked at it. "Cute little bugger."

I said, "What happened? To all your algorithms?"

"There was no commercial use for them," he said. "Back in the eighties, American companies like RCA and GE got out of commercial electronics entirely. My image enhancement programs didn't have much use in America." He shrugged. "So I tried to sell them to Sony, in Japan."

"And?"

"The Japanese had already patented the products. In Japan."

"You mean they already had the algorithms?"

"No. They just had patents. In Japan, patenting is a form of war. The Japanese patent like crazy. And they have a strange system. It takes eight years to get a patent in Japan, but your application is made public after eighteen months, after which royalties are moot. And of course Japan doesn't have reciprocal licensing agreements with America. It's one of the ways they keep their edge.

"Anyway, when I got to Japan I found Sony and Hitachi had some related patents and they had done what is called 'patent flooding.' Meaning they covered possible related uses. They didn't have the rights to use my algorithms—but I discovered I didn't have the rights, either. Because they had already patented the *use* of my invention." He shrugged. "It's complicated to explain. Anyway, that's ancient history. By now the Japanese have devised *much* more complicated video software, far surpassing anything we have. They're years ahead of us now. But we struggle along in this lab. Ah. Just the person we need. Dan. Are you busy?"

A young woman looked up from the computer console. Large eyes, horn-rim glasses, dark hair. Her face was partially blocked by the ceiling pipes.

"You're not Dan," Sanders said, sounding surprised. "Where's Dan, Theresa?"

"Picking up a midterm," Theresa said. "I'm just helping run the real-time progressions. They're finishing now." I had the impression that she was older than the other students. It was hard to say why, exactly. It certainly wasn't her clothes: she wore a bright colored headband and a U2

T-shirt under a jeans jacket. But she had a calm quality that made her seem older.

"Can you switch to something else?" Sanders said, walking around the table to look at the monitor. "Because we have a rush job here. We have to help out the police." I followed Sanders, ducking pipes.

"Sure, I guess," the woman said. She started to shut down units on the desk. Her back was turned to me, and then finally I could see her. She was dark, exotic-looking, almost Eurasian. In fact she was beautiful, drop-dead beautiful. She looked like one of those high cheek-boned models in magazines. And for a moment I was confused, because this woman was too beautiful to be working in some basement electronics laboratory. It didn't make sense.

"Say hello to Theresa Asakuma," he said. "The only Japanese graduate student working here."

"Hi," I said. I blushed. I felt stupid. I felt that information was coming at me too fast. And all things considered, I would rather not have a Japanese handling these tapes. But her first name wasn't Japanese, and she didn't look Japanese, she looked Eurasian or perhaps part Japanese, so exotic, maybe she was even—

"Good morning, Lieutenant," she said. She extended her left hand, the wrong hand, for me to shake. She held it out to me sideways, the way someone does when their right hand is injured.

I shook hands with her. "Hello, Miss Asakuma."

"Theresa."

"Okay."

"Isn't she beautiful?" Sanders said, acting as if he took credit for it. "Just beautiful."

"Yes," I said. "Actually, I'm surprised you're not a model."

There was an awkward moment. I couldn't tell why. She turned quickly away.

"It never interested me," she said.

And Sanders immediately jumped in and said, "Theresa, Lieutenant Smith needs us to copy some tapes. *These* tapes." Sanders held one out to her. She took it in her left hand

and held it to the light. Her right hand remained bent at the elbow, pressed to her waist. Then I saw that her right arm was withered, ending in a fleshy stump protruding beyond the sleeve of her jeans jacket. It looked like the arm of a Thalidomide baby.

"Quite interesting," she said, squinting at the tape. "Eight-millimeter high density. Maybe it's the proprietary digital format we've been hearing about. The one that includes real-time image enhancement."

"I'm sorry, I don't know," I said. I was feeling foolish for having said anything about being a model. I dug into my box and brought out the playback machine.

Theresa immediately took a screwdriver and removed the top. She bent over the innards. I saw a green circuit board, a black motor, and three small crystal cylinders. "Yes. It's the new setup. Very slick. Dr. Sanders, look: they're doing it with just three heads. The board must generate component RGB, because over here—you think this is compression circuitry?"

"Probably digital to analog converter," Sanders said. "Very neat. So small." He turned to me, holding up the box. "You know how the Japanese can make things this way and we can't? They *kaizen* 'em. A process of deliberate, patient, continual refinements. Each year the products get a little better, a little smaller, a little cheaper. Americans don't think that way. Americans are always looking for the quantum leap, the big advance forward. Americans try to hit a home run—to knock it out of the park—and then sit back. The Japanese just hit singles all day long, and they never sit back. So with something like this, you're looking at an expression of philosophy as much as anything."

He talked like this for a while, pivoting the cylinders, admiring it. Finally I said, "Can you copy the tapes?"

"Sure," Theresa said. "From the converter, we can run a signal out of this machine and lay it down on whatever media you like. You want three-quarter? Optical master? VHS?"

"VHS," I said.

"That's easy," she said.

"But will it be an accurate copy? The people at JPL said they couldn't guarantee the copy would be accurate."

"Oh, hell, JPL," Sanders said. "They just talk like that because they work for the government. We get things *done* here. Right Theresa?"

But Theresa wasn't listening. I watched her plugging cables and wires, moving swiftly with her good hand, using her stump to stabilize and hold the box. Like many disabled people, her movements were so fluid it was hardly noticeable that her right hand was missing. Soon she had the small playback machine hooked to a second recorder, and several different monitors.

"What're all these?"

"To check the signal."

"You mean for playback?"

"No. The big monitor there will show the image. The others let me look at the signal characteristics, and the data map: how the image has been laid down on the tape."

I said, "You need to do that?"

"No. I just want to snoop. I'm curious about how they've set up this high-density format."

Sanders said to me, "What is the actual source material?"

"It's from an office security camera."

"And this tape is original?"

"I think so. Why?"

"Well, if it's original material we want to be extra careful with it," Sanders said. He was talking to Theresa, instructing her. "We don't want to set up any feedback loops scrambling the media surface. Or signal leaks off the heads that will compromise the integrity of the data stream."

"Don't worry," she said. "I got it handled." She pointed to her setup. "See that? It'll warn of an impedance shift. And I'm monitoring the central processor too."

"Okay," Sanders said. He was beaming like a proud parent.

"How long will this take?" I said.

"Not long. We can lay down the signal at very high speed. The rate limit is a function of the playback device, and it seems to have a fast-forward scan. So, maybe two or three minutes per tape."

I glanced at my watch. "I have a ten-thirty appointment I can't be late for, and I don't want to leave these . . ."

"You need all of them done?"

"Actually, just five are critical."

"Then let's do those first."

We ran the first few seconds of each tape, one after another, looking for the five that came from the cameras on the forty-sixth floor. As each tape started, I saw the camera image on the central monitor of Theresa's table. On the side monitors, signal traces bounced and jiggled like an intensive care unit. I mentioned it.

"That's just about right," she said. "Intensive care for video." She ejected one tape, stuck in another, and started it up. "Oops. Did you say this material was original? It's not. These tapes are copies."

"How do you know?"

"Because we got a windup signature." Theresa bent over the equipment, staring at the signal traces, making fine adjustments with her knobs and dials.

"I think that's what you got, yes," Sanders said. He turned to me. "You see, with video it's difficult to detect a copy in the image itself. The older analog video shows some degradation in successive generations, but in a digital system like this, there is no difference at all. Each copy is literally identical to the master."

"Then how can you say the tapes are copies?"

"Theresa isn't looking at the picture," Sanders said. "She's looking at the signal. Even though we can't detect a copy from the image, sometimes we can determine the image came from another video playback, instead of a camera."

I shook my head. "How?"

Theresa said, "It has to do with how the signal is laid down in the first half-second of taping. If the recording video is started before the playback video, there is sometimes a slight fluctuation in the signal output as the playback machine starts up. It's a mechanical function: the playback motors can't get up to speed instantaneously.

There are electronic circuits in the playback machine to minimize the effect, but there's always an interval of getting up to speed."

"And that's what you detected?"

She nodded. "It's called a windup signature."

Sanders said, "And that never happens if the signal is coming direct from a camera, because a camera has no moving parts. A camera is instantaneously up to speed at all times."

I frowned. "So these tapes are copies."

"Is that bad?" Sanders said.

"I don't know. If they were copied, they might also be changed, right?"

"In theory, yes," Sanders said. "In practice, we'd have to look carefully. And it would be very hard to know for certain. These tapes come from a Japanese company?"

"Yes."

"Nakamoto?"

I nodded. "Yes."

"Frankly I'm not surprised they gave you copies," Sanders said. "The Japanese are extremely cautious. They're not very trusting of outsiders. And Japanese corporations in America feel the way we would feel doing business in Nigeria: they think they're surrounded by savages."

"Hey," Theresa said.

"Sorry," Sanders said, "but you know what I mean. The Japanese feel they have to put up with us. With our ineptitude, our slowness, our stupidity, our incompetence. That makes them self-protective. So if these tapes have any legal significance, the last thing they'd do is turn the originals over to a barbarian policeman like you. No, no, they'd give you a copy and keep the original in case they need it for their defense. Fully confident that with your inferior American video technology, you'd never be able to detect that it was a copy, anyway."

I frowned. "How long would it take to make copies?"

"Not long," Sanders said, shaking his head. "The way Theresa is scanning now, five minutes a tape. I imagine the Japanese can do it much faster. Say, two minutes a tape."

"In that case, they had plenty of time to make copies last night."

As we talked, Theresa was continuing to shuffle the tapes, looking at the first portions of each. As each image came up, she'd glance at me. I would shake my head. I was seeing all the different security cameras. Finally, the first of the tapes from the forty-sixth floor appeared, the familiar office image I had seen before.

"That's one."

"Okay. Here we go. Laying it onto VHS." Theresa started the first copy. She ran the tape forward at high speed, the images streaky and quick. On the side monitors, the signals bounced and jittered nervously.

She said, "Does this have something to do with the murder last night?"

"Yes. You know about that?"

She shrugged. "I saw it on the news. The killer died in a car crash?"

"That's right," I said.

She was turned away. The three-quarter profile of her face was strikingly beautiful, the high curve of her cheekbone. I thought of what a playboy Eddie Sakamura was known to be. I said, "Did you know him?"

"No," she said. After a moment she added, "He was Japanese."

Another moment of awkwardness descended on our little group. There was something that both Theresa and Sanders seemed to know that I did not. But I didn't know how to ask. So I watched the video.

Once again, I saw the sunlight moving across the floor. Then the room lights came up as the office personnel thinned. Now the floor was empty. And then, at high speed, Cheryl Austin appeared, followed by the man. They kissed passionately.

"Ah ha," Sanders said. "Is this it?"

"Yes."

He frowned as he watched the action progress. "You mean the murder is *recorded?*"

"Yes," I said. "On multiple cameras."

"You're kidding."

Sanders fell silent, watching events proceed. With the streaky high-speed image, it was difficult to see more than the basic events. The two people moving to the conference room. The sudden struggle. Forcing her back on the table. Stepping away suddenly. Leaving the room in haste.

Nobody spoke. We all watched the tape.

I glanced at Theresa. Her face was blank. The image was reflected in her glasses.

Eddie passed the mirror, and went into the dark passageway. The tape ran on for a few more seconds, and then the cassette popped out.

"That's one. You say there are multiple cameras? How many all together?"

"Five, I think," I said.

She marked the first cassette with a stick-on label. She started the second tape in the machine, and began another high-speed duplication.

I said, "These copies are exact?"

"Oh, yes."

"So they're legal?"

Sanders frowned. "Legal in what sense?"

"Well, as evidence, in a court of law—"

"Oh, no," Sanders said. "These tapes would never be admissible in a court of law."

"But if they're exact copies—"

"It's nothing to do with that. All forms of photographic evidence including video, are no longer admissible in court."

"I haven't heard that," I said.

"It hasn't happened yet," Sanders said. "The case law isn't entirely clear. But it's coming. All photographs are suspect these days. Because now, with digital systems, they can be changed perfectly. *Perfectly*. And that's something new. Remember years ago, how the Russians would remove politicians from photographs of their May Day line ups? It was always a crude cut-and-paste job—and you could always see that something had been done. There was a funny space between the shoulders of the remaining people. Or a discoloration on the back wall. Or you could see the brushstrokes of the retoucher who tried to smooth over the damage. But anyway, you could see it—fairly easily. You could *see* the picture had been altered. The whole business was laughable."

"I remember," I said.

"Photographs always had integrity precisely because they were impossible to change. So we considered photographs to represent reality. But for several years now, computers have allowed us to make seamless alterations of photographic images. A few years back the *National Geographic* moved the Great Pyramid of Egypt on a cover photo. The editors didn't like where the pyramid was, and they thought it would compose better if it was moved. So they just altered the photograph and moved it. Nobody could tell. But if you go back to Egypt with a camera and try to duplicate that picture, you'll find you can't. Because there is no place in the real world where the pyramids line up that way. The photograph no longer represents reality. But you can't tell. Minor example."

"And someone could do the same thing to this tape?"

"In theory, any video can be changed."

On the monitor, I watched the murder occurring a second time. This camera was from the far end of the room. It didn't show the actual murder very well, but afterward, Sakamura was clearly visible as he walked toward the camera.

I said, "The image could be changed how?"

Sanders laughed. "These days, you can make any damn change you want."

"Could you change the identity of the murderer?"

"Technically, yes," Sanders said. "Mapping a face onto a complex moving object is now possible. Technically possible. But as a practical matter, it'd be a bitch to do."

I said nothing. But it was just as well. Sakamura was our leading suspect and he was dead; the chief wanted the case finished. So did I.

"Of course," Sanders said, "the Japanese have all sorts of fancy video algorithms for surface mapping and three-dimensional transformations. They can do things that we can't begin to imagine." He drummed his fingers on the table again. "What is the timetable of these tapes? What's their history?"

I said, "The murder happened at eight-thirty last night, as shown on the clock. We were told the tapes were removed from the security office around eight forty-five p.m. We asked for them, and there was some back-and-forth with the Japanese."

"As always. And when did you finally take possession?"

"They were delivered to division headquarters around one-thirty a.m."

"Okay," Sanders said. "That means they had the tapes from eight forty-five to one-thirty."

"Right. A little less than five hours."

Sanders frowned. "Five tapes, with five different camera angles, to change in five hours?" Sanders shook his head. "No way. It just can't be done, Lieutenant."

"Yeah," Theresa said. "It's impossible. Even for them. It's just too many pixels to change."

I said, "You're sure about that."

"Well," Theresa said, "the only way it could be done that fast is with an automated program, and even the most sophisticated programs need you to polish the details by hand. Things like bad blur can give it all away."

"Bad blur?" I said. I found I liked asking her questions. I liked looking at her face.

"Bad motion blur," Sanders said. "Video runs at thirty frames a second. You can think of each frame of video as a picture that's shot at a shutter speed of one-thirtieth of a second. Which is very slow—much slower than pocket cameras. If you film a runner at a thirtieth of a second, the legs are just streaks. Blurs.

"That's called motion blur. And if you alter it by a mechanical process, it starts to look wrong. The image appears too sharp, too crisp. Edges look odd. It's back to the Russians: you can see it's been changed. For realistic motion, you need the right amount of blur."

"I see."

Theresa said, "And there's the color shift."

"Right," Sanders said. "Inside the blur itself, there is a color shift. For example, look there on the monitor. The man is wearing a blue suit, and his coat is swinging out as he spins the girl around the room. Now. If you take a frame of that action, and blow it up to its pixels, you will find that the coat is navy, but the blur is progressive shades of lighter blue, until at the edge it seems almost transparent—you can't tell from a single frame exactly where the coat ends and the background begins."

I could vaguely imagine it. "Okay . . ."

"If the edge colors don't blend smoothly, you will notice it immediately. It can take hours to clean up a few seconds of tape, as in a commercial. But if you don't do it, you will see it like *that*." He snapped his fingers.

"So even though they duplicated the tapes, they couldn't have altered them?"

"Not in five hours," Sanders said. "They just didn't have time."

"Then we are seeing what actually happened."

"No doubt about it," Sanders said. "But we'll poke around with this image, anyway, after you go. Theresa wants to fiddle with it, I know she does. So do I. Check in with us later today. We'll tell you if there's anything funny. But basically, it can't be done. And it wasn't done here."

As I pulled into the parking circle at the Sunset Hills Country Club, I saw Connor standing in front of the big stucco clubhouse. He bowed to the three Japanese golfers standing with him, and they bowed back. Then he shook hands with them all, tossed the clubs into the back seat, and got into my car.

"You're late, *kōhai*."

"Sorry. It's only a few minutes. I was held up at U.S.C."

"Your lateness inconvenienced everyone. As a matter of politeness, they felt obliged to keep me company in front of the club while I waited for you. Men of their position are not comfortable standing around. They are busy. But they felt obligated and could not leave me there. You embarrassed me very much. And you reflected poorly on the department."

"I'm sorry. I didn't realize."

"Start to realize, *kōhai*. You're not alone in the world."

I put the car in gear, and drove out. I looked at the Japanese in the rearview mirror. They were waving as we left. They did not appear unhappy, or in a rush to leave.

"Who were you playing with?"

"Aoki-san is the head of Tokio Marine in Vancouver. Hanada-san is a vice-president of Mitsui Bank in London. And Kenichi Asaka runs all of Toyota's Southeast Asian plants from K.L. to Singapore. He's based in Bangkok."

"What are they doing here?"

"They're on vacation," Connor said. "A short holiday in the States for golf. They find it pleasant to relax in a slower-paced country like ours."

I drove up the winding drive to Sunset Boulevard, and stopped to wait for the light. "Where to?"

"The Four Seasons Hotel."

I turned right, heading toward Beverly Hills. "And why are these men playing golf with you?"

"Oh, we go way back," he said. "A few favors here and there, over the years. I'm nobody important. But relationships must be maintained. A phone call, a small gift, a game when you're in town. Because you never know when you will need your network. Relationships are your source of information, your safety valve, and your early warning system. In the Japanese way of seeing the world."

"Who asked for this game?"

"Hanada-san was already intending to play. I just joined him. I'm quite a good golfer, you know."

"Why did you want to play?"

"Because I wanted to know more about the Saturday meetings," Connor said.

I remembered the Saturday meetings. On the video we had seen at the newsroom, Sakamura had grabbed Cheryl Austin and said: You don't understand, this is all about the Saturday meetings.

"And did they tell you?"

Connor nodded. "Apparently they began a long time ago," he said. "Nineteen eighty or so. First they were held in the Century Plaza, and later in the Sheraton, and finally in the Biltmore."

Connor stared out the window. The car jounced over the potholes on Sunset Boulevard.

"For several years, the meetings were a regular event. Prominent Japanese industrialists who happened to be in town would attend an ongoing discussion of what should be done about America. Of how the American economy should be managed."

"*What?*"

"Yes."

"That's outrageous!"

"Why?" Connor said.

"*Why*? Because this is *our* country. You can't have a

bunch of foreigners sitting around in secret meetings and deciding how to manage it!"

"The Japanese don't see it that way," Connor said.

"I'm sure they don't! I'm sure they think they have a goddamn right!"

Connor shrugged. "As a matter of fact, that's exactly what they think. And the Japanese believe they have earned the right to decide—"

"*Christ*—"

"Because they have invested heavily in our economy. They have lent us a lot of money, Peter: a *lot* of money. Hundreds of billions of dollars. For most of the last fifteen years, the United States has run a billion dollars of trade deficit a *week* with Japan. That's a billion dollars every week that they must do something with. A torrent of money roaring toward them. They don't especially want so many dollars. What can they do with all their excess billions?

"They decided to lend the money back to us. Our government was running a budget deficit, year after year. We weren't paying for our own programs. So the Japanese financed our budget deficit. They invested in us. And they lent their money, based on certain assurances from our government. Washington assured the Japanese that we would set our house in order. We would cut our deficit. We would improve education, rebuild our infrastructure, even raise taxes if necessary. In short, we would clean up our act. Because only then does an investment in America make sense."

"Uh-huh," I said.

"But we did none of those things. We let the deficit get worse, and we devalued the dollar. We cut its value in half in 1985. You know what that did to Japanese investments in America? It fucked them. Whatever they invested in 1984 now paid half its previous return."

I vaguely remembered something about this. I said, "I thought we did that to help our trade deficit, to boost exports."

"We did, but it didn't work. Our trade balance with Japan got worse. Normally, if you devalue your currency by half, the cost of everything imported doubles. But the Japanese slashed prices on their VCRs and copiers, and held their market share. Remember, business is war.

"All we really accomplished was to make American land and American companies cheap for the Japanese to buy, because the yen was now twice as strong as it had been. We made the biggest banks in the world all Japanese. And we made America a poor country."

"What does this have to do with the Saturday meetings?"

"Well," Connor said, "suppose you have an uncle who is a drunk. He says if you lend him money he'll stop drinking. But he doesn't stop drinking. And you'd like to get your money. You want to salvage what you can from your bad investment. Also, you know that your uncle, being a drunk, is likely to get loaded and hurt somebody. Your uncle is out of control. So something has to be done. And the family sits down together to decide what to do about their problem uncle. That's what the Japanese decided to do."

"Uh-huh." Connor must have heard the skepticism in my voice.

"Look," he said. "Get this conspiracy stuff out of your head. Do you want to take over Japan? Do you want to run their country? Of course not. No sensible country wants to take over another country. Do business, yes. Have a relationship, yes. But not *take over*. Nobody wants the responsibility. Nobody wants to be bothered. Just like with the drunken uncle—you only have those meetings when you're forced to. It's a last resort."

"So that's how the Japanese see it?"

"They see billions and billions of their dollars, *kōhai*. Invested in a country that's in deep trouble. That's filled with strange individualistic people who talk constantly. Who confront each other constantly. Who argue all the time. People who aren't well educated, who don't know much about the world, who get their information from television. People who don't work very hard, who tolerate violence and drug use, and who don't seem to object to it. The Japanese have billions of dollars in this peculiar land and they would like a decent return on their investment. And even though the American economy is collapsing—it will soon be third in the world after Japan and Europe—it's still important to try and hold it together. Which is all they're trying to do."

"That's it?" I said. "They're just doing the good work of saving America?"

"Somebody needs to do it," Connor said. "We can't go on this way."

"We'll manage."

"That's what the English always said." He shook his head. "But now England is poor. And America is becoming poor, too."

"Why is it becoming poor?" I said, speaking louder than I intended.

"The Japanese say it's because America has become a land without substance. We let our manufacturing go. We don't make things anymore. When you manufacture products, you add value to raw materials, and you literally create wealth. But America has stopped doing that. Americans make money now by paper manipulation, which the Japanese say is bound to catch up to us because paper profits don't reflect real wealth. They think our fascination with Wall Street and junk bonds is crazy."

"And therefore the Japanese ought to manage us?"

"They think *someone* ought to manage us. They'd prefer we do it ourselves."

"Jesus."

Connor shifted in his seat. "Save your outrage, *kōhai*. Because according to Hanada-san, the Saturday meetings stopped in 1991."

"Oh?"

"Yes. That was when the Japanese decided not to worry about whether America would clean up its act. They saw advantages in the present situation: America is asleep, and inexpensive to buy."

"So there aren't Saturday meetings any more?"

"There are occasional ones. Because of *nichibei kankei*: the ongoing Japanese-American relationship. The economies of the two countries are interlocked by now. Neither country can pull out, even if they wanted to. But the meetings are no longer important. They are basically social functions. So what Sakamura said to Cheryl Austin is wrong. And her death had nothing to do with the Saturday meetings."

"What does it have to do with?"

"My friends seemed to think it was personal. A *chijou no motsure*, a crime of passion. Involving a beautiful, *irokichigai* woman and a jealous man."

"And you believe them?"

"Well, the thing is, they were unanimous. All three of these businessmen. Of course Japanese are reluctant to express disagreement among themselves, even on the golf course of an underdeveloped peasant country. But I have learned that unanimity toward a *gaijin* may cover a multitude of sins."

"You think they were lying?"

"Not exactly." Connor shook his head. "But I had the impression they were telling me something by not telling me. This morning was a game of *hara no saguriai*. My friends were not forthcoming."

Connor described his golf game. There had been long silences all morning. Everyone in the foursome was polite and considerate, but spoken comments were rare and reserved. Most of the time, the men walked over the course in complete silence.

"And you had gone there for information?" I said. "How could you stand it?"

"Oh, I was getting information." But as he explained it, it was all unspoken. Basically, the Japanese have an understanding based on centuries of shared culture, and they are able to communicate feelings without words. It's the closeness that exists in America between a parent and child—a child often understands everything, just from a parent's glance. But Americans don't rely on unspoken communication as a general rule, and the Japanese do. It is as if all Japanese are members of the same family, and they can communicate without words. To a Japanese, silences have meaning.

"It's nothing mystical or wonderful," Connor said. "For the most part it is because the Japanese are so hemmed in by rules and conventions, they end up unable to say anything at all. For politeness, to save face, the other person is obliged to read the situation, the context, and the subtle signs of body posture and unstated feeling. Because the first person feels he can't actually put anything into words. Any speaking at all would be indelicate. So the point must be gotten across in other ways."

I said, "And that's how your morning was spent? Not talking?"

Connor shook his head. He felt he had quite clear communication with the Japanese golfers, and wasn't troubled by the silences at all.

"Because I was asking them to talk about other Japanese—members of their family—I had to frame my questions with great delicacy. Just as I would if I were asking whether your sister was in jail or any subject that was painful or awkward for you. I would be attentive to how long it took you to answer, and the pauses between your statements, the tone of your voice—all sorts of things. Beyond the literal communication. Okay?"

"Okay."

"It means you get the feeling by an intuition."

"And what was the intuition you got?"

"They said, 'We are mindful that you have performed services for us in the past. We feel a desire to help you now. But this murder is a Japanese matter and thus we are unable to tell you everything that we might like to. From our reticence, you may draw useful conclusions about the underlying issue.' That's what they said to me."

"And what is the underlying issue?"

"Well," Connor said. "They mentioned MicroCon several times."

"That high-tech company?"

"Yes. The one that's being sold. Apparently it's a small company in Silicon Valley that makes specialized computer machinery. And there are political problems about the sale. They referred to those problems several times."

"So this murder has something to do with MicroCon?"

"I think so." He shifted in his chair. "By the way, what did you learn at U.S.C. about the tapes?"

"For one thing, that they were duplicated."

Connor nodded. "I assumed that," he said.

"You did?"

"Ishiguro would never give us the originals. The Japanese think everybody who is not Japanese is a barbarian. They mean it, literally: *barbarian*. Stinking, vulgar, stupid barbarian. They're polite about it, because they know you can't help the misfortune of not being born Japanese. But they still think it."

I nodded. That was more or less what Sanders had said, too.

"The other thing," Connor said, "is that the Japanese are extremely successful, but they are not daring. They are plotters and plodders. So they're not going to give us the originals because they don't want to take any chances. Now. What else did you learn about the tapes?"

"What makes you think there was something else?" I said.

"When you looked at the tapes," he said, "I'm sure you noticed an important detail that—"

And then we were interrupted by the telephone.

"Captain Connor," said a cheerful voice, over the speaker phone. "This is Jerry Orr. Over at Sunset Hills Country Club? You left without taking the papers with you."

"The papers?"

"The application," Orr said. "You need to fill it out, Captain. Of course it's just routine. I can assure you, there won't be any problem with it, considering who your sponsors are."

"My sponsors," Connor said.

"Yes, sir," Orr said. "And congratulations. As you know, it's almost impossible to obtain a membership at Sunset these days. But Mr. Hanada's company had already bought a corporate membership some time ago, and they have decided to put it in your name. I must say, it's a very nice gesture from your friends."

"Yes, it is," Connor said, frowning.

I was looking at him.

"They know how fond you are of playing golf here," Orr said. "You know the terms, of course. Hanada will purchase the membership over five years, but after that time, it'll be transferred to your name. So when you retire from club membership, you're free to sell it. Now: will you be picking up the paperwork here, or should I send it to your home?"

Connor said, "Mr. Orr, please convey my heartfelt appreciation to Mr. Hanada for his very great generosity. I hardly know what to say. But I will have to call you back about this."

"That's fine. You just let us know where to send it."

"I'll call you back," Connor said.

He pushed the button to end the call, and stared forward, frowning. There was a long silence.

I said, "How much is a membership at that club worth?"

"Seven fifty. Maybe a million."

I said, "Pretty nice gift from your friends." I was thinking again of Graham, and the way Graham had always implied that Connor was in the pocket of the Japanese. There didn't seem to be much doubt of it now.

Connor was shaking his head. "I don't get it."

"What's not to get?" I said. "Jesus, Captain. Seems pretty straightforward to me."

"No, I don't get it," Connor said.

And then the phone rang again. This time, it was for me.

"Lieutenant Smith? It's Louise Gerber. I'm *so* glad I was able to reach you."

I didn't recognize her name. I said, "Yes?"

"Since tomorrow is Saturday, I was wondering if you had any time to look at a house."

Then I remembered who she was. A month earlier I had gone out with a broker to look at houses. Michelle is getting older, and I wanted to get her out of an apartment. To get her a backyard if I could. It was pretty discouraging. Even with a real estate slump, the smallest houses were four and five hundred thousand. I couldn't possibly qualify for that, on my salary.

"This is a very special situation," she said, "and I thought of you and your little girl. It's a small house in Palms—very small—but it's a corner lot and it has a charming backyard. Flowers and a lovely lawn. The asking is three hundred. But the reason I thought of you is that the seller is willing to take back all the paper on it. I think you could get it for very little down. Do you want to see it?"

I said, "Who is the seller?"

"I don't really know. It's a special situation. The house is owned by an elderly woman who has gone into a nursing home and her son who lives in Topeka intends to sell it, but he wants an income flow instead of an outright sale. The property's not formally listed yet, but I know the seller is motivated. If you could get in tomorrow, you might be able to do something. And the backyard is charming. I can just see your little girl there."

Now Connor was looking at me. I said, "Miss Gerber, I'd have to know more about it. Who the seller is, and so on."

She sounded surprised. "Gee, I thought you'd jump at it. A situation like this doesn't come along very often. Don't you want to look at it?"

Connor was looking at me, nodding. He mouthed, say yes.

"I'll have to get back to you about this," I said.

"All right, Lieutenant," she said. She sounded reluctant. "Please let me know."

"I will."

I hung up.

"What the hell is going on?" I said. Because there wasn't any way to get around it. Between us, we had just been offered a lot of money. A *lot* of money.

Connor shook his head. "I don't know."

"Is it to do with MicroCon?"

"I don't know. I thought MicroCon was a small company. This doesn't make sense." He looked very uneasy. "What exactly *is* MicroCon?"

I said, "I think I know who to ask."

◈ "MicroCon?" Ron Levine said, lighting a big cigar. "Sure, I can tell you about MicroCon. It's an ugly story."

We were sitting in the newsroom of American Financial Network, a cable news operation located near the airport. Through the window of Ron's office, I could see the white satellite dishes on the roof of the adjacent garage. Ron puffed on his cigar and grinned at us. He had been a financial reporter at the *Times* before taking an on-camera job here. AFN was one of the few television operations where the on-camera people weren't scripted; they had to know what they were talking about, and Ron did.

"MicroCon," he said, "was formed five years ago by a consortium of American computer manufacturers. The company was intended to develop the next generation of X-ray lithography machines for computer chips. At the time MicroCon started up, there were no American manufacturers of lithography machines—they'd all been put out of business in the eighties, under intense competition from the Japanese. MicroCon developed new technology, and has been building machines for American companies. Okay?"

"Okay," I said.

"Two years ago, MicroCon was sold to Darley-Higgins, a management company in Georgia. Darley's other operations were foundering; the company decided to sell Micro-Con to raise cash. They found a buyer in Akai Ceramics, an Osaka company that already made lithography machines in Japan. Akai had plenty of cash, and was willing to acquire the American company for a high price. Then Congress moved to stop the sale."

"Why?"

"The decline of American business is starting to disturb even Congress. We've lost too many basic industries to Japan—steel and shipbuilding in the sixties, television and computer chips in the seventies, machine tools in the eighties. One day somebody wakes up and realizes these industries are vital for American defense. We've lost the ability to make components essential to our national security. We're entirely dependent on Japan to supply them. So Congress starts to worry. But I hear the sale is going through, anyway. Why? Do you guys have something to do with the sale?"

"In a sense," Connor said.

"Lucky you," Ron said, puffing on his cigar. "If you're involved in a sale to the Japanese, it's like striking oil. Everybody gets rich. You two are looking at some pretty big gifts, I imagine."

Connor nodded. "Very big."

"I'm sure," Ron said. "They'll take care of you: buy you a house or a car, get you cheap financing, something like that."

I said, "Why would they do that?"

Ron laughed. "Why would they eat sushi? It's the way they conduct business."

Connor said, "But isn't MicroCon a small sale?"

"Yeah, pretty small. The company's worth a hundred million. Akai's buying it for a hundred and fifty. On top of that, they probably have another twenty million in incentives to the current corporate officers, maybe ten million in legal, ten million in consultant fees spread around Washington, and ten million in miscellaneous gifts for people like you. So call it two hundred million, in total."

I said, "Two hundred million for a hundred-million company? Why are they paying more than it's worth?"

"They're not," Ron said. "As far as they're concerned, they're getting a bargain."

"Why?"

"Because," Ron said, "if you own the machines that are

used to make something, like computer chips, you own the downstream industries that depend on those machines. MicroCon will give them control over the American computer industry. And as usual, we're allowing it to happen. Just the way we lost our television industry, and our machine-tool industry."

"What happened to the TV industry?" I said.

He glanced at his watch. "After World War II, America was the world's leading manufacturer of televisions. Twenty-seven American companies like Zenith, RCA, GE, and Emerson had a solid technological lead over foreign manufacturers. American companies were successful around the world, except in Japan. They couldn't penetrate the closed Japanese market. They were told if they wanted to sell in Japan, they had to license their technology to Japanese companies. And they did, reluctantly, under pressure from the American government, which wanted to keep Japan as a friendly ally against Russia. Okay?"

"Okay . . ."

"Now, licensing is a bad idea. It means Japan gets our technology for their own use, and we lose Japan as an export market. Pretty soon Japan begins to make cheap black-and-white TVs and exports them to America—something we can't do in Japan, right? By 1972, sixty percent of American black-and-white sales are imports. By 1976, one hundred percent are imports. We've lost the black-and-white market. American workers don't make those sets any more. Those jobs are gone from America.

"We say it doesn't matter: our companies have moved on to color. But the Japanese government starts an intensive program to develop a color-television industry. Once again, Japan licenses American technology, refines it in their protected markets, and floods us with exports. Once again, exports drive out American companies. Exactly the same story. By 1980 only three American companies still make color TVs. By 1987, there's only one, Zenith."

"But Japanese sets were better and cheaper," I said.

"They may have been better," Ron said, "but they were only cheaper because they were sold below production cost, to wipe out American competitors. That's called dumping. It's illegal under both American and international law."

"Then why didn't we stop it?"

"Good question. Especially since dumping was only one of many illegal Japanese marketing techniques. They also fixed prices: they had something called the Tenth-Day Group. Japanese managers met every ten days in a Tokyo hotel to set prices in America. We protested, but the meetings continued. They also pushed distribution of their products by collusive arrangements. The Japanese allegedly paid millions in kickbacks to American distributors like Sears. They engaged in massive customs fraud. And they destroyed the American industry, which could not compete.

"Of course, our companies protested, and sued for relief—there were dozens of cases of dumping, fraud, and antitrust brought against Japanese companies in federal court. Dumping cases are usually resolved within a year. But our government provided no help—and the Japanese are skilled foot-draggers. They paid American lobbyists millions to plead their case. By the time the suits came to trial twelve years later, the battle was over in the marketplace. And of course all during this time, American companies could never fight back in Japan. They couldn't even get a foot in the door in Japan."

"You're saying the Japanese took over the television industry illegally?"

Ron shrugged. "They couldn't have done it without our help," he said. "Our government was coddling Japan, which they saw as a tiny emerging country. And American industry was perceived as not needing government help. There's always been a strain of antibusiness sentiment in America. But our government never seemed to realize, it's just not the same here. When Sony develops the Walkman, we don't say, 'Nice product. Now you have to license it to GE and sell it through an American company.' If they seek distribution, we don't tell them, 'I'm sorry, but American stores all have preexisting arrangements with American suppliers. You'll have to distribute through an American company here.' If they seek patents, we don't say, 'Patents take eight years to be awarded, during which time your application will be publicly available so that our companies can read what you've invented and copy it free of charge, so that by the time we issue a patent our companies will already have their own version of your technology.'

"We don't do any of those things. Japan does all of them. Their markets are closed. Our markets are wide open. It's not a level playing field. In fact, it's not a playing field at all. It's a one-way street.

"And by now we have a defeatist business climate in this country. American companies got their asses handed to them in black-and-white television. They got their asses handed to them in color television. The U.S. government refused to help our companies fight illegal Japanese trade practices. So when Ampex invented the VCR, they didn't even try to make a commercial product. They just licensed the technology to Japan and moved on. And pretty soon you find that American companies don't do research. Why develop new technology if your own government is so hostile to your efforts that you won't be able to bring it to market?"

"But isn't American business weak and badly managed?"

"That's the standard line," Ron said. "As promoted by the Japanese and their American spokesmen. It's only with a few episodes that people ever glimpsed how outrageous the Japanese really were. Like the Houdaille case. You know that one? Houdaille was a machine-tool company that claimed its patents and licenses were being violated by companies in Japan. A federal judge sent Houdaille's lawyer to Japan to gather evidence. But the Japanese refused to issue him a visa."

"You're kidding."

"What do they care?" Ron said. "They know we'll never retaliate. When the Houdaille case came before the Reagan administration, it did nothing. So Houdaille got out of machine tools. Because nobody can compete against dumped products—that's the whole point of doing it."

"Don't you lose money if you dump?"

"For a while, yes. But you're selling millions of units, so

you can refine your production lines, and get your costs down. A couple of years later, you really can make the products for a lower cost. Meanwhile you've wiped out the competition and you control the market. You see, the Japanese think strategically—they're in for the long haul, for how things will look fifty years from now. An American company has to show a profit every three months or the CEO and the officers will be out on the street. But the Japanese don't care about short-term profits at all. They want market share. Business is like warfare to them. Gaining ground. Wiping out the competition. Getting control of a market. That's what they've been doing for the last thirty years.

"So the Japanese dumped steel, televisions, consumer electronics, computer chips, machine tools—and nobody stopped them. And we lost those industries. Japanese companies and the Japanese government target specific industries, which they take over. Industry after industry, year after year. While we sit around and spout off about free trade. But free trade is meaningless unless there is also fair trade. And the Japanese don't believe in fair trade at all. You know, there's a reason the Japanese love Reagan. They cleaned up during his presidency. In the name of free trade, he spread our legs real wide."

"Why don't Americans understand this?" I said.

Connor laughed. "Why do they eat hamburgers? It's the way they are, *kōhai*."

From the newsroom, a woman called, "Somebody named Connor here? Call for you from the Four Seasons Hotel."

Connor glanced at his watch and stood up. "Excuse me." He walked out into the newsroom. Through the glass I saw him talking on the phone, making notes.

"You realize," Ron said, "it's all still going on. Why is a Japanese camera cheaper in New York than in Tokyo? You ship it halfway around the world, pay import duty and distribution costs, and it's still cheaper? How is that possible? Japanese tourists buy their own products here because they're cheaper. Meanwhile, American products in Japan cost seventy percent more than here. Why doesn't the American government get tough? I don't know. Part of the answer is up there."

He pointed to the monitor in his office; a distinguished-looking man was talking above a running tickertape. The sound was turned low. "You see that guy? That's David Rawlings. Professor of business at Stanford. Specialist in the Pacific Rim. He's a typical—turn that up, will you? He might be talking about MicroCon."

I turned the knob on the set. I heard Rawlings say: " . . . think American attitudes are completely irrational. After all, Japanese companies are providing jobs for Americans, while American companies are moving jobs offshore, taking them away from their own people. The Japanese can't understand what the complaints are about."

Ron sighed. "Typical bullshit," he said.

On the screen, Professor Rawlings was saying, "I think the American people are rather ungrateful for the help our country is getting from foreign investors."

Ron laughed. "Rawlings is part of the group we call the Chrysanthemum Kissers. Academic experts who deliver the Japanese propaganda line. They don't really have a choice, because they need access to Japan to work, and if they start to sound critical, their contacts in Japan dry up. Doors are closed to them. And in America, the Japanese will whisper in certain ears that the offending person is not to be trusted, or that their views are 'out of date.' Or worse—that they're racist. Anybody who criticizes Japan is a racist. Pretty soon these academics begin to lose speaking engagements and consulting jobs. They know that's happened to their colleagues who step out of line. And they don't make the same mistake."

Connor came back into the room. He said, "Is there anything illegal about this MicroCon sale?"

"Sure," Ron said. "Depending on what Washington decides to do. Akai Ceramics already has sixty percent of the American market. MicroCon will give it a virtual monopoly. If Akai were an American company, the government would block the sale on antitrust grounds. But since Akai is not an American company, the sale isn't scrutinized closely. In the end, it'll probably be allowed."

"You mean a Japanese company can have a monopoly in America but an American company can't?"

"That's the usual outcome these days," Ron said. "But American laws often promote the sale of our companies to foreigners. Like Matsushita buying Universal Studios. Universal's been for sale for years. Several American companies tried to buy it, but couldn't. Westinghouse tried in 1980. No deal: violates antitrust. RCA tried. No deal: violates conflict of interest. But when Matsushita came in, there were no laws against it at all. Recently our laws changed. Under present law, RCA could buy Universal. But back then, no. MicroCon is just the latest example of crazy American regulations."

I said, "But what do American computer companies say about the MicroCon sale?"

Ron said, "American companies don't like the sale. But they don't oppose it, either."

"Why not?"

"Because American companies feel over-regulated by the government already. Forty percent of all American exports are covered by security regulations. Our government doesn't allow our computer companies to sell to Eastern Europe. The cold war is over but the regulations still exist. Meanwhile the Japanese and Germans are selling products like mad. So the Americans want less regulation. And they see any attempt to block the MicroCon sale as government interference."

I said, "It still doesn't make sense to me."

"I agree," Ron said. "The American companies are going to get killed in the next few years. Because if Japan is the sole source of chip-making machines, they're in a position to withhold the machines from American companies."

"Would they do that?"

"They've done it before," Ron said. "Ion implanters and other machines. But the American companies can't get together. They squabble among themselves. And meanwhile the Japanese are buying high-tech companies at the rate of about one every ten days. For the last six years. We're being disemboweled. But our government doesn't pay attention, because we have something called CFIUS—the Committee on Foreign Investment in the United States—that monitors the sale of high-tech companies. Except CFIUS never does anything. Of the last five hundred sales, only one was blocked. Company after company gets sold, and nobody in Washington says boo. Finally, Senator Morton makes a stink, and says 'Wait a minute here.' But nobody's listening to him."

"The sale is going through anyway?"

"That's what I heard today. The Japanese PR machine is hard at work, cranking out favorable publicity. And they are tenacious. They are on top of everything. I mean everything—"

There was a knock at the door, and a blond woman stuck her head in. "Sorry to disturb you, Ron," she said, "but Keith just got a call from the Los Angeles representative for NHK, Japanese national television. He wants to know why our reporter is bashing Japan."

Ron frowned. "Bashing Japan? What's he talking about?"

"He claims our reporter said on air, 'The damn Japanese are taking over this country.' "

"Come on," Ron said. "Nobody would say that—on air. Who's supposed to have said that?"

"Lenny. In New York. Over the backhaul," the woman said.

Ron shifted in his chair. "Uh-oh," he said. "Did you check the tapes?"

"Yeah," she said. "They're tracing the download now in the main control room. But I assume it's true."

"Hell."

I said, "What's the backhaul?"

"Our satellite feed. We pick up segments from New York and Washington every day, and replay them. There's always about a minute before and after that isn't aired. We cut it out, but the raw transmission can be picked up by anybody with a private dish who wants to hunt for our signal. And people do. We warn the talent to be careful what they do in front of a camera. But last year, Louise unbuttoned her blouse and miked herself—and we got calls from all over the country."

Ron's phone rang. He listened for a moment, and said, "Okay. I understand," and hung up. "They checked the tape. Lenny was talking on camera before the feed, and he said to Louise, 'The goddamn Japanese are going to own this country if we don't wise up.' It wasn't on air, but he did say it." He shook his head ruefully. "The NHK guy knows we didn't run it?"

"Yeah. But he's saying it can be picked up and he's protesting on that basis."

"Hell," Ron said. "So they even monitor our backhaul. Jesus. What does Keith want to do?"

"Keith says he's tired of warning New York talent. He wants you to handle it."

"Does he want me to call the NHK guy?"

"He says use your judgment, but we have a deal with NHK for the half-hour show we send them every day and he doesn't want that risked. He thinks you should apologize."

Ron sighed. "Now I have to apologize for what wasn't even on air. God *damn* it." He looked at us. "Guys, I have to go. Was there anything else?"

"No," I said. "Good luck."

"Listen," Ron said. "We all need good luck. You know NHK is starting Global News Network with a billion dollars in capitalization. They're going to take on Ted Turner's CNN around the world. And if past history is any guide . . ." He shrugged. "Kiss the American media goodbye."

As we were leaving, I heard Ron say on the phone, "Mr. Akasaka? Ron Levine, over here at AFN. Yes, sir. Yes, Mr. Akasaka. Sir, I wanted to express my concern and deep apologies about what our reporter said over the satellite—"

We closed the door, and left.

"Where now?" I said.

The Four Seasons Hotel is favored by stars and politicians, and it has a graceful entrance, but we were parked around the corner by the service entrance. A large dairy truck was pulled up to a loading dock, and kitchen staff was unloading cartons of milk. We had been waiting here for five minutes. Connor glanced at his watch.

I said, "Why are we here?"

"We're complying with the Supreme Court, *kōhai*."

At the loading dock, a woman in a business suit came out, looked around, and waved. Connor waved back. She disappeared again. Connor got out his billfold and took out a couple of twenties.

"One of the first things I learned as a detective," Connor said, "is that hotel staff can be extremely helpful. Particularly since the police have so many restrictions these days. We can't go into a hotel room without a warrant. If we did, whatever we found in a search would be inadmissible, right?"

"Right."

"But the maids can go in. Valet and housekeeping and room service can go in."

"Uh-huh."

"So I've learned to maintain contacts at all the big hotels." He opened the door. "I'll only be a moment."

He walked to the loading dock and waited. I tapped the steering wheel with my hands. The words came into my head:

I changed my mind, this love is fine.
Goodness, gracious, great balls of fire.

On the loading dock, a maid in uniform came out, and
talked to Connor briefly. He took notes. She held something
golden in the palm of her hand. He didn't touch it, he just
looked at it, and nodded. She slipped it back in her pocket.
Then he gave her money. She went away.

You shake my nerves and you rattle my brain.
Too much love drives a man insane.
You broke my will, but what a thrill—

A valet came out onto the loading dock, carrying a man's
blue suit on a hanger. Connor asked a question, and the
valet looked at his watch before he answered. Then Connor
crouched down and peered closely at the lower edges of the
suit coat. He opened the jacket and examined the trousers
on the hanger.

The valet took away the first suit, and brought a second
one out onto the dock. This one was a blue pinstripe suit.
Connor repeated his inspection. He seemed to find something on the coat, and scraped it carefully into a small glassine bag. Then he paid the valet and walked back to the car.

I said, "Checking Senator Rowe?"

"Checking a number of things," he said. "But, yes, Senator Rowe."

"Rowe's aide had white panties in his pocket last night.
But Cheryl was wearing black panties."

"That's true," Connor said. "But I think we are making
progress."

"What've you got in the bag?"

He took the little glassine bag out, and held it to the light.
I saw small dark strands through the plastic. "Carpet fibers, I
think. Dark, like the carpet at the Nakamoto conference
room. Have to check with the lab to be sure. Meanwhile, we
have another problem to solve. Start the car."

"Where are we going?"

"Darley-Higgins. The company that owns MicroCon."

In the lobby beside the receptionist, a workman was mounting large gold letters on the wall: DARLEY-HIGGINS INC. Beneath that it read EXCELLENCE IN MANAGEMENT. More workmen were laying carpet in the hallway.

We showed our badges and asked to see the head of Darley-Higgins, Arthur Greiman.

The receptionist had a Southern accent and an upturned nose. "Mr. Greiman is in meetings all day. Is he expecting you?"

"We're here about the MicroCon sale."

"Then you want Mr. Enders, our vice-president for publicity. He speaks to people about MicroCon."

"All right," Connor said.

We sat down on a couch in the reception area. On a couch across the room sat a pretty woman in a tight skirt. She had a roll of blueprints under her arm. The workmen continued to hammer. I said, "I thought the company was in financial trouble. Why're they redecorating?"

Connor shrugged.

The secretary answered the phone, routing the calls. "Darley-Higgins, one moment, please. Darley-Higgins . . . Oh, please hold, Senator . . . Darley-Higgins, yes, thank you . . ."

I picked up a brochure from the coffee table. It was the annual report of Darley-Higgins Management Group, with offices in Atlanta, Dallas, Seattle, San Francisco, and Los Angeles. I found a picture of Arthur Greiman. He looked happy and self-satisfied. The report included an essay signed by him entitled, "A Commitment to Excellence."

The secretary said to us, "Mr. Enders will be right with you."

"Thank you," Connor said.

A moment later, two men in business suits walked out into the hallway. The woman with the blueprints stood. She said, "Hello, Mr. Greiman."

"Hello, Beverly," the older man said. "I'll be with you in a minute."

Connor stood up, too. The secretary immediately said, "Mr. Greiman, these men—"

"Just a minute," Greiman said. He turned to the man with him, who was younger, in his early thirties. "Just make sure you get it straight with Roger," Greiman said.

The younger man was shaking his head. "He won't like it."

"I know he won't. But tell him anyway. Six million four in direct compensation for the CEO is the minimum."

"But Arthur—"

"Just tell him."

"I will, Arthur," the younger man said, smoothing his tie. He lowered his voice. "But the board may balk at raising you above six when company earnings are down so much—"

"We're not talking about *earnings*," Greiman said. "We're talking about compensation. It has nothing to do with earnings. The board has to match current compensation levels for chief executives. If Roger can't bring the board into line on this, I'm going to cancel the March meeting and ask for changes. You tell him *that*."

"Okay, I will, Arthur, but—"

"Just do it. Call me tonight."

"Right, Arthur."

They shook hands. The younger man walked off unhappily. The receptionist said, "Mr. Greiman, these gentlemen—"

Greiman turned to us. Connor said, "Mr. Greiman, we'd

like to speak to you for a minute about MicroCon." And he turned slightly aside, and showed his badge.

Greiman exploded in rage. "Oh, for Christ's sake. Not *again.* This is goddamned *harassment*."

"Harassment?"

"What would you call it? I've had senatorial staffers here, I've had the F.B.I. here. Now I have the L.A. police? We're not criminals. We own a company and we have the right to sell it. Where is Louis?"

The receptionist said, "Mr. Enders is coming."

Connor said calmly, "Mr. Greiman, I'm sorry to disturb you. We have only one question. It'll just take a minute."

Greiman glowered. "What's your question?"

"How many bidders were there for MicroCon?"

"That's none of your business," he said. "Anyway, our agreement with Akai stipulates that we can't discuss the sale publicly in any way."

Connor said, "Was there more than one bidder?"

"Look, you have questions, you talk to Enders. I'm busy." He turned to the woman with blueprints. "Beverly? What have you got for me?"

"I have a revised layout for the boardroom, Mr. Greiman, and tile samples for the washroom. A very nice gray I think you'll like."

"Good, good." He led her down the hallway away from us.

Connor watched them go, and then abruptly turned toward the elevator. "Come on, *kōhai.* Let's get some fresh air."

■☀ "Why does it matter if there were other bidders?" I said, when we were back in the car.

"It goes back to the original question we had," Connor said. "Who wants to embarrass Nakamoto? We know the sale of MicroCon has strategic significance. That's why Congress is upset. But that almost certainly means other parties are upset, too."

"In Japan?"

"Exactly."

"Who will know that?"

"Akai."

The Japanese receptionist tittered when she saw Connor's badge. Connor said, "We would like to see Mr. Yoshida." Yoshida was the head of the company.

"One moment, please." She got up and hurried away, almost running.

Akai Ceramics was located on the fifth floor of a bland office-block in El Segundo. The decor was spare and industrial-looking. From the reception area, we could see into a large space, which was not partitioned: lots of metal desks and people at the phones. The soft click of word processors.

I looked at the office. "Pretty bare."

"All business," Connor said, nodding. "In Japan, ostentation is frowned on. It means you are not serious. When old Mr. Matsushita was the head of the third biggest company in Japan, he still took the regular commercial jet between his head offices in Osaka and Tokyo. He was the head of a fifty-billion-dollar company. But no private jets for him."

As we waited, I looked at the people working at the desks. A handful were Japanese. Most were Caucasian. Everyone wore blue suits. There were almost no women.

"In Japan," Connor said, "if a company is doing poorly, the first thing that happens is the executives cut their own salaries. They feel responsible for the success of the company, and they expect their own fortunes to rise and fall as the company succeeds or fails."

The woman came back, and sat at her desk without speaking. Almost immediately, a Japanese man wearing a blue suit came toward us. He had gray hair, horn-rimmed glasses, and a solemn manner. He said, "Good morning. I am Mr. Yoshida."

Connor made the introductions. We all bowed and exchanged business cards. Mr. Yoshida took each card with both hands, bowing each time, formally. We did the same. I noticed that Connor did not speak Japanese to him.

Yoshida led us to his office. It had windows looking toward the airport. The furnishings were austere.

"Would you like coffee, or tea?"

"No, thank you," Connor said. "We are here in an official capacity."

"I understand." He gestured for us to sit down.

"We would like to talk to you about the purchase of MicroCon."

"Ah, yes. A troubling matter. But I am not aware that it should involve the police."

"Perhaps it doesn't," Connor said. "Can you tell us about the sale, or is the agreement sealed?"

Mr. Yoshida looked surprised. "Sealed? Not at all. It is all very open, and has been from the beginning. We were approached by Mr. Kobayashi, representing Darley-Higgins in Tokyo, in September of last year. That was the first we learned the company was for sale. Frankly, we were surprised that it would be offered. We began negotiations in early October. The negotiating teams had the basis of a rough agreement by mid-November. We proceeded to the final stage of negotiations. But then the Congress raised objections, on November sixteenth."

Connor said, "You said you were surprised that the company would be offered for sale?"

"Yes. Certainly."

"Why is that?"

Mr. Yoshida spread his hands on his desk and spoke slowly. "We understood that MicroCon was a government-owned company. It had been financed in part by funds from the American government. Thirteen percent of capitalization, if I remember. In Japan, that would make it a government-owned company. So naturally we were cautious to enter into negotiations. We do not want to offend. But we received assurance from our representatives in Washington there would be no objection to the purchase."

"I see."

"But now there are difficulties, as we feared. I think now we make a cause for Americans. In Washington, some people are upset. We do not wish this."

"You didn't expect Washington would make objections?"

Mr. Yoshida gave a diffident shrug. "The two countries are different. In Japan we know what to expect. Here, there is always an individual who may have another opinion, and speak it. But Akai Ceramics does not wish a high profile. It is awkward now."

Connor nodded sympathetically. "It sounds as if you want to withdraw."

"Many in the home office criticize me, for not knowing what would happen. But I tell them, it is impossible to know. Washington has no firm policy. It changes every day, according to the politics." He smiled and added. "Or, I would say, that is how it seems to us."

"But you expect the sale to go forward?"

"This I cannot say. Perhaps the criticism from Washington will be too much. And you know the Tokyo government wants to be friends with America. They give pressure on business, not to make purchases that will upset America. Rockefeller Center and Universal Studios, these purchases that make criticism for us. We are told to be *yōjinbukai*. It means . . ."

"Discreet," Connor said.

"Careful. Yes. Wary." He looked at Connor. "You speak Japanese?"

"A little."

Yoshida nodded. For a moment he seemed to consider switching to Japanese, but did not. "We wish to have friendly relations," he said. "These criticisms of us, we feel they are not fair. The Darley-Higgins company has many financial difficulties. Perhaps bad management, perhaps some other reason. I cannot say. But that is not our fault. We are not responsible for that. And we did not seek Micro-Con. It was offered to us. Now we are criticized for trying to help." He sighed.

Outside, a big jet took off from the airport. The windows rattled.

Connor said, "And the other bidders for MicroCon? When did they drop out?"

Mr. Yoshida frowned. "There were no other bidders. The company was privately offered. Darley-Higgins did not wish to make known their financial difficulties. So we cooperated with them. But now . . . the press makes many distortions about us. We feel very . . . *kizu tsuita*. Wounded?"

"Yes."

He shrugged. "That is how we feel. I hope you understand my poor English."

There was a pause. In fact, for the next minute or so, nobody said anything. Connor sat facing Yoshida. I sat beside Connor. Another jet took off, and the windows vibrated again. Still nobody spoke. Yoshida gave a long sigh. Connor nodded. Yoshida shifted in his chair, and folded his hands over his belly. Connor sighed, and grunted. Yoshida sighed. Both men seemed to be entirely focused. Something was taking place, but I was not clear what. I decided it must be this unspoken intuition.

Finally, Yoshida said, "Captain, I wish no misunderstanding. Akai Ceramics is an honorable company. We have no part in any . . . complications that have occurred. Our position is difficult. But I will assist you in whatever way I can."

Connor said, "I am grateful."

"Not at all."

Then Yoshida stood up. Connor stood up. I stood up. We all bowed, and then we all shook hands.

"Please do not hesitate to contact me again, if I can be of assistance."

"Thank you," Connor said.

Yoshida led us to the door to his office. We bowed again, and he opened the door.

Outside was a fresh-faced American man in his forties. I recognized him at once. He was the blond man who had been in the car with Senator Rowe the night before. The man who hadn't introduced himself.

"Ah, Richmond-san," Yoshida said. "Very good luck you are here. These gentlemen are just asking about Micro-Con *baishū*." He turned to us. "Perhaps you will like to talk to Mr. Richmond. His English is much better than mine. He can give you many more details you may wish to know."

"Bob Richmond. Myers, Lawson, and Richmond." His handshake was firm. He was suntanned, and looked as though he played a lot of tennis. He smiled cheerfully. "Small world, isn't it?"

Connor and I introduced ourselves. I said, "Did Senator Rowe get back all right?"

"Oh yes," Richmond said. "Thanks for your help." He smiled. "I hate to think how he's feeling this morning. But I guess it's not the first time." He shifted back and forth on the balls of his feet, like a tennis player waiting for a serve. He looked slightly concerned. "I must say, you two are the last people I ever expected to see here. Is there anything I should know about? I represent Akai in the MicroCon negotiations."

"No," Connor said mildly. "We're just getting general background."

"Is this to do with what happened at Nakamoto last night?"

Connor said, "Not really. Just background."

"If you like, we can talk in the conference room."

"Unfortunately," Connor said, "we're late for an appointment. But perhaps we can talk later."

"You bet," Richmond said. "Happy to. I'll be back in my office in about an hour." He gave us his card.

"That's fine," Connor said.

But Richmond still seemed worried. He walked with us to the elevator. "Mr. Yoshida is from the old school," he said. "I'm sure he was polite. But I can tell you he is furious about what happened with this MicroCon thing. He's taking a lot of heat from Akai Tokyo. And it's very unfair. He really was sandbagged by Washington. He got assurances there would be no objection to the sale, and then Morton pulled the rug out from under him."

Connor said, "Is that what happened?"

"No question about it," Richmond said. "I don't know what Johnny Morton's problem is, but he came right out of left field on this. We made all the proper filings. CFIUS registered no objection until long after the negotiations were concluded. You can't do business like this. I just hope John sees the light, and lets this thing go through. Because at the moment it looks pretty racist."

"Racist? Really?"

"Sure. It's exactly like the Fairchild case. Remember that one? Fujitsu tries to buy Fairchild Semiconductor in eighty-six, but Congress blocks the sale, saying it's against national security. Congress doesn't want Fairchild sold to a foreign company. Couple of years later Fairchild is going to be sold to a French company, and this time there's not a peep from Congress. Apparently, it's okay to sell to a foreign company—just not a *Japanese* company. I'd say that's racist policy, pure and simple." We came to the elevator. "Anyway, call me. I'll make myself available."

"Thank you," Connor said.

We got on the elevator. The doors closed.

"Asshole," Connor said.

I was driving north toward the Wilshire exit, to meet Senator Morton. I said, "Why is he an asshole?"

"Bob Richmond was the assistant trade negotiator for Japan under Amanda Marden until last year. He was privy to all the strategy meetings of the American government. One year later, he turns around and starts working for the Japanese. Who now pay him five hundred thousand a year plus bonuses to close this deal. And he's worth it, because he knows everything there is to know."

"Is that legal?"

"Sure. It's standard procedure. They all do it. If Richmond worked for a high-tech company like Microsoft, he'd have to sign an agreement that he wouldn't work for a competing company for five years. Because you shouldn't be able to peddle trade secrets to the opposition. But our government has easier rules."

"Why is he an asshole?"

"This racist stuff." Connor snorted. "He knows better. Richmond knows exactly what happened with the Fairchild sale. And it had nothing to do with racism."

"No?"

"And there's another thing Richmond knows: the Japanese are the most racist people on earth."

"They are?"

"Absolutely. In fact, when the Japanese diplomats—"

The car phone rang. I pushed the speaker button and said, "Lieutenant Smith."

Over the speaker, a man said, "Jesus, *finally*. Where the hell have you guys been? I want to get to sleep."

I recognized the voice: Fred Hoffmann, the watch commander from the night before.

Connor said, "Thanks for getting back to us, Fred."

"What is it you wanted?"

"Well, I'm curious," Connor said, "about the Nakamoto calls you got last night."

"You and everybody else in this town," Hoffmann said. "I got half the department on my ass about this. Jim Olson is practically camping on my desk, going through the paperwork. Even though it was all routine at the time."

"If you'd just review what happened . . ."

"Sure. First thing, I got the transmittal from metro. That was the original phone-in. Metro wasn't sure what it meant, because the caller had an Asian accent and sounded confused. Or maybe on drugs. He kept talking about 'problems with the disposition of the body.' They couldn't get it clear what he was talking about. Anyway, I dispatched a black and white about eight-thirty. Then when they confirmed a homicide, I assigned Tom Graham and Roddy Merino— for which I got all *kinds* of shit later."

"Uh-huh."

"But what the hell, they were up on the roster next. You know we're supposed to stay in strict rotation for detective assignments. To avoid the appearance of special treatment. That's policy. I was just following it."

"Uh-huh."

"Anyway. Then Graham calls in at nine o'clock, and reports there's trouble at the scene, and there is a request for the Special Services liaison. Again, I check the list. Pete Smith is the SSO on call. So I give Graham his number at home. And I guess he called you, Pete."

"Yes," I said. "He did."

"All right," Connor said. "What happened after that?"

"About two minutes after Graham calls, maybe nine oh-five, I get a call from somebody with an accent. I would say it sounds like an Asian accent, but I don't know for sure.

And the guy says that on behalf of Nakamoto he is requesting Captain Connor be assigned to the case."

"The caller didn't identify himself?"

"Sure he did. I made him identify himself. And I wrote down the name. Koichi Nishi."

"And he was from Nakamoto?"

"That's what he said," Hoffmann said. "I'm just sitting there, working the phone, what the hell do I know. I mean, this morning Nakamoto is formally protesting the fact that Connor was assigned to the case and saying they have nobody named Koichi Nishi employed by them. They're claiming it's all a fabrication. But let me tell you, somebody called me. I'm not making it up."

"I'm sure you're not," Connor said. "You say the caller had an accent?"

"Yeah. His English was pretty good, you know, almost hip, but there was a definite accent. The only thing I thought was funny was that he seemed to know a hell of a lot about you."

"Oh?"

"Yeah. First thing he says to me, do I know your phone number or should he give it to me. I say I know the number. I'm thinking, I don't need some Japanese to tell me the phone numbers of people on the force. Then he says, you know, Captain Connor doesn't always answer his phone. Be sure to send somebody down there to pick him up."

"Interesting," Connor said.

"So I called Pete Smith, and told him to swing by and pick you up. And that's all I knew. I mean, this is all in the context of some political problem they're having at Nakamoto. I knew Graham was unhappy. I figured other people were unhappy, too. And everybody knows Connor has special relationships with the community, so I put it through. And now there is all this shit coming down. Fucking beats me."

"Tell me about the shit," Connor said.

"It starts maybe eleven o'clock last night, when the chief called me about Graham. Why did I assign Graham. I tell him why. But he's still not happy. Then right at the end of my watch, maybe five a.m., there is the business about how Connor got brought in. How did it happen, why did it happen. And now there's a story in the *Times* and this whole thing about racism by the police. I don't know which way to turn here. I keep explaining I did the routine thing. By the book. Nobody is buying that. But it's true."

"I'm sure it is," Connor said. "Just one more thing, Fred. Did you ever listen to the original metro call?"

"Damn right I did. I heard it about an hour ago. Why?"

"Did the voice that called in sound like Mr. Nishi?"

Hoffmann laughed. "Christ. Who knows, Captain. Maybe. You're asking me if one Asian voice sounds like another Asian voice I heard earlier. Honestly, I don't know. The original voice on the call sounded pretty confused. Maybe in shock. Maybe on drugs. I'm not sure. All I know is, whoever Mr. Nishi actually was, he knew a hell of a lot about you."

"Well, that's very helpful. Get some rest." Connor thanked him, and hung up. I pulled off the freeway and headed down Wilshire, to our meeting with Senator Morton.

☀ "Okay, Senator, now look this way, please . . . a little more . . . that's it, that's *very* strong, very *masculine*, I like it a lot. Yes, bloody good. Now I will need three minutes, please." The director, a tense man wearing a bomber jacket and a baseball cap, climbed down off the camera and barked orders in a British accent. "Jerry, get a scrim there, the sun is too bright. And can we do something about his eyes? I need a little fill in the eyes, please. Ellen? You see the shine on his right shoulder. Flag it, love. Pull the collar smooth. The microphone is visible on his tie. And I can't see the gray in his hair. Bring it up. And straighten out the carpeting on the ground so he doesn't trip when he walks, people. *Please*. Come on now. We're losing our lovely light."

Connor and I were standing to one side, with a cute production assistant named Debbie who held a clipboard across her breasts and said meaningfully, "The director is Edgar Lynn."

"Should we recognize that name?" Connor said.

"He's the *most* expensive and *most* sought-after commercial director in the world. He is a *great* artist. Edgar did the *fantastic* Apple 1984 commercial, and . . . oh, lots of others. And he has directed famous movies, too. Edgar is *just* the *best*." She paused. "And not too crazy. Really."

Across from the camera, Senator John Morton stood patiently while four people fussed with his tie, his jacket, his hair, his makeup. Morton was wearing a suit. He was standing under a tree with the rolling golf course and the skyscrapers of Beverly Hills in the background. The production crew had laid down a strip of carpet for him to walk on as he approached the camera.

I said, "And how is the senator?"

Debbie nodded. "Pretty good. I think he has a shot."

Connor said, "You mean a chance for the presidency?"

"Yeah. Especially if Edgar can do his magic. I mean, let's face it, Senator Morton is not exactly *Mel Gibson*, you know what I mean? He's got a big nose, and he's a little bald, and those freckles are a *problem* because they photograph so prominently. They distract you from his eyes. And the eyes are what sell a candidate."

"The eyes," Connor said.

"Oh, yeah. People get elected on their eyes." She shrugged, as if it was common knowledge. "But if the senator puts himself in Edgar's hands . . . Edgar is a great artist. He can make it happen."

Edgar Lynn walked past us, huddled with the cameraman. "Christ, clean up the luggage under his eyes," Lynn said. "And get the chin. Firm that chin with a hard inky low and up."

"Okay," the cameraman said.

The production assistant excused herself and we waited, watching. Senator Morton was still some distance away, being worked over by the makeup and wardrobe people.

"Mr. Connor? Mr. Smith?" I turned. A young man in a blue pinstripe suit was standing beside us. He looked like a Senate staffer: well turned-out, attentive, polite. "I'm Bob Woodson. With the senator's office. Thank you for coming."

"You're welcome," Connor said.

"I know the senator is eager to talk to you," Woodson said. "I'm sorry, this seems to be running a little late. We were supposed to finish shooting by one." He glanced at his watch. "Now, I guess it may be quite a while. But I know the senator wants to talk to you."

Connor said, "Do you know what about?"

Someone shouted, "Run-through! Run-through for sound and camera, please!"

The cluster around Senator Morton vanished, and Woodson turned his attention to the camera.

Edgar Lynn was back looking through the lens. "There still isn't enough gray. Ellen? You will have to add gray to his hair. It isn't reading now."

Woodson said, "I hope he doesn't make him look too old."

Debbie, the production assistant, said, "It's just for the shot. It isn't reading for the shot, so we add some gray. See, Ellen is just putting it at the temples. It'll make him distinguished."

"I don't want him old. Especially when he's tired, he sometimes looks old."

"Don't worry," the assistant said.

"All right now," Lynn said. "That's enough for now. Senator? Shall we try a run-through?"

Senator Morton said, "Where does this begin?"

"Line?"

A script girl said, " 'Perhaps like me . . .' "

Morton said, "Then we've already done the first part?"

Edgar Lynn said, "That's right, love. We start here with your turn to the camera, and you give us a very strong, very direct *masculine* look, and begin 'Perhaps like me.' Right?"

"Okay," Morton said.

"Remember. Think *masculine*. Think *strong*. Think *in control*."

Morton said, "Can we shoot it?"

Woodson said, "Lynn's going to piss him off."

Edgar Lynn said, "All right. Shoot the rehearsal. Here we go."

Senator Morton walked toward the camera. "Perhaps like me," he said, "you're concerned about the erosion of our national position in recent years. America is still the greatest military power, but our security depends on our ability to defend ourselves militarily *and* economically. And it is economically that America has fallen behind. How far behind? Well, under the last two administrations, America has gone from the greatest creditor nation to the greatest debtor nation the world has ever seen. Our industries have fallen behind the rest of the world. Our workers are less educated than workers in other countries. Our investors demand short-term gain and cripple our industries' ability to plan for the future. And as a result, our standard of living is declining rapidly. The outlook for our children is bleak."

Connor murmured, "Somebody is actually saying it."

"And in this time of national crisis," Morton continued, "many Americans have another concern, as well. As our economic power fades, we are vulnerable to a new kind of invasion. Many Americans fear that we may become an economic colony of Japan, or Europe. But especially Japan. Many Americans feel that the Japanese are taking over our industries, our recreation lands, and even our cities." He gestured to the golf course with skyscrapers in the background.

"And in doing so, some fear that Japan now has the power to shape and determine the future of America."

Morton paused, beneath the tree. He gave the appearance of thinking.

"How justified are these fears for the American future? How much should we be concerned? There are some who will tell you foreign investment is a blessing, that it helps our nation. Others take the opposite view, and feel we are selling our precious birthright. Which view is correct? Which should—which is—which—oh, *fuck!* What's the line again?"

"Cut, cut," Edgar Lynn called. "Take five, everybody. I need to clean up a few things, and then we can do it for real. Very good, Senator. I liked it."

The script girl said, " 'Which should we believe for the future of America,' Senator."

He repeated, "Which should we believe for the future of . . ." He shook his head. "No wonder I can't remember it. Let's change that line. Margie? Let's change that line, please. Never mind, bring me a script, I'll change it myself."

And the crowd of makeup and wardrobe people descended on him again, touching him up and fluffing him down.

Woodson said, "Wait here, I'll try and get you a few minutes with him."

We stood beside a humming trailer, with power cables coming out of it. As soon as Morton approached us, two aides came running up, brandishing thick books of computer printout. "John, you better look at this."

"John, you better consider this."

Morton said, "What is it?"

"John, this is the latest Gallup and Fielding."

"John, this is the cross-referenced analysis by voter age-brackets."

"And?"

"Bottom line, John, the president is *right*."

"Don't tell me that. I'm running *against* the president."

"But John, he's right about the C-word. You can't say the C-word in your television ad."

"I can't say 'conservation'?"

"You can't say it, John."

"It's death, John."

"The figures show it."

"You want us to run over the figures, John?"

"No," Morton said. He glanced at Connor and me. "I'll be right with you," he said, with a smile.

"But look here, John."

"It's very clear, John. Conservation means diminution of life-style. People are already experiencing diminution of life-style. They don't want any more of it."

"But that's wrong," Morton said. "That's not how it works."

"John, it's what the voters *think*."

"But they're wrong about this."

"John, you want to educate the voters, well and good."

"Yes, I do want to educate the voters. Conservation is not synonymous with diminution of life-style. It is synonymous with more wealth, power, and freedom. The idea is not to make do with less. The idea is to do all the things you are doing now—heat your house, drive your car—using less gas and oil. Let's have more efficient heaters in our houses, more efficient cars on our streets. Let's have cleaner air, better health. It can be done. Other countries have done it. Japan has done it."

"John, please."

"Not Japan."

"In the last twenty years," Morton said. "Japan cut the energy cost of finished goods by sixty percent. America has done nothing. Japan can now make goods cheaper than we can, because Japan has pushed investment in energy-efficient technology. Conservation is competitive. And we aren't being competitive—"

"Fine, John. Conservation *and* statistics. *Really* boring."

"Nobody cares, John."

"The American people care," Morton said.

"John: they absolutely don't."

"And they aren't going to listen. Look, John. We have age-regressions here, particularly among the over fifty-fives, which is the most solid voting block, and they are straight ahead on this issue. They want no decreases. No conservation. The old people of America don't want it."

"But older people have children, and grandchildren. They must care about the future."

"Older people don't give a flying fuck, John. It's right here in black and white. They think their kids don't care about them, and they're right. So they don't care about their kids. It's that simple."

"But certainly the children—"

"Children don't vote, John."

"Please, John. Listen to us."

"No conservation, John. Competitiveness, yes. Look to the future, yes. Face our problems, yes. A new spirit, yes. But no conservation. Just look at the numbers. Don't do it."

"Please."

Morton said, "I'll think about it, fellas."

The two aides seemed to realize that that was all they were going to get. They closed their printouts with a snap.

"You want us to send Margie over to rewrite?"

"No. I'm thinking about it."

"Maybe Margie should just rough out a few lines."

"No."

"Okay, John. Okay."

"You know," Morton said, as they were leaving, "some day an American politician is going to do what he thinks is right, instead of what the polls tell him. And it's going to look revolutionary."

The two aides turned back together. "John, come on. You're tired."

"It's been a long trip. We understand."

"John. Trust us on this, we have the figures. We are telling you with ninety-five percent confidence intervals how the people feel."

"I know damn well how they feel. They feel frustrated. And I know why. It's been fifteen years since they've had any *leadership*."

"John. Let's not do this one again. This is the twentieth century. Leadership is the quality of telling people what they want to hear."

They walked away.

Immediately, Woodson came up, carrying a portable phone. He started to speak, but Morton held up his hand. "Not now, Bob."

"Senator, I think you need to take this—"

"*Not now.*"

Woodson backed away. Morton glanced at his watch. "You're Mr. Connor and Mr. Smith?"

"Yes," Connor said.

"Let's walk," Morton said. He started away from the film crew, toward a hill overlooking the rolling course. It was Friday. Not many people were playing. We stood about fifty meters from the crew.

"I asked you to come," Morton said, "because I understand you're the officers in charge of the Nakamoto business."

I was about to protest that it wasn't true, that Graham was the officer in charge, when Connor said, "That's true, we are."

"I have some questions about that case. I gather it's been resolved now?"

"It seems to be."

"Is your investigation finished?"

"For all practical purposes, yes," Connor said. "The investigation is concluded."

Morton nodded. "I'm told you officers are particularly knowledgeable about the Japanese community, is that right? One of you has even lived in Japan?"

Connor gave a slight bow.

"You were the one playing golf with Hanada and Asaka today?" Morton said.

"You're well informed."

"I spoke with Mr. Hanada this morning. We have had contact in the past, on other matters." Morton turned abruptly and said, "My question is this. Is the Nakamoto business related to MicroCon?"

"How do you mean?" Connor said.

"The sale of MicroCon to the Japanese has come before the Senate Finance Committee, which I chair. We've been asked for a recommendation by staff from the Committee on Science and Technology, which must actually authorize the sale. As you know, the sale is controversial. In the past I have gone on record as opposing the sale. For a variety of reasons. You're familiar with all this?"

"Yes," Connor said.

"I still have problems about it," Morton said. "Micro-Con's advanced technology was developed in part with American taxpayer money. I'm outraged that our taxpayers should pay for research that is being sold to the Japanese— who will then use it to compete against our own companies. I feel strongly we should be protecting American capacity in high-tech areas. I feel we should be protecting our intellectual resources. I feel we should be limiting foreign investment in our corporations and our universities. But I seem to be alone in this. I can't find support in the Senate or in industry. Commerce won't help me. The trade rep's worried it'll upset the rice negotiations. *Rice*. Even the Pentagon is against me on this. And I just wondered, since Nakamoto is the parent company of Akai Ceramics, whether the events of last night had any relationship to the proposed sale."

He paused. He was looking at us in an intense way. It was almost as if he expected that we would know something.

Connor said, "I'm not aware of any linkage."

"Has Nakamoto done anything unfair or improper to promote the sale?"

"Not that I am aware, no."

"And your investigation is formally concluded?"

"Yes."

"I just want to be clear. Because if I back down on my opposition to this sale, I don't want to find that I've stuck my hand in a box of snakes. One could argue that the party at Nakamoto was an attempt to win over opponents to the sale. So a change of position can be worrisome. You know in Congress they can get you coming and going, with a thing like this."

Connor said, "Are you abandoning your opposition to the sale?"

From across the lawn, an aide said, "Senator? They're ready for you, sir."

"Well." Morton shrugged. "I'm out on a limb with this thing. Nobody agrees with my position on MicroCon. Personally, I think it's another Fairchild case. But if this battle can't be won, I say, let's not fight it. Plenty of other battles to be fought, anyway." He straightened, smoothed his suit.

"Senator? When you're ready, sir." And he added, "They're concerned about the light."

"They're concerned about the light," Morton said, shaking his head.

"Don't let us keep you," Connor said.

"Anyway," Morton said. "I wanted your input. I understand you to say that last night had nothing to do with MicroCon. The people involved had nothing to do with it. I'm not going to read next month that someone was working behind the scenes, trying to promote or block the sale. Nothing like that."

"Not as far as I know," Connor said.

"Gentlemen, thank you for coming," he said. He shook both of our hands, and started away. Then he came back. "I appreciate your treating this matter as confidential. Because, you know, we have to be careful. We are at war with Japan." He smiled wryly. "Loose lips sink ships."

"Yes," Connor said. "And remember Pearl Harbor."

"Christ, that too." He shook his head. He dropped his voice, becoming one of the boys. "You know, I have colleagues who say sooner or later we're going to have to drop another bomb. They think it'll come to that." He smiled. "But I don't feel that way. Usually."

Still smiling, he headed back to the camera crew. As he walked, he collected people, first a woman with script changes, then a wardrobe man, then a sound man fiddling with his microphone and adjusting the battery pack at his waist, and the makeup woman, until finally the senator had disappeared from view, and there was just a cluster of people moving awkwardly across the lawn.

◈ I said, "I like him."

I was driving back into Hollywood. The buildings were hazy in the smog.

"Why shouldn't you like him?" Connor said. "He's a politician. It's his job to make you like him."

"Then he's good at his job."

"Very good, I think."

Connor stared out the window silently. I had the sense that something was troubling him.

I said, "Didn't you like what he was saying in the commercial? It sounded like all the things you say."

"Yes. It did."

"Then what's the matter?"

"Nothing," Connor said. "I was just thinking about what he actually *said*."

"He mentioned Fairchild."

"Of course," Connor said. "Morton knows the real story about Fairchild, very well."

I started to ask him what it was, but he was already telling me.

"Have you ever heard of Seymour Cray? For years, he was the best designer of supercomputers in the world. Cray Research made the fastest computers in the world. The Japanese were trying to catch up with him, but they just couldn't do it. He was too brilliant. But by the mid-eighties, Japanese chip dumping had put most of Cray's domestic suppliers out of business. So Cray had to order his custom-designed chips from Japanese manufacturers. There was nobody in America to make them. And his Japanese suppliers experienced mysterious delays. At one point, it took them a *year* to deliver certain chips he had ordered—and during that time, his Japanese competitors made great strides forward. There was also a question of whether they had stolen his new technology. Cray was furious. He knew they were fucking with him. He decided that he had to form a liaison with an American manufacturer, and so he chose Fairchild Semiconductor, even though the company was financially weak, far from the best. But Cray couldn't trust the Japanese anymore. He had to make do with Fairchild. So now Fairchild was making his next generation of custom chips for him—and then he learned that Fairchild was going to be sold to Fujitsu. His big competitor. It was concern about situations like that, and the national security implications, that led Congress to block the sale to Fujitsu."

"And then?"

"Well, blocking the sale didn't solve Fairchild's financial problems. The company was still in trouble. And it eventually had to be sold. There was a rumor it was going to be bought by Bull, a French company that didn't compete in supercomputers. That sale might have been permitted by Congress. But in the end, Fairchild was sold to an American company."

"And MicroCon is another Fairchild?"

"Yes, in the sense that MicroCon will give the Japanese a monopoly on vital chip-making machinery. Once they have a monopoly, they can withhold the machines from American companies. But now I think—"

That was when the phone rang. I left it on the speakerphone.

It was Lauren. My ex-wife.

"Peter?"

I said, "Hello, Lauren."

"Peter, I am calling to inform you that I'm going to pick up Michelle early today." Her voice sounded tense, formal.

"You are? I didn't know you were picking her up at all."

"I never said that, Peter," she answered quickly. "Of course I'm picking her up."

I said, "Okay, fine. By the way, who's Rick?"

There was a pause. "Really. That is beneath you, Peter."

"Why?" I said. "I'm just curious. Michelle mentioned it this morning. She said he has a black Mercedes. Is he the new boyfriend?"

"Peter. I hardly think that is on the same level."

I said, "The same level as what?"

"Let's not play games," she said. "This is difficult enough. I'm calling to tell you I have to pick up Michelle early because I'm taking her to the doctor."

"Why? She's over her cold."

"I'm taking her for an examination, Peter."

"For what?"

"An *examination*."

"I heard you," I said. "But—"

"The physician who will examine her is Robert Strauss. He is an expert, I'm told. I have been asking people in the office who is the best person. I don't know how this is going to turn out, Peter, but I want you to know I am concerned, particularly in the light of your history."

"Lauren, what are you talking about?"

"I'm talking about child abuse," she said. "I'm talking about sexual molestation."

"What?"

"There's no getting around it, at this point. You know you've been accused of it in the past."

I felt churning nausea. Whenever a relationship goes sour, there's always some residue of resentment, some pockets of bitterness and anger—as well as lots of private things that you know about the other person, that you can use against them. If you choose to do that. Lauren never had.

"Lauren, you know that abuse charge was trumped up. You know everything about that. We were married at the time."

"I only know what you told me." Her voice sounded distant now, moralistic, a little sarcastic. Her prosecutor's voice.

"Lauren, for Christ's sake. This is ridiculous. What's going on?"

"It is not ridiculous. I have my responsibilities as a mother."

"Well, for God's sake, you've never been particularly worried about your responsibilities as a mother before. And now you—"

"It's true that I have a demanding career," she said, in an icy tone, "but there has never been any question that my daughter comes first. And I deeply, *deeply* regret if my past behavior in any way contributed to this unpleasant circumstance now." I had the feeling that she wasn't talking to me. She was rehearsing. Trying out the words to see how they would sound before a judge. "Clearly, Peter, if there is child abuse, Michelle cannot continue to live with you. Or even to see you."

I felt pain in my chest. A wrenching.

"What are you talking about? Who told you there was child abuse?"

"Peter, I don't think it's appropriate for me to comment at this point in time."

"Was it Wilhelm? Who called you, Lauren?"

"Peter, there's no point in going into this. I'm officially notifying you that I'm going to pick Michelle up at four p.m. I want her ready to go at four this afternoon."

"Lauren—"

"I have my secretary, Miss Wilson, listening on the line and making stenographic notes of our conversation. I'm giving you formal notice of my intention to pick up my daughter and take her for a physical examination. Do you have any questions about my decision?"

"No."

"Four o'clock, then. Thank you for your cooperation. And let me add on a personal note, Peter, I'm truly sorry that it has come to this."

And she hung up.

I had been involved in sex abuse cases when I was a detective. I knew how it worked. The fact is, you usually can't determine anything from a physical exam. It's always equivocal. And if a kid is questioned by a psychologist who hammers her with questions, the kid will eventually start to go along, and make up answers to please the psychologist. Normal procedure requires the psychologist to videotape the kids, to prove that the questioning wasn't leading. But the situation is almost always unclear when it finally comes before a judge. And the judge must therefore rule conservatively. Which means, if there is a possibility of abuse, to keep the child away from the accused parent. Or at least, not allow unsupervised visitation. No overnight visits. Or perhaps not even—

"That's enough," Connor said, sitting beside me in the car. "Come back now."

"Sorry," I said. "But it's upsetting."

"I'm sure. Now: what haven't you told me?"

"About what?"

"The molestation charge."

"Nothing. There's nothing to it."

"*Kōhai,*" he said quietly. "I can't help you if you won't tell me."

"It had nothing to do with sexual molestation," I said. "It was something else entirely. It was about money."

Connor said nothing. He just waited. Looking at me.

"Ah, hell," I said.

And I told him.

You have these times in your life when you believe you know what you're doing, but you really don't. Later on, you can look back, and you see you weren't acting right at all. You drifted into something, and you were completely screwed up. But at the time, you thought everything was fine.

What happened to me was, I was in love. Lauren was one of those patrician-acting girls, lean and graceful and understated. She looked like she grew up with horses. And she was younger than me, and beautiful.

I always knew it wouldn't work between us, but I was trying to make it work anyway. We had gotten married and had begun living together and she was starting to be dissatisfied. Dissatisfied with my apartment, where it was located, how much money we had. All of that. She was throwing up, which didn't help. She had crackers in the car, crackers by the bed, crackers everywhere. She was so miserable and so unhappy that I tried to please her in little ways. Get her things. Bring her things. Cook her meals. Do little domestic things. It wasn't my usual way, but I was in love. I was drifting into this habit of pleasing her. Trying to please her.

And there was constant pressure. More this, more that. More money. More, more.

We also had a specific problem. Her health insurance through the D.A.'s office didn't cover pregnancy and neither did mine. After we got married, we couldn't get coverage in time to pay for the baby. It was going to cost eight thousand dollars and we had to come up with it. Neither of us had the money. Lauren's father was a doctor in Virginia but she didn't want to ask him for the money because he disapproved of her marrying me in the first place. My family doesn't have any money. So. There wasn't any money. She worked for the D.A. I worked for the department. She had a lot of debts on her MasterCard and owed money on her car. We had to come up with eight thousand dollars. It's hanging over our heads. How we are going to do this. And it gets to be an unspoken thing, at least from her. That I should handle it.

So one night in August I'm out on a domestic violence call in Ladera Heights. Hispanic couple. They've been drinking and going at it pretty good, she's got a split lip and he's got a black eye, and their kid's screaming in the next room, but pretty soon we calm them down and we can see that nobody is seriously injured, so we're about to leave. And the wife sees we're about to leave. At that point she starts yelling that the husband has been fooling with the daughter. Physically abusing the daughter. When the husband hears this, he looks really pissed, and I think it's bullshit, the wife is just doing something to harass him. But the wife insists we check the daughter, so I go into the kid's room and the kid is about nine months old and screaming red in the face, and I pull the covers back to check for bruises and there I see a kilo of white brick. Under the covers with the kid.

So.

I don't know, it's one of those situations, they're married so she'd have to testify against her husband, there's no probable cause, the search is invalid, on and on. If he's got a halfway decent lawyer he can beat this, no problem. So I go out and call the guy in. I know I can't do anything. All I'm thinking is that if his kid ever got this brick in her mouth, chewed on it, it would kill her. I want to talk to him about that. I figure I'll fuck him over a little. Scare him a little.

So now it's him and me in the kid's room. The wife is still out in the living room with my partner, and suddenly the guy pulls out an envelope two centimeters thick. He cracks it open. I see hundred-dollar bills. An inch thick of hundred-dollar bills. And he says, "Thanks for your help, officer."

There's got to be ten thousand dollars in that envelope. Maybe more. I don't know. The guy holds out the envelope and looks at me. Expecting me to take it.

I say something lame about how it's dangerous to hide shit in a kid's bed. Right away, the guy picks up the brick, puts it on the floor, kicks it out of sight under the bed. Then he says, "You are right. Thank you, officer. I would hate something happens to my daughter." And he holds out the envelope.

So.

Everything is in turmoil. The wife is outside screaming at my partner. The kid is in here screaming at us. The guy is holding the envelope. He smiles and nods. Like, go ahead and take it. It's yours. And I think . . . I don't know what I thought.

Next thing I know, I'm out in the living room and I say everything is fine with the kid, and now the woman starts to scream in her drunken way that *I* abused her child—now it's me, not the husband—and that I am in a conspiracy with the husband, that we are both child abusers. My partner figures she's crazy drunk and we leave, and that's it. My partner says, "You were in that room a while." And I say, "I had to check the kid." And that's it. Except the next day she comes in and makes a formal complaint that I abused her child. She's hung over and she has a record, but even so it's a serious charge and it goes through the system as far as the preliminary, where it gets thrown out as entirely without merit.

That's it.

That's what happened.

That's the whole story.

"And the money?" Connor said.

"I went to Vegas for the weekend. I won big. I paid taxes on thirteen thousand in unearned income that year."

"Whose idea was that?"

"Lauren. She told me how to handle it."

"So she knows what happened?"

"Sure."

"And the department investigation? Did the preliminary board issue a report?"

"I don't think it got that far. They just heard it orally and dismissed it. There's probably a notation in the file, but not an actual report."

"All right," Connor said. "Now tell me the rest."

So I told him about Ken Shubik, and the *Times*, and the Weasel. Connor listened silently, frowning. As I talked, he began to suck air through his teeth, which was the Japanese way of expressing disapproval.

"*Kōhai*," he said, when I finished, "you are making my life extremely difficult. And certainly you make me appear foolish when I should not. Why didn't you tell me this earlier?"

"Because it has nothing to do with you."

"*Kōhai*." He was shaking his head. "*Kōhai* . . ."

I was thinking about my daughter again. About the possibility—just the possibility—that I would not be able to see her—that I would not be able to—

"Look," Connor said, "I told you it could be unpleasant. Take my word for it. It can get much more unpleasant than this. This is only the beginning. It can get *nasty*. We must proceed quickly and try to wrap everything up."

"I thought everything *was* wrapped up."

Connor sighed, and shook his head. "It's not," he said. "And now we must resolve everything before you meet your wife at four o'clock. So let's make sure we are done by then."

✦ "Christ, I'd say it's pretty fucking wrapped up," Graham said. He was walking around Sakamura's house in the Hollywood hills. The last of the SID teams was packing up cases to leave.

"I don't know why the chief has such a bug up his ass on this," Graham said. "The SID boys have been doing most of their work right here, on the spot, because he's in such a rush. But thank God: everything ties up perfect. Sakamura is our boy. We combed his bed for pubic hair—it matches the pubic hair found on the girl. We got dried saliva off his toothbrush. It matches blood type and genetic markers for the sperm inside the dead girl. Matchup is ninety-seven percent sure. It's his come inside her, and his pubic hair on her body. He fucked her and then he killed her. And when we came to arrest him, he panicked, made a break for it, and died as a result. Where is Connor?"

"Outside," I said.

Through the windows, I could see Connor standing down by the garage, talking to policemen in a black-and-white patrol car. Connor was pointing up and down the street; they were answering questions.

"What's he doing down there?" Graham said.

I said I didn't know.

"Damn, I don't understand him. You can tell him the answer to his question is no."

"What question?"

"He called me an hour ago," Graham said. "Said he wanted to know how many pairs of reading glasses we found here. We checked. The answer is, no reading glasses.

268

Lots of sunglasses. Couple of pairs of women's sunglasses. But that's it. I don't know why he cared. Strange man, isn't he? What the hell is he doing now?"

We watched as Connor paced back and forth around the squad car, then pointed up and down the road again. One man was in the car, talking on the radio. "Do you understand him?" Graham said.

"No, I don't."

"He's probably trying to track down the girls," Graham said. "Christ, I wish we had gotten the ID on that redhead. Especially now it's turned out this way. She must have fucked him, too. We could have gotten some sperm from her, and made an exact match with all the factors. And I look like a horse's ass, letting the girls get away. But shit, who knew it was going to go that way. It was all so fast. Naked girls up here, prancing around. A guy gets a little confused. It's natural. Shit, they were good-looking, weren't they?"

I said they were.

"And there's nothing left of Sakamura," Graham said. "I talked to the PEO boys an hour ago. They're downtown, cutting the corpse out of the car, but I guess he's burned beyond identification. The M.E.'s office is going to try, but good luck." He stared unhappily out the window. "You know what? We did the best we could with this fucking case," he said. "And I think we did pretty good. We got the right guy. We did it fast, no fuss no muss. But all I hear now is a lot of Japan-bashing. Fuck. You can't win."

"Uh-huh," I said.

"And *Christ* they have juice now," Graham said. "The heat on my ass is terrific. I got the chief calling me, wanting this thing wrapped up. I got some reporter at the *Times* investigating me, hauling out some old shit about a questionable use of force on a Hispanic back in 1978. Nothing to it. But this reporter, he's trying to show I've always been a racist. And what is the background of his story? That last night was a 'racist' incident. So I am now an example of racism rearing its ugly head again. I tell you. The Japanese are masters of the smear job. It's fucking scary."

"I know," I said.

"They getting to you, too?"

I nodded.

"For what?"

"Child abuse."

"Christ," Graham said. "And you got a daughter."

"Yes."

"Doesn't it piss you off? Innuendo and smear tactics, Petey-san. Nothing to do with reality. But try and tell that to a reporter."

"Who is it?" I asked. "The reporter talking to you."

"Linda Jensen, I think she said."

I nodded. Linda Jensen was the Weasel's protégé. Somebody once said that Linda didn't fuck her way to the top. She fucked other people's reputations to the top. She had been a gossip columnist in Washington before graduating to the big time in Los Angeles.

"I don't know," Graham said, shifting his bulk. "Personally, I think it's not worth it. They're turning this country into another Japan. You've already got people afraid to speak. Afraid to say anything against them. People just won't talk about what's happening."

"It would help if the government passed a few laws."

Graham laughed. "The government. They *own* the government. You know what they spend in Washington every year? Four hundred million fucking dollars a year. That's enough to pay the campaign costs of everybody in the United States Senate *and* the House of Representatives. That is a lot of fucking money. Now you tell me. Would they spend all that money, year after year, if it wasn't paying off for them? Of course they wouldn't. Shit. The end of America, buddy. Hey. Looks like your boss wants you."

I looked out the window. Connor was waving to me.

I said, "I better go."

"Good luck," Graham said. "Listen. I may take a couple of weeks off."

"Yeah? When?"

"Maybe later today," Graham said. "The chief mentioned it. He said as long as the fucking *Times* is on my ass, maybe I should. I'm thinking of a week in Phoenix. I got family there. Anyway, I wanted you to know, I might be going."

"Okay, sure," I said.

Connor was still waving to me. He seemed impatient. I hurried down to see him. As I came down the steps, I saw a black Mercedes sedan pull up, and a familiar figure emerge.

It was Weasel Wilhelm.

By the time I got down there, the Weasel had his notepad and tape recorder out. A cigarette hung from the corner of his mouth. "Lieutenant Smith," he said. "I wonder if I could talk to you."

"I'm pretty busy," I said.

"Come on," Connor called to me. "Time's a'wasting." He was holding the door open for me.

I started toward Connor. The Weasel fell in step with me. He held a tiny black microphone toward my face. "I'm taping, I hope you don't mind. After the Malcolm case, we have to be extra careful. I wonder if you would comment on racial slurs allegedly made by your associate Detective Graham during last night's Nakamoto investigation?"

"No," I said. I kept walking.

"We've been told he referred to them as 'fucking Japs.' "

"I have no comment," I said.

"He also called them 'little Nips.' Do you think that kind of talk is appropriate to an officer on duty?"

"Sorry. I don't have a comment, Willy."

He held the microphone up to my face as we walked. It was annoying. I wanted to slap it away, but I didn't. "Lieutenant Smith, we're preparing a story on you and we have some questions about the Martinez case. Do you remember that one? It was a couple of years back."

I kept walking. "I'm pretty busy now, Willy," I said.

"The Martinez case resulted in accusations of child abuse brought by Sylvia Morelia, the mother of Maria Martinez. There was an internal affairs investigation. I wondered if you had any comment."

"No comment."

"I've already talked to your partner at that time, Ted Anderson. I wondered if you had any comment on that."

"Sorry. I don't."

"Then you aren't going to respond to these serious allegations against you?"

"The only one I know that's making allegations is you, Willy."

"Actually, that's not entirely accurate," he said, smiling at me. "I'm told the D.A.'s office has started an investigation."

I said nothing. I wondered if it was true.

"Under the circumstances, Lieutenant, do you think the court made a mistake in granting you custody of your young daughter?"

All I said was, "Sorry. No comment, Willy." I tried to sound confident. I was starting to sweat.

Connor said, "Come on, come on. No time." I got into the car. Connor said to Wilhelm, "Son, I'm sorry, but we're busy. Got to go." He slammed the car door. I started the engine. "Let's go," Connor said.

Willy stuck his head in the window. "Do you think that Captain Connor's Japan-bashing represents another example of the department's lack of judgment in racially sensitive cases?"

"See you, Willy." I rolled up the window, and started driving down the hill.

"A little faster wouldn't bother me," Connor said.

"Sure," I said. I stepped on the gas.

In the rearview mirror, I saw the Weasel running for his Mercedes. I took the turn faster, tires squealing. "How did that lowlife know where to find us? He monitoring the radio?"

"We haven't been on the radio," Connor said. "You know I'm careful about the radio. But maybe the patrol car phoned in something when we arrived. Maybe we have a bug in this car. Maybe he just figured we'd turn up here. He's a scumbag. And he's connected to the Japanese. He's their plant at the *Times*. Usually the Japanese are a little more classy about who they associate with. But I guess he'll do everything they want done. Nice car, huh?"

"I notice it's not Japanese."

"Can't be obvious," Connor said. "He following us?"

"No. I think we lost him. Where are we going now?"

"U.S.C. Sanders has had enough time screwing around by now."

We drove down the street, down the hill, toward the 101 freeway. "By the way," I said. "What was all that about the reading glasses?"

"Just a small point to be verified. No reading glasses were found, right?"

"Right. Just sunglasses."

"That's what I thought," Connor said.

"And Graham says he's leaving town. Today. He's going to Phoenix."

"Uh-huh." He looked at me. "You want to leave town, too?"

"No," I said.

"Okay," Connor said.

I got down the hill and onto the 101 going south. In the old days it would be ten minutes to U.S.C. Now it was more like thirty minutes. Especially now, right at midday. But there weren't any fast times, anymore. Traffic was always bad. The smog was always bad. I drove through haze.

"You think I'm being foolish?" I said. "You think I should pick up my kid and run, too?"

"It's one way to handle it." He sighed. "The Japanese are masters of indirect action. It's their instinctual way to proceed. If someone in Japan is unhappy with you, they never tell you to your face. They tell your friend, your associate, your boss. In such a way that the word gets back. The Japanese have all these ways of indirect communication. That's why they socialize so much, play so much golf, go drinking in *karaoke* bars. They need these extra channels of communication because they can't come out and say what's on their minds. It's tremendously inefficient, when you think about it. Wasteful of time and energy and money. But since they cannot confront—because confrontation is almost like death, it makes them sweat and panic—they have no other choice. Japan is the land of the end run. They never go up the middle."

"Yeah, but . . ."

"So behavior that seems sneaky and cowardly to Americans is just standard operating procedure to Japanese. It doesn't mean anything special. They're just letting you know that powerful people are displeased."

"Letting me know? That I could end up in court over my daughter? My relationship with my kid could be ruined? My own reputation could be ruined?"

"Well, yes. Those are normal penalties. The threat of social disgrace is the usual way you're expected to know of displeasure."

"Well, I think I know it, now," I said. "I think I get the fucking picture."

"It's not personal," Connor said. "It's just the way they proceed."

"Yeah, right. They're spreading a lie."

"In a sense."

"No, not in a sense. It's a fucking lie."

Connor sighed. "It took me a long time to understand," he said, "that Japanese behavior is based on the values of a farm village. You hear a lot about samurai and feudalism, but deep down, the Japanese are farmers. And if you lived in a farm village and you displeased the other villagers, you were banished. And that meant you died, because no other village would take in a troublemaker. So. Displease the group and you die. That's the way they see it.

"It means the Japanese are exquisitely sensitive to the group. More than anything, they are attuned to getting along with the group. It means not standing out, not taking a chance, not being too individualistic. It also means not necessarily insisting on the truth. The Japanese have very little faith in truth. It strikes them as cold and abstract. It's like a mother whose son is accused of a crime. She doesn't care much about the truth. She cares more about her son. The same with the Japanese. To the Japanese, the important thing is relationships between people. That's the real truth. The factual truth is unimportant."

"Yeah, fine," I said. "But why are they pushing now? What's the difference? This murder is solved, right?"

"No, it's not," Connor said.

"It's not?"

"No. That's why we have all the pressure. Obviously, somebody badly *wants* it to be over. They want us to give it up."

"If they are squeezing me and squeezing Graham—how come they're not squeezing you?"

"They are," Connor said.

"How?"

"By making me responsible for what happens to you."

"How are they making you responsible? I don't see that."

"I know you don't. But they do. Believe me. They do."

I looked at the line of cars creeping forward, blending into the haze of downtown. We passed electronic billboards for Hitachi (#1 IN COMPUTERS IN AMERICA), for Canon (AMERICA'S COPY LEADER), and Honda (NUMBER ONE RATED CAR IN AMERICA!). Like most of the new Japanese ads, they were bright enough to run in the daytime. The billboards cost thirty thousand dollars a day to rent; most American companies couldn't afford them.

Connor said, "The point is the Japanese know they can make it very uncomfortable. By raising the dust around you, they are telling me, 'handle it.' Because they think I can get this thing done. Finish it off."

"Can you?"

"Sure. You want to finish it off now? Then we can go have a beer, and enjoy some Japanese truth. Or do you want to get to the bottom of why Cheryl Austin was killed?"

"I want to get to the bottom."

"Me, too," Connor said. "So let's do it, *kōhai*. I think Sanders's lab will have interesting information for us. The tapes are the key, now."

Phillip Sanders was spinning like a top. "The lab is shut down," he said. He threw up his hands in frustration. "And there's nothing I can do about it. *Nothing*."

Connor said, "When did it happen?"

"An hour ago. Buildings and Grounds came by and told everybody in the lab to leave, and they locked it up. Just like that. There's a big padlock on the front door, now."

I said, "And the reason was?"

"A report that structural weakness in the ceiling has made the basement unsafe and will invalidate the university's insurance if the skating rink comes crashing down on us. Some talk about how student safety comes first. Anyway, they closed the lab, pending an investigation and report by a structural engineer."

"And when will that happen?"

He gestured to the phone. "I'm waiting to hear. Maybe some time next week. Maybe not until next month."

"Next *month*."

"Yeah. Exactly." Sanders ran his hand through his wild hair. "I went all the way to the dean on this one. But the dean's office doesn't know. It's coming from high up in the university. Up where the board of governors knows rich donors who make contributions in multi-million-dollar chunks. The order came from the highest levels." Sanders laughed. "These days, it doesn't leave much mystery."

I said, "Meaning what?"

"You realize Japan is deeply into the structure of American universities, particularly in technical departments. It's happened everywhere. Japanese companies now endow twenty-five professorships at M.I.T., far more than any other nation. Because they know—after all the bullshit stops—that they can't innovate as well as we can. Since they need innovation, they do the obvious thing. They buy it."

"From American universities."

"Sure. Listen, at the University of California at Irvine, there's two floors of a research building that you can't get into unless you have a Japanese passport. They're doing research for Hitachi there. An American university closed to Americans." Sanders swung around, waving his arms. "And around here, if something happens that they don't like, it's just a phone call from somebody to the president of the university, and what can he do? He can't afford to piss the Japanese off. So whatever they want, they get. And if they want the lab closed, it's closed."

I said, "What about the tapes?"

"Everything is locked in there. They made us leave everything."

"Really?"

"They were in a hell of a rush. It was gestapo stuff. Pushing and prodding us to get out. You can't imagine the panic at an American university if it thinks it may lose some funding." He sighed. "I don't know. Maybe Theresa managed to take some tapes with her. You could ask her."

"Where is she?"

"I think she went ice skating."

I frowned. "Ice skating?"

"That's what she said she was going to do. So you could check over there."

And he looked right at Connor. In a particularly meaningful way.

Theresa Asakuma wasn't ice skating. There were thirty little kids in the rink, with a young teacher trying in vain to control them. They looked like fourth graders. Their laughter and yells echoed in the high ceiling of the rink.

The building was almost deserted, the bleachers empty. A handful of fraternity boys sat up in one corner, looking down and punching each other on the shoulder. On our side, up high, near the ceiling, a janitor mopped. A couple of adults who looked like parents stood at the railing, down near the ice. Opposite us, a man was reading a newspaper.

I didn't see Theresa Asakuma anywhere.

Connor sighed. Wearily, he sat on the wooden bleachers and leaned back. He crossed his legs, taking his ease. I stood there, watching him. "What are you doing? She's obviously not here."

"Have a seat."

"But you're always in such a rush."

"Have a seat. Enjoy life."

I sat down next to him. We watched the kids skating around the perimeter of the ice. The teacher was shouting, "Alexander? Alexander! I've told you before. No hitting! Don't you hit her!"

I leaned back against the bleachers. I tried to relax. Connor watched the kids and chuckled. He appeared entirely at ease, without a care in the world.

I said, "Do you think Sanders is right? The Japanese squeezed the university?"

"Sure," Connor said.

"And all that business about Japan buying into American technology? Buying professorships at M.I.T.?"

"It's not illegal. They're supporting scholarship. A noble ideal."

I frowned. "So you think it's okay?"

"No," he said. "I don't think it's okay at all. If you give up control of your own institutions you give up everything. And generally, whoever pays for an institution controls it. If the Japanese are willing to put up the money—and if the American government and American industry aren't—then the Japanese will control American education. You know they already *own* ten American colleges. Own them outright. Bought them for the training of their young people. So that they can be assured of the ability to send young Japanese to America."

"But they already can do that. Lots of Japanese go to American universities."

"Yes. But as usual, the Japanese are planning ahead. They know in the future it may get tougher. They know that sooner or later, there will be a backlash. No matter how diplomatically they play it—and they are in the acquisition phase now, so they're playing it very diplomatically. Because the fact is, countries don't like to be dominated. They don't like to be occupied—economically or militarily. And the Japanese figure some day the Americans will wake up."

I watched the kids skating in the rink. I listened to their laughter. I thought of my daughter. I thought of the four o'clock meeting.

I said, "Why are we sitting here?"

"Because," he said.

So we sat there. The teacher was rounding the kids up now, leading them off the ice. "Skates off here. Skates off here, please. That means you too, Alexander! Alexander!"

"You know," Connor said, "if you wanted to buy a Japanese company, you couldn't do it. The people in the company would consider it shameful to be taken over by foreigners. It would be a disgrace. They would never allow it."

"I thought you could. I thought the Japanese had liberalized their rules."

Connor smiled. "*Technically*. Yes. Technically, you can buy a Japanese company. But as a practical matter, you can't. Because if you want to take over a company, you first have to approach its bank. And get the agreement of the bank. That's what is necessary, in order to proceed. And the bank doesn't agree."

"I thought General Motors owns Isuzu."

"GM owns a third of Isuzu. Not a controlling interest. And yes, there are isolated instances. But overall, foreign investment in Japan has declined by half in the last ten years. One company after another finds the Japanese market just too tough. They get tired of the bullshit, the hassles, the collusion, the rigged markets, the *dangō*, the secret agreements to keep them out. They get tired of the government regulations. The run around. And eventually they give up. They just . . . give up. Most other countries have given up:

Germans, Italians, French. Everybody's getting tired of trying to do business in Japan. Because no matter what they tell you, Japan is closed. A few years ago, T. Boone Pickens bought one-fourth of the stock of a Japanese company, but he couldn't get on the board of directors. Japan is *closed*."

"So what are we supposed to do?"

"The same thing the Europeans are doing," Connor said. "Reciprocity. Tit for tat. One of yours for one of mine. Everybody in the world has the same problem with Japan. It's just a question of what solution works best. The European solution is pretty direct. Works well, at least so far."

On the rink, some teenage girls began to do warmups and a few tentative leaps. Now the schoolteacher was leading her charges along the corridor past us. As she went by, she said, "Is one of you Lieutenant Smith?"

"Yes, ma'am," I said.

One kid said, "Do you have a gun?"

The teacher said, "That woman asked me to tell you that what you're looking for is in the men's locker room."

"It is?" I said.

The kid said, "Can I see it?"

The teacher said, "You know, the Oriental woman? I think she was Oriental."

"Yes," Connor said. "Thank you."

"I want to see the gun."

Another kid said, "Quiet, stupid. Don't you know anything? They're *undercover*."

"I want to see the gun."

Connor and I started walking away. The kids trailed after us, still asking to see our guns. Across the rink, the man with the newspaper looked up curiously. He watched us leave.

"Nothing like an inconspicuous exit," Connor said.

The men's locker room was deserted. I started going through the green metal lockers, one after another, looking for the tapes. Connor didn't bother. I heard him call to me, "Back here."

He was in the rear by the showers. "You found the tapes?"

"No."

He was holding open a door.

We went down a flight of concrete stairs to a landing. There were two doors. One opened onto a below-grade truck entrance. The other went into a dark hallway with wooden beams. "This way," Connor said.

We went down this hallway, crouched over. We were underneath the rink again. We passed throbbing stainless-steel machinery, and then came to a series of doors.

"Do you know where we're going?" I said.

One of the doors was ajar. He pushed it open. The room lights were out, but I could see that we were in the lab. Off in a corner, I saw a faint monitor glow.

We walked toward it.

Theresa Asakuma leaned back from the table, pushed her glasses up on her forehead, and rubbed her beautiful eyes. "It's okay as long as we don't make much noise," she said. "They had a guard outside the main door earlier. I don't know if he's still there."

"A guard?"

"Yeah. They were serious about shutting down the lab. It was spectacular, like a drug bust. It really surprised the Americans."

"And you?"

"I don't have the same expectations about this country."

Connor pointed to the monitor in front of her. It showed a freeze-frame image of the couple, embracing as they moved toward the conference room. The same image, seen from other camera angles, was reproduced on other monitors on the desk. Some of the monitors had superimposed red lines, radiating out from the night lights. "What have you learned from the tapes?"

Theresa pointed to the main screen. "I'm not certain," she said. "To be completely certain, I would have to run 3-D modeling sequences to match the dimensions of the room and keep track of all the light sources, and the shadows cast by all the sources. I haven't done that, and I probably can't with the equipment in this room. It would probably require an overnight run on a mini. Maybe I could get time next week from the astrophysics department. The way things are going, maybe not. But in the meantime, I have a strong feeling."

"Which is?"

"The shadows don't match."

In the darkness, Connor nodded slowly. As if that made sense to him.

I said, "Which shadows don't match?"

She pointed to the screen. "As these people move around the floor, the shadows they cast don't line up exactly. They're in the wrong place, or the wrong shape. Often it's subtle. But I think it is there."

"And the fact that the shadows don't match means . . . ."

She shrugged. "I'd say the tapes have been altered, Lieutenant."

There was a silence. "Altered how?"

"I'm not sure how much has been done. But it seems clear that there was another person in that room, at least part of the time."

"Another person? You mean a third person?"

"Yes. Someone watching. And that third person has been systematically erased."

"No *shit*," I said.

It was making my head spin. I looked at Connor. He was staring intently at the monitors. He seemed completely unsurprised. I said, "Did you already know this?"

"I suspected something of the sort."

"Why?"

"Well, early in the investigation it seemed likely that the tapes were going to be altered."

"Why?" I said.

Connor smiled. "Details, *kōhai*. Those little things we forget." He glanced at Theresa, as if he was reluctant to talk too much in front of her.

I said, "No, I want to hear this. When did you first know the tapes were altered?"

"In the Nakamoto security room."

"Why?"

"Because of the missing tape."

"What missing tape?" I said. He had mentioned it before.

"Think back," Connor said. "In the security room, the guard told us that he changed the tapes when he came on duty, around nine o'clock."

"Yes . . ."

"And the tape recorders all had timers, showing an elapsed time of about two hours. Each recorder started about ten or fifteen seconds later than the previous one. Because that was the time interval it took him to change each tape."

"Right . . ." I remembered all that.

"And I pointed out to him one tape recorder that didn't fit the sequence. Its tape was only running for half an hour. So I asked if it was broken."

"And the guard seemed to think it was."

"Yes. That's what he said. I was letting him off the hook. Actually, he knew perfectly well it was not broken."

"It wasn't?"

"No. It was one of the few mistakes that the Japanese have made. But they only made it because they were stuck—they couldn't get around it. They couldn't beat their own technology."

I leaned back against the wall. I looked apologetically at Theresa. She looked beautiful in the semidarkness of the monitors. "I'm sorry. I'm lost."

"That's because you are rejecting the obvious explanation, *kōhai*. Think back. If you saw a line of tape recorders, each one running a few seconds later than the one before, and you saw one recorder way out of sequence, what would you think?"

"That someone had changed the tape in that one recorder at a later time."

"Yes. And that's exactly what happened."

"One tape was switched later?"

"Yes."

I frowned. "But why? All of the tapes were replaced at nine o'clock. So none of the replacements showed the murder, anyway."

"Correct," Connor said.

"Then why switch one tape after that?"

"Good question. It's puzzling. I couldn't make sense of it for a long time. But now I know," Connor said. "You have to remember the timing. The tapes were all changed at nine.

Then one tape was changed again at ten-fifteen. The obvious assumption was that something important happened between nine o'clock and ten-fifteen, that it was recorded on the tape, and the tape was therefore taken away for some reason. I asked myself: what could this important event be?"

I thought back. I frowned. I couldn't think of anything.

Theresa began to smile and nod, as if something had just amused her. I said, "You know?"

"I can guess," she said, smiling.

"Well," I said. "I'm glad everyone seems to know the answer except me. Because I can't think of anything important being recorded on that tape. By nine o'clock, the yellow barrier was up, isolating the crime scene. The girl's body was on the other side of the room. There were a lot of Japanese standing by the elevators, and Graham was calling me on the phone for help. But nobody actually began an investigation until I got there at about ten. Then we had a lot of back and forth with Ishiguro. I don't think anybody crossed the tape until almost ten-thirty. Say ten-fifteen at the earliest. So if somebody looked at a recording, all it would show is a deserted room, and a girl lying on the table. That's all."

Connor said, "Very good. Except you have forgotten something."

Theresa said, "Did anybody cross the room? Anybody at all?"

"No," I said. "We had the yellow barrier up. Nobody was allowed on the other side of the tape. In fact—"

And then I remembered. "Wait a minute! There was somebody! That little guy with the camera," I said. "He was on the other side of the barrier, taking pictures."

"That's right," Connor said.

"What little guy?" she said.

"A Japanese guy. He was taking pictures. We asked Ishiguro about him. He said his name was, ah . . ."

"Mr. Tanaka," Connor said.

"That's right, Mr. Tanaka. And you asked Ishiguro for the film from his camera." I frowned. "But we never got it."

"No," Connor said. "And frankly, I never thought we would."

Theresa said, "This man was taking pictures?"

"I doubt that he was actually taking pictures," Connor said. "Perhaps he was, because he was using one of those little Canons—"

"The ones that shoot video stills, instead of film?"

"Right. Would there be any use for those, in retouching?"

"There might be," she said. "The images might be used for texture mapping. They'd go in fast, because they were already digitized."

Connor nodded. "Then perhaps he was taking pictures, after all. But it was clear to me that his picture-taking was just an excuse to allow him to walk on the other side of the yellow line."

"Ah," Theresa said, nodding.

I said, "How do you know that?"

"Think back," Connor said.

I had been standing facing Ishiguro when Graham yelled: Aw, Christ, what is this? And I looked back over my shoulder and saw a short Japanese man about ten meters beyond the yellow tape. The man's back was turned to me. He was taking pictures of the crime scene. The camera was very small. It fitted into the palm of his hand.

"Do you remember how he moved?" Connor said. "He moved in a distinctive way."

I tried to recall it. I couldn't.

Graham had gone forward to the tape, saying: For Christ's sake, you can't be in there. This is a goddamned crime scene. You can't take pictures! And there was a general uproar. Graham was yelling at Tanaka, but he continued to be entirely focused on his work, shooting the camera and backing toward us. Despite all the yelling, Tanaka didn't do what a normal person would do—turn around and walk toward the tape. Instead, he backed up to the yellow stripe and, still turned away, ducked his head and went under it.

I said, "He never turned around. He backed up all the way."

"Correct. That is the first mystery. Why would he back up? Now, I think, we know."

"We do?"

Theresa said, "He was repeating the walk of the girl and the killer in reverse, so it would be laid down on videotape and he would have a good record of where the shadows in the room were."

"That's right," Connor said.

I remembered that when I protested, Ishiguro had said to me: This is our employee. He works for Nakamoto Security.

And I had said: This is outrageous. He can't take pictures.

And Ishiguro had explained: But this is for our corporate use.

And meanwhile the man had disappeared in the crowd, slipping through the knot of men at the elevator.

But this is for our corporate use.

"Damn it!" I said. "So Tanaka left us, went downstairs, and removed a single tape, because that tape had a record of his own walk across the room, and the shadows he cast?"

"Correct."

"And he needed that tape to make changes in the original tapes?"

"Correct."

I was finally beginning to understand. "But now, even if we can figure out how the tapes were altered, they won't stand up in a court of law, is that right?"

"That's right," Theresa said. "Any good lawyer will make sure they're inadmissible."

"So the only way to go forward is to get a witness who can testify to what was done. Sakamura might know, but he's dead. So we're stuck unless we can somehow get our hands on Mr. Tanaka. I think we better get him in custody right away."

"I doubt that will ever happen," Connor said.

"Why not? You think they'll keep him from us?"

"No, I don't think they have to. It is very likely that Mr. Tanaka is already dead."

Connor immediately turned to Theresa. "Are you good at your job?"

"Yes," she said.

"Very good?"

"I think so."

"We have little time left. Work with Peter. See what you can extract from the tape. *Gambatte:* try very hard. Trust me that your efforts will be rewarded. In the meantime, I have some calls to make."

I said, "You're leaving?"

"Yes. I'll need the car."

I gave him the keys. "Where are you going?"

"I'm not your *wife*."

"I'm just asking," I said.

"Don't worry about it. I need to see some people." He turned to go.

"But why do you say Tanaka is dead?"

"Well, perhaps he's not. We'll discuss it when there is more time. Right now, we have a lot to finish before four o'clock. That is our true deadline. I think you have surprises in store for you, *kōhai*. Just call it my *chokkan*, my intuition. Okay? You have trouble, or something unexpected, call me on the car phone. Good luck. Now work with this lovely lady. *Urayamashii ne!*"

And he left. We heard the rear door close.

I said to Theresa, "What did he say?"

"He said he envies you." She smiled in the darkness. "Let's begin."

She pressed buttons on the equipment in rapid succession. The tape rolled back to the beginning of the sequence.

I said, "How are we going to do this?"

"There are three basic approaches to learn how video has been doctored. The first is blur and color edges. The second is shadow lines. We can try to work with those elements, but I've been doing that for the last two hours, and I haven't gotten very far."

"And the third method?"

"Reflected elements. I haven't looked at them yet."

I shook my head.

"Basically, reflected elements—REs—are portions of the scene that are reflected within the image itself. Like when Sakamura walks out of the room, and his face is reflected in the mirror. There are almost certainly other reflections in that room. A desk lamp may be chrome, and it may show the people, distorted, as they pass. The walls of the conference room are glass. We may be able to pull a reflection off the glass. A silver paperweight on a desk, with a reflection in it. A glass vase of flowers. A plastic container. Anything shiny enough to make a reflection."

I watched her reset the tapes, and prepare to run forward. Her one good hand moved quickly from one machine to the next as she talked. It was odd to stand next to a woman so beautiful, who was so unselfconscious of her beauty.

"In most images, there is something reflective," Theresa said. "Outside, there are car bumpers, wet streets, glass windowpanes. And inside a room there are picture frames, mirrors, silver candlesticks, chrome table-legs. . . . There's always something."

"But won't they fix the reflections, too?"

"If they have time, yes. Because now there are computer programs to map an image onto any shape. You can map a picture onto a complicated, twisted surface. But it takes time. So. Let's hope they had no time."

She started the tapes forward. The first portion was dark, as Cheryl Austin first appeared by the elevators. I looked at Theresa. I said, "How do you feel about this?"

"What do you mean?"

"Helping us. The police."

"You mean, because I am Japanese?" She glanced at me, and smiled. It was an odd, crooked smile. "I have no illusions about Japanese. Do you know where Sako is?"

"No."

"It is a city—a town, really—in the north. In Hokkaido. A provincial place. There is an American airfield there. I was born in Sako. My father was a *kokujin* mechanic. You know that word, *kokujin*? *Niguro*. A black man. My mother worked in a noodle shop where the air force personnel went. They married, but my father died in an accident when I was two years old. There was a small pension for the widow. So we had some money. But my grandfather took most of it, because he insisted he had been disgraced by my birth. I was *ainoko* and *niguro*. They are not nice words, what he called me. But my mother wanted to stay there, to stay in Japan. So I grew up in Sako. In this . . . *place* . . ."

I heard the bitterness in her voice.

"You know what the *burakumin* are?" she said. "No? I am not surprised. In Japan, the land where everyone is supposedly equal, no one speaks of *burakumin*. But before a marriage, a young man's family will check the family history of the bride, to be sure there are no *burakumin* in the past. The bride's family will do the same. And if there is any doubt, the marriage will not occur. The *burakumin* are the untouchables of Japan. The outcasts, the lowest of the low. They are the descendants of tanners and leather workers, which in Buddhism is unclean."

"I see."

"And I was lower than *burakumin*, because I was deformed. To the Japanese, deformity is shameful. Not sad, or a burden. *Shameful*. It means you have done something wrong. Deformity shames you, and your family, and your community. The people around you wish you were dead. And if you are half black, the *ainoko* of an American big nose . . ." She shook her head. "Children are cruel. And this was a provincial place, a country town."

She watched the tape go forward.

"So I am glad to be here. You Americans do not know in

what grace your land exists. What freedom you enjoy in your hearts. You cannot imagine the harshness of life in Japan, if you are excluded from the group. But I know it very well. And I do not mind if the Japanese suffer a little now, from my efforts with my *one good hand*."

She glared at me. The intensity turned her face to a mask. "Does that answer your question, Lieutenant?"

"Yes," I said. "It does."

"When I come to America, I think the Americans are very foolish about the Japanese—but never mind. Here is the sequence now. You watch the top two monitors. I will watch the bottom three. Look carefully for objects that reflect. Look closely. Here it comes."

I watched the monitors in the darkness.

Theresa Asakuma was feeling bitter about the Japanese, but so was I. The incident with Weasel Wilhelm had made me angry. Angry the way somebody who's scared can be angry. One sentence he had said kept coming back to my mind, again and again.

Under the circumstances, don't you think the court made a mistake in granting you custody of your young daughter?

I never wanted custody. In all the turmoil of the divorce, of Lauren moving out, packing up, this is yours, this is mine—in all that, the last thing I wanted was custody of a seven-month-old baby. Shelly was just starting to move around the living room, holding onto the furniture. She would say "Mama." Her first word. But Lauren didn't want the responsibility and kept saying, "I can't handle it, Peter. I just can't handle it." So I took custody. What else could I do?

But now it was almost two years later. I had changed my life. I had changed my job, my schedule. She was *my* daughter now. And the thought of giving her up was like twisting a knife in my stomach.

Under the circumstances, Lieutenant, don't you think . . .

On the monitor, I watched as Cheryl Austin waited in the darkness for the arrival of her lover. I watched the way she looked around the room.

The court made a mistake . . .

No, I thought, the court didn't make a mistake. Lauren couldn't handle it, and had never been able to handle it. Half the time, she skipped on her weekends. She was too

293

busy to see her own daughter. Once after a weekend she
returned Michelle to me. Michelle was crying. Lauren said,
"I just don't know what to do with her." I checked. Her
diapers were wet and she had a painful rash. Michelle always gets a rash when her diapers aren't changed promptly.

Lauren hadn't changed her diapers often enough during
the weekend. So I changed her, and there were streaks of
shit in Michelle's vagina. She hadn't cleaned her own daughter properly.

Don't you think the court made a mistake?

No, I didn't.

Under the circumstances, don't you think—

"Fuck it," I said.

Theresa stabbed a button, stopped the tapes. The images
froze on the monitors all around us. "What is it?" she said.
"What did you see?"

"Nothing."

She looked at me.

"I'm sorry. I was thinking of something else."

"Don't."

She started the tape again.

On multiple monitors, the man embraced Cheryl Austin.
Images from the different cameras were coordinated in an
eerie way. It was as if we could see all sides of the event—
front and back, top and sides. It was like a moving architec-
tural blueprint.

And it felt creepy, to watch.

My two monitors showed the view from the far end of the
room, and from high above, looking straight down. Cheryl
and her lover were small in one monitor, and in the other
one, I saw only the tops of their heads. But I watched.

Standing alongside me, Theresa Asakuma breathed
slowly, regularly. In and out. I glanced at her.

"Pay attention."

I looked back.

The lovers were in a passionate embrace. The man
pressed Cheryl back against a desk. In my top view, I could
see her face, looking straight up as she lay back. Beside her,
a framed picture on the desk fell over.

"There," I said.

Theresa stopped the tape.

"What?" she said.

"There." I pointed to the framed picture. It lay flat, facing upward. Reflected in the glass, we could see the outline of the man's head as he bent over Cheryl. It was very dark. Just a silhouette.

"Can you get an image from that?" I said.

"I don't know. Let's try."

Her hand moved swiftly across the controls, touching them briefly. "The video image is digital," she said. "It's in the computer now. We'll see what we can do with it." The image began to jump, growing larger in increments as she zoomed in on the picture frame. The image moved past Cheryl's frozen, grainy face, her head thrown back in an instant of passion. Moved down from her shoulder, toward the frame.

As the picture enlarged, it became more grainy. It began to decompose into a pattern of dots, like a newspaper photo held too close to your face. Then the dots themselves enlarged, formed edges, turned into small blocks of gray. Pretty soon I couldn't tell what we were looking at.

"Is this going to work?"

"I doubt it. But there's the edge of the frame, and there's the face."

I was glad she could see it. I couldn't.

"Let's sharpen."

She pressed buttons. Computer menus dropped down, flashed back. The image became crisper. Grittier. But I could see the frame. And the outline of the head.

"Sharpen again."

She did that.

"All right. Now we can adjust our grayscale . . ."

The face in the frame began to emerge from the gloom. It was chilling.

Enlarged so much, the grain was severe—each pupil of the eyes was a single black spot—and we really couldn't see who it was. The man's eyes were open, and his mouth was twisted, distorted in passion, or arousal, or hate. But we couldn't really tell.

Not really.

"Is that a Japanese face?"

She shook her head. "There's not enough detail in the original."

"You can't bring it out?"

"I'll work on it later. But I think, no. It won't ever be there. Let's go on."

The images snapped back into full movement. Cheryl suddenly shoved the man away, pushing his chest with the flat of her hand. The face disappeared from the picture frame.

We were back to the original five views.

The couple broke and she complained, pushing him repeatedly. Her face looked angry. Now that I had seen the man's face reflected in the frame, I wondered if she had become frightened of what she saw. But it was impossible to tell.

The lovers stood in the deserted room, discussed where to go. She was looking around. He nodded his head. She pointed toward the conference room. He seemed to agree or accept.

They kissed, clinched again. There was a familiarity in the way they joined and parted, joined again.

Theresa saw it, too. "She knows him."

"Yes. I'd say."

Still kissing, the couple moved awkwardly toward the conference room. At this point my monitors were no longer very useful. The far camera showed the whole room, and the couple moving laterally across it, from right to left. But the figures were tiny, and difficult to see. They were moving between the desks, heading toward—

"Wait," I said. "What was that?"

She went back, frame by frame.

"There," I said.

I pointed to the image. "See that? What's that?"

As the couple moved across the room, the camera tracked past a large Japanese calligraphy scroll hanging on the wall near the elevator. The scroll was encased in glass. For a brief moment, there was a glint of light in the glass. That was what had caught my eye.

A glint of light.

Theresa frowned. "It's not a reflection from the couple," she said.

"No."

"Let's look."

She began zooming again. The image jumped toward the hanging scroll, growing grittier with each step. The glint enlarged, broke in two fragments. There was a fuzzy spot of light in one corner. And a vertical slit of light, running almost the length of the picture.

"Let's rock it," she said.

She began to make the image go forward and back, one frame at a time. Flipping from one to the other. In one frame, the vertical slit was missing. In the next frame, it was there. The vertical bar lasted for the next ten frames. Then it was gone, never to reappear. But the fuzzy spot in the corner was always present.

"Hmmm."

She pushed in on the spot. Under ever-increasing magnification, it disintegrated until it looked like a cluster of stars from an astronomy picture. But it seemed to have some kind of internal organization. I could almost imagine an X shape to it. I said so.

"Yes," she said. "Let's sharpen."

She did that. The computers worked on the data. The fuzzy cluster resolved itself. Now it looked like Roman numerals.

ΓΙΧ⅃

"What the hell is that?" I said.

She kept working. "Edge trace," she said. The outline of the Roman numerals appeared more clearly.

ΓΙΧ⅃

Theresa continued to try and resolve it. As she worked, in some ways the image seemed to get better, and in some ways, less clear. But eventually we could recognize it.

"It's the reflection of an exit sign," she said. "There's an exit at the far end of the room opposite the elevators, is that right?"

"Yes," I said.

"It's being reflected in the glass of the scroll. That's all it is." She flipped to the next frame. "But this vertical bar of light. That's interesting. See? It appears, and is gone." She ran it back and forth several times.

And then I figured it out.

"There's a fire exit back there," I said. "And a staircase going downstairs. That must be the reflection of the light from the stairwell as someone opens the door and closes it again."

"You mean someone came into the room," she said. "From the back stairs?"

"Yes."

"Interesting. Let's try and see who it is."

She ran the tapes forward. At this high magnification, the grainy image spattered and popped like fireworks on the screen. It was as if the smallest components of the image had a life of their own, their dance independent of the image they assembled to make. But it was exhausting to watch. I rubbed my eyes. "Jesus."

"Okay. *There*."

I looked up. She had frozen the image. I couldn't see anything but erratic black-and-white dots. There seemed to be a pattern but I couldn't tell what it was. It reminded me of the sonograms when Lauren was pregnant. The doctor would say, The head is here, that's the baby's stomach there. . . . But I couldn't see anything. It was just abstract. My daughter still in the womb.

The doctor had said, See? She wiggled her fingers. See? Her heart is beating.

I had seen that. I had seen the heart beating. The little heart and the little ribs.

Under the circumstances, Lieutenant, don't you think—

"See?" Theresa said. "That's his shoulder. That's the outline of the head. Now he is moving forward—see him getting larger?—and now he is standing in that far passageway, looking around the corner. He is cautious. You can see the profile of his nose for a moment as he turns to look. See that? I know it's hard. Watch carefully. Now he is looking at them. He is watching them."

And suddenly, I could see it. The spots seemed to fall into place. I saw a silhouetted man standing in the hallway by the far exit.

He was watching.

Across the room, the lovers were wrapped up in their kiss. They didn't notice the new arrival.

But someone was watching them. It gave me a chill.

"Can you see who he is?"

She shook her head. "Impossible. We are at the limits of everything. I cannot even resolve eyes, a mouth. Nothing."

"Then let's go on."

The tapes snapped back, full speed. I was jarred by the sudden return to normal size and normal movement. I watched as the lovers, kissing passionately, continued to cross the room.

"So now they are being watched," Theresa said. "Interesting. What kind of a girl is this?"

I said, "I believe the term is *torigaru onnai*."

She said, "She is light in her bird? *Tori* what?"

"Never mind. I mean she is a loose woman."

Theresa shook her head. "Men always say things like that. To me, it looks like she loves him, but she is troubled in her mind."

The lovers were approaching the conference room, and Cheryl suddenly twisted away, attempting to break free from the man.

"If she loves him, she's got a strange way of showing it," I said.

"She senses something is wrong."

"Why?"

"I don't know. Perhaps she hears something. The other man. I don't know."

Whatever the reason, Cheryl was struggling with the lover, who now had both arms around her waist and was almost dragging her into the conference room. Cheryl twisted once more at the door, as the man tried to pull her in.

"A good chance here," Theresa said.

The tape froze again.

All the walls of the conference room were glass. Through the outer walls, the lights of the city were visible. But the inner walls, facing the atrium, were dark enough to act as a black mirror. Since Cheryl and her lover were near the inner glass walls, their images were reflected in the glass as they struggled.

Theresa ran the tape forward, frame by frame, looking for an image that might hold up. From time to time, she zoomed in, probed the pixels, zoomed back out. It was difficult. The two people were moving quickly, and they were often blurred. And the lights from the skyscrapers outside sometimes obscured otherwise good images.

It was frustrating.

It was slow.

Stop. Zoom in. Slide around in the image, trying to locate a section that had enough detail. Give up. Go forward again. Stop again.

Finally, Theresa sighed. "It's not working. That glass is murder."

"Then let's keep going."

I saw Cheryl grab the door frame, trying to keep from being pulled into the conference room. The man finally pulled her free, she slid backward with a look of terror on her face, and then she swung her arms back to hit the man. Her purse went flying. Then they were both inside the room. Silhouettes moving quickly, turning.

The man shoved her back against the table, and Cheryl appeared in the camera that aimed straight down on the conference room. Her short blond hair contrasted with the dark wood of the table. Her mood changed again, she stopped struggling for a minute. She had a look of expectation. Excitement. She licked her lips. Her eyes followed the man as he leaned over her. He slid her skirt up her hips.

She smiled, pouted, whispered in his ear.

He pulled her panties away, a quick jerk.

She smiled at him. It was a tense smile, half-aroused, half-pleading.

She was excited by her own fear.

His hands caressed her throat.

☀ Standing in the darkened laboratory, with the hiss of skaters on the ice above, we watched the final violent act, again and again. It played on five monitors, different angles, as her pale legs went up, onto his shoulders, and he crouched over her, hands fumbling at his trousers. With repetition, I noticed small things not seen before. The way she slid down the table to meet him, wiggling her hips. The way his back arched at the moment of penetration. The change in her smile, catlike, knowing. Calculating. How she urged him on, saying something. Her hands around his back, caressing. The sudden change in mood, the flash of anger in her eyes, the abrupt slap. The way she fought him, first to arouse him, and then later, struggling in a different way, because then something was wrong. The way her eyes bulged, and she had a look of real desperation. Her hands pushing his arms, shoving his coat sleeves up, revealing the tiny metallic sparkle of cuff links. The glint of her watch. Her arm falling back, palm open. Five fingers pale against the black of the table. Then a tremor, the fingers twitching, and stillness.

His slowness to understand something was wrong. The way he went rigid for a moment, then took her head in his hand, moved it back and forth, trying to arouse her, before he finally pulled away. Even looking at his back, you could almost feel his horror. He remained slow, as if in a trance. Pacing around the room in aimless half steps, first this way, then that. Trying to recover his wits, to decide what to do.

Each time I saw the sequence repeated, I felt a different way. The first few times, there was a tension, a voyeuristic sensation, itself almost sexual. And then later, I felt progressively more detached, more analytical. As if I was drifting away, moving back from the monitor. And finally, the entire sequence seemed to break down before my eyes, the bodies losing their human identities altogether, becoming abstractions, elements of design, shifting and moving in dark space.

Theresa said, "This girl is sick."

"It looks that way."

"She is not a victim. Not this one."

"Maybe not."

We watched it again. But I no longer knew why we were watching. Finally I said, "Let's go forward, Theresa."

We had been running the sequence to a certain point on the tape counter, and then going back to run again. So we had seen a part of the tape again and again, but we hadn't gone farther. Almost immediately as we went forward, something remarkable happened. The man stopped pacing and looked sharply off to one side—as if he had seen something, or heard something.

"The other man?" I said.

"Perhaps." She pointed to the monitors. "This is the area in the tapes where the shadows do not seem to match up. Now, we know why."

"Something was erased?"

She ran the tape backward. On the side monitor view, we could see the man look up, in the direction of the exit. He gave every appearance that he had seen someone. But he did not appear frightened or guilty.

She zoomed in. The man was just a silhouette. "You can't see anything, can you?"

"Profile."

"What about it?"

"I am looking at the jaw line. Yes. See? The jaw is moving. He is talking."

"Talking to the other man?"

"Or to himself. But he is certainly looking off. And now see? He has sudden new energy."

The man was moving around the conference room. His

behavior purposeful. I remembered how confusing this part had been, when I saw it the night before at the police station. But with five cameras, it was clear. We could see exactly what he was doing. He picked up the panties from the floor.

And then he bent over the dead girl, and removed her watch.

"No kidding," I said. "He took her watch."

I could only think of one reason why: the watch must have an inscription. The man put the panties and the watch in his pocket, and was turning to go, when the image froze again. Theresa had stopped it.

"What is it?" I said.

She pointed to one of the five monitors. "There," she said.

She was looking at the side view, from the overall camera. It showed the conference room as seen from the atrium. I saw the silhouette of the girl on the table, and the man inside the conference room.

"Yeah? So?"

"*There*," she said, pointing. "They forgot to erase that one." In the corner of the screen, I saw a ghostly form. The angle and the lighting were just right to enable us to see him. It was a man.

The third man.

He had come forward, and now was standing in the middle of the atrium, looking toward the killer, inside the conference room. The image of the third man was complete, reflected in the glass. But it was faint.

"Can you get that? Can you make it out?"

"I can try," she said.

The zooms began. She punched in, saw the image decompose. She sharpened it, heightened contrast. The image streaked, and went dull, flat. She coaxed it back, reconstituted it. She moved closer, enlarging it. It was tantalizing. We could almost make an identification.

Almost, but not quite.

"Frame advance," she said.

Now, one by one, the frames clicked ahead. The image of the man was alternately sharper, blurred, sharp.

And then at last, we saw the waiting man clearly.

"No *shit*," I said.

"You know who he is?"

"Yes," I said. "It's Eddie Sakamura."

After that, we made swift progress. We knew, without a doubt, that the tapes had been altered and the identity of the killer had been changed. We watched as the killer came out of the room, and moved toward the exit, with a regretful look back at the dead girl.

I said, "How could they change the killer's face in just a few hours?"

"They have very sophisticated mapping software," she said. "It's by far the most advanced in the world. The Japanese are becoming much better in software. Soon they will surpass the Americans in that, as they already have in computers."

"So they did it with better software?"

"Even with the best software it would be daring to try it. And the Japanese are not daring. So I suspect this particular job was not so hard. Because the killer spends most of his time kissing the girl, or in shadow, so you can't see his face. I am guessing they had the idea very late, as an afterthought, to make a change of identity. Because they saw that they only had to change this part coming up. . . . There, where he passes the mirror."

In the mirror, I saw the face of Eddie Sakamura, clearly. His hand brushing the wall, showing the scar.

"You see," she said, "if they changed that, the rest of the tape could pass. In all the cameras. It was a golden opportunity, and they took it. That is what I think."

On the monitors, Eddie Sakamura went past the mirror, into shadow. She ran it back. "Let's look."

She put up the reflection in the mirror, and step-zoomed

in to the face until it broke into blocks. "Ah," she said. "You see the pixels. You see the regularity. Someone has done some retouching here. Here, on the cheekbone, where there is a shadow beneath his eye. Normally you get some irregularity at the edge between two gray scales. Here, the line is cleaned up. It has been repaired. And let me see—"

The image spun laterally.

"Yes. Here, too."

More blocks. I couldn't tell what she was looking at. "What is it?"

"His right hand. Where the scar is. You see, the scar has been added, you can tell from the way the pixels configure."

I couldn't see it, but I took her word for it. "Then who was the actual killer?"

She shook her head. "It will be difficult to determine. We have searched the reflections and we have not found it. There is a final procedure which I did not try, because it is the easiest of all, but it is also the easiest to change. That is to search the shadow detail."

"Shadow detail?"

"Yes. We can try to do image intensification in the black areas of the picture, in the shadows and the silhouettes. There may be a place where there is enough ambient light to enable us to derive a recognizable face. We can try."

She didn't sound enthusiastic about the prospects.

"You don't think it will work?"

She shrugged. "No. But we might as well try. It is all that is left."

"Okay," I said. "Let's do it."

She started to run the tape in reverse, walking Eddie Sakamura backward from the mirror toward the conference room. "Wait a minute," I said. "What happens after the mirror? We haven't looked at that part."

"I looked earlier. He goes under an overhang, and moves away, toward the staircase."

"Let's see it anyway."

"All right."

The tape ran forward. Quickly, Eddie Sakamura went toward the exit. His face flashed in the mirror as he went past it. The more often I saw it, the more fake that moment looked. It even seemed as if a small delay, a tiny pause, had been added to his movement. To help us make the identification.

Now the killer walked on, into a dark passage leading toward the staircase, which was somewhere around the corner, out of view. The far wall was light, so he was silhouetted. But there was no detail visible in the silhouette. He was entirely dark.

"No," she said. "I remember this part. Nothing here. Too dark. *Kuronbō.* What they used to call me. Black person."

"I thought you said you could do shadow detail."

"I can, but not here. Anyway, I am sure this part has been retouched. They know we will examine the section of tape on either side of the mirror. They know we will go in with pixel microscopes and scan every frame. So they will have fixed that area carefully. And they will blacken the shadows on this person."

"Okay, but even so—"

"Hey!" she said suddenly. "What was that?"

The image froze.

I saw the outline of the killer, walking away toward the white wall in the background, the exit sign above his head.

"Looks like a silhouette."

"Yes, but something is wrong."

She ran the tape backward, slowly.

As I watched, I said, "*Machigai no umi oshete kudasaii.*" It was a phrase I had learned from one of my early classes.

She smiled in the darkness. "I must help you with your Japanese, Lieutenant. Are you asking me if there has been a mistake?"

"Yes."

"The word is *umu,* not *umi. Umi* is ocean. *Umu* means you are asking yes or no about something. And yes, I believe there may have been a mistake."

The tape continued backward, the silhouette of the killer coming back toward us. She sucked in her breath, in surprise.

"There *is* a mistake. I cannot believe it. Do you see it now?"

"No," I said.

She ran the tape forward for me. I watched as the man walked away in silhouette.

"There, do you see it now?"

"No, I'm sorry."

She was becoming irritable. "Pay attention. Look at the shoulder. Watch the shoulder of the man. See how it rises and falls with each step, in a rhythmic way, and then suddenly . . . There! You see it?"

I did. Finally. "The outline seemed to jump. To get bigger."

"Yes. Exactly. To jump bigger." She adjusted the controls. "Quite a lot bigger, Lieutenant. They tried to blend the jump into the up-step, to make it less conspicuous. But they did not try very hard. It is clear anyway."

"And what does that mean?"

"It means they are arrogant," she said. She sounded angry. I couldn't tell why.

So I asked her.

"Yes. Now it pisses me off," she said. She was zooming in on the image, her one hand moving quickly. "It is because they have made an obvious mistake. They expect we will be sloppy. We will not be thorough. We will not be intelligent. We will not be *Japanese*."

"But—"

"Oh, I *hate* them." The image moved, shifted. She was concentrating on the outline of the head, now. "You know Takeshita Noboru?"

I said, "Is that a manufacturer?"

"No. Takeshita was prime minister. A few years ago, he made a joke about visiting American sailors on a Navy ship. He said America is now so poor, the Navy boys cannot afford to come ashore to enjoy Japan. Everything is too expensive for them. He said they could only remain on their ship and give each other AIDS. Big joke in Japan."

"He said that?"

She nodded. "If I was American, and someone said that

to me, I would take this ship away, and tell Japan to go fuck itself, pay for its own defense. You didn't know Takeshita said this?"

"No . . ."

"American news." She shook her head. "Such nothing."

She was furious, working quickly. Her fingers slipped on the controls, the image jumped back, lost definition. "Shit fuck."

"Take it easy, Theresa."

"Fuck, take it easy. We're going to score now!"

She moved in on the silhouetted head, isolating it, then following it, frame by frame. I saw the image jump larger, distinctly.

"You see, that is the join," she said. "That is where the changed image goes back to the original. Here on, it's original material on the tape. This is the original man walking away from us, now."

The silhouette moved toward the far wall. She proceeded frame by frame. Then the outline began to change shape.

"Ah. Okay. Good, what I hoped for . . ."

"What is it?"

"He is taking a last look. A look back at the room. See? The head is turning. There is his nose, and now, the nose is gone again, because he has turned completely. Now he is looking back at us."

The silhouette was dense black.

"Lot of good it does us."

"Watch."

More controls.

"The detail is there," she said. "It is like dark exposure on film. The detail has been recorded, but we cannot see it yet. So. . . . Now I have enhancement. And now I will get the shadow detail. . . . Now!"

And in a sudden, shocking moment, the dark silhouette blossomed, the wall behind flaring white, making a kind of halo around the head. The dark face became lighter, and we could see the face for the first time, distinctly and clearly.

"Huh, white man." She sounded disappointed.

"My God," I said.

"You know who he is?"

"Yes," I said.

The features were twisted with tension, the lip turned up in a kind of snarl. But the identity was unmistakable.

I was looking at the face of Senator John Morton.

I sat back, staring at the frozen image. I heard the hum of the machinery. I heard water dripping into buckets, somewhere in the darkness of the laboratory. I heard Theresa breathing alongside me, panting like a runner who has finished a race.

I sat there and just stared at the screen. Everything fell into place, like a jigsaw puzzle that assembled itself before my eyes.

Julia Young: She has a boyfriend who travels a lot. She's always traveling. New York, Washington, Seattle . . . she meets him. She's madly in love with him.

Jenny, in the TV studio: Morton has a young girlfriend that's driving him crazy. Makes him jealous. Some young girl.

Eddie: She likes to cause trouble, this girl. She likes to make turmoil.

Jenny: I've seen this girl hanging around at parties with some of the Washington types for about six months now.

Eddie: She was a sick girl. She liked pain.

Jenny: Morton heads the Senate Finance Committee. The one that's been having hearings about this MicroCon sale.

Cole, the security guard, in the bar: They have the big guys in their pocket. They own 'em. We can't beat 'em now.

And Connor: Somebody wants this investigation to be over. They want us to give it up.

And Morton: So your investigation is formally concluded?

"Hell," I said.

She said, "Who is he?"

"He's a senator."

"Oh." She looked at the screen. "And why do they care about him?"

"He has a powerful position in Washington. And I think he has something to do with the sale of a company. Maybe other reasons, too."

She nodded.

I said, "Can we print a picture of this?"

"No. We don't have equipment for hard copies. The lab can't afford it."

"Then what can we do? I need something to take with me."

"I can take a Polaroid for you," she said. "Not great, but okay for now." She started poking around the lab, stumbling in the dark. Finally she came back with a camera. She moved close to the screen and shot several copies.

We waited for them to come out, standing in the blue light from the monitors.

"Thanks," I said. "For all your help."

"You are welcome. And I'm sorry."

"Why?"

"I know you expected it would be a Japanese man."

I realized she was speaking for herself. I didn't answer her. The pictures darkened. They were good quality, the image clear. As I slipped them in my pocket, I felt something hard there. I brought it out.

"You have a Japanese passport?" she said.

"No. It's not mine. It's Eddie's." I put it back in my pocket. "I have to go," I said. "I have to find Captain Connor."

"All right." She turned back to the monitors.

"What are you going to do?" I said.

"I will stay, and work more."

I left her, went out the back door, and made my way down the dark passageway to the outside.

Blinking in the harsh daylight, I went to a pay phone and called Connor. He was in the car.

"Where are you?" I said.

"Back at the hotel."

"What hotel?"

"The Four Seasons," Connor said. "It's Senator Morton's hotel."

"What are you doing there?" I said. "Do you know that—"

"*Kōhai*," he said. "Open line, remember? Call yourself a taxi and meet me at 1430 Westwood Boulevard. We will meet there in twenty minutes."

"But how—"

"No more questions." And he hung up.

I looked at the building at 1430 Westwood Boulevard. It had a plain brown facade, just a door with a painted number. On one side was a French bookstore. On the other side was a watch repair place.

I went up and knocked on the door. I noticed a small sign in Japanese characters beneath the numbers.

Nothing happened, so I opened the door. I found myself in an elegant, tiny sushi bar. It had only four seats for customers. Connor was alone there, sitting at the far end. He waved to me. "Say hello to Imae. The best sushi chef in Los Angeles. Imae-san, Sumisu-san."

The chef nodded and smiled. He put something on the shelf before my seat. "*Kore o dōzo, Sumisu-san.*"

I sat down. "*Dōmo, Imae-san.*"

"*Hai.*"

I looked at the sushi. It was some kind of pink fish eggs, with a raw yellow egg yolk sitting on top. I thought it looked revolting.

I turned to Connor.

He said "*Kore o tabetakoto arukai?*"

I shook my head. "Sorry. You lost me."

"You'll have to work on your Japanese, for your new girlfriend."

"What new girlfriend?"

Connor said, "I thought you would thank me. I gave you all that time with her."

"You mean Theresa?"

He smiled. "You can do much worse, *kōhai*. And I gather you have, in the past. Anyway, I asked you if you knew what that was." He pointed to the sushi.

"No, I don't."

"Quail egg and salmon roe," he said. "Good protein. Energy. You need it."

I said, "Do I have to?"

Imae said, "Make you strong for girlfriend." And he laughed. He said something quickly in Japanese to Connor.

Connor replied, and the two had a good laugh.

"What's funny?" I said. But I wanted to change the subject, so I ate the first of the sushi. If you got past the slimy texture, it was actually very good.

Imae said, "Good?"

"Very good," I said. I ate the second one, and turned to Connor. "You know what we found on those tapes? It's unbelievable."

Connor held up his hand. "Please. You must learn the Japanese way to have relaxation. Everything in its place. *Oaisō onegai shimasu.*"

"*Hai, Connor-san.*"

The sushi chef produced the bill, and Connor peeled off money. He bowed and there was a rapid exchange in Japanese.

"We're leaving now?"

"Yes," Connor said. "I've already eaten, and you, my friend, can't afford to be late."

"For what?"

"For your ex-wife, remember? We'd better go to your apartment now, and meet her."

I was driving again. Connor was staring out the window. "How did you know it was Morton?"

"I didn't," Connor said. "At least, not until this morning. But it was clear to me last night that the tape had been altered."

I thought of all the effort that Theresa and I had gone to, all the zooming and inspection and image manipulation.

"You're telling me you just looked at the tape, and you could tell?"

"Yes."

"How?"

"There was one glaring error. Remember when you met Eddie at the party? He had a scar on his hand."

"Yes. It looked like an old burn scar."

"Which hand was it on?"

"Which hand?" I frowned. I thought back to the meeting. Eddie in the cactus garden at night, smoking cigarettes, flicking them away. Eddie turning, moving nervously. Holding the cigarettes. The scar had been on . . . "His left hand," I said.

"That's right," Connor said.

"But the scar appears on the tape, too," I said. "You see it clearly when he walks past the mirror. His hand touches the wall for a moment—"

I stopped.

On the tape, his *right* hand had touched the wall.

"Jesus," I said.

"Yes," Connor said. "They made a mistake. Maybe they got confused about what was a reflection and what wasn't. But I imagine they were working hastily, and they couldn't remember which hand it was, and they just added the scar anyway. Mistakes like that happen."

"So last night, you saw the scar on the wrong hand . . ."

"Yes. And I knew at once that the tape was changed," Connor said. "I had to prepare you to analyze the tape in the morning. So I sent you to SID, to get names of places that would work on the tape. And then I went home to bed."

"But you allowed us to arrest Eddie. Why? You must have known that Eddie wasn't the killer."

"Sometimes, you have to let things play out," Connor said. "It was clear we were meant to think that Eddie killed the girl. So: play it out."

"But an innocent man died," I said.

"I wouldn't call Eddie innocent," Connor said. "Eddie was in this up to his neck."

"And Senator Morton? How did you know it was Morton?"

"I didn't, until he called us in for that little meeting today. Then he gave himself away."

"How?"

"He was smooth. You have to think about what he actually said," Connor said. "Wedged in between all the bullshit, he asked us three times if our investigation was finished. And he asked us if the murder had anything to do with MicroCon. When you think about it, that's a very peculiar question."

"Why? He has contacts. Mr. Hanada. Other people. He told us that."

"No," Connor said, shaking his head. "If you take away all the bullshit, what Senator Morton told us was his train of thought: Is the investigation over? And can you connect it to MicroCon? Because I am now going to change my position on the MicroCon sale."

"Okay . . ."

"But he never explained a crucial point. Why was he changing his position on the MicroCon sale?"

"He told us why," I said. "He had no support, nobody cares."

Connor handed me a Xerox. I glanced at it. It was a page from a newspaper. I gave it back. "I'm driving. Tell me."

"This is an interview Senator Morton gave in *The Washington Post*. He repeats his stand on MicroCon. It's against the interest of national defense and American competitiveness to sell the company. Blah blah. Eroding our technology base and selling off our future to the Japanese. Blah blah. That was his position on Thursday morning. On Thursday night he attends a party in California. By Friday morning, he has a different view of MicroCon. The sale is fine with him. Now you tell me why."

"Jesus," I said. "What are we going to do?"

Because there is a thing about being a policeman. Most of the time, you feel pretty good. But at certain points, it comes back to you that you are just a cop. The truth is, you're pretty far down the ladder. And you are reluctant to take on certain kinds of people, certain kinds of power. It gets messy. It gets out of control. You can have your ass handed to you.

"What do we do?" I said again.

"One thing at a time," Connor said. "Is this your apartment building up here?"

The TV minivans were lined up along the street. There were several sedans with PRESS signs behind the windshield. A knot of reporters stood outside the front door to my apartment, and along the street. Among the reporters I saw Weasel Wilhelm, leaning against his car. I didn't see my ex-wife.

"Keep driving, *kōhai*," Connor said. "Go to the end of the block and turn right."

"Why?"

"I took the liberty of calling the D.A.'s office a while ago. I arranged for you to meet your wife in the park down here."

"You did?"

"I thought it would be better for everybody."

I drove around the corner. Hampton Park was adjacent to the elementary school. At this hour of the afternoon, kids were outside, playing baseball. I drove slowly along the street, looking for a parking place. I passed a sedan with two people inside. There was a man in the passenger seat, smoking a cigarette. There was a woman behind the wheel, drumming her fingers on the dashboard. It was Lauren.

I parked the car.

"I'll wait here," Connor said. "Good luck."

She always favored pale colors. She was wearing a beige suit and a cream silk blouse. Her blond hair was pulled back. No jewelry. Sexy and businesslike at the same time, her particular talent.

We walked along the sidewalk on the edge of the park, looking at the kids playing ball. Neither of us said anything. The man who had come with her waited in the car. A block away, we could see the press clustered outside my apartment.

Lauren looked at them and said, "Jesus *Christ*, Peter. I can't believe you, I really can't. This is very badly handled. This is very insensitive to my position."

I said, "Who told them?"

"Not me."

"Someone did. Someone told them you were coming at four o'clock."

"Well, it wasn't me."

"You just happened to show up with full makeup on?"

"I was in court this morning."

"Okay. Fine."

"Fuck you, Peter."

"I said, fine."

"Such a fucking detective."

She turned, and we walked back the way we had come. Moving away from the press.

She sighed. "Look," she said. "Let's try and be civil about this."

"Okay."

"I don't know how you managed to get yourself into this

319

mess, Peter. I'm sorry, but you're going to have to give up custody. I can't permit my daughter to be raised in a suspect environment. I can't allow that. I have my position to think of. My reputation in the office."

Lauren was always preoccupied with appearances. "Why is the environment suspect?"

"Why? Child abuse is an extremely serious allegation, Peter."

"There's no child abuse."

"The allegations from your past must be dealt with."

"You know all about those allegations," I said. "You were married to me. You know everything about it."

She said stubbornly, "Michelle has to be tested."

"Fine. The exam will be negative."

"At this point, I don't really care what the exam shows. It's gone beyond that, Peter. I'm going to have to get custody. For my peace of mind."

"Oh, for Christ's sake."

"Yes, Peter."

"You don't know what it's like to raise a child. It'll take too much time away from your career."

"I have no choice, Peter. You have left me no choice." Now she sounded long suffering. Martyrdom was always one of her strong suits.

I said, "Lauren, you know the past accusations are false. You're just running with this thing because Wilhelm called you."

"He didn't call *me*. He called the assistant D.A. He called my *boss*."

"Lauren."

"I'm sorry, Peter. But you brought it on yourself."

"Lauren."

"I mean it."

"Lauren, this is very dangerous."

She laughed harshly. "Tell me. You think I don't know how dangerous this is, Peter? This could be my ass."

"What are you talking about?"

"What do you *think* I'm talking about, you son of a bitch?" she said, furiously. "I'm talking about Las Vegas."

I was silent. I didn't follow her line of thought at all.

"Look," she said. "How many times have you been to Las Vegas?"

"Just once."

"And the one time you went, you won big?"

"Lauren, you know all about that—"

"Yes, I do. Clearly I do. And what is the timing of your big winning trip to Las Vegas, and the accusations against you of child abuse? A week apart? Two weeks apart?"

So that was it. She was worried that somebody could put those two things together, that it could be traced back, somehow. And that it would implicate her.

"You should have made another trip, last year."

"I was busy."

"If you remember, Peter, I told you to go every year, for the next couple of years. Establish a pattern."

"I was busy. I had a child to raise."

"Well." She shook her head. "Now we're here."

I said, "What's the problem? They'll never figure it out."

That was when she really exploded. "Never figure it out? They've *already* figured it out. They already *know*, Peter. I'm sure they've already talked to Martinez or Hernandez or whoever that couple is."

"But they can't possibly—"

"For Christ's *sake*. How do you think somebody gets a job as Japanese liaison? How did *you* get the job, Peter?"

I frowned, thinking back. It was more than a year ago. "There was a posting of the job in the department. A list of candidates applied for it . . ."

"Yes. And then what?"

I hesitated. The truth was, I wasn't sure exactly what happened administratively. I had just applied for the job and had forgotten all about it, until it came through. I had been busy in those days. Working in the press section was a hectic job.

"I'll tell you what happens," Lauren said. "The chief of Special Services for the department makes a final determination of appropriate candidates, *in consultation with members of the Asian community*."

"Well, that's probably true, but I don't see—"

"And do you know how long the members of the Asian community take to review the list of candidates? *Three months*, Peter. That's long enough to learn everything about the people on that list. *Everything*. They know everything from the size of your shirt collar to your financial status. And believe me, they know about the allegations of child abuse. And your trip to Las Vegas. And they can put it together. *Anybody* can put it together."

I was going to protest, when I found myself remembering what Ron said earlier in the day: Now they watch the back-haul.

She said, "You're going to stand there and tell me you don't know how all this works? That you weren't paying attention to the process? Christ, Peter, come on. You understood what was involved in that liaison job: *you wanted the money*. Just like everybody else who has anything to do with the Japanese. You know how they make their deals. There's something for everyone. You get something. The department gets something. The chief gets something. Everybody gets taken care of. And in return they get to pick exactly the kind of person they want as a liaison. They know they have a handle on you going in. And now they have a handle on me, too. All because you didn't take your goddamn trip to Las Vegas last year and establish a pattern, the way I told you to."

"So now you think you have to get custody of Michelle?"

She sighed. "At this point, we're just playing out our roles."

She glanced at her watch, and looked toward the reporters. I saw that she was impatient to get on with it, to meet the press and make the speech she had already prepared for herself. Lauren had always had a strong sense of drama.

"Are you sure what your role is, Lauren? Because it's going to get very messy around here in the next few hours. You may not want to be involved."

"I *am* involved."

"No." I took the Polaroid out of my pocket and showed it to her.

"What's this?"

"That's a video frame from the Nakamoto security tapes, taken last night. At the time of the murder of Cheryl Austin."

She frowned at the picture. "You're kidding."

"No."

"You're going with this?"

"We have to."

"You're going to arrest Senator Morton? You're *out* of your *fucking mind*."

"Maybe."

"You'll never see daylight, Peter."

"Maybe."

"They'll bury you so fast and so deep you'll never know what hit you."

"Maybe."

"You can't make this work. You know you can't. In the end, it's only going to harm Michelle."

I didn't say anything to that. I found I liked her less all the time. We walked along, her spike heels clicking on the sidewalk.

Finally she said, "Peter, if you insist on following this reckless course of action, there's nothing I can do. As your friend, I advise you not to. But if you insist, there is nothing I can do to help you."

I didn't answer. I waited and watched her. In the hard sunlight, I saw she was starting to get wrinkles. I saw the dark roots of her hair. The fleck of lipstick on her tooth. She took off her sunglasses and glanced at me, her eyes worried. Then she turned away, looking toward the press. She tapped the sunglasses in the palm of her hand.

"If this is really what's happening, Peter, I think maybe I had better hold off a day and let events take their course."

"All right."

"You understand: I'm not dropping my concerns, Peter."

"I understand."

"But I don't think the question of Michelle's custody should be mixed up in some other, crazy controversy."

"Of course not."

She put her sunglasses back on. "I feel sorry for you, Peter. I really do. At one time you had a promising future in the department. I know you've been mentioned for a position under the chief. But nothing can save you if you do this."

I smiled. "Well."

"You have anything besides photographic evidence?"

"I don't know if I should give you too many details."

"Because if you only have photographic evidence, you have no case, Peter. The D.A. won't touch it. Photographic evidence doesn't fly anymore. It's too easily doctored. The courts know it. If all you have is a picture of this guy doing the crime, it won't wash."

"We'll see."

"Peter," she said. "You are going to lose everything. Your job, your career, your child, everything. Wake up. Don't do it."

She started back toward her car. I walked with her. We didn't say anything. I waited for her to ask how Michelle was, but she never did. It wasn't surprising. She had other things to think about. Finally we arrived at her car, and she went around to the driver's side to get in.

"Lauren."

She looked at me over the top of the car.

"Let's keep it clean for the next twenty-four hours, okay? No well-placed calls to anybody."

"Don't worry," she said. "I never heard any of this. Frankly, I wish I never heard of *you*."

And she got in the car and drove off. As I watched her go, I felt my shoulders drop, and a tension leave me. It was more than the fact that I'd done what I set out to do—I had talked her out of it, at least for a while. It was more than that. There was something else, finally gone.

■ Connor and I went up the rear stairs of my apartment building, avoiding the press. I told him what had happened. He shrugged.

"This was a surprise to you? How the liaisons are chosen?"

"Yeah. I guess I never paid attention."

He nodded. "That's how it happens. The Japanese are very skilled at providing what they call incentives. Originally, the department had qualms about letting outsiders say anything about which officers would be chosen. But the Japanese said they simply wanted to be consulted. Their recommendations wouldn't be binding. And they pointed out that it made sense for them to have some input in the choice of liaisons."

"Uh-huh . . ."

"And just to show they were even-handed, they proposed a contribution to the officers' relief fund, to benefit the whole department."

"How much was that?"

"I think half a million. And the chief was asked to come to Tokyo and consult on criminal record-keeping systems. Three-week trip. One-week stopover in Hawaii. All first class. And lots of publicity, which the chief loves."

We got to the second-floor landing. Went up to the third.

"So," Connor said, "by the time it's all finished, it's rather difficult for the department to ignore the recommendations of the Asian community. Too much is at stake."

"I feel like quitting," I said.

"That's always an option," he said. "Anyway, you got your wife to back off?"

"My ex-wife. She got the point right away. She's a finely tuned political animal, Lauren is. But I had to tell her who the murderer was."

He shrugged. "There's not much she can do in the next couple of hours."

I said, "But what about these pictures? She says they won't stand up in court. And Sanders said the same thing: the day of photographic evidence is over. Do we have any other evidence?"

"I've been working on that," Connor said. "I think we're all right."

"How?"

Connor shrugged.

We came to the back entrance to my apartment. I unlocked the door, and we went into the kitchen. It was empty. I went down the corridor to the front hall. My apartment was quiet. The doors to the living room were closed. But there was the distinct smell of cigarette smoke.

Elaine, my housekeeper, was standing in the front hall, looking out the window at the reporters on the street below. She turned when she heard us. She looked frightened.

I said, "Is Michelle all right?"

"Yes."

"Where is she?"

"Playing in the living room."

"I want to see her."

Elaine said, "Lieutenant, there's something I have to tell you first."

"Never mind," Connor said. "We already know."

He threw open the door to the living room. And I had the biggest shock of my life.

John Morton sat in the makeup chair at the television studio, a Kleenex tucked around his collar, while the girl powdered his forehead. Standing at his side, his aide Woodson said, "This is how they recommend you handle it." He handed a fax to Morton.

"The basic through-line," Woodson said, "is that foreign investment invigorates America. America is made stronger by the influx of foreign money. America has much to learn from Japan."

"And we aren't learning it," Morton said gloomily.

"Well, the argument can be made," Woodson said. "It's a viable position and as you can see, the way Marjorie shaped it, it doesn't read as a change of position so much as a refinement of your previous view. You can skate on this one, John. I don't think it is going to be an issue."

"Is the question even going to come up?"

"I think so. I've told the reporters you are prepared to discuss a modification of your position on MicroCon. How you now favor the sale."

"Who'll ask it?"

"Probably Frank Pierce of the *Times*."

Morton nodded. "He's okay."

"Yeah. Business orientation. Should be fine. You can talk about free markets, fair trade. Lack of national security issues on this sale. All that."

The makeup girl finished, and Morton stood up from the chair.

"Senator, I'm sorry to bother you, but could I have your autograph?"

"Sure," he said.

"It's for my son."

"Sure," he said.

Woodson said, "John, we have a rough assembly of the commercial if you want to see it. It's very rough, but you might like to give comments. I've set it up for you in the next room."

"How much time have I got?"

"Nine minutes to airtime."

"Fine."

He started out the door and saw us. "Good evening, gentlemen," he said. "You need me for anything?"

"Just a short conversation, Senator," Connor said.

"I've got to look at a tape," Morton said. "Then we can talk. But I've only got a couple of minutes . . ."

"That's all right," Connor said.

We followed him into another room, which overlooked the studio below. Down there, on a beige-colored set that said NEWSMAKERS, three reporters were shuffling through their notes and being fitted with microphones. Morton sat in front of a television set, and Woodson plugged in a cassette.

We saw the commercial that was shot earlier in the day. It had a timecode running at the bottom of the frame, and it opened with Senator Morton, looking determined, walking over the golf course.

The basic message was that America had lost its economic competitiveness, and that we had to get it back.

"It's time for all of us to pull together," Morton said, on the monitor. "Everyone from our politicians in Washington, to our leaders of business and labor, to our teachers and children, to all of us in our homes. We need to pay our bills as we go, and cut the government deficit. We need to increase savings. To improve our roads and education. We need a government policy of energy conservation—for our environment, for our children's lungs, and for our global competitiveness."

The camera moved close to the senator's face, for his closing remarks.

"There are some who say that we are entering a new era

of global business," he said. "They say it no longer matters where companies are located, or where things are made. That ideas of national economies are old-fashioned and out of date. To those people, I say—Japan doesn't think so. Germany doesn't think so. The most successful countries in the world today maintain strong national policies for energy conservation, for the control of imports, for promotion of exports. They nourish their industries, protecting them against unfair competition from abroad. Business and government work together to look after their own people and their jobs. And those countries are doing better than America, because those economic policies reflect the real world. Their policies work. Ours don't. We do not live in an ideal world, and until we do, America had better face the truth. We had better build our own brand of hard-nosed economic nationalism. We had better take care of Americans. Because nobody else will.

"I want to make it clear: the industrial giants of Japan and Germany are not the cause of our problems. Those countries are challenging America with new realities—and it is up to us to face those realities, and meet their economic challenge head on. If we do so, our great country will enter an era of unparalleled prosperity. But if we continue as we are, mouthing the ancient platitudes of a free market economy, disaster awaits us. The choice is ours. Join me in choosing to meet the new realities—and to make a better economic future for the American people."

The screen went blank.

Morton sat back. "When does this run?"

"It'll start in nine weeks. Test run in Chicago and the Twin Cities, associated focus groups, any modifications, then the national break in July."

"Long after MicroCon . . ."

"Oh, yes."

"Okay, good. Go with it."

Woodson took the tape, and left the room. Morton turned to us. "Well? What can I do for you?"

Connor waited until the door had closed. Then he said, "Senator, you can tell us about Cheryl Austin."

* * *

There was a pause. Morton looked at each of us. A blank expression came over his face. "Cheryl Austin?"

"Yes, Senator."

"I'm not sure that I know who—"

"Yes, Senator," Connor said. And he handed Morton a watch. It was a woman's gold Rolex.

"Where did you get this?" Morton said. His voice was low now, icy.

A woman knocked on the door. "Six minutes, Senator." She closed the door.

"Where did you get this?" he repeated.

"Don't you know?" Connor said. "You haven't even looked at the back. At the inscription."

"*Where did you get this?*"

"Senator, we'd like you to talk to us about her." He took a glassine bag from his pocket, and set it on the table next to Morton. It contained a pair of women's black panties.

"I have nothing to say to you gentlemen," Morton said. "Nothing at all."

Connor took a videotape from his pocket, and set it next to the senator. "This is a tape from one of five different cameras which recorded the incident on the forty-sixth floor. The tape has been altered, but it was still possible to extract an image that shows who the person with Cheryl Austin was."

"I have nothing to say," Morton said. "Tapes can be edited and changed and then changed again. It doesn't mean anything. This is all lies and baseless allegation."

"I'm sorry, Senator," Connor said.

Morton stood up and began to pace. "I want to impress upon you gentlemen the severity of the charges that you are considering. Tapes can be altered. These particular tapes have been in the custody of a Japanese corporation which, it could be argued, has a wish to exert influence over me. Whatever they may or may not show, I assure you they will not stand up to scrutiny. The public will clearly see this as an attempt to blacken the name of one of the few Americans willing to speak up against the Japanese threat. And as far as I am concerned, you two are pawns in the hands of foreign powers. You don't understand the consequences of your actions. You are making damaging allegations without proof. You have no witnesses to anything that may allegedly have happened. In fact, I would even say—"

"Senator." Connor's voice was soft but insistent. "Before you go any farther, and say anything you may regret, would you look down at the studio? There's somebody there you need to see."

"What is the meaning of this?"

"Just look, Senator. If you would, please."

Snorting angrily, Morton strode to the window and looked down at the studio. I looked too. I saw the reporters swiveling in their chairs, laughing and joking with each other as they waited to ask questions. I saw the moderator, adjusting his tie and clipping on his mike. I saw a workman wiping the shiny sign that said NEWSMAKERS. And in the corner, standing right where we had told him to stand, I saw a familiar figure with his hands in his pockets, looking up at us.

Eddie Sakamura.

Of course Connor had put it all together. When he opened the door to my living room and saw my daughter sitting on the floor, playing with her Tinkertoys with Eddie Sakamura, he hadn't even blinked. He just said, "Hello, Eddie. I was wondering how long it'd take you to get here."

"I've been here all day," Eddie said. He sounded put out. "You guys. Never come here. I wait and wait. Have a peanut butter jelly sandwich with Shelly. You have nice girl, Lieutenant. Cute girl."

"Eddie is funny," my daughter said. "He smokes, Daddy."

"I see that," I said. I felt slow and stupid. I was still trying to understand.

My daughter came over and held her arms up. "Pick me up, Daddy." I picked her up.

"Very nice girl," Eddie said. "We made a windmill. See?" He spun the spokes of the Tinkertoy. "Works."

I said, "I thought you were dead."

"Me?" He laughed. "No. Never dead. Tanaka dead. Mess hell out of my car, too." He shrugged. "I have bad luck with Ferraris."

"So does Tanaka," Connor said.

I said, "Tanaka?"

Michelle said, "Daddy, can I watch Cinderella?"

"Not right now," I said. "Why was Tanaka in the car?"

"Panicky guy," Eddie said. "Very nervous guy. Maybe guilty, too. Must have got scared, I don't know for sure."

Connor said, "You and Tanaka took the tapes."

332

"Yes. Sure. Right after. Ishiguro says to Tanaka: Get the tapes. So Tanaka gets them. Sure. But I know Tanaka, so I go along. Tanaka takes them to some lab."

Connor nodded. "And who went to the Imperial Arms?"

"I know Ishiguro sends some men, to clean up. I don't know who."

"And you went to the restaurant."

"Sure, yes. Then I went to the party. Rod's party. No problem."

"And what about the tapes, Eddie?"

"I told you. Tanaka takes them. I don't know where. He's gone. He works for Ishiguro. For Nakamoto."

"I understand," Connor said. "But he didn't take all the tapes, did he."

Eddie gave a crooked grin. "Hey."

"You kept some?"

"No. Just one. Just a mistake, you know. In my pocket." He smiled.

Michelle said, "Daddy, can I watch Disney channel?"

"Sure," I said. I put her down. "Elaine will help you."

My daughter went away. Connor kept talking to Eddie. Slowly the sequence of events came out. Tanaka had gone off with the tapes, and at some point in the evening, apparently realized that one was missing. He figured it out, Eddie said, and he came back to Eddie's house to collect the missing tape. He had interrupted Eddie with the girls. He had demanded the tape.

"I don't know for sure, but after I talk to you, I figure they set me up. We have a big argument."

"And then the police came. Graham came."

Eddie nodded slowly. "Tanaka-san shit a brick. Hey! He's unhappy Japanese man."

"So you made him tell you everything . . ."

"Oh yeah, Captain. He tells me very fast—"

"And in return you told him where the missing tape was."

"Sure. In my car. I give him the keys. So he can unlock it. He has the keys."

Tanaka had gone into the garage to get the tape. The

patrolmen downstairs ordered him to halt. He started the car and drove off.

"I watch him go, John. Drives like shit."

So it had been Tanaka who was driving the car when it hit the embankment. It was Tanaka who had burned to death. Eddie explained that he hid in the shrubbery behind the swimming pool and waited until everybody left.

"Cold as shit out there," he said.

I said to Connor, "You knew all this?"

"I suspected. The reports of the crash said that the body was badly burned, and that even the glasses had melted."

Eddie said, "Hey, I don't wear glasses."

"Exactly," Connor said. "Even so, I asked Graham to check, the next day. He never found any glasses in Eddie's house. So it couldn't have been Eddie in the car. The next day, when we went to Eddie's house, I had the patrolmen check the license plates on all the cars parked on the street. Sure enough: there was a yellow Toyota sedan, a short distance up the road, registered to Akira Tanaka."

"Hey, pretty good," Eddie said. "Smart."

I said, "Where were you, all this time?"

"At Jasmine's house. Very nice house."

"Who's Jasmine?"

"Redhead number. Very nice woman. Got a Jacuzzi, too."

"But why did you come here?"

Connor said to me, "He had to. You have his passport."

"Right," Eddie said. "And me, I have your business card. You give me. Home address and phone. I need my passport, Lieutenant. I got to go now. So I come here, and wait. And holy shit, all the reporters. Cameras. Everything. So I stay low, play with Shelly." He lit a cigarette, turned nervously. "So. What do you say, Lieutenant? How about you give me my passport? *Netsutuku*. No harm done. I'm dead anyway. Okay?"

"Not just yet," Connor said.

"Come on, John."

"Eddie, you have to do a little job first."

"Hey. What job? I got to go, Captain."

"Just one job, Eddie."

Morton took a deep breath, and turned away from the studio window. I had to admire his self-control. He seemed completely calm. "It appears," he said, "that my options at this moment are somewhat reduced."

"Yes, Senator," Connor said.

He sighed. "You know it was an accident. It really was."

Connor nodded sympathetically.

"I don't know what it was about her," Morton said. "She was beautiful, of course, but it wasn't . . . it wasn't that. I only met her a short time ago. Four, five months ago. I thought she was a nice girl. Texas girl, sweet. But it was . . . one of those things. It just happened. She had this way of getting under your skin. It was crazy. Unexpected. I started to think about her all the time. I couldn't . . . she would call me, when I was on a trip. She would find out when I was on a trip, somehow. And pretty soon, I couldn't tell her to stay away. I couldn't. She always seemed to have money, always had a plane ticket. She was crazy. Sometimes, she would make me so *mad*. It was like my . . . I don't know. Demon. Everything changed when she was around. Crazy. I had to stop seeing her. And eventually I had the feeling she was paid for. Someone was paying her. Someone knew all about her. And me. So I had to stop it. Bob told me. Hell, everybody in the office told me. I couldn't. Finally I did. It was over. But when I came to that reception, there she was. Shit." He shook his head. "It just happened. What a mess."

The girl stuck her head in the door. "Two minutes, Senator. They're asking for you downstairs if you're ready."

Morton said to us, "I'd like to do this first."

"Of course," Connor said.

His self-possession was extraordinary. Senator Morton conducted a televised interview with three reporters for half an hour, without a trace of tension or discomfort. He smiled, cracked jokes, bantered with the reporters. It was as if he had no problems at all.

At one point he said, "Yes, it's true that the British and the Dutch both have larger investments in America than the Japanese. But we can't ignore the reality of targeted, adversarial trade as practiced by Japan—where business and government make a planned attack on some segment of the American economy. The British and Dutch don't operate that way. We haven't lost basic industries to those countries. But we've lost many to Japan. That is a real difference—and that's the reason for concern."

He added, "And, of course, if we want to buy a Dutch or English company, we can. But we can't buy a Japanese company."

The interview continued, but nobody asked him about MicroCon. So he steered it: in reply to a question, he said, "Americans should be able to criticize Japan without being called racists or bashers. Every country has conflicts with other countries. It's inevitable. Our conflicts with Japan should be freely discussed, without these ugly epithets. My opposition to the MicroCon sale has been termed racist, but it is nothing of the sort."

Finally, one reporter asked him about the MicroCon sale. Morton hesitated, then he leaned forward across the table.

"As you know, George, I have opposed the MicroCon sale from the beginning. I still oppose it. It is time for Americans to take steps to preserve the assets of this nation. Its real assets, its financial assets, and its intellectual assets. The MicroCon sale is unwise. My opposition continues. Therefore, I am pleased to say that I have just learned Akai Ceramics has withdrawn its bid to purchase the MicroCon Corporation. I think this is the best solution all around. I applaud Akai for its sensitivity on this matter. The sale will not go forward. I am very pleased."

I said, "What? The bid was withdrawn?"

Connor said, "I guess it is now."

Morton was cheerful as the interview drew to a close. "Since I've been characterized as so critical of Japan, perhaps you'll let me express my admiration for a moment. The Japanese have a wonderful lighthearted side, and it shows up in the most unlikely places.

"You probably know that their Zen monks are expected to write a poem close to the moment of death. It's a very traditional art form, and the most famous poems are still quoted hundreds of years later. So you can imagine, there's a lot of pressure on a Zen *roshi* when he knows he's nearing death and everyone expects him to come up with a great poem. For months, it's all he can think about. But my favorite poem was written by one particular monk who got tired of all the pressure. It goes like this."

And then he quoted this poem.

> *Birth is thus,*
> *Death is thus,*
> *Poem or no poem*
> *What's the fuss?*

All the reporters started laughing. "So let's not take all this Japan business too seriously," Morton said. "That's another thing we can learn from the Japanese."

At the end of the interview, Morton shook hands with the three reporters and stepped away from the set. I saw that Ishiguro had arrived in the studio, very red-faced. He was sucking air through his teeth in the Japanese manner.

Morton said cheerfully, "Ah, Ishiguro-san. I see you have heard the news." And he slapped him on the back. Hard.

Ishiguro glowered. "I am extremely disappointed, Senator. It will not go well from this point." He was clearly furious.

"Hey," Morton said. "You know what? Tough shit."

"We had an *arrangement*," Ishiguro hissed.

"Yes, we did," Morton said. "But you didn't keep your end of it, did you?"

The senator came over to us and said, "I suppose you want me to make a statement. Let me get this makeup off, and we can go."

"All right," Connor said.

Morton walked away, toward the makeup room.

Ishiguro turned to Connor and said, "*Totemo taihenna koto ni narimashita ne.*"

Connor said, "I agree. It is difficult."

Ishiguro hissed through his teeth. "Heads will roll."

"Yours first," Connor said. "*Sō omowa nakai.*"

The senator was walking toward the stairway going up to the second floor. Woodson came over to him, leaned close, and whispered something. The senator threw his arm around his shoulder. They walked arm in arm a moment. Then the senator went upstairs.

Ishiguro said bleakly, "*Konna hazuja nakatta no ni.*"

Connor shrugged. "I am afraid I have little sympathy. You attempted to break the laws of this country and now there is going to be big trouble. *Eraikoto ni naruyo, Ishiguro-san.*"

"We will see, Captain."

Ishiguro turned and gave Eddie a frosty look. Eddie shrugged and said, "Hey, I got no problems! Know what I mean, compadre? You got all problems now." And he laughed.

The floor manager, a heavyset guy wearing a headset, came over. "Is one of you Lieutenant Smith?"

I said I was.

"A Miss Asakuma is calling you. You can take it over there." He pointed to a living-room set. Couch and easy chairs, against a morning city skyline. I saw a blinking telephone by one chair.

I walked over and sat in the chair and picked up the phone. "Lieutenant Smith."

"Hi, it's Theresa," she said. I liked the way she used her first name. "Listen, I've been looking at the last part of the tape. The very end. And I think there may be a problem."

"Oh? What kind of a problem?" I didn't tell her Morton had already confessed. I looked across the stage. The senator had already gone upstairs; he was out of sight. Woodson, his aide, was pacing back and forth at the foot of the stairs, a pale, stricken look on his face. Nervously, he fingered his belt, feeling it through his suit coat.

Then I heard Connor say, "Ah, *shit!*" and he broke into a run, sprinting across the studio toward the stairs. I stood up, surprised, dropped the phone, and followed him. As Connor passed Woodson, he said "You *son of a bitch,*" and then he was taking the stairs two at a time, racing upward. I was right behind him. I heard Woodson say something like, "I *had* to."

When we got to the second floor hallway Connor shouted "Senator!" That was when we heard the single, cracking report. It wasn't loud: it sounded like a chair falling over.

But I knew that it was a gunshot.

SECOND NIGHT

◼ The sun was setting on the *sekitei*. The shadows of the rocks rippled over the concentric circles of raked sand. I sat and stared at the patterns. Connor was somewhere inside, still watching television. I could faintly hear the newscast. Of course, a Zen temple would have a television set on the premises. I was starting to become accustomed to these contradictions.

But I didn't want to watch TV any more. I had seen enough, in the last hour, to know how the media was going to play it. Senator Morton had been under a great deal of stress lately. His family life was troubled; his teenage son had recently been arrested for drunk driving, after an accident in which another teenager had been seriously injured. The senator's daughter was rumored to have had an abortion. Mrs. Morton was not available for comment, although reporters were standing outside the family townhouse in Arlington.

The senator's staff all agreed that the senator had been under enormous pressure lately, trying to balance family life and his own impending candidacy. The senator had not been himself; he had been moody and withdrawn, and in the words of one staffer, "He seemed to have been troubled by something personal."

While no one questioned the senator's judgment, one colleague, Senator Dowling, said that Morton had "become a bit of a fanatic about Japan lately, perhaps an indication of the strain he was under. John didn't seem to think accommodation with Japan was possible anymore, and of course we all know that we have to make an accommodation. Our two nations are now too closely bound together. Unfortunately, none of us could have known the strain he was really under. John Morton was a private man."

I sat watching the rocks in the garden turn gold, then red. An American Zen monk named Bill Harris came out and asked me if I wanted tea, or perhaps a Coke. I said no. He went away. Looking back inside, I saw flickering blue light from the tube. I couldn't see Connor.

I looked back at the rocks in the garden.

The first gunshot had not killed Senator Morton. When we kicked open the bathroom door, he was bleeding from the neck, staggering to his feet. Connor shouted "Don't!" just as Morton put the gun in his mouth and fired again. The second shot was fatal. The gun kicked out of his hands and went spinning across the tile floor of the bathroom. It came to rest near my shoes. There was a lot of blood on the walls.

Then people started screaming. I had turned back and I saw the makeup girl in the doorway, holding her hands to her face and screaming at the top of her lungs. Eventually, when the paramedics came, they sedated her.

Connor and I had stayed until the division sent Bob Kaplan and Tony Marsh. They were the detectives in charge, and we were free to go. I told Bob we'd give statements whenever he wanted them, and we left. I noticed that Ishiguro had already gone. So had Eddie Sakamura.

That had bothered Connor. "That damn Eddie," he said. "Where is he?"

"Who cares?" I said.

"There's a problem with Eddie," Connor said.

"What problem?"

"Didn't you notice how he acted around Ishiguro? He was too confident," Connor said. "*Much* too confident. He should have been frightened and he wasn't."

I shrugged. "You said it yourself, Eddie's crazy. Who knows why he does what he does." I was tired of the case, and tired of Connor's endless Japanese nuances. I said I thought Eddie had probably gone back to Japan. Or to Mexico, where he had said earlier that he wanted to go.

"I hope you're right," Connor said.

He led me toward the rear entrance to the station. Connor said he wanted to leave before the press arrived. We got into our car and left. He directed me to the Zen center. We had been there ever since. I had called Lauren but she was out of the office. I called Theresa at the lab but her line was busy. I called home, and Elaine said that Michelle was fine, and the reporters had all gone. She asked if I wanted her to stay and give Michelle dinner. I said yes, that I might be home late.

And then for the next hour, I watched television. Until I didn't want to watch any more.

It was almost dark. The sand was purple-gray. My body was stiff from sitting, and it was growing chilly. My beeper went off. I was getting a call from the division. Or perhaps it was Theresa. I got up and went inside.

On the television set, Senator Stephen Rowe was expressing sympathy for the bereaved family, and talking about the fact that Senator Morton had been overstressed. Senator Rowe pointed out that the Akai offer had not been withdrawn. The sale was, so far as Rowe knew, still going through, and there would not now be any serious opposition.

"Hmmm," Connor said.

"The sale is back on?" I said.

"It seems it was never off." Connor was obviously worried.

"You don't approve of the sale?"

"I'm worried about Eddie. He was so cocky. It's a question of what Ishiguro will do now."

"Who cares?" I was tired. The girl was dead, Morton was dead, and the sale was going forward.

Connor shook his head. "Remember the stakes," he said. "The stakes are huge. Ishiguro isn't concerned about a sordid little murder, or even the strategic purchase of some high-tech company. Ishiguro is concerned about Nakamoto's reputation in America. Nakamoto has a large corporate presence in America, and it wants it to be larger. Eddie can damage that reputation."

"How?"

He shook his head. "I don't know, for sure."

My beeper went off again. I called in. It was Frank Ellis, the watch officer at division headquarters for the evening.

"Hey, Pete," he said. "We got a call for Special Services. Sergeant Matlovsky, down at vehicle impound. He's asking for language assistance."

"What is it?" I said.

"He says he's got five Japanese nationals down there, demanding to inspect the wrecked vehicle."

I frowned. "What wrecked vehicle?"

"That Ferrari. The one in the high-speed pursuit. Apparently it's pretty ragged: the impact crushed it, and there was a fire. And the body was cut out with torches by the VHDV teams this morning. But the Japanese insist on inspecting the vehicle anyway. Matlovsky can't tell from the paperwork whether it's okay to let somebody look at it or not. You know, whether it's material to an ongoing investigation or not. And he can't speak the language to understand the Japanese. One of the Japanese claims to be related to the deceased. So, you want to go down there and handle it?"

I sighed. "Am I on tonight? I was on last night."

"Well, you're on the board. You traded nights with Allen, looks like."

I dimly remembered. I had traded nights with Jim Allen so he could take his kid to a Kings hockey game. I had agreed to it a week ago, but it seemed like something from my distant past.

"Okay," I said. "I'll handle it."

I went back to tell Connor I had to leave. He listened to the story and suddenly jumped to his feet, "Of course! Of *course!* What was I thinking of? Damn!" He pounded his hand in his fist. "Let's go, *kōhai.*"

"We're going to impound?"

"Impound? Absolutely not."

"Then what are we doing?"

"Oh, damn it, I'm a fool!" he said. He was already heading for the car.

I hurried after him.

* * *

As I pulled up in front of Eddie Sakamura's house, Connor leapt from the car, and raced up the steps. I parked and ran after him. The sky was deep blue. It was almost night.

Connor was taking the steps two at a time. "I blame myself," he said. "I should have seen it earlier. I should have understood what it meant."

"What *what* meant?" I said. I was panting a little, at the top of the steps.

Connor threw open the front door. We went inside. The living room was exactly as I had last seen it, earlier in the day, when I had stood there talking to Graham.

Connor went quickly from room to room. In the bedroom, a suitcase lay open. Armani and Byblos jackets lay on the bed, waiting to be packed. "The little idiot," Connor said. "He should never have come back here."

The pool lights were on outside. They cast a green rippling pattern on the ceiling. Connor went outside.

The body lay face down in the water, naked, floating in the center of the pool, a dark silhouette in the glowing green rectangle. Connor got a skimmer pole and pushed Eddie toward the far edge. We hauled him up onto the concrete lip.

The body was blue and cold, beginning to stiffen. He appeared unmarked.

"They would be careful about that," Connor said.

"About what?"

"About not letting anything show. But I'm sure we can find the proofs . . ." He got out his penlight and peered inside Eddie's mouth. He inspected the nipples, and the genitals. "Yes. There. See the rows of red dots? On the scrotum. And there on the side of the thigh . . ."

"Alligator clips?"

"Yes. For the electric shock coil. *Damn!*" Connor said. "Why didn't he tell me? All that time, when we were driving from your apartment to the television station to see the senator. He could have said something then. He could have told me the truth."

"About what?"

Connor didn't answer me. He was lost in his own thoughts. He sighed. "You know, in the end, we are just *gaijin*. Foreigners. Even in his desperation, we're excluded. And anyway, he probably wouldn't tell us because . . ."

He fell silent. He stared at the corpse. Finally, he slid the body back into the water. It floated out again.

"Let somebody else do the paperwork," Connor said, standing up. "We don't need to be the ones who found the body. It doesn't matter." He watched Eddie drift back to the center of the pool. The head tilted down slightly. The heels bobbed on the surface.

"I liked him," Connor said. "He did favors for me. I even met his family when I was in Japan. Some of his family. Not the father." He watched the body rotate slowly. "But Eddie was okay. And now, I want to *know*."

I was lost. I had no idea what he was talking about, but I didn't think I should say anything. Connor looked angry.

"Come on," he said finally. "We have to move fast. There's only a couple of possibilities. And once again, we have fallen behind events. But if it's the last thing I do, I want to get that son of a bitch."

"What son of a bitch?"

"Ishiguro."

We were driving back to my apartment. "You take the night off," he said.

"I'm going with you," I said.

"No. I'll do this alone, *kōhai*. It's better if you don't know."

"Know what?" I said.

We went on like this for a while. He didn't want to tell me. Finally he said, "Tanaka went to Eddie's house last night because Eddie had the tape. Presumably, the original."

"Right . . ."

"And Tanaka wanted it back. That's why they had an argument. When you and Graham came, and all hell broke loose, Eddie told Tanaka the tape was in the Ferrari. So Tanaka went down there, panicked when he saw the police, and drove the car away."

"Right."

"I always assumed the tape was destroyed in the crash, and the fire."

"Yes . . ."

"But obviously it wasn't. Because Eddie wouldn't dare be so cocky around Ishiguro unless he still had a tape. The tape would be his ace in the hole. He knew it. But he obviously didn't understand how ruthless Ishiguro would be."

"They tortured him for the tape?"

"Yes. But Eddie must have surprised them. He didn't tell them."

"How do you know?"

"Because," Connor said, "otherwise, there wouldn't be

five Japanese nationals asking to inspect the wreck of a
Ferrari in the middle of the night."

"So they're still looking for the tape?"

"Yes. Or evidence of the tape. They may not even know
how many are missing, at this point."

I thought it over.

"What are you going to do?" I said.

"Find the tape," Connor said. "Because it matters. People are dying for that tape. If we can find the original . . ."
He shook his head. "It'll put Ishiguro in deep shit. Which is
just where he belongs."

I pulled up in front of my apartment building. As Elaine
had said, all the reporters were gone. The street was quiet.
Dark.

"I still want to go with you," I said again.

Connor shook his head. "I'm on extended leave," he said.
"You're not. You've got your pension to think of. And
you don't want to know exactly what I am going to do tonight."

"I can guess," I said. "You're going to retrace Eddie's
steps from last night. Eddie left his house and went to stay
with the redhead. Maybe he went somewhere else, too—"

"Look," Connor said. "Let's not waste more time, *kōhai*.
I have some contacts and some people I can lean on. Leave
it at that. If you need me, you can call me on the car
phone. But don't call unless you have to. Because I'll be
busy."

"But—"

"Come on, *kōhai*. Out of the car. Spend a nice night
with your kid. You did a good job, but your job is finished
now."

Finally, I got out of the car.

"*Sayonara*," Connor said, with an ironic wave. And he
drove off.

"Daddy! Daddy!" She ran toward me, arms outstretched.
"Pick me up, Daddy."

I picked her up. "Hi, Shelly."

"Daddy, can I watch *Sleeping Beauty*?"

"I don't know. Have you had dinner yet?"

"She ate two hot dogs and an ice cream cone," Elaine said. She was washing dishes in the kitchen.

"Jeez," I said. "I thought we were going to stop feeding her junk food."

"Well, it's all she would eat," Elaine said. She was irritable. It was the end of a long day with a two-year-old.

"Daddy, can I watch *Sleeping Beauty*?"

"Just a minute, Shelly, I'm talking to Elaine."

"I tried that soup," Elaine said, "but she wouldn't touch it. She wanted a hot dog."

"Daddy, can I watch Disney channel?"

"Michelle," I said.

Elaine said, "So I thought it was better that she eat something. I think she was thrown off. You know, the reporters and everything. All the excitement."

"Daddy? Can I? *Sleeping Beauty*?" She was squirming in my arms. Patting my face to get my attention.

"Okay, Shel."

"Now, Daddy?"

"Okay."

I put her down. She ran into the living room and turned on the TV, pushing the remote without hesitation. "I think she watches too much television."

"They all do," Elaine said, shrugging.

"Daddy?"

I went into the living room and plugged in the cassette. I fast-forwarded to the credits, then let it run.

"Not this part," she said impatiently.

So I fast-forwarded to the beginning of the action. Pages turning in a book.

"This part, this part," she said, tugging at my hand.

I let the tape run at normal speed. Michelle sat in the chair and started sucking her thumb. She pulled her thumb out of her mouth and patted the seat beside her. "Here, Daddy," she said.

She wanted me to sit with her.

I sighed. I looked at the room. It was a mess. Her crayons

and coloring books were scattered over the floor. And the large Tinkertoy windmill.

"Let me clean up," I said. "I'll be right here, with you."

She popped her thumb back in her mouth, and turned to the screen. Her attention was total.

I cleaned up the crayons and put them back in the cardboard box. I folded up her coloring books and set them on the shelf. I was suddenly tired and sat down for a minute on the floor next to Michelle. On the screen, three fairies, red, green, and blue, were flying into the throne room of the castle.

"That's Merryweather," Michelle said, pointing. "She's the blue one."

From the kitchen, Elaine said, "Can I fix you a sandwich, Lieutenant?"

"That'd be great," I said. I found I just wanted to sit there and be with my daughter. I wanted to forget everything, at least for a while. I was grateful that Connor had dropped me off. I sat and watched the TV dumbly.

Elaine brought in a salami sandwich with lettuce and mustard. I was hungry. Elaine looked at the TV, shook her head, and went back into the kitchen. I ate my sandwich, and Michelle insisted on a few bites. She likes salami. I worry about the additives in it, but I guess it's no worse than hot dogs.

After I had the sandwich, I felt a little better. I got up to finish cleaning up the room. I picked up the Tinkertoy windmill and started taking it apart, putting the sticks back into the cardboard tube. Michelle said, "No this, no this!" in a pained voice. I thought she didn't want me to take apart the windmill, but that wasn't it at all. She was cupping her hands over her eyes. She didn't like to see Maleficent, the bad witch. I fast-forwarded past the witch, and she relaxed again.

I dismantled the Tinkertoy windmill and put everything back into the tube container. I put the metal cap on the tube and set it on the lowest shelf of the bookcase. That was where it always went. I like to keep the toys low, so Michelle can get to them herself.

The tube fell off the shelf, onto the carpet. I picked it up again. There was something on the shelf. A small gray rectangle. I knew at once what it was.

It was an eight-millimeter video cassette, with Japanese writing on the label.

Elaine said, "Lieutenant? Do you need anything else?" She had her coat on; she was ready to go.

"Hang on a minute," I said.

I went to the phone, and called the switchboard downtown. I asked them to connect me to Connor in my car. I waited impatiently. Elaine looked at me.

"Just another minute, Elaine," I said.

On the TV, the prince was singing a duet with Sleeping Beauty while birds chirped. Michelle was sucking her thumb.

The operator said, "I'm sorry, there is no answer from the car."

"Okay," I said. "Do you have a forwarding number for Captain Connor?"

A pause. "He's not on our active roster."

"I know that. But did he leave a number?"

"I don't have anything, Lieutenant."

"I'm trying to find him."

"Wait a minute." She put me on hold. I swore.

Elaine stood in the front hallway. She was waiting to go.

The operator came back on. "Lieutenant? Captain Ellis says that Captain Connor has gone."

"Gone?"

"He was here a while ago, but he's gone now."

"You mean he was *downtown*?"

"Yes, but he's gone now. I don't have a number for him. I'm sorry."

I hung up. What the hell was Connor doing downtown?

Elaine was still standing in the front hallway. "Lieutenant?"

I said, "Just a minute, Elaine."

"Lieutenant, I have a—"

"I said, *just a minute.*"

I started pacing. I didn't know what to do. I was suddenly overwhelmed with fear. They had killed Eddie for the tape. They wouldn't hesitate to kill anybody else. I looked at my daughter, watching television with her thumb in her mouth. I said to Elaine, "Where's your car?"

"In the garage."

"Okay. Look. I want you to take Michelle and I want you to go—"

The phone rang. I grabbed it, hoping it was Connor. "Hello."

"*Moshi moshi. Connor-san desu ka?*"

"He's not here," I said. As soon as the words were out of my mouth, I cursed myself. But it was too late, the damage was done.

"Very good, Lieutenant," the voice said, heavily accented. "You have what we want, don't you?"

I said, "I don't know what you are talking about."

"I think you do, Lieutenant."

I could hear a faint hiss on the line. The call was coming from a car phone. They could be anywhere.

They could be right outside.

Damn!

I said, "Who is this?"

But I heard only a dial tone.

Elaine said, "What is it, Lieutenant?"

I was running to the window. I saw three cars doubleparked in the street below. Five men getting out of them, dark silhouettes in the night.

I tried to stay calm. "Elaine," I said. "I want you to take Michelle, and both of you go into my bedroom. Get under the bed. I want you to stay under there and be very quiet, no matter what happens. Do you understand?"

"No, Daddy!"

"Do it now, Elaine."

"No, Daddy! I want to watch Sleeping Beauty."

"You can watch it later." I had taken out my gun and was checking the clip. Elaine's eyes were wide.

She took Michelle. "Come on, honey."

Michelle squirmed in her arms, protesting. "No, Daddy!"

"*Michelle*."

She went silent, shocked at my tone. Elaine carried her into the bedroom. I loaded another clip, and put it in my jacket pocket.

I turned off the lights in the bedroom, and in Michelle's room. I looked at her crib, and the covers with little elephants sewn into it. I turned off the lights in the kitchen.

I went back into the living room. The TV was still playing. The wicked witch was instructing her raven to find Sleeping Beauty. "You are my last hope, my pet, do not fail me," she said to the bird. The bird flew away.

I stayed low. I moved toward the door. The phone rang again. I crawled back to answer it.

"Hello."

"*Kōhai*." It was Connor's voice. I heard the static hiss of the car phone.

I said, "Where are you?"

"You have the tape?"

"Yes, I have the tape. Where are you?"

"At the airport."

"Well, *get here*. Right away. And call for backup! Jesus!"

I heard a sound on the landing, outside my door. A soft sound, like footsteps.

I hung up the phone. I was sweating.

Christ.

If Connor was at the airport, he was twenty minutes away from me. Maybe more.

Maybe more.

I was going to have to handle this on my own.

I watched the door, listening intently. But I didn't hear anything else on the landing outside.

From the bedroom, I heard my daughter say, "I want Sleeping Beauty. I want *Daddy*." I heard Elaine whispering to her. Michelle whimpered.

Then it was quiet.

The phone rang again.

"Lieutenant," the heavily accented voice said, "there is no need for backups."

Christ, they were listening to the car phone.

"We want no harm, Lieutenant. We want only one thing. Will you be so kind, to bring the tape out to us?"

"I have the tape," I said.

"We know."

I said, "You can have it."

"Good. It will be better."

I knew I was on my own. I was thinking fast. My sole idea was: Get them away from here. Get them away from my daughter.

"But not here," I said.

There was a knock at the front door. Quick, insistent rapping.

Damn!

I could feel events closing in around me. Things were happening too fast. I was crouched down on the floor, with the phone pulled down from the table above. Trying to stay below the windows.

The knock came again.

I said into the phone, "You can have the tape. But first call off your boys."

"Say again, please?"

Christ, a fucking language problem!

"Call your men away. Get them out in the street. I want to see."

"Lieutenant, we must have tape!"

"I know that," I said. "I'll give it to you." While I talked, I kept my eyes on the door. I saw the knob turning. Someone was trying to open the front door. Slowly, quietly. Then the knob was released. Something white slid under the door.

A business card.

"Lieutenant, please cooperate."

I crawled forward and picked up the card. It said: Jonathan Connor, Captain, Los Angeles Police Department.

Then I heard a whisper from the other side.

"*Kōhai.*"

I knew it was a trick. Connor said he was at the airport, so it had to be a trick—

"Perhaps I can be of assistance, *kōhai.*"

Those were the words he had used before, at the start of the case. I was confused to hear them.

"Open the fucking door, *kōhai.*"

It was Connor. I reached up and opened the door. He slipped into the room, bent over. He was dragging something blue: a Kevlar vest. I said, "I thought you were—"

He shook his head, and whispered, "Knew they must be here. Had to be. I've been waiting in the car in the alley behind the house. How many are there in front?"

"I think, five. Maybe more."

He nodded.

The accented voice on the phone said, "Lieutenant? You are there? Lieutenant?"

I held the receiver away from my ear so Connor could listen while I talked. "I'm here," I said.

On the TV, there was a loud witch's cackle.

"Lieutenant, I hear something with you."

"It's just Sleeping Beauty," I said.

"What? Sreeping Booty?" the voice said, puzzled. "What is this?"

"Television," I said. "It's the *television*."

Now I heard whispers at the other end of the line. The rush of a car going by on the street. It reminded me that the men were in an exposed position outside. Standing there on a residential street lined with apartment buildings on both sides. Lots of windows. People that might look out at any time. Or people walking by. The men would have to move quickly.

Perhaps they already were.

Connor was tugging at my jacket. Signaling me to undress. I slid out of my coat as I spoke into the phone.

"All right," I said. "What do you want me to do?"

"You bring tape to us."

I looked at Connor. He nodded. Yes.

"All right," I said. "But first get your people back."

"I am sorry?"

Connor made a fist. His face turned to a snarl. He wanted me to be angry. He covered the phone and whispered in my ear. A Japanese phrase.

"Pay attention!" I said. "*Yoku kike!*"

At the other end, there was a grunt. Surprise.

"*Wakatta*. The men come away. And now, you come, Lieutenant."

"Okay," I said. "I'm coming."

I hung up the phone.

Connor whispered, "Thirty seconds," and disappeared out the front door. I was still buttoning up my shirt around the vest. Kevlar is bulky and hot. Immediately I started to sweat.

I waited thirty seconds, staring at the face of my watch. Watching the hand go around. And then I went outside.

Someone had turned the lights out in the hallway. I tripped over a body. I got to my feet, and looked at a slender Asian face. It was just a kid, surprisingly young. A teenager. He was unconscious, breathing shallowly.

I moved slowly down the stairs.

There wasn't anybody on the second-floor landing. I kept going down. I heard canned laughter from a television, behind one of the doors on the second floor. A voice said, "So tell us, where did you go on this first date?"

I continued down to the ground floor. The front door of the apartment building was glass. I looked out and saw only parked cars, and a hedge. A short section of lawn in front of the building. The men and the cars were somewhere off to the left.

I waited. I took a breath. My heart was pounding. I didn't want to go out there, but all I could think was to get them away from my daughter. To move the action away from my—

I stepped out into the night.

The air was cold on my sweating face and neck.

I took two steps forward.

Now I could see the men. They stood about ten meters away, beside their cars. I counted four men. One of them waved to me, beckoning me over. I hesitated.

Where were the others?

I couldn't see anybody except the men by the cars. They waved again, beckoning me. I started toward them when suddenly a heavy thumping blow from behind knocked me flat onto my face on the wet grass.

It was a moment before I realized what had happened.

I had been shot in the back.

And then the gunfire erupted all around me. Automatic weapons. The street was lit up like lightning from the gunfire. The sound echoed off the apartment buildings on both sides of the street. Glass was shattering. I heard people shouting all around me. More gunfire. I heard the sound of ignitions, cars roaring down the street past me. Almost immediately there was the sound of police sirens and tires squealing, and the glare of searchlights. I stayed where I was, face down on the grass. I felt like I was there for about an hour. Then I realized that the shouts now were all in English.

Finally someone came and crouched over me and said,

"Don't move, Lieutenant. Let me look first." I recognized Connor's voice. His hand touched my back, probing. Then he said, "Can you turn over, Lieutenant?"

I turned over.

Standing in the harsh light of the searchlights, Connor looked down at me. "They didn't penetrate," he said. "But you're going to have a hell of a sore back tomorrow."

He helped me to my feet.

I looked back to see the man who had shot me. But there was nobody there: just a few shell casings, glinting dull yellow in the green grass, by the front door.

THIRD DAY

The headline read VIETNAMESE GANG VIOLENCE ERUPTS ON WESTSIDE. The story reported that Peter Smith, an L.A.P.D. Special Services officer, was the target of a vicious grudge attack by an Orange County gang known as the Bitch Killers. Lieutenant Smith had been shot twice before backup police units arrived on the scene to disperse the attacking youths. None of the suspects had been apprehended alive. But two had been killed in the shooting.

I read the papers in the bathtub, soaking my aching back. I had two large, ugly bruises on either side of my spine. It hurt to breathe.

I had sent Michelle to stay with my mother in San Diego for the weekend, until things were sorted out. Elaine had driven her down, late last night.

I continued reading.

According to the story, the Bitch Killers was thought to be the same gang that had walked up to a black two-year-old boy, Rodney Howard, and shot the child in the head while he was playing on his tricycle in the front yard of his Inglewood home a week earlier. That incident was rumored to be an initiation into the gang, and the viciousness of it had touched off a furor about whether the L.A.P.D. was able to handle gang violence in southern California.

There were a lot of reporters outside my door again, but I wasn't talking to any of them. The phone rang constantly, but I let the answering machine take it. I just sat in the tub, and tried to decide what to do.

In the middle of the morning I called Ken Shubik at the *Times*.

"I wondered when you'd check in," he said. "You must be pleased."

"About what?"

"About being alive," Ken said. "These kids are murder."

"You mean the Vietnamese kids last night?" I said. "They spoke Japanese."

"No."

"Yes, Ken."

"We didn't get that story right?"

"Not really."

"That explains it," he said.

"Explains what?"

"That was the Weasel's story. And the Weasel is in bad odor today. There's even talk of firing him. Nobody can figure it out, but something's happening around here," he said. "Somebody high in editorial all of a sudden has a bug up his ass about Japan. Anyway, we're starting a series investigating Japanese corporations in America."

"Oh, yeah?"

"Of course you'd never know it from today's paper. You see the business section?"

"No, why?"

"Darley-Higgins announced the sale of MicroCon to Akai. It's on page four of the business section. Two-centimeter story."

"That's it?"

"Not worth any more, I guess. Just another American company sold to the Japanese. I checked. Since 1987, there have been a hundred and eighty American high-tech and electronics companies bought by the Japanese. It's not news any more."

"But the paper is starting to investigate?"

"That's the word. It won't be easy, because all the emotional indicators are down. The balance of payments with Japan is dropping. Of course it only looks better because they don't export so many cars to us now. They make them here. And they've farmed out production to the little dragons, so the deficits appear in their columns, not Japan's. They've stepped up purchases of oranges and timber, to make things look better. Basically, they treat us as an under-developed country. They import our raw materials. But they don't buy our finished goods. They say we don't make anything they want."

"Maybe we don't, Ken."

"Tell it to the judge." He sighed. "But I don't know if the public gives a damn. That's the question. Even about the taxes."

I was feeling a little dull. "Taxes?"

"We're doing a big series on taxes. The government is finally noticing that Japanese corporations do a lot of business here, but they don't pay much tax in America. Some of them pay none, which is ridiculous. They control their profits by overpricing the Japanese subcomponents that their American assembly plants import. It's outrageous, but of course, the American government has never been too swift about penalizing Japan before. And the Japanese spend half a billion a year in Washington, to keep everybody calmed down."

"But you're going to do a tax story?"

"Yeah. And we're looking at Nakamoto. My sources keep telling me Nakamoto's going to get hit with a price-fixing suit. Price-fixing is the name of the game for Japanese companies. I pulled a list of who's settled lawsuits. Nintendo in 1991, price-fixing games. Mitsubishi that year, price-fixing TVs. Panasonic in 1989. Minolta in 1987. And you know that's just the tip of the iceberg."

"Then it's good you're doing the story," I said.

He coughed. "You want to go on record? About the Vietnamese who speak Japanese?"

"No," I said.

"We're all in this together," he said.

"I don't think it would do any good," I said.

I had lunch with Connor at a sushi bar in Culver City. As we were pulling up, someone was placing a CLOSED sign in the window. He saw Connor, and flipped it to say OPEN.

"They know me here," Connor said.

"You mean they like you?"

"It's hard to know about that."

"They want your business?"

"No," Connor said. "Probably Hiroshi would prefer to close. It won't be profitable for him to keep his people on, just for two *gaijin* customers. But I come here often. He is honoring the relationship. It doesn't really have to do with business or liking."

We got out of the car.

"Americans don't understand," he said. "Because the Japanese system is fundamentally different."

"Yeah, well, I think they're starting to understand," I said. I told him Ken Shubik's story about price-fixing.

Connor sighed. "It's a cheap shot to say the Japanese are dishonest. They're not—but they play by different rules. Americans just don't get it."

"That's fine," I said. "But price-fixing is illegal."

"In America," he said. "Yes. But it's normal procedure in Japan. Remember, *kōhai*: fundamentally different. Collusive agreements are the way things are done. The Nomura stock scandal showed that. Americans get moralistic about collusion, instead of just seeing it as a different way of doing business. Which is all it is."

We went into the sushi bar. There was a lot of bowing and greeting. Connor spoke Japanese and we sat at the bar. We didn't order.

I said, "Aren't we going to order?"

"No," Connor said. "It would be offensive. Hiroshi will decide for us what we would like."

So we sat at the bar and Hiroshi brought us dishes. I watched him cutting fish.

The phone rang. From the far end of the sushi bar, a man said, "*Connor-san, onna no hito ga matteru to ittemashita yo.*"

"*Dōmo,*" Connor said, nodding. He turned to me, and pushed back from the bar. "Guess we won't eat, after all. Time for us to go to our next appointment. You brought the tape with you?"

"Yes."

"Good."

"Where are we going?"

"To see your friend," he said. "Miss Asakuma."

◼ We were bouncing along the potholes of the Santa Monica freeway, heading downtown. The afternoon sky was gray; it looked like rain. My back hurt. Connor was looking out the window, humming to himself.

In all the excitement, I had forgotten about Theresa's call the night before. She had said she was looking at the last part of the tape, and she thought there was a problem.

"Have you talked to her?"

"Theresa? Briefly. I gave her some advice."

"Last night, she said there was a problem with the tape."

"Oh? She didn't mention that to me."

I had the feeling he wasn't telling me the truth, but my back was throbbing and I wasn't in the mood to press him. There were times when I thought Connor had become Japanese himself. He had that reserve, that secretive manner.

I said, "You never told me why you left Japan."

"Oh, that." He sighed. "I had a job, working for a corporation. Advising on security. But it didn't work out."

"Why not?"

"Well, the job was all right. It was fine."

"Then what was it?"

He shook his head. "Most people who've lived in Japan come away with mixed feelings. In many ways, the Japanese are wonderful people. They're hardworking, intelligent, and humorous. They have real integrity. They are also the most racist people on the planet. That's why they're always accusing everybody else of racism. They're so prejudiced, they assume everybody else must be, too. And living in Japan . . . I just got tired, after a while, of the way things worked.

370

I got tired of seeing women move to the other side of the street when they saw me walking toward them at night. I got tired of noticing that the last two seats to be occupied on the subway were the ones on either side of me. I got tired of the airline stewardesses asking Japanese passengers if they minded sitting next to a *gaijin*, assuming that I couldn't understand what they were saying because they were speaking Japanese. I got tired of the exclusion, the subtle patronizing, the jokes behind my back. I got tired of being a nigger. I just . . . got tired. I gave up."

"Sounds to me like you don't really like them."

"No," Connor said. "I do. I like them very much. But I'm not Japanese, and they never let me forget it." He sighed again. "I have many Japanese friends who work in America, and it's hard for them, too. The differences cut both ways. They feel excluded. People don't sit next to them, either. But my friends always ask me to remember that they are human beings first, and Japanese second. Unfortunately, in my experience that is not always true."

"You mean, they're Japanese first."

He shrugged. "Family is family."

We drove the rest of the way in silence.

■ We were in a small room on the third floor of a boardinghouse for foreign students. Theresa Asakuma explained it was not her room; it belonged to a friend who was studying in Italy for a term. She had set up the small VCR and a small monitor on a table.

"I thought I should get out of the lab," she said, running the machine fast forward. "But I wanted you to see this. This is the end of one of the tapes you brought me. It begins right after the senator has left the room."

She slowed the tape, and I saw the wide view of the forty-sixth floor of the Nakamoto building. The floor was deserted. The pale body of Cheryl Austin lay on the dark conference table.

The tape continued to roll.

Nothing happened. It was a static scene.

I said, "What are we looking at?"

"Just wait."

The tape continued. Still nothing happened.

And then I saw, clearly, the girl's leg twitch.

"What was *that*?"

"A spasm?"

"I'm not sure."

Now the girl's arm, outlined against the dark wood, moved. There was no question about it. The fingers closed and opened.

"She's still alive!"

Theresa nodded. "That's the way it looks. Now watch the clock."

The clock on the wall said 8:36. I watched it. Nothing happened. The tape ran for two more minutes.

Connor sighed.

"The clock isn't moving."

"No," she said. "I first noticed the grain pattern, on a close scan. The pixels were jumping back and forth."

"Meaning what?"

"We call it rock and roll. It's the usual way to disguise a freeze-frame. A normal freeze is visible to the eye, because the smallest units of the image are suddenly static. Whereas in a regular picture, there's always some small movement, even if it's just random. So what you do is you rock and roll, cycling three seconds of image over and over. It gives a little movement, makes the freeze less obvious."

"You're saying the tape was frozen at eight thirty-six?"

"Yes. And the girl was apparently still alive at that time. I don't know for sure. But maybe."

Connor nodded. "So that's why the original tape is so important."

"What original tape?" she said.

I produced the tape I had found in my apartment the night before.

"Run it," Connor said.

In crisp color, we saw the forty-sixth floor. It was from the side camera, with a good view of the conference room. And it was one of the original tapes: we saw the murder, and we saw Morton leave the girl behind on the table.

The tape ran on. We watched the girl.

"Can you see the wall clock?"

"Not in this angle."

"How much time do you think has gone by?"

Theresa shook her head. "It's time lapse. I can't say. A few minutes."

Then, the girl moved on the table. Her hand twitched, and then her head moved. She was alive. There was no question about it.

And in the glass of the conference room, we saw the shape of a man. He walked forward, appearing from the right. He entered the room, looking back once to make sure he was alone. It was Ishiguro. Very deliberately, he walked to the edge of the table, placed his hands on the girl's neck, and strangled her.

"Jesus."

It seemed to take a long time. The girl struggled toward the end. Ishiguro held her down, long after she had stopped moving.

"He's not taking any chances."

"No," Connor said. "He's not."

Finally, Ishiguro stepped back from the body, shot his cuffs, straightened his suit jacket.

"All right," Connor said. "You can stop the tape now. I've seen enough."

We were back outside. Weak sunlight filtered through the smoggy haze. Cars roared by, bouncing in the potholes. The houses along the street looked cheap to me, in disrepair.

We got in our car.

"What now?" I said.

He handed me the car phone. "Call downtown," he said, "and tell them we have a tape that shows Ishiguro did the murder. Tell them we're going to Nakamoto now, to arrest Ishiguro."

"I thought you didn't like car phones."

"Just do it," Connor said. "We're about finished, anyway."

So I did it. I told the dispatcher what our plan was, where we were going. They asked if we wanted backup. Connor shook his head, so I said we didn't need backup.

I hung up the phone.

"Now what?"

"Let's go to Nakamoto."

☀ After seeing the forty-sixth floor so many times on videotape, it was strange to find myself there again. Although it was Saturday, the office was busy and active, secretaries and executives were hurrying about. And the office looked different during the day; sunlight poured in through the large windows on all sides, and the surrounding skyscrapers looked close, even in the L.A. haze.

Looking up, I saw that the surveillance cameras had been removed from the walls. To the right, the conference room where Cheryl Austin had died was being remodeled. The black furniture was gone. Workmen were installing a blond wood table and new beige chairs. The room looked completely different.

On the other side of the atrium, a meeting was being held in the large conference room. Sunlight streamed in through the glass walls on forty people sitting on both sides of a long table covered in green felt. Japanese on one side, Americans on the other. Everyone had a neat stack of documents in front of them. Prominent among the Americans, I noticed the lawyer, Bob Richmond.

Standing beside me, Connor sighed.

"What is it?"

"The Saturday meeting, *kōhai.*"

"You mean *that*'s the Saturday meeting Eddie was talking about?"

Connor nodded. "The meeting to conclude the MicroCon sale."

There was a receptionist seated near the elevators. She

watched us staring for a moment, then said politely, "Can I help you, gentlemen?"

"Thank you," Connor said. "But we're waiting for someone."

I frowned. From where we were standing, I could clearly see Ishiguro inside the conference room, seated near the center of the table on the Japanese side, smoking a cigarette. The man to his right leaned over to whisper something to him; Ishiguro nodded and smiled.

I glanced over at Connor.

"Just wait," Connor said.

Several minutes passed, and then a young Japanese aide hurried across the atrium and entered the conference room. Once inside, he moved more slowly, circling the table unobtrusively until he was standing behind the chair of a distinguished, gray-haired man seated toward the far end of the table. The aide bent and whispered something to the older man.

"Iwabuchi," Connor said.

"Who is he?"

"Head of Nakamoto America. Based in New York."

Iwabuchi nodded to the young aide, and got up from the table. The aide pulled his chair out for him. Iwabuchi moved down the line of Japanese negotiators. As he passed one man, he brushed him lightly on the shoulder. Iwabuchi continued to the end of the table, then opened the glass doors and walked outside, onto a terrace beyond the conference room.

A moment later, the second man stood to leave.

"Moriyama," Connor said. "Head of the Los Angeles office."

Moriyama also went outside onto the terrace. The two men stood in the sun and smoked cigarettes. The aide joined them, speaking quickly, his head bobbing. The senior men listened intently, then turned away. The aide remained standing there.

After a moment, Moriyama turned back to the aide and said something. The aide bowed quickly and returned to the conference room. He moved to the seat of another man, dark-haired with a mustache, and whispered in his ear.

"Shirai," Connor said. "Head of finance."

Shirai stood up, but did not go onto the terrace. Instead, he opened the inner door, crossed the atrium, and disappeared into an office on the far side of the floor.

In the conference room, the aide went to still a fourth man, whom I recognized as Yoshida, the head of Akai Ceramics. Yoshida also slipped out of the room, going into the atrium.

"What's going on?" I said.

"They're distancing themselves," Connor said. "They don't want to be there when it happens."

I looked back at the terrace, and saw the two Japanese men outside moving casually along the length of the terrace, toward a door at the far end.

I said, "What are we waiting for?"

"Patience, *kōhai.*"

The young aide departed. The meeting in the conference room proceeded. But in the atrium, Yoshida pulled the young aide over and whispered something.

The aide returned to the conference room.

"Hmmm," Connor said.

This time the aide went to the American side of the table, and whispered something to Richmond. I couldn't see Richmond's face, because his back was to us, but his body jerked. He twisted and leaned back to whisper something to the aide. The aide nodded and left.

Richmond remained seated at the table, shaking his head slowly. He bent over his notes.

And then he passed a slip of paper across the table to Ishiguro.

"That's our cue," Connor said. He turned to the receptionist, showed her his badge, and we walked quickly across the atrium toward the conference room.

A young American in a pinstripe suit was standing in front of the table and saying, "Now, if you will direct your attention to Rider C, the summary statement of assets and—"

Connor came into the room first. I was right after him.

Ishiguro looked up, showing no surprise. "Good afternoon, gentlemen." His face was a mask.

Richmond said smoothly, "Gentlemen, if this can wait, we're in the middle of something rather complicated here—"

Connor interrupted him. "Mr. Ishiguro, you are under arrest for the murder of Cheryl Lynn Austin," and then he read him his Miranda rights, while Ishiguro stared fixedly at him. The others in the room were entirely silent. Nobody moved at the long table. It was like a still life.

Ishiguro remained seated. "This is an absurdity."

"Mr. Ishiguro," Connor said, "would you please stand?"

Richmond said softly, "I hope you guys know what you are doing."

Ishiguro said, "I know my rights, gentlemen."

Connor said, "Mr. Ishiguro, would you please stand?"

Ishiguro did not move. The smoke from his cigarette curled up in front of him.

There was a long silence.

Then Connor said to me, "Show them the tape."

One wall of the conference room consisted of video equipment. I found a playback machine like the one I had used, and plugged the tape in. But no image came up on the big central monitor. I tried pushing various buttons, but couldn't get a picture.

From a rear corner, a Japanese secretary who had been taking notes hurried up to help me. Bowing apologetically, she pushed the proper buttons, bowed again, and returned to her place.

"Thank you," I said.

On the screen, the image came up. Even in the bright sunlight, it was clear. It was right at the moment we had seen in Theresa's room. The moment where Ishiguro approaches the girl and holds the struggling body down.

Richmond said, "What is this?"

"It's a fake," Ishiguro said. "It's a fraud."

Connor said, "This is a tape taken by Nakamoto security cameras on the forty-sixth floor Thursday night."

Ishiguro said, "It's not legal. It's a fraud."

But nobody was listening. Everybody was looking at the monitor. Richmond's mouth was open. "Jesus," he said.

On the tape, it seemed to take a long time for the girl to die.

Ishiguro was glaring at Connor. "This is nothing but a sensational publicity stunt," he said. "It is a fabrication. It means *nothing*."

"Jesus Christ," Richmond said, staring at the screen.

Ishiguro said, "It has no legal basis. It is not admissible. It will never stand up. This is just a disruption—"

He broke off. For the first time, he had looked down to the other end of the table. And he saw that Iwabuchi's chair was empty.

He looked the other way. His eyes darted around the room.

Moriyama's chair was empty.

Shirai's chair.

Yoshida's chair.

Ishiguro's eyes twitched. He looked at Connor in astonishment. Then he nodded, gave a guttural grunt, and stood. Everyone else was staring at the screen.

He walked up to Connor. "I'm not going to watch this, Captain. When you are through with your charade, you will find me outside." He lit a cigarette, squinting at Connor. "Then we will talk. *Kicchiirito na*." He opened the door and walked onto the terrace. He left the door open behind him.

I started to follow him out, but Connor caught my eye. He shook his head fractionally. I remained where I was.

I could see Ishiguro outside, standing at the railing. He smoked his cigarette and turned his face to the sun. Then he glanced back at us and shook his head pityingly. He leaned against the railing, and put his foot on it.

In the conference room, the tape continued. One of the American lawyers, a woman, stood up, snapped her briefcase shut, and walked out of the room. Nobody else moved.

And finally, the tape ended.

I popped it out of the machine.

There was silence in the room. A slight wind ruffled the papers of the people at the long table.

I looked out at the terrace.

It was empty.

By the time we got out to the railing, we could hear the sirens faintly, on the street below.

Down on ground level, the air was dusty and we heard the deafening sound of jackhammers. Nakamoto was building an annex next door, and construction was in full swing. A line of big cement trucks was pulled up along the curb. I pushed my way through the cluster of Japanese men in blue suits, and broke through to look down into the pit.

Ishiguro had landed in a wet concrete pouring. His body lay sideways, just the head and one arm sticking above the soft concrete surface. Blood ran in spreading fingers across the gray surface. Workmen in blue hardhats were trying to fish him out, using bamboo poles and ropes. They weren't having much success. Finally a workman in thigh-high rubber boots waded in to pull the body out. But it proved more difficult than he expected. He had to call for help.

Our people were already there, Fred Perry and Bob Wolfe. Wolfe saw me and walked up the hill. He had his notebook out. He shouted over the din of the jackhammers. "You know anything about this, Pete?"

"Yeah," I said.

"Got a name?"

"Masao Ishiguro."

Wolfe squinted. "Spell that?"

I started to try to spell it, talking over the sound of the construction. Finally I just reached in my pocket and fished out his card. I gave it to Wolfe.

"This is him?"

"Yeah."

"Where'd you get it?"

"Long story," I said. "But he's wanted for murder."

Wolfe nodded. "Let me get the body out and we'll talk."

"Fine."

Eventually, they used the construction crane to pull him out. Ishiguro's body, sagging and heavy with concrete, was lifted into the air, and swung past me, over my head.

Bits of cement dripped down on me, and spattered on the sign at my feet. The sign was for the Nakamoto Construction Company, and it said in bold letters: BUILDING FOR A NEW TOMORROW. And underneath, PLEASE EXCUSE THE INCONVENIENCE.

■ It took another hour to get everything settled at the site. And the chief wanted our reports by the end of the day, so afterward we had to go down to Parker to do the paperwork.

It was four o'clock before we went across the street to the coffee shop next to Antonio's bail bond shop. Just to get away from the office. I said, "Why did Ishiguro kill the girl in the first place?"

Connor sighed. "It's not clear. The best I can understand it is this. Eddie was working for his father's *kaisha* all along. One of the things he did was supply girls for visiting dignitaries. He'd been doing that for years. It was easy—he was a party guy; he knew the girls; the congressmen wanted to meet the girls, and he got a chance to make friends with the congressmen. But in Cheryl he had a special opportunity, because Senator Morton, head of the Finance Committee, was attracted to her. Morton was smart enough to break off the affair, but Eddie kept sending her in private jets to meet him unexpectedly, keeping the thing alive. Eddie liked her, too: he had sex with her that afternoon. And it was Eddie who arranged for her to come to the party at Nakamoto, knowing that Morton would be there. Eddie was pushing Morton to block the sale, so Eddie was preoccupied with the Saturday meeting. By the way, on the news-station tape you thought he said 'no cheapie' to Cheryl. He was saying *nichibei*. The Japanese-American relationship.

"But I think Eddie just intended for Cheryl to meet Morton. I doubt he had any idea about the forty-sixth floor. He certainly didn't expect her to go up there with Morton. The idea of going there must have been suggested during the party by someone from Nakamoto. The company left the floor accessible for a very simple reason: there's a bedroom suite up there that executives sometimes use. Somewhere in the back."

I said, "How did you know that?"

Connor smiled. "Hanada-san mentioned he had once used it. Apparently it's quite luxurious."

"So you *do* have contacts."

"I have a few. I imagine Nakamoto was probably just being accommodating, too. They may have installed cameras up there with the idea of blackmail, but I'm told there were no cameras in the bedroom suite. And the fact that they had a camera right in the conference room suggests to me that Phillips was right—the cameras were placed to *kaizen* the office workers. Certainly they couldn't have expected the sexual encounter to occur where it did.

"Anyway, when Eddie saw Cheryl going off with Morton to another part of the Nakamoto building, it must have alarmed the hell out of him. So he followed them. He witnessed the murder, which I believe was probably accidental. And Eddie then helped out his friend Morton, calling him over, getting him out of there. Eddie went back to the party with Morton."

"What about the tapes?"

"Ah. You remember we talked about bribery. One of Eddie's bribes was to a low-level security officer named Tanaka. I believe Eddie supplied him with drugs. Anyway, Eddie had known him for a couple of years. And when Ishiguro ordered Tanaka to pull the tapes, Tanaka told Eddie."

"And Eddie went down and got the tapes himself."

"Yes. Together with Tanaka."

"But Phillips said Eddie was alone."

"Phillips lied, because he knew Tanaka. That's also why he didn't make more of a fuss—Tanaka said it was all right. But when Phillips told us the story, he left Tanaka out."

"And then?"

"Ishiguro sent a couple of guys to clean out Cheryl's

apartment. Tanaka took the tapes someplace to get them copied. Eddie went to the party in the hills."

"But Eddie kept one."

"Yes."

I thought it over. "But when we talked to Eddie at the party, he told a completely different story."

Connor nodded. "He lied."

"Even to you, his friend?"

Connor shrugged. "He thought he could get away with it."

"What about Ishiguro? Why did he kill the girl?"

"To get Morton in his pocket. And it worked—they got Morton to change his position on MicroCon. For a while there, Morton was going to allow the sale to go forward."

"Ishiguro would kill her for that? For some corporate sale?"

"No, I don't think it was calculated at all. Ishiguro was high-strung, under great pressure. He felt he had to prove himself to his superiors. He had much at stake—so much, that he behaved differently from an ordinary Japanese under these circumstances. And in a moment of extreme pressure, he killed the girl, yes. As he said, she was a woman of no importance."

"Jesus."

"But I think there's more to it than that. Morton was very ambivalent about the Japanese. I had the sense there was a lot of resentment—those jokes about dropping the bomb, all that. And having sex on the boardroom table. It's . . . disrespectful, wouldn't you say? It must have infuriated Ishiguro."

"And who called in the murder?"

"Eddie."

"Why?"

"To embarrass Nakamoto. Eddie got Morton safely back to the party, and then called in. Probably from a phone somewhere at the party. When he called, he didn't know about the security cameras yet. Then Tanaka told him about them, and Eddie started to worry that Ishiguro might set him up. So he called back."

"And he asked for his friend John Connor."

"Yes."

I said, "So Eddie was Koichi Nishi?"

Connor nodded. "His little joke. Koichi Nishi is the name of a character in a famous Japanese movie about corporate corruption."

Connor finished his coffee and pushed away from the counter.

"And Ishiguro? Why did the Japanese abandon him?"

"Ishiguro had played it too fast and loose. He acted too independently Thursday night. They don't like that. Nakamoto would have sent him back pretty soon. He was destined to spend the rest of his life in Japan in a *madogiwa-zoku*. A window seat. Somebody who's bypassed by corporate decisions, and stares out the window all day. In a way, it's a life sentence."

I thought it over. "So when you used the car phone, calling the station, telling them what you planned . . . who was listening?"

"Hard to say." Connor shrugged. "But I liked Eddie. I owed him one. I didn't want to see Ishiguro go home."

Back in the office there was an elderly woman waiting for me. She was dressed in black and she introduced herself as Cheryl Austin's grandmother. Cheryl's parents died in a car crash when she was four, and she had raised the little girl afterward. She wanted to thank me for my help in the investigation. She talked about what Cheryl had been like, as a little girl. How she had grown up in Texas.

"Of course, she was pretty," she said, "and the boys surely did like her. Always a bunch of them hanging around, you couldn't shake them off with a stick." She paused. "Of course, I never thought she was entirely right in the head. But she wanted to keep those boys around. And she liked them to fight over her, too. I remember she was seven or eight, she'd get those kids brawling in the dust, and she'd clap her hands and watch them go at it. By the time she was teenage, she was real good at it. Knew just what to do. It wasn't real nice to see. No, something was wrong in the head. She could be mean. And that song, she always played it, day and night. About lose my mind, I'd think."

"Jerry Lee Lewis?"

"Of course, I knew why. That was her Daddy's favorite song. When she was just a little bit of a thing, he'd drive her to town in his convertible, with his arm around her, and the radio making that awful racket. She'd have her best sundress on. She was such a pretty thing when she was a child. The image of her mother."

Then the woman started to cry, thinking about that. I got her a Kleenex. Tried to be sympathetic.

And pretty soon she wanted to know what had happened. How Cheryl had died.

I didn't know what to say to her.

As I was coming out of the ground-floor entrance to Parker Center, walking out by the fountains, a Japanese man in a suit stopped me. He was about forty, with dark hair and a mustache. He greeted me formally, and gave me his card. It took a moment to realize that this was Mr. Shirai, the head of finance for Nakamoto.

"I wanted to see you in person, Sumisu-san, to express to you how much my company regrets the behavior of Mr. Ishiguro. His actions were not proper and he acted without authority. Nakamoto is an honorable company and we do not violate the law. I want to assure you that he does not represent our company, or what we stand for in doing business. In this country, the work of Mr. Ishiguro put him in contact with many investment bankers, and men who make leveraged buy-outs. Frankly, I believe he was too long in America. He adopted many bad habits here."

So there it was, an apology and an insult in the same moment. I didn't know what to say to him, either.

Finally, I said, "Mr. Shirai, there was the offer of financing, for a small house . . ."

"Oh, yes?"

"Yes. Perhaps you didn't hear of it."

"Actually, I believe I have heard something of that."

I said, "I was wondering what you intended to do about that offer now."

There was a long silence.

Just the splash of the fountains off to my right.

Shirai squinted at me in the hazy afternoon light, trying to decide how to play it.

Finally he said, "Sumisu-san, the offer is improper. It is of course withdrawn."

"Thank you, Mr. Shirai," I said.

Connor and I drove back to my apartment. Neither of us talked. I was driving on the Santa Monica freeway. The signs overhead had been spray-painted by gangs. I was aware of how uneven and bumpy the roadway was. To the right, the skyscrapers around Westwood stood hazy in smog. The landscape looked poor and decrepit.

Finally I said, "So is that all this was? Just competition between Nakamoto and some other Japanese company? Over MicroCon? Or what?"

Connor shrugged. "Multiple purposes, probably. The Japanese think in those ways. And to them, America is now only an arena for their competition. That much is true. We're just not very important, in their eyes."

We came to my street. There was a time when I thought it was pleasant, a little tree-lined street of apartments, with a playground at the end of the block for my daughter. Now I wasn't feeling that way. The air was bad, and the street seemed dirty, unpleasant.

I parked the car. Connor got out, shook my hand. "Don't be discouraged."

"I am."

"Don't be. It's very serious. But it can all change. It's changed before. It can change again."

"I guess."

"What are you going to do now?" he asked.

"I don't know," I said. "I feel like going somewhere else. But there's nowhere to go."

He nodded. "Leave the department?"

"Probably. Certainly leave Special Services. It's too . . . unclear for me."

He nodded. "Take care, *kōhai*. Thanks for your help."

"You, too, *sempai*."

I was tired. I climbed the stairs to my apartment and went inside. It was quiet, with my daughter gone. I got a can of Coke from the refrigerator and walked into the living room, but my back hurt when I sat in the chair. I got up again, and turned on the television. I couldn't watch it. I thought of how Connor said everybody in America focused on the unimportant things. It was like the situation with Japan: if you sell the country to Japan, then they will own it, whether you like it or not. And people who own things do what they want with them. That's how it works.

I walked into my bedroom and changed my clothes. On the bedside table, I saw the pictures from my daughter's birthday that I had been sorting when all this started. The pictures that didn't look like her, that didn't fit the reality anymore. I listened to the tinny laughter from the television in the other room. I used to think things were basically all right. But they're not all right.

I walked into my daughter's room. I looked at her crib, and her covers with the elephants sewn on it. I thought of the way she slept, so trustingly, lying on her back, her arms thrown over her head. I thought of the way she trusted me to make her world for her now. And I thought of the world that she would grow into. And as I started to make her bed, I felt uneasy in my heart.

Transcript of: March 15 (99)

INT: All right, Pete, I think that about does it for us. Unless you have anything else.

SUBJ: No. I'm done.

INT: I understand you resigned from the Special Services.

SUBJ: That's right.

INT: And you made a written recommendation to Chief Olson that the Asian liaison program be changed. You said the connection with the Japan-America Amity Foundation should be severed?

SUBJ: Yes.

INT: Why is that?

SUBJ: If the department wants specially trained officers, we should pay to train them. I just think it's healthier.

INT: Healthier?

SUBJ: Yes. It's time for us to take control of our country again. It's time for us to start paying our own way.

INT: Have you had a response from the Chief?

SUBJ: Not yet. I'm still waiting.

If you don't want Japan to buy it, don't sell it.
—AKIO MORITA

Afterword

"People deny reality. They fight against real feelings caused by real circumstances. They build mental worlds of shoulds, oughts, and might-have-beens. Real changes begin with real appraisal and acceptance of what is. Then realistic action is possible."

These are the words of David Reynolds, an American exponent of Japanese Morita psychotherapy. He is speaking of personal behavior, but his comments are applicable to the economic behavior of nations, as well.

Sooner or later, the United States must come to grips with the fact that Japan has become the leading industrial nation in the world. The Japanese have the longest lifespan. They have the highest employment, the highest literacy, the smallest gap between rich and poor. Their manufactured products have the highest quality. They have the best food. The fact is that a country the size of Montana, with half our population, will soon have an economy equal to ours.

But they haven't succeeded by doing things our way. Japan is not a Western industrial state; it is organized quite differently. And the Japanese have invented a new kind of trade—adversarial trade, trade like war, trade intended to wipe out the competition—which America has failed to understand for several decades. The United States keeps insisting the Japanese do things our way. But increasingly, their response is to ask, why should *we* change? We're doing better than you are. And indeed they are.

What should the American response be? It is absurd to blame Japan for successful behavior, or to suggest that they slow down. The Japanese consider such American reactions childish whining, and they are right. It is more appropriate for the United States to wake up, to see Japan clearly, and to act realistically.

In the end, that will mean major changes in the United States, but it is inevitably the task of the weaker partner to adjust to the demands of a relationship. And the United States is now without question the weaker partner in any economic discussion with Japan.

A century ago, when Admiral Perry's American fleet opened the nation, Japan was a feudal society. The Japanese realized they had to change, and they did. Starting in the 1860s, they brought in thousands of Western specialists to advise them on how to change their government and their industries. The entire society underwent a revolution. There was a second convulsion, equally dramatic, after World War II.

But in both cases, the Japanese faced the challenge squarely, and met it. They didn't say, let the Americans buy our land and our institutions and hope they will teach us to do things better. Not at all. The Japanese invited thousands of experts to visit—and then sent them home again. We would do well to take the same approach. The Japanese are not our saviors. They are our competitors. We should not forget it.

Acknowledgments

For advice and assistance during my research, I am grateful to Nina Easton, James Flanigan, Ken Reich, and David Shaw, all of the *Los Angeles Times*; Steve Clemons of the Japan America Society of Southern California; Senator Al Gore; Jim Wilson of the Jet Propulsion Laboratory; Kevin O'Connor of Hewlett-Packard; Lieutenant Fred Nixon of the Los Angeles Police Department; Ron Insana of CNBC/FNN; and Keith Manasco. For suggestions and corrections of the manuscript at various points, I am indebted to Mike Backes, Douglas Crichton, James Fallows, Karel van Wolferen, and Sonny Mehta. Valery Wright shepherded the manuscript through seemingly endless revisions, Shinoi Osuka and later Sumi Adachi Sovak assisted ably with the Japanese text, and Roger McPeek gave me his understanding of video technology and future security systems.

The subject of Japanese-American relations is highly controversial. I wish to state clearly that the views expressed in this novel are my own, and are not to be attributed to any of the individuals listed above.

Bibliography

This novel questions the conventional premise that direct foreign investment in American high technology is by definition good, and therefore should be allowed to continue without restraint or limitation. I suggest things are not so simple.

Although this book is fiction, my approach to Japan's economic behavior, and America's inadequate response to it, follows a well-established body of expert opinion, much of it listed in the bibliography. Indeed, in preparing this novel, I have drawn heavily from a number of the sources below.

I hope readers will be provoked to read further from more knowledgeable authors. I have listed the principal texts in rough order of readability and pertinence to the issues raised in this novel.

PRINCIPAL SOURCES

Clyde V. Prestowitz, Jr., *Trading Places: How We Are Giving Our Future to Japan and How to Reclaim It* (New York: Basic Books, 1989).

James Fallows, *More Like Us: Putting America's Native Strengths and Traditional Values to Work to Overcome the Asian Challenge* (Boston: Houghton Mifflin, 1989).

———, "Containing Japan," *The Atlantic*, May 1989, pp. 40–54.

———, "Getting Along with Japan," *The Atlantic*, December 1989, pp. 53–64.

Peter F. Drucker, *The New Realities* (New York: Harper & Row, 1989).

Ezra F. Vogel, *Japan as Number One: Lessons for America* (Cambridge, Mass.: Harvard University Press, 1979).

Karel van Wolferen, *The Enigma of Japanese Power* (New York: Alfred A. Knopf, 1989).

Chalmers Johnson, *MITI and the Japanese Miracle* (Stanford: Stanford University Press, 1982).

Michael T. Jacobs, *Short-Term America: The Causes and Cures of Our Business Myopia* (Boston: Harvard Business School Press, 1991).

Robert Kuttner, *The End of Laissez-Faire: National Purpose and the Global Economy after the Cold War* (New York: Alfred A. Knopf, 1991).

Michael L. Dertouzos, Richard K. Lester, and Robert M. Solow, *Made in America: Regaining the Productive Edge,* The Report of the M.I.T. Commission on Industrial Productivity (Cambridge, Mass.: M.I.T. Press, 1989).

Pat Choate, *Agents of Influence* (New York: Alfred A. Knopf, 1990).

Dorinne K. Kondo, *Crafting Selves: Power, Gender and Discourses of Identity in a Japanese Workplace* (Chicago: University of Chicago Press, 1990).

Kenichi Ohmae, *Fact and Friction: Kenichi Ohmae on U.S.-Japan Relations* (Tokyo: *The Japan Times*, Ltd., 1990).

Donald M. Spero, "Patent Protection or Piracy—A CEO Views Japan," *Harvard Business Review*, September–October 1990, pp. 58–67.

OTHER SOURCES

Daniel E. Bob and SRI International, *Japanese Companies in American Communities: Cooperation, Conflict and the Role of Corporate Citizenship* (New York: Japan Society, 1990).

Bryan Burrough and John Helyar, *Barbarians at the Gate: The Fall of RJR Nabisco* (New York: Harper & Row, 1990).

Alfred D. Chandler, Jr., *Scale and Scope: The Dynamics of Industrial Capitalism* (Cambridge, Mass.: Belknap Press of Harvard University Press, 1990).

Ronald Dore, *Taking Japan Seriously: A Confucian Perspective on Leading Economic Issues* (Stanford: Stanford University Press, 1987).

David Halberstam, *The Next Century* (New York: William Morrow and Co., 1991).

Kichiro Hayashi, editor, *The U.S.-Japanese Economic Relationship: Can It Be Improved?* (New York: New York University Press, 1989).

Kanji Ishizumi, *Acquiring Japanese Companies* (Toyko: *The Japan Times*, Ltd., 1988).

Gary Katzenstein, *Funny Business: An Outsider's Year in Japan* (New York: Prentice Hall Press, 1989).

Maryann Keller, *Rude Awakening: The Rise, Fall and Struggle for Recovery of General Motors* (New York: William Morrow and Co., 1989).

Paul Kennedy, *The Rise and Fall of the Great Powers* (New York: Random House, 1987).

W. Carl Kester, *Japanese Takeovers: The Global Contest for Corporate Control* (Cambridge, Mass.: Harvard Business School Press, 1991).

Philip Kotler, Liam Fahey, and S. Jatusripitak, *The New Competition: What Theory Z Didn't Tell You About Marketing* (New Jersey: Prentice Hall, 1985).

Paul Krugman, *The Age of Diminished Expectations: U.S. Economic Policy in the 1990's* (Cambridge, Mass.: M.I.T. Press, 1990).

Takie Sugiyama Lebra, *Japanese Patterns of Behavior* (Honolulu: University of Hawaii Press, 1976).

Michael Lewis, *Liar's Poker* (New York: Penguin Books, 1989).

Charles A. Moore, *The Japanese Mind: Essentials of Japanese Philosophy and Culture* (Honolulu: University of Hawaii Press, 1967).

Kenichi Ohmae, *The Borderless World: Power and Strategy in the Interlinked Economy* (New York: Harper Business, 1990).

Daniel I. Okimoto, *Between MITI and the Market: Japanese Industrial Policy for High Technology* (Stanford: Stanford University Press, 1989).

L. Craig Parker, Jr., *The Japanese Police System Today: An American Perspective* (New York: Kodansha, 1987).

Michael E. Porter, *The Competitive Advantage of Nations* (New York: Free Press, 1990).

Jim Powell, *The Gnomes of Tokyo: The Positive Impact of Foreign Investment in North America* (New York: American Management Association, 1989).

Clyde V. Prestowitz, Jr., Alan Tonelson, and Robert W. Jerome, "The Last Gasp of GATTism," *Harvard Business Review*, March–April 1991, pp. 130–38.

Michael Random, *Japan: Strategy of the Unseen* (Wellingborough, England: Thorsons Publishing Group, 1987).

Donald Richie, *The Films of Akira Kurosawa* (Berkeley: University of California Press, 1970).

Robert M. Stern, *Trade and Investment Relations Among the United States, Canada, and Japan* (Chicago: University of Chicago Press, 1989).

Sheridan M. Tatsuno, *Created in Japan: From Imitators to World-Class Innovators* (New York: Harper & Row, 1990).

Peter Trasker, *The Japanese: Portrait of a Nation* (New York: New American Library, 1987).

Thomas R. Zengage and C. Tait Ratcliffe, *The Japanese Century: Challenge and Response* (Hong Kong: Longman Group [Far East] Ltd., 1988).

Don't miss these bestselling novels
of adventure and suspense by
MICHAEL CRICHTON....

CONGO

Deep in the heart of the Congo, near the legendary
ruins of the Lost City of Zinj, an eight-person field
expedition dies mysteriously and brutally in a matter of minutes. Ten thousand miles away, in
Houston, Karen Ross watches a gruesome video
transmission of that ill-fated team: a camp
destroyed, tents crushed and torn, and the grainy,
moving image of a dark, blurred shape. In San
Francisco, Amy, an extraordinary gorilla with a 620
"sign" vocabulary and a fondness for finger painting,
has recently drawn a replica of the frayed, brittle
pages of a Portuguese print dating back to 1642, a
drawing of the ancient lost city.

Immediately, a new expedition is sent into the
Congo, descending into a secret world where the
only way out may be through the grisliest death.
"Thrilling."
—*The New York Times Book Review*

THE ANDROMEDA STRAIN

Five prominent biophysicists warn the U.S. government that returning space probes may be reentering
the atmosphere contaminated. After Project Scoop
sends seventeen satellites into space to "collect
organisms for study," a probe satellite falls in deso-
late northeastern Arizona. Nearby, bodies lie
heaped and flung across the ground, faces locked in
frozen surprise. The terror has begun.
"Hideously plausible suspense...Will glue you to
your chair."
—*Detroit Free Press*

MICHAEL CRICHTON
RISING SUN

On the forty-fifth floor of the new American head-quarters of a Japanese conglomerate, a grand opening celebration is in full swing. On the forty-sixth floor, the dead body of a beautiful young woman is discovered. The investigation begins, and the Japanese saying "business is war" takes on a terrifying reality.

> "Dazzling...As well built a thrill machine as a suspense novel can be."
> —*The New York Times Book Review*

JURASSIC PARK

An astonishing technique for recovering and cloning dinosaur DNA has been discovered. Now, one of mankind's most thrilling fantasies has come true. Creatures extinct for eons now roam Jurassic Park, and all the world can visit them—for a price.

Until something goes wrong.

> "Wonderful...Powerful."
> —*The Washington Post Book World*

SPHERE

In the middle of the South Pacific, a thousand feet below the surface of the water, a huge vessel is discovered resting on the ocean floor. A group of American scientists rushes to investigate, and what they find defies their imaginations: a spaceship of phenomenal dimensions, apparently undamaged by its fall from the sky. And, most startling, it appears to be at least three hundred years old.

> "A page-turner...
> Powerful visual images and non-stop action."
> —*Newsweek*

MICHAEL CRICHTON

THE TERMINAL MAN

Harry Benson has been cured of his violent seizures by a surgical procedure known as a stage three: Electrodes are placed deep in the brain to send monitored soothing pulses to its pleasure canyons. But Benson has discovered how to get the pulses with increasing frequency. By the time he escapes from the hospital, he's a homicidal maniac with a deadly agenda.

> "A fascinating, splendidly
> documented thriller."
> —*The New Yorker*

EATERS OF THE DEAD

In the year A.D. 922, Arab courtier Ahmad Ibn Fadlan accompanies a party of Vikings to the barbaric North. Ibn Fadlan is appalled by Viking customs—their wanton sexuality, their disregard for cleanliness, their cold-blooded human sacrifices. And then he learns the horrifying truth: he has been enlisted to combat a terror that slaughters the Vikings and devours their flesh.

> "Crichton excels at storytelling."
> —*Newsday*

RANDOM HOUSE AUDIO PUBLISHING

RISING SUN
**by Michael Crichton
is now available on audiocassette!**

Keith Szarabajka reads this fast-paced, heart-stopping whodunit that unfolds in the arena of volatile Japanese-American relationships—where control of the international electronics industry is the fiercely coveted prize.

Running time: 3 hours, abridged, 2 cassettes

Available at your bookstore or use this convenient coupon.